09-CFT-226

DISCARD

IRENE INGLE
PUBLIC LIBRARY
P.O. BOX 679
WRANGELL, AK 99929

DATE DUE		
MAY 2 1 2002		
JUN 2 6 2002		
AUG 1 2 2002		
SEP 1 6 2002		
JUN 0 2 2003		
MAY 0 2 2005		
MAR 2 8 2009		

PERMA-BOUND

02-453

J
Dun

Duncan, Lois.
Down a dark hall

AK5.3 (7)

LOIS DUNCAN is the author of forty best-selling books for young people and adults. Her novels have won her high acclaim, and many have been chosen as American Library Association Best Books for Young Adults. Six of her books have been Junior Literary Guild selections, and three have received *Parents' Choice* awards. She has received five Special Awards from the Mystery Writers of America and is a recipient of the Margaret A. Edwards Award, sponsored by *School Library Journal* and the ALA Young Adult Library Services Association (YALSA).

Among her most popular suspense stories for young people are *Daughters of Eve, Don't Look Behind You, Down a Dark Hall, Killing Mr. Griffin, Locked in Time, Ransom, Stranger with My Face, Summer of Fear, They Never Came Home, The Third Eye,* and *The Twisted Window,* all available in Dell Laurel-Leaf editions. In addition, Lois Duncan is the author of the nonfiction *Who Killed My Daughter?,* the true story of her own search for her daughter's murderer, and, with William Roll, *Psychic Connections: A Journey into the Mysterious World of Psi.*

Irene Ingle Public Library
P.O. Box 679
Wrangell, AK 99929

ALSO AVAILABLE BY LOIS DUNCAN
IN LAUREL-LEAF BOOKS:

THE THIRD EYE
LOCKED IN TIME
DON'T LOOK BEHIND YOU
KILLING MR. GRIFFIN
SUMMER OF FEAR
STRANGER WITH MY FACE
DAUGHTERS OF EVE
RANSOM
THE TWISTED WINDOW
THEY NEVER CAME HOME
GALLOWS HILL
A GIFT OF MAGIC
I KNOW WHAT YOU DID LAST SUMMER

Down
a
Dark
Hall

LOIS DUNCAN

LAUREL-LEAF BOOKS

Published by
Bantam Doubleday Dell Books for Young Readers
a division of
Bantam Doubleday Dell Publishing Group, Inc.
1540 Broadway
New York, New York 10036

Copyright © 1974 by Lois Duncan

All rights reserved. No part of this book may be reproduced
or transmitted in any form or by any means, electronic or
mechanical, including photocopying, recording, or by any
information storage and retrieval system, without the written
permission of the Publisher, except where permitted by law.
For information address Little, Brown and Company, Inc.,
Boston, Massachusetts 02106.

The trademark Laurel-Leaf Library® is registered in the U.S.
Patent and Trademark Office.

The trademark Dell® is registered in the U.S. Patent and
Trademark Office.

ISBN: 0-440-91805-7
RL: 6.0

Reprinted by arrangement with Little, Brown and Company,
Inc.

Printed in the United States of America.
One previous edition
October 1990

OPM 37 36 35 34 33 32 31 30 29 28

02-453

For Dan and Betty Sabo

Down
A
Dark
Hall

Chapter 1

They had been driving since dawn, and for the past two hours, since they had turned off the highway onto the winding road that led through the hill country, Kit Gordy had been sleeping. Perhaps not completely sleeping — there had been a part of her mind that had remained awake, conscious of the curves of the road, of the faint warmth of the September sunlight slanting through the window to lie upon her hair, of the two voices in the front seat, her mother's light and lilting, Dan's low-pitched and even.

But she rode with her eyes closed and her head settled against the back of the seat. In this way she could keep from entering into the conversation.

I will not talk to them, she told herself. I have nothing to say to them.

Yet when the car drew to a stop, she could not keep herself from opening her eyes. When she did, she found her mother turned sideways, looking back at her.

"Hi, sleepyhead," she said. "You've been missing a lot of pretty countryside — pastures and brooks and rolling hills. It's been like something out of a picture book."

"Has it?" Kit said with disinterest. She straightened in the seat and glanced out of the window. "Are we stopping for gas?"

"That and directions," Dan Rheardon told her. "According to the map, this must be Blackwood Village, though I'm darned if I can find a sign to tell us so. It shouldn't be far to the school now. Madame Duret's letter said it was only about ten miles past the town limits."

The service station was small, with only one pump and one attendant who could be seen through the open door, sitting with his feet propped on the cash register, reading a magazine. Kit glanced down the narrow street where the one block was lined with storefronts — a grocery, a pharmacy, a hardware store, a shop with a display of dress goods in the window.

"It's the middle of nowhere," she said. "There isn't even a movie theater."

"I think it's nice," Mrs. Rheardon said. "I grew up in a little town like this one and it was delightful, with no noise, no pressure, everybody knowing everybody else. I didn't realize places like this existed anymore."

"When we get back from Europe," Dan said, "maybe we can find one. To live in, I mean." His voice was gentle — *sloshy*, Kit thought — like something from a Sunday afternoon television program. But her mother did not seem to think so, for she smiled and tilted her head, looking almost girlish, despite the lines at the corners of her eyes and the faint sheen of silver in her dark hair.

"Could we?" she asked. "But, Dan, your work —"

"They have lawyers in little towns as well as big ones. Or I could just drop law altogether and open a movie theater in Blackwood Village."

They laughed together, and Kit turned her head.

"Nowhere," she grumbled again. "A whole year here! I won't be able to stand it."

4

"I wouldn't worry." The gentleness was gone from Dan's voice. "I doubt that you'll be getting into the village very often. Your life will be pretty well centered around the school."

He gave the horn a beep and the attendant looked up startled, took a moment to adjust to the summons, and slowly laid his magazine on the counter. He stretched, yawned, and finally got to his feet to come begrudgingly out to the car.

"Want some gas, Mister?"

"Fill it up, please," Dan said. "Can you direct us to Blackwood School for Girls?"

"Around here?" The man looked bewildered.

"It's a boarding school run by a Madame Duret. The post office address is Blackwood Village, but the school itself is supposed to be out of town a way. It used to be a private home owned by a man named Brewer."

"Oh, the Brewer place!" The man nodded in recognition. "Well, sure, I know where that is. I did hear that some foreign lady had bought the place. She's had some of the town people up there during the summer putting it in shape, fixing the roof and the grounds and all. I think she's hired Bob Culler's girl Natalie to do kitchen work."

"Can you tell us how to get there?" Dan asked patiently.

"That's easy enough. Just follow this road through town and out the other side. It'll take you up into the hills, and you'll see a private road cutting in from the left."

The man moved to the gas pump, and Kit sighed, leaning her head back against the seat.

"Honey, please." Her mother turned to look at her with worried eyes. "Just give the school a chance. The pictures were so lovely with that marvelous old house and the pond and the woods all around it, and Madame Duret was so charming when we met her last spring. You seemed happy enough about going when we first suggested it."

"That's when I thought Tracy was going," Kit said. "I still don't see why I couldn't go to Europe with you and Dan. I wouldn't be any trouble. I'm fourteen and can look after myself; it wouldn't be as though you were dragging a child around with you."

"Kit, that's enough." There was an edge to Dan's voice. "We've been over it and over it. I know your position in the family has been different from that of most girls; with just the two of you, your mother has treated you as an equal rather than as a child. You're strong-willed and independent and very used to running things. But you are *not* going along with us on our honeymoon."

"But, I don't see —" Kit began.

Dan interrupted her. "No more, now. You're upsetting your mother."

The attendant came to the car window and Dan paid him and started the engine. They pulled out onto the street and drove past the block of shopfronts and past another two blocks of small white houses, and then across a bridge over a narrow river where water swirled in frothy tumult between gray stones. Then the town was behind them and they began to climb.

Trees grew thicker along the sides of the road as the fields gave way to woodland. Dense and dark and still smelling of summer, they laced their branches across the road. Like guards, Kit thought, protecting something that lies beyond.

Growing up in the city, she had never had a chance to really know trees, only the ones in the park and the few small, thin ones in front of the public library. If you watched those carefully you could mark the seasons by

6

their leaves — translucent green ones in the springtime which drooped in the summer and crinkled and fell with the autumn frost.

The trees they passed now were different, wild and strange, living a separate life of their own. Country trees. Mountain trees.

"There's nothing lovelier than upper New York State in the autumn," Kit's mother had said when the brochure describing Blackwood had arrived in the mail. "The school sounds perfect — a small, select number of students, individual instruction in music and art, and all sorts of advanced studies that you wouldn't get in a public high school. When you graduate from Blackwood, Kit, you should be able to get into any college in the country."

"This Madame Duret has an impressive background," Dan had added, studying the written material. "She was formerly owner and headmistress of a girls' school in London and before that she had one in Paris. And she has a fantastic knowledge of art. I recall reading an article about her once in *Newsweek*. One of the paintings she picked up somewhere at an auction turned out to be an original Vermeer."

"That would interest Tracy," Kit had said. Her best friend, Tracy Rosenblum, hoped someday to become an artist.

"I wonder," her mother had said thoughtfully, "if the Rosenblums might want to consider sending Tracy to Blackwood. They can certainly afford it, and the two of you have been inseparable."

"Do you suppose they might?" Kit's enthusiasm had perked up tremendously. She and Tracy had been close friends since grammar school. Going away to boarding school wouldn't be so bad if Tracy were going also.

So for six weeks she had drifted along, accepting what came — her mother's marriage to Dan, their plan for a European honeymoon, the reams of tests that were necessary for entrance to Blackwood.

Then the notice had arrived that Tracy had not been accepted. It was as though the bottom had dropped out of Kit's world.

"I'm not going!" she had stormed. "It won't be any fun without Tracy." But for the first time in her life, she had found herself faced with a stubbornness that matched her own.

"Of course, you're going," Dan had told her firmly. "You'll make new friends. Knowing you, I won't be surprised if you're elected president of the student body the first week you get there." He had smiled when he said it but the tone of his voice had left no room for argument.

Kit had clung to one last hope that her mother might intercede for her, but that had faded today with each passing mile. Now they were on the final lap of the journey, with Blackwood only a matter of minutes away. There could be no turning back at this point; it was time to face the inevitable.

They almost missed the road because it was not paved. Dan hit the brakes, brought the car to a stop, and backed it up again.

"Do you suppose that's it?" he asked, frowning. "There isn't any name on it. You'd think there would be a sign of some sort directing us in."

"Let's give it a try," Kit's mother suggested. "We've come a good ten miles, and there haven't been any other roads."

"Nothing to lose, I guess." Dan pulled into the lane, and Kit could feel the tires sink a little in the rich, damp soil.

8

They inched their way along for several yards, and then the road curved and suddenly the trees had closed in around them. The highway behind them might never have existed, for they were in a world of cool darkness where the only sound was the rustle of leaves and the only odor the wild, sweet smell of earth and woods.

"This can't be right," Dan said.

They continued inching forward as the road twisted and rose and turned again, and suddenly they were passing through an open gate in a high spiked fence. Gravel crunched beneath the wheels.

"This is it," Kit exclaimed, startled into speech. "There's the sign — this is Blackwood!"

For a moment she forgot that she did not want to be there and simply sat, staring wide-eyed at the vista that had opened before them. There on a rise above them stood a house such as she had never envisioned in her strangest dreams.

It was huge, three stories tall with a black slate roof so steep that it seemed to fall rather than slope to its outer edge. The walls were of gray stone, no two of the same size and shape, yet arranged somehow, one upon another, so as to fit together like a child's jigsaw puzzle. The great front door was flanked by stone lions and the steps leading down to the driveway were fashioned of the same stone. Centered on the second-floor level there was a deep-set window of stained glass. The other windows were more ordinary in construction, but the late afternoon sunlight struck them now in such a way that it seemed as though the entire interior of the mansion was ablaze with orange flames.

"Good grief," Dan said slowly, letting his breath out in a low whistle. "You won't be missing a thing, Kit, by not going with us to Europe. You're going to be living in a castle the like of which you'd never see along the Rhine River."

"It couldn't have looked like this in the brochure," Kit said. "It just couldn't have."

She tried to picture the photograph of the school that had been part of the folder, but she could not see it in her mind. It seemed to her that it had been of an ordinary-enough-looking building, large, of course, as a school would have to be, but nothing to cause one to gasp and stare.

"The picture didn't do it justice," her mother said now. "And to think, this was once a private residence! It's hard to imagine what sort of people must have lived here, way up in the hills so far from the nearest little town."

Dan shifted into first gear and they continued up the driveway.

But for some reason it seemed to Kit that they were not covering any distance. The house stood above them still, no closer than it had been when they had turned in at the gate. It was an illusion, she knew, something to do with the curve of the driveway and the angle at which they were approaching, but the car itself did not seem to be moving. It was as if the house were growing larger, reaching out its great gray arms to gather them in.

She could not move her eyes from the glowing windows, dancing before her like a hundred miniature suns.

Kit shivered with the sensation of an icy wind blowing across her heart.

"Mother," she said softly, and then, more loudly, "Mom?"

"What is it, honey?" Her mother turned in the seat to look back at her.

"I don't want to stay here," Kit said.

"Now, look," Dan said impatiently, "there's no use rehashing this. We're not taking you abroad with us, and that's final. You'd better accept it, Kit. Your mother and I —"

"That's not it," Kit said frantically. "I don't care where I stay, Dan. I'll go back to the city and live with the Rosenblums while you and Mom are gone. Or I'll go to another boarding school. There must be plenty of schools that would take me."

"Whatever is wrong, darling?" her mother asked with concern. "It's a quaint-looking place, but it's really rather wonderful. You'll get used to it. Before you know it, you'll be as much at home here as you were in P.S. 37."

"I'll never be at home here!" Kit cried. "Can't you feel it, Mom? There's something about the place — something —"

She could not find the word she was seeking, and so she fell silent as the house grew nearer and nearer and then was upon them.

Dan stopped the car and got out and came around to open the doors.

"Here we are," he said. "Hop out. We may as well check in with Madame Duret, and I'll come back out for the luggage."

And then Kit knew the word for which she had been searching. The word was "evil."

Chapter 2

The woman who answered the door was completely gray. Her hair was like gray straw, pulled back into a tight bun, and she had the sharp little eyes of a gray mouse. She wore a gray dress, hemmed low, and covered by a starched white apron.

Her eyes flicked quickly from Kit to her mother and then to Dan. For a moment Kit had the impression that she was going to close the door in their faces.

"I'm Mr. Rheardon," Dan said to block this possibility. "This is my wife and her daughter, Kathryn Gordy. Madame Duret is expecting us."

"This is Monday." The gray woman spoke with a voice so heavily accented that it was difficult to comprehend the words. "Until tomorrow the school it does not open."

"We're aware of that," Dan said. "We've made special arrangements for Kit to arrive a day early. Mrs. Rheardon and I are leaving the country tomorrow and we need to start back to the coast tonight."

"This is not the day," the woman said again. "The classes, they do not begin yet."

"Lola!" A voice spoke from the hallway beyond. "These people are expected."

A moment later the maid had moved aside and Madame Duret herself stood framed in the doorway, smiling a greeting.

She had not changed, Kit thought, in the months since they had first seen her. That had been in May when she had come into the city to give Kit and Tracy entrance examinations. She had seemed an imposing figure then, and now, against the setting of Blackwood, she was even more so.

Madame Duret was a tall woman, five foot nine or ten, with olive coloring and a striking, high-boned face. Her height was increased by a pile of rich, black hair which she wore high on her head like a crown, and the strength of her face was accentuated by black brows and a sharp, straight nose. But her most striking feature was her eyes. They were dark and deep-set with a gaze so intense that it could almost be felt physically.

"How nice it is to see you again." Madame's voice was low-pitched and gracious, with only the slightest suggestion of a French accent. "You must forgive us. Life here has been so disorganized this week with all the preparations for our influx of young people that I did not have the opportunity to mention to Lola that one of our girls would be coming early."

"I hope we're not inconveniencing you," Mrs. Rheardon said. "Our ship sails tomorrow. There was simply no way —"

"But, of course! Of course! Please come in. Did you have any trouble finding us?"

"Not really," Dan said. "We got directions from the village."

They fell into step behind Madame Duret as she moved ahead of them through a hallway with a high, arched ceiling into a pleasantly furnished room with a fireplace and a color television set.

13

"Please, sit down." Madame gestured them to chairs. "What may I offer you? Coffee, perhaps, or wine? What about a glass of sherry?"

"That would be great," Dan said. "Ginny?"

"Lovely," said Kit's mother. "Thank you. Really, Madame Duret, I can't get over this fantastic place. Was it actually once a private home?"

"Indeed, it was," Madame said. "Lola —" She addressed an aside to the little gray woman who had appeared silently in the doorway as though in response to a silent summons, "Please to bring three sherries and a Coke. You would like a soft drink, Kathryn, would you not?"

"Yes, please," Kit said.

"This entire estate," Madame continued, turning back to the Rheardons, "was owned by a man named Brewer who died over ten years ago. Since that time it has stood vacant. The heirs, distant cousins of some kind, live on the West Coast and placed it in the hands of a realtor. No one has wanted to buy it, which is understandable; it is no normal one-family residence, as you can see, and standing empty all that time it picked up something of an unusual reputation. Teenagers from the village used to come up here to park on dates and they would go home with all sorts of weird stories about lights in the windows and bodiless creatures floating through the garden."

She laughed, and the Rheardons laughed with her.

"It sounds exciting," Kit's mother said. "I'm going to expect marvelous letters from my daughter telling us about the adventures she has here."

There was a break in the conversation as Lola came in with a tray. Kit took her glass, glad of something to hold in her hands. The dreadful feeling that had come upon her at her first glimpse of Blackwood had somewhat faded, but the shadow of it still remained.

"How many students are there going to be?" she asked.

"That is never a certainty," Madame Duret told her. "There are always first-day dropouts who get homesick at the thought of leaving their parents. We'll know the final count at Orientation tomorrow. Personally, I think that going away to school is an educational experience that should be part of the life of every young woman."

The conversation continued, and Kit sat, sipping her Coke, only half listening. Tomorrow, she thought, there would be other girls in this room, laughing and chatting and tuning in favorite programs on the giant television. Perhaps, with young voices ringing through the halls, the atmosphere at Blackwood would be different. Maybe, as Dan had suggested, there would be someone among the new arrivals who would be the same kind of friend as Tracy, close and companionable and always ready to share a good time.

Dan glanced at his watch. "I hate to rush things, but we have a long drive ahead of us. I'd better go out and bring in Kit's suitcases."

"Lola will show you where to bring them." Madame Duret rose from her chair. "While you are getting the luggage, perhaps Mrs. Rheardon would enjoy a quick look at Blackwood."

"I'd love it," Kit's mother told her. "This is a fascinating old mansion. Did you have to do a great deal of renovating?"

"Not as much as one might suppose," Madame said, leading the way out into the hall. "The original building was well constructed. The only actual rebuilding that had to be done was in the upstairs dormitory wing where there had once been a fire. The stone structure withstood

15

it well, but the wooden paneling was burned away and the furniture had to be replaced. I tried as well as I could to duplicate the style of the original pieces."

As she led the way down the hall, she gestured to various doorways, some closed, some open.

"The room we just left is the living room or, as I prefer to call it, the parlor. This door to my right leads to my office and beyond that lies a suite of rooms which I share with my son Jules. There is a guest residence out behind which has been converted to apartments for the other members of the faculty.

"Here is the dining room, and on the far side of that is the kitchen. These doors lead to classrooms."

She paused at one door, opened it, and flicked on the light. A baby grand piano took up one whole corner of the room, while along the far wall there stood an array of musical instruments. Music racks, comfortable chairs, and a large and intricate-looking tape recorder completed the furnishings.

"This, of course, is the music room," Madame Duret said. "Are you musically inclined, Kathryn?"

"I had a year of piano," Kit said, "back when I was eleven. I can't say I did too well at it."

"You just got impatient," her mother said. "You didn't want to take the time to practice. I hope that here at Blackwood you'll take advantage of the chance to get some musical training. It's something that will give you pleasure all your life."

"We devote much time and effort to the study of the arts," Madame told them, turning off the light and drawing the door closed. "If you had more time you would enjoy browsing through the library, and the paintings throughout the house represent a hobby of mine, collecting little-known works of famous artists. But I know that

16

what you are most interested to see is where it is that Kathryn herself will be living."

The stairway was curved and at its head an immense mirror seemed to double the length of the upstairs hallway. At the hall's end was the stained-glass window that had been evident from the driveway, and the sun slanted through it, lighting the hallway in rainbow hues.

A series of doors opened onto the hall from both sides. Madame Duret stopped in front of one of these, fumbled in her skirt pocket for a key, and inserted it in the brass lock. She turned it, withdrew it, and handed the key to Kit.

"We believe in privacy at Blackwood," she said. "Each student carries her own room-key and is encouraged to keep her room locked when she is not in it. And here, Kathryn, is where you will be making your nest."

She pushed the door open, and Kit heard her mother catch her breath. She herself could not contain a small gasp of surprise, for the room was far more elaborate than anything she could have imagined.

The largest piece of furniture was a bed of carved dark wood with a high, rich canopy of red velvet. Beside it sat a small table bearing an ornate lamp with a ruffled shade. Heavy gold draperies bordered a window and against the wall opposite there stood a walnut bureau, over which hung an oval mirror with a gilded frame. A Persian carpet covered the floor, and under the window there stood a rolltop desk with a study lamp.

"If this is a dorm room," Mrs. Rheardon exclaimed, "it's the kind I never dreamed of when I was a schoolgirl!"

"It's beautiful," Kit agreed, stunned in spite of herself. Tentatively she reached out and let her hand caress the bedspread. "Is this real velvet?"

"It is, indeed," Madame Duret told her. "We want Blackwood to be more than just a school for our students; we want it to be an experience they will carry with them long after they have left its halls. We feel that beauty enriches the spirit and that young people should learn to be at ease with lovely things."

"But there's just one bed." The thought occurred to Kit suddenly. "Won't I be having a roommate?"

"Not at Blackwood," Madame said. "All our girls have private rooms and baths. I think that privacy makes for better study habits, don't you?"

"I guess so," Kit said, recalling the plans she and Tracy had made to room together. It was true that they would probably have done more talking than studying, but it would have been fun.

"Hello, there!" Dan's voice called from the top of the stairs. "I've got a couple of bags here that feel as though they must be stuffed with bricks. Where do you want them?"

"Down here, dear," Kit's mother called back. "Come and see Kit's room. You won't believe it!"

"Good grief!" Dan appeared in the doorway, a suitcase in each hand. "This looks more like a palace than a school. You won't be able to toss your stuff all over the place here, Kit."

"We trust our girls to take care of their rooms," Madame Duret said easily. "And now, if you will excuse me, I must go down and speak to our kitchen help about dinner. We dine fairly early, Kathryn, because the girl who does the cooking lives in the village and has to drive home every evening. Dinner will be served at six-thirty in the dining room."

"Okay," Kit said. "Thank you."

"Thank you, Madame Duret," Kit's mother said. "We'll stop and say good-bye before we leave."

They all stood quiet, listening to her quick, strong footsteps as the headmistress hurried off down the hall.

"Quite a woman," Dan commented in a low voice. "Imagine what a job it must have been to turn this ancient place into a modern school."

"I'm certainly impressed." Kit's mother turned to her. "Honey —" And then suddenly she pulled her daughter to her, and Kit could hear the note of pleading in her voice. "Kit, dear, you will be happy here, won't you? I'd never enjoy a moment of our trip if I thought you weren't. We *can* make other arrangements, even if it means taking another ship later. Your happiness is the most important thing."

At that moment, Kit felt her resentment leave her. She had won, and she could not take advantage of the winning. Putting her arms around her mother, she gave her a warm hug.

"Of course, I'll like it," she said thickly. "You and Dan have a wonderful honeymoon. You deserve it, Mom, if anybody ever did. I'm sorry I've been such a pill. I'll be happy here — I promise."

There had been a question nagging at the back of her mind. It slid away now and was forgotten. It did not really matter why her bedroom at Blackwood had a lock on the outside — but not on the inside — of its door.

Chapter 3

———◆———

The bed was high and beautiful, but not particularly comfortable. Kit lay back upon the velvet bedspread and stared up at the wine-colored canopy. Somebody — was it Poe? — had written a story about a bed exactly like this one in which the canopy had sunk slowly at night to smother the person unlucky enough to be sleeping beneath it. They had read it last year in literature class and there had been a barrage of squeals and laughter.

Now the story didn't seem so funny.

I don't like canopies, Kit decided, and I don't like hard mattresses. But I am going to like it at Blackwood if it kills me. I gave Mom my promise.

Her mother and Dan had been gone for over an hour now, and still she had not begun to unpack her suitcases. She had climbed onto the bed at first simply to see what it felt like and, once there, she had remained, staring up at the canopy and thinking.

She *had* been a pill over the past weeks. She could admit it now, and she was ashamed of herself. Her mother had been through enough in the way of hard work and loneliness since the death of Kit's father to deserve any happiness that fell her way. Maybe Dan wasn't the person Kit herself would have gone out and selected for a stepfather, but if her mother loved him, that was all that mattered. In all fairness, no one whom her mother chose as a second husband would have pleased Kit completely. She had been close to her father and to her no one would ever take his place.

She had been the last one to see him. No one had ever believed that, but it was true. She had been seven at the time and had awakened in the night to find her father standing at the foot of her bed, gazing down at her. Although the room had been dark, she had been able to see him clearly, his head bent, his gray eyes wistful, and a world of love reflected in his square, strong-featured face.

Kit had drawn herself up upon her elbows and stared at him.

"Dad?" she had said. "What are you doing here? I thought you were in Chicago on business."

When he had not answered she had shivered, realizing suddenly how cold the room had become even though it was midsummer. She had lain back upon the pillow, pulling the sheet and spread up to her chin, and had let her eyes close for a moment. When she had opened them again it was morning, and sunlight streamed through the windows, falling in bright golden patterns upon the bedroom rug.

She had gotten up and dressed in shorts and a T-shirt and gone downstairs. The house had been filled with people.

One of her aunts had come over and put an arm around her and said, "Poor baby! Poor little love!"

"What is it?" Kit had asked. "What's happened?" Her eyes had taken in the group before her. "Why is Mom crying?"

"It's your father, dear," her aunt had told her. "There was an accident last night and your mother only got the call about it this morning. Your father was in a taxi headed back to his hotel, when the driver went through a stop sign —"

"But that can't be true," Kit had interrupted in bewilderment. "He was here last night. I saw him. He came into my bedroom."

"You were dreaming, dear," her aunt told her gently.

"I wasn't," Kit had insisted. "I was awake. Dad was here. I saw him." Across the room she had cried to her mother, "Daddy did come home last night, didn't he? You must have gone to pick him up at the airport. Mom —"

Her mother's face had been white and terrible in grief, but she had come quickly and taken Kit in her arms.

"I wish he had, honey," she had said in a choking voice. "If only he had."

The year that followed had seen many changes in their lives. Her mother, who had never worked before, had taken a course in business school and found a secretarial job with a law firm. She had sold the house — "The payments are too high for me to manage," she had said, "and I can't keep up the yard by myself" — and had rented an apartment in the city close to the office where she worked.

Kit knew it had not been easy. Her mother was a pretty, vivacious woman, and much as she loved her daughter, there was bound to be a void in her life, a terrible longing for adult companionship. This had been proven by the change in her spirits since she had found Dan.

Mom's happy now, and I must be also, Kit told herself determinedly. If I'm not, I'll put a damper on everything.

But she could not forget that feeling in the driveway, the sudden sense of evil chill as though a cloud had slid across the sun.

If Tracy were here, they would have laughed about it. They would even have made a joke of the crimson canopy; Tracy would probably have suggested attaching bells to it so that the tinkle would wake them when it descended in the night. Tracy Rosenblum was level-headed and bright and funny, and the possibility that she might not be accepted at Blackwood had never occurred to either of them.

When the notice arrived, Kit had not been able to believe it.

"But you're an honor student!" she had exclaimed incredulously. "You always get better grades than I do!"

"Maybe it was the psychological tests," Tracy had said. "Or the interview. It's possible the woman just didn't like me."

"That's ridiculous. Everybody likes you. Besides, you knew all about her art collection and you could talk to her about the Vermeer she discovered, and she kept calling you 'chérie' with every other breath. She liked you better than she did me."

"Well, you come up with a reason then." Tracy had shrugged her shoulders philosophically. "I just didn't make it, and that's that. So back I go to old P.S. 37, and off you go to Blackwood, and it's a good thing you're good at composition because I'm going to expect a lot of letters."

"You'll get them," Kit had promised. "But there's still a chance I can talk Mom out of sending me."

Well, that chance was gone. Here she was, stretched out on velvet, staring up at more velvet, watching the room grow dim as dusk settled outside the window. I should unpack, she thought, but she made no move to do so; she felt lulled and heavy, weighted down with a strange weariness which she could not explain.

There was a rap on the door. A voice said, "Miss Kathryn?"

"Yes?" Kit came to life with a start. Guiltily she shoved her feet over the edge of the bed so that her shoes were no longer in touch with the spread. "Yes — what is it?"

"Dinner, miss." The voice was unmistakably Lola's. "The others are already down."

"Oh, thanks. I guess I lost track of time." Pushing her legs the rest of the way over the edge of the bed, Kit sat up. To her surprise she saw that in only a moment's time the twilight outside had deepened into night. The room was very dark.

Reaching over, she fumbled with the lamp on the bedside table, found a knob at its base, and turned it. The light went on and shadows leapt high against the opposite wall.

I wish there was an overhead, Kit thought, getting to her feet. There's such a thing as being too old-fashioned and charming.

She crossed to the desk and turned on the study lamp, which helped slightly. She knew she should change from her travel-wrinkled clothes, but with dinner already waiting, it seemed better not to take the time. She compromised by scrubbing her hands and face and running a comb through her thick mane of blond hair.

The face that looked back at her from the bathroom mirror was not conventionally pretty. The mouth was a little too wide, the chin too square. But the gray eyes were direct and friendly and the cheeks flushed with the glow of vitality and good health. It was a likable face, and the only time Kit really thought about it was when she saw its growing resemblance to her father's.

Leaving the lights burning in the bedroom, she stepped out into the hall and drew the door closed behind her.

Immediately she found herself standing in a tunnel of

darkness. The hall was unlighted except for a single bulb encased in a frosted globe at the top of the stairwell. Kit began to walk slowly toward it, and to her astonishment, she saw a slim, pale figure moving toward her as though out of the wall beyond the stairs.

She stopped, and the figure stopped. She took one tentative step, and realized suddenly that she was seeing her own reflection in the mirror beyond the stairs.

"I'm a great one," she said aloud, disgusted with herself. "Next thing you know I'll be seeing goblins."

Placing her hand on the smooth mahogany banister, she descended the stairs to the hall below. This was well lighted, and though it was empty she could hear the sound of voices and the clink of glasses and silverware in a room beyond. Following the sounds, she made her way down the hall to the door of the dining room and looked inside.

The room was massive with high, arched ceilings and a crystal chandelier of such grandeur that it might have been stolen from the set of a period movie. Beneath it stood a large, circular table covered with a white linen cloth and set with candles and china. Three people were seated around it, and there was a fourth place setting.

Madame Duret glanced up from the conversation to see Kit standing in the doorway.

"Come in, my dear. Forgive us for starting without you, but dinner at Blackwood is served promptly at six-thirty."

"I'm sorry," Kit said contritely. "I think I must have fallen asleep."

As she entered the room the two men at the table rose to their feet and Madame made the introductions.

"Kathryn Gordy, may I present Professor Farley and my son, Jules."

"How do you do," Kit said.

The elderly gentleman across from her had a receding hairline and a short, white beard, trimmed into a point. Kit shook his hand politely, but her eyes had already shifted past him to Jules Duret.

Slim and fine-boned, with glossy black hair which framed a face so perfect in feature that it might have belonged to a television star, he was without doubt the handsomest young man she had ever seen.

"Won't you sit down?" Madame Duret asked pleasantly. She reached over and lifted the little silver bell which stood by her water glass.

At the tinkle, a swinging door in the back of the room opened and a plain, flat-faced girl in a blue uniform appeared.

"Miss Kathryn is here now, Natalie," Madame said. "She will have her soup." She smiled at Kit as she took her place at the table. "It is pleasant to have you with us a day early, Kathryn. Professor Farley will be your instructor in math and sciences. Jules has just received his degree from a music conservatory in England and will be teaching piano."

"Are the other teachers not here yet?" Kit asked, unfolding her napkin and placing it in her lap.

There was a slight pause.

"There are not to be any others," Jules said. His voice had the same charming blend of accents as his mother's, so subtle as to be almost undetectable, yet adding a note of color to his speech.

Kit regarded him with surprise. "You're kidding, aren't you?"

"I, too, will be teaching," Madame told her. "I will instruct in languages and literature, and, of course, in art, if there should be an interest."

"But the brochure said 'small classes,' " Kit exclaimed. "How can they be with only three people to teach them?"

26

"You mustn't worry about that, Kathryn." Professor Farley's wise old eyes seemed to twinkle in the candlelight. "You will receive all the personal attention at Blackwood that you could possibly ask for. I had the pleasure of visiting Madame Duret's school in England several years ago and was so impressed by her achievements there that I convinced her to open a school here in the United States."

"How is your room, chérie?" Madame asked. "There is a supply of extra blankets if you need them. Are there enough hangers in the closet?"

"Everything seems fine," Kit said. She hesitated and then added, "There's one thing — the light in the hall seems awfully dim. I didn't notice it this afternoon because of the light from the window, but now at night it's really pretty black."

"That's one of the problems that comes with renovating an old place," Professor Farley said. "That upstairs wiring just doesn't do the trick. Madame has been trying to get electricians out from the village, but that's easier said than done."

"Perhaps we could remove the globe," Madame Duret said, "and use a bulb of a higher wattage. As a temporary measure, of course, until we can have another fixture installed."

"Oh, that's all right," Kit said in sudden embarrassment. "I didn't mean to make a big deal out of it. I'm not usually worried about things like that, it's just that the dorm floor is so empty right now. It won't matter at all tomorrow when the other girls get here and it's all filled up with people."

There was a moment's silence. Madame Duret lifted her napkin to dab at her lips. Professor Farley took a sip from his water glass.

Kit turned to Jules, whose head was bent over his plate.

"It will be different tomorrow," she said again, "after everybody gets here."

"Naturally," Jules said. "It will seem different then." He lifted his head, but his eyes did not meet hers, and there was a strange, closed-in look on his face.

She dreamed that the canopy was lowering. Twice she dreamed it. Slowly, softly, the air was pressing down upon her as the great, billowing bubble of wine-colored velvet descended to settle over her face.

The first time she woke, shaking, she groped frantically for the lamp on the bedside table. She pressed the button at its base, and at once the room was filled with dim, yellow light.

Sitting up, Kit stared about her at the room. It lay in perfect order except for a pile of her own clothing which she had tossed in her usual careless manner onto a chair, and the two suitcases, still only partially unpacked, which lay open on the floor before the closet.

The canopy stood high above her, just where it should have been.

Kit turned off the light and lay back upon the pillow, and after a bit she slept. When she woke again, from the same dream, she turned the lamp on and left it burning for the rest of the night.

Chapter 4

————◆————

When she awoke in the morning, Kit could laugh at herself for her midnight foolishness. Bright sunshine poured in the window, falling in golden splashes across the rich hues of the carpet and picking up the gleam of the woodwork in a way that made the room seem aglow with beauty. The canopy was only a canopy, a regal decoration for what must undoubtedly be classed as one of the world's most elegant beds.

Kit swung her legs over the side and placed her bare feet on the rug. It felt thick and luxurious, and she dug her toes into it as she crossed the room to the window. Once there, she wondered how she could possibly not have looked out of it before, for the view was so spectacular that her heart leapt with pleasure.

Below her lay a garden, still partially abloom with late summer flowers, and through it ran a narrow, gravel walkway which wound about like a maze, splitting and turning and meeting itself once again. Beyond this lay a stretch of lawn that led down to a pond. The pond was not large, but it shimmered like silver in the morning light, smooth and flat and luminous as a mirror. Past that rose the woods, circling protectively around the opposite shore and coming in a full curve to border Blackwood on all sides.

Above everything rose the sky, blue and clear in a high, rich arc. The air smelled fresh and sweet.

From this side of the house, Kit was not able to catch sight of the driveway. She could imagine it filled with cars from which harried fathers were busily extracting suitcases. In a short time now there would be other girls rollicking about the hall, laughing and chattering, comparing backgrounds and rushing inquisitively in and out of each other's rooms.

I'm just as glad I got here early, Kit thought as she dressed. This way I have sort of a head start.

She made her bed and unpacked her suitcases, hanging the dresses in the closet and folding other clothing to place in bureau drawers. In the second suitcase she had packed her photographs. One was of Tracy and herself, taken three years before at Tracy's eleventh birthday party. They were giggling and posing self-consciously with their arms around each other's shoulders and a mammoth cake in front of them.

The other picture was of her parents on their honeymoon. Her mother had had it enlarged and framed for her soon after her father's death.

"I want you to remember him," she had said.

As though I could ever *not* remember, Kit thought now, studying the picture. Her father's clear eyes laughed out at her and the stubborn chin, so much like her own, gave a look of strength to a face still curved and boyish. The girl clinging to his arm was harder to remember. Had her mother ever really been that young and carefree, so radiant with joy?

Be happy, Mom, Kit told her silently. Please, be happy

with Dan. For no matter what companionship and security her mother found in her second marriage, Kit knew in her heart that she would never again be the girl in this picture.

She set the photograph of her parents on the bureau and tucked the snapshot of herself and Tracy into the rim of the mirror. Why, she wondered, hadn't she brought any pictures of boys? She had a batch of them at home, for last spring everybody had traded class pictures, and a mass of snapshots had been taken at parties. From what she had heard they were standard decorations for dorm rooms.

Oh, well, Kit thought resignedly, any specimens I could have come up with would have looked pretty scroungy with Jules Duret for contrast. I bet Blackwood turns out to have a lot of dedicated piano students.

Yesterday's doldrums were over. Today the world was bright and shining. When she left the room she found the hallway flooded with rainbow light as it had been the afternoon before. The figure approaching from the depths of the mirror did not startle her now; instead she looked like a friend. Kit waved and smiled at her, pleased with the neat, bright-faced image who waved back.

There was no one in the downstairs hall, but a murmur of voices came from behind the closed door of Madame's office. Kit swung on past it and into the dining room, and found it empty. The rattle of pans and the sound of running water came to her from the room beyond. Crossing through the dining room, Kit pushed open the swinging door and entered the kitchen.

The thin girl who had served dinner the night before was standing at the sink, washing dishes. She glanced up and frowned as Kit came in.

"Breakfast is over, miss, but the lady says I'm to fix you

something if you want it. They had their breakfasts at eight o'clock. It's past ten now."

"I slept late," Kit said apologetically, "and then I unpacked. My name's Kit Gordy. You're Natalie, aren't you?"

The girl nodded. "Natalie Culler. What do you want to eat?"

"Don't worry about fixing me breakfast," Kit said. "I'll just make myself some toast if that's okay."

The girl made a gesture to forestall her.

"That's my job. I do the cooking." She removed two slices of bread from a wrapped loaf and placed them in the toaster. "After all, it's what I'm getting paid for."

"You wait table and do the cooking too?" Kit exclaimed. "That's an awfully big job for one person. Will there be somebody to help you when all the students get here?"

"There won't be that many," Natalie said. "I'm eighteen now and I've done cooking off and on since I was twelve. A few extra don't make much difference."

"But, gosh — a whole school full of girls!" Kit regarded her with awe. "Won't that mean —"

The girl interrupted. "Your toast's up, miss. Here's the butter, and there's jam over there on the counter." She paused and then added in a more friendly manner, "The lady — Madame Duret — she doesn't want the village help talking with the students. She told us all that when she hired us. I can ask people what they want and things like that, but that's all the talking I'm supposed to do."

"Oh," Kit said awkwardly. "Well, I didn't mean to do anything to get you in trouble."

"I know that, miss, but this job means a lot to me. Full-time work isn't easy to find in a place like Blackwood Village. So maybe it's best you take your breakfast and go eat it in the dining room, all right?"

"Okay," Kit said. "Sure."

She pushed open the kitchen door and went through into the room beyond. The door swung closed behind her, shutting off the everyday world of the kitchen area, and immediately the dark beauty of the Blackwood dining room surrounded her. The room's floor-level windows were shielded from the outside by shrubbery so that the light that did slip through between the leaves was dim and diffused. The round table glowed gently with polish and the crystal chandelier hung silent and pale above it.

The room was so empty, so devoid of movement or sound, that Kit hurried through it without being tempted to sit down and went out once again into the entrance hall.

The door to the office stood open now. Madame stood just inside, talking to a slight, red-haired girl.

She turned as Kit came opposite the doorway and said, "Here is one of our students now. Kathryn, come here, dear. I want you to meet Sandra Mason."

"Hello," Kit said, pleased to see a young face.

"Hi." The bright-haired girl smiled shyly. She had a narrow, elfin face and an uptilted nose that was sprinkled with freckles.

"Sandra came by bus as far as the village," Madame Duret explained, "and Professor Farley met her there and drove her the rest of the way to Blackwood. Would you show her upstairs, Kathryn? Her room will be 211, the corner room at the end of the hall."

"I'll be glad to," Kit said, suddenly feeling ridiculous with her hands full of toast. She glanced about for a place to deposit it, saw none, and decided to make the best of the situation. "Would you like some breakfast?"

"No, thank you," the girl said seriously. "I ate in the village." A few moments later, as they mounted the stairs, she said, "I didn't really."

"Didn't really what?" Kit asked.

"I ordered some coffee and a doughnut at a drugstore, but I couldn't eat them. I guess I was too excited. You see, I've never been away to school before."

"Neither have I," Kit told her. "I got here yesterday, and I wasn't exactly prepared for what it would be like."

"The house waiting at the end of the drive — when I saw it from the car I couldn't believe it —"

"If you think that was something," Kit said, "wait until you see the bedrooms."

Room 211 was identical to Kit's, except that it was a corner room with one window facing the driveway. It was done in greens and golds instead of red, but the ornate furnishings, the plush carpet and the heavy draperies were the same.

Kit could see on Sandra's face the same amazement that she herself had experienced the day before.

"It's so — different!" the girl exclaimed. "I guess I should have realized from the brochure, but somehow it just didn't come across as — as quite like this."

"It sure didn't," Kit agreed. "It's like living in a palace. I was the only one sleeping on the hall last night, and I kept having funny dreams. I hope they don't come with the bedrooms as built-in accessories."

"I hope not too. I'm not exactly the world's soundest sleeper." The girl smiled nervously. "By the way, I go by 'Sandy.' I can't remember anyone's ever calling me 'Sandra' except Madame Duret."

"And I'm never 'Kathryn,'" Kit said. "I'm 'Kit.' Do you know what's funny? The morning's almost over and I haven't seen anybody but you. Wouldn't you think that a lot of the students would have gotten here by this time?"

"Someone's arriving now," Sandy said. "I can hear a

34

car in the driveway." She crossed to the window and stood, looking out. "There are two girls and a man. He must be the chauffeur; he's wearing a uniform."

"But no parents?" Kit went over to stand beside her. "That seems funny, doesn't it? You'd think any parents would want to see their daughters get settled and take a look at where they'll be living." She caught herself and grew red with embarrassment. "I'm sorry. I wasn't thinking."

"That's all right," Sandy said. "My family would have liked to have brought me but they don't drive. I live with my grandparents. They're moving into a retirement village that doesn't take teenagers, and it seemed as though it would be best for me to come away to school and just visit them on vacations."

"My mother just got married," Kit said, feeling she had to volunteer something or seem unfriendly. "She and my stepfather are honeymooning in Europe." She leaned forward, studying the two girls who had climbed from the car and were watching the chauffeur unload their belongings. "That blond's pretty, isn't she? I bet she hooks Jules right out from under our noses."

"Jules?" Sandy said blankly.

"Madame Duret's son. Young, dark and handsome — a real dream guy. He's going to be our music instructor."

"That sounds like a challenge for somebody," Sandy said. "Did you date much back home?"

"A fair amount. I didn't leave a steady or anything if that's what you mean. How about you?"

"My grandparents are old-fashioned. They don't think a girl should go out until she's old enough to get married." Sandy sighed. "Not that it mattered. Nobody's ever asked me."

"They will," Kit said comfortingly.

35

"I suppose." Sandy turned away from the window and went to open the door to the hall.

A few moments later they could hear the clatter of footsteps on the stairs and the sound of excited voices. Lola's expressionless voice was saying, "Rooms 208 and 206, on your left, ladies."

"What a funny hall! The window at the end makes it all different colors!" The high, light voice of the blond girl rose liltingly as she hurried ahead of her companions.

"Why, hi!" she said as she saw Kit and Sandy. "I'm glad somebody's here! I was beginning to think we'd come on the wrong day!"

"We're glad to see you too," Kit told her. "I'm Kit Gordy and this is Sandy Mason."

"I'm Lynda Hannah," the girl said, "and this is Ruth Stark. We're both old hands at boarding schools but, I swear, I've never seen one like this!" Her exquisite, china-doll face was bright with excitement, and the pale hair framed it like a halo.

Her friend was a complete contrast, a short, heavy-set girl with a smooth, dark cap of hair and a downy shadow across her upper lip. Her thick brows met each other across the bridge of her nose, and her eyes were sharp and alert behind wire-rimmed glasses.

She acknowledged Kit's greeting with a nod and turned to open the door of her room.

"Cripes!" she exclaimed as the interior became visible to her. "Will you look at that, Lynda!"

"Oh, let me see mine!" the blond girl gasped. "I wonder if it's the same!" She hurried down the hall to the next door.

"Come on," Kit said to Sandy. "Let's look out and see who's coming next."

They reentered Sandy's room and crossed to the window. The driveway below was empty. Even the chauffeured car that had brought Lynda and Ruth had disappeared. The drive stretched flat and straight, bordered by shrubbery, down to the black iron fence, and beyond that the trees crowded close like a line of sentinels. The sun was high in the sky and threw no shadows.

"I guess it'll be a real mob scene this afternoon," said Sandy. "The people who plan to drive up in one day won't be coming till later. I wonder, though, why there weren't any other students on the bus this morning. After all, there can't be many buses coming through a little place like Blackwood Village."

"It does seem strange," Kit said. She gazed out past the driveway to the fence. Something was different. Something had changed since the last time she had looked through this window.

"Sandy," she said slowly, "I — I think — there aren't going to be any other students."

"No more students?" Her new friend turned to her incredulously. "You've got to be kidding. *Four* students in this great huge place? That's ridiculous!"

"Ridiculous or not," Kit said, "I don't think they're expecting anybody else. The gate at the end of the driveway has been closed."

"Yes, it is true. We have only accepted four students for our first session." Madame Duret smiled at them across the dining table. The candles flickered above the white cloth, and an unfelt breeze seemed to touch the crystals of the chandelier, moving them against each other with a faint tinkle as of distant music.

They had just completed the soup course, and Natalie had not come in yet to clear the table.

"There were many applicants," Professor Farley inter-

37

jected. "The problem was that most of them didn't fill our requirements."

"You mean they couldn't pass the tests?" Kit asked in bewilderment. "I don't understand. The examinations weren't that hard. *I* passed them, and I'm not an all-A student."

"None of you are, except for Ruth." Professor Farley nodded toward the dark-haired girl, who reacted with a little smile of satisfaction. "Your selection was not based entirely upon your academic accomplishments. There were other considerations."

"Like what?" Lynda Hannah asked. "Like who our parents are?"

"It can't be that," Sandy said softly from her seat on Kit's right. "I don't have parents."

"Let us just say that we found you four very special girls." Madame's eyes were like mirrors, reflecting the glow of the candles. When Kit leaned forward, she could see her own image peering back at her from the luminous pupils. "You have just the attributes we want our students to possess. Does it displease you to be part of a small class?"

"I like the idea," Ruth said in her clipped, no-nonsense way. "This way we'll get individual attention and advance faster. That's the whole reason I'm here. I was bored to death in the last school I attended."

"I don't know," Lynda said hesitantly. "I kind of wish there were more people. I mean, what kind of social affairs will we be having with so few of us? We can't have dances or get together with boys' schools for parties."

"You will not be bored at Blackwood. I can assure you of that." Madame lifted the little silver bell and shook it.

Immediately the kitchen door opened and Natalie came in.

38

"We are ready for the main course," Madame told her.

Kit was seated directly across from Jules Duret. How much, she found herself wondering, did he have to do with the selection of the students?

She glanced over and flushed to find him studying her. He did not shift his gaze when their eyes met, but continued looking at her, as though trying to fathom some part of her that did not show upon the surface.

"My mother is right," he said slowly. "You will not be bored."

Chapter 5

———◆———

It was twelve-thirty — half past midnight — on the eighth day of September, and Kit lay sprawled across the bed, writing a letter to Tracy. She knew it was late to be writing letters. If she had been at home with her light on at this hour her mother would have been rapping at the door, calling in a worried voice, "Kit? Is anything wrong, honey? It's much too late for you to be up."

At Blackwood nobody sounded a lights-off curfew, and Kit was glad. Although she had been at the school for well over a week now and was adjusting well on most counts, she still did not feel at ease at night. The light at the end of the hall had not been fixed — "It's almost impossible to get electricians to come out this far," Madame explained apologetically — and though Kit's own room was often lightened by moonlight, she could not shut out a strange nervousness about the oppressive darkness on the far side of her closed door.

She did not sleep well at Blackwood. She dreamed. She knew that she dreamed, for when she woke in the mornings the feeling of the dreams still clung to the edges of her mind, and yet in most cases she could not remember what they had been. She needed to be very sleepy to turn off the light and settle into slumber, and so she had begun to form the habit of studying and writing letters during the early part of the night.

"Dear Tracy," she wrote now, "I'm sorry to have been so long in writing. I got a note off to Mom the first day here so that she would have mail waiting for her in Cherbourg, and then I got snowed under with schoolwork. The work here is harder than it was in public school, mostly, I guess, because the classes are so small. There are only four of us here — can you believe it? Four students in the entire school! So it's almost like having private tutors. I'm taking math and science from Professor Farley, a dear old goat of a man with a funny little beard — really sweet — and literature from Madame Duret. And piano from *Jules!* I guess I'd better put a row of exclamation marks — !!!!!!!! — to give you an idea of what *he* looks like. All of a sudden I'm getting interested in music.

"The three other girls here are very different. My favorite is Sandy Mason — she's shy and quiet, but nice, and I've started to stir her up a little with plans to short-sheet the other girls' beds and maybe raid the kitchen one night and bring the food up to the rooms for a midnight feast. Lynda Hannah and Ruth Stark knew each other before. They went to the same prep school last year, and when Ruth's parents decided to switch her to Blackwood, Lynda persuaded her mother to let her change schools too. Ruth is homely but very bright, and Lynda is the opposite, awfully pretty but not much in the brains department. They seem to balance each other.

"I still don't understand how we four were selected. Professor Farley says we have the special attributes they were looking for in their students, but I can't imagine what they might be. We seem to have nothing in common with each other, and I don't see how you could have failed to get accepted if I was. I tried to ask Madame Duret about it, but she only said that she didn't discuss test results.

"I wish I could say I like it here. In a way I do. Everybody's very nice to me, and the classes are interesting. But there's something — I don't know how to put it into words, and you'd probably laugh if I did — but I've got this creepy feeling that something's wrong. I felt it first when we entered the gates and started up the driveway, and I feel it more and more every day, as though —"

Somebody screamed. Somewhere in the blackness on the far side of the door. It was a funny scream, choked off in an instant as though a hand had been pressed suddenly to cover the mouth.

It went through Kit like an electric shock. Her hand jerked, and the pen made a lurch across the page, so that the word "though" ran off the side of the paper.

Pulling herself upright on the bed, she sat, tense and shaken, listening. There was nothing but silence.

But I heard it, she told herself. I know I heard it.

Somewhere in the quiet dormitory someone had shrieked. In pain? In terror? Perhaps only from a nightmare, and yet, perhaps for some other reason. For — *help?*

I won't, Kit thought. I can't. I just can't open that door and go out there.

And yet, what if one of the other girls were ill? No one screamed without reason. Was someone lying even now in one of the rooms along the hall, wretched with fear or in physical agony, praying that her cry had been heard and would be answered?

Slowly, as though impelled by something other than her own will, Kit got off the bed and crossed the room and opened the door. The terrible blackness of the hall stretched before her, lessened only by the patch of lamplight that fell from her own doorway. Beyond this there was nothing but stillness and dark.

Kit stood with one hand on the door jamb, listening. The only sounds she could hear were the thud of her own heart and the quick, sharp noise of her breathing.

Perhaps I imagined it, she thought. Perhaps I dozed off a little, there on the bed, and dreamed.

And then she heard it — not a scream this time but a little moaning sound, half a sob, half a wail. It seemed to come from the end of the hall where Sandy had her room.

Well, that does it, Kit told herself resignedly. I have to go.

Drawing a deep breath as if in readiness for a dive into icy water, she stood poised for a moment on the edge of the patch of light. Then, bracing herself, she stepped out into the darkness.

For an instant she felt that she actually had plunged into water. The dark rose about her, filling her eyes and nose and ears, pressing on all sides so that she could not catch her breath. As her initial panic began to subside, she forced herself to fill her chest with air. Stretching out one hand, she groped for the wall. She found it and steadied herself against it and then, carefully, one step at a time, she began to work her way down the hall toward Sandy's room.

With each step she tested the floor ahead of her. It was ridiculous, she knew, and yet the darkness was so total that it seemed that she was moving forward into nothingness, that suddenly the boards of the floor might be gone as though they had never existed and she would find herself stepping off into infinite space. Or, even worse, what if there were something — something whose existence she could not even begin to contemplate — waiting for her up ahead? A shudder ran through her, and she turned her head to glance back at the comforting light from her room.

As she stared back at it, she saw the pattern of light grow smaller. Slowly, steadily, the edge of darkness was encroaching upon it.

That's impossible, Kit thought frantically. And then there was the short, strong click of the door coming closed and the entire hall was in darkness.

Steady, Kit told herself firmly. You mustn't panic. The door blew closed, that's all.

But how could it have blown shut when there was no wind? The air in the hall was absolutely still. The stained-glass window at its end was sealed tight.

Should she keep moving forward or turn and work her way back to her room? Just the thought of the bright security of that lighted haven was enough to make her long to reverse her steps. But it would not alter the fact of the scream, of the moaning sob.

There's no way, Kit thought, except to keep going. I've got to find out what's wrong.

Step by cautious step, always keeping one hand upon the wall to orient herself, she moved down the hallway. The floorboards creaked slightly under her feet, and the sound seemed a shriek in the silence. When at last her hand touched the edge of Sandy's door, she drew a deep, shuddering breath of relief.

She groped for the knob and found it. Closing her hand upon it, she tried to turn it. It would not move.

"It's locked!" Kit spoke the words aloud, unable to believe them. How could Sandy possibly have managed to secure the door when the locks were located on the outside? Kit released the knob and rapped hard with her knuckles upon the thick wood. The sound seemed to fill the night.

From somewhere within the room there came a small moan.

"Sandy!" Truly concerned now, Kit called the name aloud. She made her hand into a fist and began to pound upon the door in earnest, heedless of whom else she might wake with the noise. "Sandy, answer me! Are you all right in there? Sandy?"

When there was no answer from within the room she grabbed for the knob again, giving it one final twist out of desperation. To her astonishment, this time it turned quite easily and the door came open. Immediately, a gust of cold air swept upon her, as damp and chilling as though it had come from the Arctic.

"Sandy?" Kit cried, and as she stepped into the room she knew, with a sharp, unexplainable certainty, that her friend was not alone in the dark interior. Someone else was with her.

Fighting a terrible desire to turn and run stumbling and staggering back along the hallway to her own room, Kit groped her way forward. The icy air was all around her, so intense that she found herself growing numb.

"Who is it?" she cried shakily. "Who's in here?"

From somewhere close she could hear the sound of breathing, long heavy breaths as though someone had been running for a long way. The closer she drew to the spot where she knew the bed should be, the more intense the cold became, until she began to wonder if she could bear to move an inch farther. Stretching out her hand, she felt for the edge of the bedside table and then for the lamp that she knew must be standing upon it. It seemed as though her hand was pressing through a wall of ice.

Then she touched the base of the lamp, fumbling along it, and found the button. She pressed it, and immediately the room was filled with blessed light.

Blinking her eyes against the sudden brilliance, Kit glanced wildly about her. The alien presence, if it had ever really existed, was gone. The room fell into place around her, as familiar as her own. The only two people in it were herself and Sandy.

Her friend was sitting straight up in the bed, staring at her. Her eyes had the blank, unfocused look of a sleepwalker, and her skin had a bluish hue, as though she had been outside for a long time in the cold.

Kit reached out tentatively and touched her arm.

"You're frozen!" she said. "My gosh, Sandy, pull up the blanket. What in the world has been going on?"

"Kit?" Sandy spoke the name in a hesitant voice. "Kit, is that you?"

"Of course it's me." Kit tugged the blanket up and hauled it over her friend's shoulders. "Cover up before you get pneumonia. How did your room ever get so cold? Sandy, are you awake? You look so — so odd —"

"Yes. Yes, I guess so." Sandy gave her head a shake as if to rid it of a dream. "What are you doing here? It's the middle of the night."

"It's later than that," Kit said. "I'm here because you yelled. Don't you remember?"

Sandy looked at her blankly. "No. No, I don't. I guess I must have been dreaming."

"Your door was locked."

"It couldn't have been. You know I can't lock it from the inside." Sandy paused, and then repeated Kit's words. "It was locked? My door?"

46

"It sure was, but then it came free again the second time I tried it. Someone was in here. I could swear it, Sandy. When I stepped into this room I could feel somebody. I don't mean I actually touched him, but you know how it is when you feel a presence, when you know a room isn't empty."

"I was dreaming," Sandy said. Her voice was thin and frightened. "At least, I think I was dreaming. There was this woman by my bed. She was young — maybe in her middle twenties — and she was wearing a long dress, kind of old-fashioned-looking. She was just standing there, looking down at me, and I could see her even in the darkness."

"Good Lord," Kit said. Her legs felt weak, and she sank down on the edge of Sandy's bed. "Of course, you were dreaming. You must have been."

"Yes," Sandy said. "But — but, Kit — it's not the first time."

"It's not?"

"Oh, it's the first time this exact thing has happened. I mean, this woman — a stranger — and the funny clothes and everything. But it's not the first time I've had odd dreams. You know how I told you that I live with my grandparents?"

"Yes."

"My parents died three years ago," Sandy said. "It was their fifteenth wedding anniversary. Daddy had arranged a trip as a surprise for Mother; it was to be a kind of second honeymoon. They were flying to the Bahamas. The plane went down in the ocean. They never even found the wreckage."

"How awful," Kit breathed. "I'm so sorry."

"I was staying with my grandparents," Sandy said. "The crazy thing was — I knew about the plane. I knew it as soon as it happened. I was in the kitchen helping Grandma with the dinner, and suddenly I *knew*. I said, 'Gran, the plane has crashed.' She looked at me as though I were nutty and said, 'What plane?' 'Dad's and Mother's,' I told her. 'It's gone down.' She kept staring at me, and then she said, 'What a terrible thing to joke about!' She was so mad she wouldn't even talk to me, and then, later that night, we heard about it on television."

"You said you had a dream," Kit reminded her.

"It wasn't that night. I don't think any of us slept that night. But the next day after the notification was official, I started crying and couldn't stop, and Grandpa got a doctor over to the house, and he gave me a shot. I did go to sleep then, and that's when I had the dream.

"Daddy and Mother were there, standing next to the bed, holding hands. Mother said, 'Sandy, you've got to get hold of yourself.' In the dream I answered her. I said, 'But, you're dead! I'm crying because you're dead!' And Daddy said, 'Your mother and I are together. To us, that's the important thing. We're happy, and you must be too.' "

Kit looked down at her own hands and saw that they were gripped together until the knuckles were white.

"Did you tell anybody?" she asked.

"I tried to," Sandy said, "but nobody would listen. They just said that everybody has funny dreams when they're emotionally upset."

"They wouldn't believe me either," Kit said quietly.

"You?" Sandy stared at her.

"After my father was killed. Except, I never thought of that as a dream. He was there in my room, *really* there. I know he was."

For a moment they sat in silence, gazing at each other. Sandy's eyes were huge in her thin face and the freckles stood out like polka dots against her pale skin.

Kit was trembling, and this time it was not from cold.

"What does it mean?" Sandy asked finally. "It can't be coincidence. The two of us — both having had experiences like that — and tonight — the locked door — the woman by my bed —"

"I don't know what it means," Kit said. "But I'll tell you one thing. I'm going to do my best to find out."

Chapter 6

They spent the rest of the night in Kit's room.

They did not talk, but Kit was too keyed up to sleep, and she could tell by the sound of her breathing that Sandy was awake also, lying still and tense in the bed beside her. Only when the first flush of dawn lightened the sky beyond the window did she finally doze off, and when she again opened her eyes she found that it was well past eight o'clock and Sandy was no longer in the room.

She got up and dressed and went down to the dining room to breakfast. Ruth and Lynda were there, finishing plates of eggs and toast.

"Yes, Sandy was here a few minutes ago," Ruth told her in answer to her query. "She said she wasn't hungry, she just wanted some coffee, and that she had an early class scheduled with Professor Farley. I guess he's giving her some remedial help in algebra."

"How did she look?" Kit asked.

"Awful," Lynda told her. "I thought maybe she was coming down with something. There were bags under her eyes and she looked exhausted. Come to think of it, you don't look too great yourself." She regarded Kit quizzically. "Is there some sort of flu bug doing the rounds at Blackwood?"

"Not that I know of," Kit said. "We were both up a big part of the night. Sandy had a dream and woke up screaming, and I was in with her for a while, and then she came back to my room with me. Didn't you hear us? Between her yelling and my banging on the door, we should have waked the dead."

Despite herself, she gave a little shiver at her choice of words.

"I didn't hear a thing," Lynda said. "Did you, Ruth?"

"I might have," the dark-haired girl said. "I had a restless night, so maybe I kind of half-consciously got waked up. I've been doing a lot of dreaming myself lately."

"You have?" Kit froze at the statement. "What — what sort of dreams?"

"I don't know," Ruth said with a shrug. "I don't remember them when I wake up. I just have this feeling in the morning that I've been at it all night."

"I know what you mean," Lynda said. "When that alarm goes off, sometimes I can hardly make myself get up."

"Well, at least let's get up from the *table*." Ruth consulted her watch. "We've got literature with Madame in just a couple of minutes. What's on your schedule this morning, Kit?"

"Music," Kit told her.

"And Jules all to yourself? Lucky you!" Lynda giggled and tossed her blond curls. "If I'd known there would be a teacher like him, I'd have signed up for piano lessons too. As it is, I can't even get him to look at me."

"He does seem the silent type," Ruth agreed. "I get the impression he's dedicated to his work. Not that I'm that interested."

"Well, *I* am," Lynda said. "After all, he's probably the only man we're going to see between now and Christmas vacation. That is, unless you count Professor Farley."

The door to the kitchen opened and Natalie came in with a pot of coffee. She nodded a curt good morning, but her face softened a little when she saw Kit.

"Morning, miss," she said. "Can I fix you some breakfast?"

"No thanks, Natalie," Kit said. "I'm not hungry this morning."

Natalie set the coffee pot on the table.

"You ought to eat something," she said. "You're getting skinny."

The aroma of the coffee rose in a cloud, and Kit, who normally found the odor enticing, felt her stomach lurch with a wave of nausea.

"There's no time for it now," she said. "I'm running late. I'll make up for it at lunchtime." With a nod of farewell to the girls, she left the room.

Jules Duret was waiting for her in the music room. He was wearing a pale blue shirt, open at the throat, and a pair of white flared pants. He was seated in a chair by the window, and a musical score lay open on his lap, but he did not seem to be reading it. He had the look of one who had been waiting for a long time.

He glanced up as Kit came in, his face solemn.

"You're late," he said by way of greeting. "I'd about given up on you."

"I'm sorry," Kit said. "I didn't sleep well last night, and I overslept this morning."

It was hard to think of this handsome young man as a teacher. He appeared hardly older than the boys she had gone out with in public school, and his dark good looks made him far more attractive than the best of them. Still, there was a quality of reserve about him that made communication difficult, and Kit, who was usually as at ease with boys as she was with girls, found herself fighting a vague feeling of discomfort in his presence.

"Have you done your practicing?" Jules asked now. "Sit down and let me hear how far you've come. Let's warm up with some scales before we get to the actual pieces."

Kit obediently took her place on the piano bench. She placed her hands on the keys. To her surprise, she found that her fingers were stiff and sore, as though she had already been playing for hours.

"Jules?" she said.

"Yes."

"I — I just don't think I want to play this morning." Kit took her hands from the keys and let them fall into her lap. I'm tired, she thought, I'm so terribly tired, and I'm scared, and I need somebody to talk to. I need a friend.

She raised her eyes to meet the dark, intense gaze of the young man across from her. Was Jules Duret a friend? For all she knew, he might not even like her. Yet whom else was there to talk to? Sandy was as upset as she was, and Lynda and Ruth could provide no help.

"Can we talk for a few minutes," she asked in a thin voice, "instead of having a lesson?"

"Talk?" Jules's eyes seemed to narrow slightly. "About what?"

"Blackwood."

"What about Blackwood?"

"I don't know," Kit said. "That's just it — I don't know. There's something odd about Blackwood, something — sinister. We all of us feel it, but it's almost impossible to put it into words. Things have been happening."

"What do you mean?" Jules asked with interest.

"Well, for one thing, we've all been having dreams. Sandy dreamed last night that someone was in her room. She cried out, and I heard her and went down the hall to find out what was wrong. Her door was locked."

"It couldn't have been," Jules said. "The doors don't lock from the inside."

"Why don't they?" Kit asked.

"What do you mean?"

"Just that. Why don't they lock from the inside the way other doors do? Your mother said that she'd had the locks put on the doors to assure us of privacy, but how can you have privacy if you can't lock up when you're in a room?"

"You can lock up when you go out of a room," Jules said. "So that no one can get into your things while you're gone."

"I'm not concerned about that," Kit said. "I don't have anything sitting around in there valuable enough for someone to want to steal it. But I *would* like to be able to lock the door when I'm inside. And last night, Sandy's door *was* locked. I tried the knob. And then, suddenly, it did come open as though somebody had released it."

"Then it wasn't locked," Jules said with certainty. "It must just have been stuck. I'll see about putting some oil on those latches. Which room did you say it was?"

Kit regarded him with frustration. "Weren't you listening at all? I'm not asking you to oil Sandy's lock — what I'm trying to tell you is that something weird is happening here at Blackwood. There was somebody in Sandy's room last night. A woman. I know it sounds crazy, but Sandy saw her with her own eyes!"

"She was dreaming," Jules said. "You just finished saying yourself that all you girls are doing a lot of that. It's nothing to be concerned about. It often happens to people who are away from home for the first time, under the strain of meeting new people and adjusting to new surroundings." He paused, and then in a lower voice asked, "Did she say anything — the woman in Sandy's room?"

Kit was surprised at the question. "Why do you ask that?"

"Well — just to get the end of the story."

"I don't think she did. At least, Sandy didn't tell me so. What do you care if you're so sure it was a dream?"

"Sandy reacted by screaming," Jules said. "I thought perhaps it was at something the woman had said to her."

"She was frightened," Kit told him, "simply by the fact that the woman was *there*. Can't you imagine what it would be like to wake up in a room where you thought you were all by yourself and find somebody standing by your bed, looking down at you? And the cold — I felt that myself. When I went into the room this great wave of cold air came sweeping over me, and Sandy was blue with it. When I touched her hand, it was like ice."

"Look, Kit," Jules said, "there just couldn't have been a stranger in Sandy's room. How could she have gotten there? The gates to Blackwood are always locked at night, and so is the building itself. Nobody is going to climb up a straight wall to come in a window. And even supposing that were possible, how did she get out again so quickly when you came bursting in the door? Did she have wings?"

"The locked door — the cold air —"

"I told you, the door was undoubtedly stuck. And, of course, the air in Sandy's room was going to be colder than the air in the hallway. She probably had her window open."

Jules leaned over and put his hand on Kit's. It was a

nice hand, warm and strong with long, fine fingers, and it felt good upon hers.

His voice was suddenly gentle. "Blackwood is an old mansion, magnificent, of course, but heavy with atmosphere. Old places are inclined to be that way. You have to get used to this place gradually. I had some dreams myself the first week or so after we came here."

"You did?" Kit asked, surprised.

"Sure. What would you expect? I'm not used to living in a place like Blackwood. I'm fresh out of music school. I've been living in an apartment with a couple of other fellows. I've spent my vacations with my mother at her various schools, but other than that I've pretty much lived my own life. When she wrote and asked if I would come to America with her to teach in her new school, I wasn't too sure I wanted to. Then she told me more about the school — how special it would be and the kind of students she would have here — and I decided to give it a try.

"When I got my first glimpse of Blackwood, I couldn't believe it. I still don't know how my mother was able to locate such a spot. The place has its own vibes. You just have to get used to them."

"And you're used to them now?" Kit asked him.

"I like them. I feel — different — here. I play better. I appreciate things more."

"Do you still dream?"

"Well, sure. Some. Everybody dreams."

"Oh, Jules." Kit tried to smile at him. "You make everything sound so sensible and normal. You must think I'm a fool."

"I don't think that at all," Jules said quietly. "I think you're a smart girl. And a pretty one. Sometimes I wish that I'd met you somewhere else, under another set of circumstances. That I wasn't your teacher. But —" He gave her hand a quick squeeze and released it, "we'll just have to take things as they are. And the way they are right now, we've wasted half the class period chattering. Are you ready to play for me?"

"As ready as I'll ever be," Kit said with a sigh. "I probably have as little talent as anyone you'll ever have as a student. Don't you get bored listening to me plow through pieces like 'Happy Leaves' and 'Swinging on the Gate'?"

"I don't get bored," Jules told her. Then, after a pause, he lowered his voice. "You *do* have talent, Kit. Maybe someday you'll realize how much. There are all sorts of talents in the world, and only one of them is music."

Chapter 7

"Hey, Kit, guess what? I've done your portrait!" Lynda stood in the entrance to the parlor, holding a sheet of paper against her chest.

"You have?" Kit glanced up from her book. "Let's have a look."

The girls generally gathered in the parlor during the hour before dinner. It was a pleasant spot, well lighted with comfortable furnishings, and a good deal more modern than the rest of the rooms at Blackwood.

Usually they chatted or watched television, but tonight no one seemed to be in a communicative mood. Kit and Ruth had been reading, and Sandy was over at the card table in the corner, dealing out a game of solitaire.

Now, with Lynda's entrance, they all looked up from their activities. There was something about Lynda's bright prettiness that wakened any room, and at this moment she looked so innocently pleased with herself that Kit found herself smiling.

"Come on, let's see it. I didn't know you were an artist."

"I didn't either," Lynda said, handing her the paper. "I really surprised myself."

Kit held the sketch out in front of her in a joking manner and then caught her breath in amazement. "Why — it *is* of me!"

"I told you it was." Lynda perched on the arm of her chair. "Do you like it?"

"Like it!" Kit exclaimed. "Why, it's — it's — incredible. I mean it, honestly. Lynda, you're great!"

"This I've got to see." Ruth got up from the couch and came over to stand behind them. She was silent a moment and then said, "You couldn't have drawn that, Lynda. You must have traced it or something."

"I didn't," Lynda said in a hurt voice. "I just sat down and drew it. I'd been taking a nap, and I woke up, and all of a sudden I wanted to draw a picture. I went over to the desk and got a pencil and a sheet of paper and sat down and did it, just like that. And the funny thing is, I didn't even know who it was going to be until it started to look like Kit, and then suddenly it *was* Kit."

"But you've never done any drawing before," Ruth said skeptically. "You never took art classes in school. This sketch — well, it's expert. The eyes have that direct, kind of challenging look that Kit's do, and the mouth — the chin — everything — it's Kit, all over. It's absolutely professional."

By this time Sandy too had come over and was studying the picture.

"You're right," she said. "It's awfully good. Would you do one of me, Lynda? I'd like to send it to my grandparents. I bet they'd frame it."

"Sure," Lynda said happily. "Now that I've caught the knack of how to do this, I'll draw everybody. Next I think I'll do Madame Duret with her eyes kind of boring right into you, the way they do. Or maybe Jules. Would anybody like a picture of him?"

"Do carbons of that one," Kit said with a laugh.

"We're all going to want them. And one of Professor Farley stroking his beard —"

"Did I hear my name mentioned?" The professor's deep voice broke into the conversation. He stood framed in the doorway, smiling in his friendly way. "Let me in on the joke. I was drawn by the laughter."

"I was drawn too," Kit said, "but in my case, it was by a pencil." She turned the picture so that he could see it. "Look what Lynda did. Isn't that something?"

"It is, indeed." Professor Farley came slowly into the room to stand, gazing down at the penciled portrait. "That's an excellent piece of work, Lynda. Have you studied art for a long time?"

"I've never studied it at all," Lynda told him. "In fact, the only drawing I've ever done was during a party game once when we were all supposed to draw each other and then have people guess who the pictures were. I drew Ruth, and won the booby prize."

"Well, you've surely improved since then," Professor Farley said admiringly. "I'm going to mention this to Madame Duret. She likes to encourage talent in our young people. I'm sure she will provide you with art supplies that will allow you to express yourself better than you can with a pencil."

"May I keep this?" Kit asked, and Lynda nodded, pleased.

"Of course. I'm glad you like it enough to want it. And I will do you, Sandy, and you too, Ruth, if you want me to. Or do you still believe that I traced?"

"No," Ruth said apologetically. "I've never known you to lie about anything. Besides, what could you possibly have traced it from? I'm sorry to have sounded so doubtful. It's just that we've known each other so long, and to suddenly discover that you're an artist comes as a shock. It's as though I've never really known you at all."

"You know me better than anybody," Lynda said fondly. "I'd never have made it through at that last boarding school if it hadn't been for your helping me. Like I said, I don't wonder you're surprised. I'm surprised myself."

"Five minutes till dinner," Kit said, glancing at her watch. "I'm going to run upstairs and put this picture in my room before something happens to it. The way we're thumbing it over, it's going to be nothing but one big smudge."

The soft glow of twilight lit the stained-glass window at the end of the hall with a gentle radiance that made the hallway itself appear like the center aisle of a cathedral.

At a moment like this, Kit thought as she walked down it, I can almost believe that all the creepiness has been in my imagination.

She reached the door of her room and opened it and went in. She flicked on the study light and laid the pencil portrait on the desk.

For a long moment she stood there, gazing down at it. It was not an intricate sketch; the lines were pure and simple, and yet it caught something beyond a surface likeness. The straight nose, the stubborn chin, the curve of the rounded cheek, all were there, but there was something more, something about the eyes. As Ruth had commented, they had a directness which was typical of Kit, but there was another quality too — a youngness, a touch of uncertainty. The eyes were those of a girl who was not as sure on the inside as she appeared outwardly to be.

"Who am I?" the eyes asked. "What is my place in life? Am I pretty? Do people like me? Does *Jules* like me? In what direction am I going? Will I accomplish anything worthwhile in my lifetime? Will I be happy? Am I worth loving?"

A multitude of questions glimmered behind the eyes, suggested by a few tiny lines and some subtle shading. It was the difference between the real Kit, the one known only to herself and possibly to Tracy, and the strong, self-confident Kathryn Gordy everyone else saw.

How did she guess? Kit asked herself wonderingly. How in the world could Lynda Hannah come to know me so well? We've never talked with each other except as part of a group.

But the girl in the picture could not be denied.

"Kit?" Sandy's voice called to her from the stairs at the end of the hall. "Madame's rung the bell for dinner. Come along or you're going to be late."

"Coming," Kit called back.

Flicking off the light, she left the room, pulling the door closed behind her. She hesitated a second and then, turning back, she reentered the room and took the key off the bureau top, where it had lain ever since Madame had given it to her upon her arrival at Blackwood, and went out again into the hall.

This time she thrust the key into the lock and turned it. She did not know exactly why, but for the first time since she had come here, she felt that her room held something of value.

Dinner hour was one of the pleasantest times at Blackwood. All meals were served in the grandeur of the dining room, but only the evening meal was eaten by candlelight with a white cloth upon the table and linen napkins and fine china. The dishes were pure white and thin to the touch, and each plate was bordered by a delicate line of gold.

"They came with Blackwood," Madame Duret explained when Kit asked about them. "The dishes and kitchenware, the furniture, the piano, the drapes and carpets, all of them have been here for years and years. The only things that were brought in from outside were the furnishings in my own apartment, which I had shipped over after I closed my school in England, and those in the reconverted carriage house which was made into an apartment for Professor Farley. And, of course, the furnishings in the rooms occupied by you girls."

"It's strange," Kit commented, examining the china, "that something so lovely would just have been left here. You'd think the owners would have wanted it for themselves."

"It is strange," Madame had agreed, "but then, people are peculiar sometimes, are they not? After Mr. Brewer died the new owners wanted nothing to do with Blackwood except to sell it. It is a shame, really, but very lucky for us."

The china set the mood of dinner. It was an elegant meal, served in several courses, and Madame Duret seemed at that time less a headmistress than a gracious hostess, entertaining her guests with interesting stories of her life abroad. Jules occasionally contributed to these, as did Professor Farley, who had taught at Madame's school in England though not at the one in France. Conversation flowed freely, with all of the girls joining in, and dinner generally ended with everyone in good spirits, ready to adjourn to the parlor or to go up to her room to study.

This night was different. The atmosphere in the dining room seemed charged with an extra quality, a kind of electricity. Conversation moved well, as always, but to Kit there seemed to be an artificiality about it, as though the speakers were playing their parts and did not really have their minds on the discussion. At one point she caught an exchange of glances between Madame and Professor Farley. As far as she could see, there had been nothing to trigger it, but when Madame Duret turned back again her eyes were shining with a kind of suppressed excitement. Or perhaps it was simply the flicker of the candles reflected in the black pupils.

When dinner was over and Kit had started down the hall to the stairs, Sandy caught up with her and laid a hand on her arm.

"Let's go out for a little while," she said softly.

"Out? At night? Whatever for?" Kit asked her.

"Just into the garden. I need to talk. Please?"

"All right," Kit said. "But we'd better slip out through the kitchen. I'm sure Madame wouldn't want us roaming around the grounds in the dark."

Natalie was putting away the silver when they entered. She glanced up sharply.

"Where do you ladies think you're going?"

"Out," Kit told her. "For air." Natalie's crispness had never bothered Kit, for she knew that the girl liked her and that this was simply her manner.

"I don't blame you," Natalie said now. "It's stuffy in this place. The rest of the help is quitting."

"You're kidding!" Kit exclaimed. "Why?"

"They just don't like it, especially the upstairs part. They say it spooks 'em, cleaning in that hall. One girl says she gets headaches."

"Are you quitting?" Kit asked.

"Not me. I need the job. I got myself and a sick dad to support. Besides, I don't go along with all that superstition stuff. Whatever happened was so long ago, you can't count it."

"What do you mean?" Kit's curiosity was piqued. "What happened here?"

"Oh, well, Mr. Brewer was sort of odd." Natalie gave

a shrug. "People blow things up. Will you be warm enough outside? My coat and sweater are in the broom closet if you want to wear them."

"Thanks," Kit said gratefully. "We won't be outside long."

Giving the coat to Sandy, she herself pulled on the worn blue sweater that hung on a nail on the inside of the closet door, and the two girls let themselves out into the night.

The path from the kitchen door led around the corner of the house and into the garden. There was a three-quarter moon hanging high over the trees, sending long bands of silver out across the lawn. The garden path was aglow with moonlight, and a faint, sweet smell rose from the bushes, as though in remembrance of recent summer flowers. Below the lawn the pond lay black and still with the moonlight making a silver path across its surface.

The night air was cold and pure, tinged with the scent of trees. The woods rose in a dark frame around the silver garden and shining pond.

"How lovely," Kit said softly. "I'm glad you wanted to come outside. It's even more beautiful at night than it is in the daytime."

"I had to come," Sandy said. "If I'd stayed cooped up inside those walls any longer I think I'd have strangled. Kit, am I crazy? What on earth is happening to me?"

"You mean, your dream?" Kit tried to sound reassuring. "I talked with Jules about that, and what he said made a lot of sense. You're away from home for the first time, adjusting to new things —"

"That's not it," Sandy interrupted. "It really isn't, I'm sure of it. It's this place — Blackwood itself. There's something weird about Blackwood. Don't tell me you haven't felt it too. I know you have."

"Well, sure —" Kit found her thoughts swept back to

that first day as she and her mother and Dan saw the mansion standing before them, huge and stark with the late afternoon sunlight glancing off the windows to make the whole place seem aflame from within.

"Can't you feel it?" she had cried to Dan and her mother. "There's something about the place — something —"

"Yes," she said to Sandy now, shivering a little despite the wool sweater. "I did say that, and I do know what it is that you're saying. But how can it be the place itself? A place doesn't have a personality."

"What was the first word that came to your mind when you saw it?"

"I — I don't remember —" Kit began.

"You do. You just don't want to remember. There was a particular word, and it jumped right into your mind. It was 'evil.' "

"You're right." Kit turned to her incredulously. "How could you know that? I never told you. I never told anybody."

"I know it because the word was *there*. I felt it too. It was as much a part of the first view of this place as the peaked roof. Professor Farley picked me up at the bus stop in the village, and we drove up here through the beautiful morning with the sunlight streaming down through the trees and the sky so blue and clear. We came through the gate and started up the driveway, and it was as though a black shadow fell in front of us. An invisible shadow. The closer we got to the house, the darker it became — the kind of darkness you can feel and not see — and when I got out of the car and walked through that front door, I almost turned and ran back out again."

"But — but we don't feel it now," Kit said. "Not all the time. At night along the hall we do, with it all so

66

black — and in our dreams — but there are lots of times when we laugh and study and go to class and it's all so nice and normal —"

"Because we're part of it now," Sandy said. "Don't you see, Kit? We're *part* of the shadow. We've been living in it for weeks and we're adjusting to it. That's why I wanted to come outside tonight, to stand back from Blackwood and be able to look at it and feel the difference."

"It does feel different from out here," Kit admitted. Standing there in the moonlight, she could look at Blackwood, at the great building with the pointed roof, towering against the paler darkness of the sky, as though it were a picture in a child's storybook. Sandy's second-floor corner room was dark. A light shone in Ruth's; evidently she had already begun her evening studying. Lynda's room was on the far side of the hall, facing off the other side of the house. And her own —

"There's a light on," she said.

"What?"

"A light in my room. There — that window there — that *is* my room, isn't it?"

"Of course," Sandy said. "Perhaps you left it on when you came down to dinner."

"I didn't," Kit said. "I remember turning the light off. Then I locked the door." She stiffened, her eyes glued to the shining window, as a dark form moved across it.

"Somebody's there!" she exclaimed. "Somebody's in my room!"

"That's impossible if you locked your door." Sandy too was staring at the window. "Maybe it's the curtain blowing."

"It's not! It's a person!" Kit whirled and started up the path at a run. "Come on, we'll catch him! There's no

67

place he can go except back along the hall. If we get to the stairs in time we can cut him off!"

But the stairs were empty, and so was the long, black hallway. The door was still locked. When she turned the key and opened it, Kit found the room dark.

She turned on the light, and before she looked, she knew what she would find. The pencil portrait was no longer on her desk.

Her dream that night was different. It was a strange dream, and oddly lovely. In it she was in the music room, sitting at the piano, and her fingers were at home on the keys. There was no sheet music in front of her, but she was playing in a way that she had never played before. It was a beautiful melody, as cool and haunting as the moonlight in the garden, as smooth as the path of silver across the pond.

It is so beautiful, she told herself in the dream, that I must try to remember it so that I can play it again. But the music had no name, and she knew that she had never before heard it.

When she woke in the morning she felt as exhausted as though she had never slept at all, and her fingers ached.

Chapter 8

The incoming mail was on a table in the entrance hall, and Kit, coming back from a class with Professor Farley, picked up her portion and carried it up to her room to read.

There were two postcards from her mother, one from Cherbourg and one from Paris, both sent airmail but with a week between mailing dates.

". . . so exciting," the first one said, ". . . marvelous trip over . . . so many interesting people on board . . . we caught up on our sleep and lay out on deck chairs." The second was filled with references to the Eiffel Tower and Montmartre and the Folies Bergères.

"Where are your letters, honey?" said a hurried postscript. "We got your note in Cherbourg but haven't had a word since. You have our itinerary. Write care of American Express, but allow enough time."

Besides the postcards, there was a letter from Tracy. The neat, round handwriting, almost as familiar as Tracy herself, gave Kit a momentary pang of homesickness.

"That must be some great place," the letter ran, "if you can't even get around to writing. What's with that promise you made to keep me up to date on everything? Things here are as usual. I got Mrs. Logan for English — hooray! — and Mr. Garfield for Latin — ugh. Advanced art is keen, we can do whatever we want. There's a cute guy in my geometry class named Kevin Weber. How are you bearing up at Blackwood without a single guy under the age of eighty?"

There's Jules, Kit thought. I wrote her about Jules in my very first letter. Could it be that it got lost in the mail? But I've written a couple of times since and mentioned him both times.

She flipped over the page and was skimming the next few paragraphs when there was a light rap at the door.

"Come on in," Kit called, assuming it was Sandy. To her surprise her visitor turned out to be Ruth Stark.

"I hope I'm not disturbing you." The dark-haired girl stood hesitantly in the doorway. "If you're in the middle of studying —"

"I'm not," Kit said. "I'm only reading some letters."

"Then I want to show you something." Ruth stepped inside and closed the door carefully behind her. "It's this."

She held out a sheet of paper. At a glance Kit could see that it was a crude sketch of a face, a wavering, childish drawing of the type that one might expect to see in a display of grammar school art.

"What is it?" she asked. "Did it come in the mail? Your little brother or sister —"

"No," Ruth said. "It's a portrait of me. Lynda did it. It's the picture she drew for that parlor game she was talking about."

"Lynda drew that?" Kit exclaimed, reaching for the paper and laying it flat on the bed in front of her. Ruth came over to stand beside her and together they studied the drawing. A round, unformed face. A triangle nose. A mouth that resembled a Halloween pumpkin. A mop of black hair.

"She got the hair right," Ruth said. "It's black. Frankly, I don't see any other resemblance. I know I'm no beauty queen, but even I have two eyes that look in the same direction. And she's forgotten to put on the ears."

"I don't understand," Kit said. "We know that Lynda can draw. That portrait she did of me was excellent."

"It was a freak," Ruth said flatly. "Lynda can't draw. Lynda doesn't have any talent in anything. She's pretty and sweet, but the day they distributed brains, Lynda was out to lunch."

Somehow from Ruth the statement did not sound brutal, simply factual.

"Sit down," Kit said slowly. "I think you and I need to talk."

Ruth nodded. She seated herself on the edge of the bed. In her lap, her square, strong hands gripped each other tightly.

"Something's going on here," she said in a low voice. "I'm aware of it, but I don't know what it is. Do you feel it too?"

"Yes," Kit said, "and so does Sandy."

"Lynda doesn't. Lynda just doesn't notice things. She's like a little kid in so many ways."

"Maybe you'd better tell me about her," Kit said. "And about yourself. The two of you seem to be good friends, but you're so different. There's nothing wrong with *your* I.Q."

"It's a hundred and fifty," Ruth said with pride. "I was ahead of myself from the beginning. I skipped two grades in grammar school, and by the time I reached junior high I'd already read so far ahead on my own that the things in the textbooks were old stuff to me. And the kids didn't like me. Who wants a fat little nine-year-old in a class of twelve-year-olds?

"My parents are both Ph.D.s. They think education is awfully important, so they decided to send me to a special, ungraded school in Los Angeles. That's where I first met Lynda Hannah."

"What was she doing there," Kit asked, "if the school was for brilliant students?"

"Well, it wasn't exactly. At least, that's what I discovered after I got there. It was just 'elite.' I don't know if you realize it or not, but Lynda's mother is Margaret Storm."

"Margaret Storm, the actress?" Kit said in surprise. "I've seen her on some of the late movies on television."

"She was pretty popular in her day," Ruth said. "Of course, a glamorous actress doesn't stay on top forever. Lynda says she's still making pictures, but the parts aren't that good anymore, and she met some Italian actor in one of them and there was some sort of scandal — well, anyway, she's living in Italy now. That's why Lynda was away at school. She was really lost there; she'd try and try and she just couldn't keep up academically. And I couldn't keep up socially. We sort of found each other, and after that it wasn't so bad for either of us."

"Why did you come to Blackwood?" Kit asked her.

"That was my parents' doing. They didn't think the school in L.A. was challenging enough, and they were right. When they read the brochure about Blackwood and saw the part about the private instruction, the way each student moves along at her own level, they got pretty excited. We talked about it during spring vacation, and Mother wrote Madame Duret and arranged for me to take the entrance tests, and then Lynda heard about it and persuaded her mother to let her take them too. She didn't want to be left behind."

"And she got in?" Kit said. "That's surprising, isn't it."

"I couldn't believe it," Ruth said. "I thought maybe they'd mixed up the scores. But Lynda likes it here. Everybody's nice to her. And now suddenly she thinks she's an artist, and she's thrilled about that. Madame Duret has given her an easel and oil paints and canvases. You should see Lynda's room! It looks like a professional studio."

"But if she doesn't have art ability," Kit said, "how could she have drawn the picture of me? You call it a 'freak,' but that's no answer. How could someone produce something as expert as that, when the best she has ever done before is *this?*" She gestured toward the dreadful sketch.

"That's what's so crazy," Ruth said. "Maybe that picture of you isn't as good as we first thought it was. Why don't you go get it so we can look at it again?"

"I can't," Kit said. "I don't have it any longer."

"You don't have it?"

"Somebody took it," Kit said. "The door was locked, but somebody got in anyway and took the picture off my desk."

"Do you know who?" Ruth asked her.

"No. I can't imagine. I can't even think who would want the picture. We all have the keys to our own rooms, but I'm sure that Madame must have duplicates. Who could get hold of one of them depends upon where she keeps them."

"Or she could have used one herself," Ruth suggested.

"Why in the world would she do a thing like that? Why would a picture of me mean that much to her? Besides, as far as I know, she wasn't even aware of the sketch. She wasn't in the parlor when Lynda brought it in to show to us. Nobody was there then except us girls."

"Professor Farley came in," Ruth reminded her. "He saw it."

"That's right, he did. But why would *he* want it? The more we talk about it, the more ridiculous the whole thing seems. Lynda, who can't draw, draws a wonderful picture. There's no reason for anyone to want it except me, yet somebody goes into a locked room to steal it. Add to that Sandy's nightmare about the woman by her bed —"

"A nightmare?"

"That's what Jules thinks it was. Sandy isn't so certain. She's had experiences like that before. There was one in particular, right after her parents were killed. They were in a plane crash, and before any report was received, Sandy knew about it. She says it just came to her from out of the blue, the absolute certainty that the plane was down and her parents were dead."

"So she has it too." Ruth spoke softly, and there was no surprise in her voice.

"Has what?" Kit asked blankly.

"ESP." Ruth paused, and then, seeing the bewilderment on Kit's face, elaborated. "Extrasensory perception. It's a sort of sixth sense that some people are born with. It's a special kind of sensitivity to things that are normally not seen or heard."

"And you think Sandy has that?" Kit exclaimed. "But you said, 'she has it *too*.' Do you mean that *you* —"

"I've had it for as long as I remember," Ruth said. "For a while I didn't realize what it was. I thought maybe it just came with being bright, my being able to sense things that other people couldn't. It was part of how I got ahead so fast in school. I could look at a book and sometimes I wouldn't even have to open it, I'd find I knew without reading it what was inside. When my teachers asked questions, I'd know the answers even if I hadn't studied the material. I could feel the answers in their minds. Then I'd tell them just what it was they wanted to hear."

"And Lynda?" Kit asked shakily. "Does Lynda have this ability too?"

"Not in the same way," Ruth said. "With Lynda it's a different thing. Lynda remembers."

"Remembers?" Kit repeated the word stupidly. "Remembers *what?*"

"This is going to sound crazy," Ruth said. "It did to me the first time she told me. But, now — after coming to know her so well — I swear, I almost believe it's true. At least, I believe that Lynda thinks it is."

"Well?"

Ruth's eyes dropped to her hands, still gripped tightly in her lap.

"Lynda," she said, "remembers another lifetime in which she was born in England and lived under Queen Victoria."

"Good grief!" Kit said in a cracked voice. There was a long moment of silence while she digested this information. Then she shook her head. "You're right, it's crazy. But it's no crazier than the night I woke to see my father standing by my bed. In the morning I found that he had been killed in an accident the night before."

"So —" Ruth said softly, "it's you too." She drew a deep breath. "I guess that now, at least, we realize what it is the four of us girls have in common, and why, out of all the applications, we were selected to be the first students at Blackwood."

At first the thought occurred to her that she might be dreaming again. Of course, she knew that she wasn't. It was midafternoon, and she was on her way to her literature class with Madame Duret. And yet, the music —

It was coming from behind the closed door of the music room. Strange and beautiful and achingly familiar, the melody swept over her, drawing from her a response she had never experienced from any music before.

She placed her hand on the knob and opened the door. Jules was seated with his back toward her, operating the tape recorder.

"What are you playing?" Kit asked him. When he did not respond, she realized that he was concentrating too hard upon the music to have heard her. She raised her voice. "Jules, what is that music?"

With a quick, startled gesture, Jules flicked the playback switch and the tape slowed to a halt. His expression when he turned was one of unreasonable anger.

"What do you mean, interrupting —" he began, and then, at the sight of Kit's surprised face, he seemed to catch himself. His voice softened. "Oh — it's you."

"You didn't have to shut it off," Kit said. "I heard the music through the door. It's beautiful. I had to know — what is it called?"

"I don't think it has a name," Jules told her.

"But it must. Everything that's published has a name."

"Well, sure. What I meant was, I don't know what it is."

"Doesn't it say on the tape?"

"It's not a commercial tape," Jules said. "It's just a collection of odds and ends I've taken from one place or another because I liked them."

"I like them too," Kit said. "Especially that last piece. Could you play it again?"

"You heard most of it." Jules made no gesture to reach again for the switch of the recorder.

Kit regarded him with bewilderment. Never had she seen Jules Duret any way but in complete control of himself. Now he looked off balance, as though he did not know how to handle the situation.

His eyes shifted from hers in a way that made him look almost guilty.

Guilty — about what? Kit could not imagine. She knew that she should continue to class. She was already late, and Madame could not stand tardiness.

Still, she stood there, anchored in the doorway, watching the play of expressions on Jules's handsome face.

"You do know that song," she said with certainty. "You're a music graduate. If you don't recall the title, you must at least know who wrote it. Who was the composer?"

"I'm not sure," Jules said. "It sounds like — well, I guess it's from something by Schubert."

"By Schubert? And you don't recognize it?" Kit was incredulous. "How can you possibly not know the work of someone so famous?"

"*You* don't recognize it," Jules said defensively.

"No, but I don't claim to be a student of music. Even so, I know that Schubert died when he was very young. He couldn't have written that much."

"Look, Kit —" Jules did meet her gaze now. His eyes were blazing, and the anger which he had shown when he had first turned and seen her lay somewhere in their depths. "I don't know what's gotten into you all of a sudden, but I don't need this kind of interrogation. You don't know a thing about music. You can't have heard this music before. It's practically unknown."

"But I have heard it," Kit said quietly.

She had not only heard it, but she knew where it had been. The melody on the tape was the same haunting song that she had been playing in her dream.

Chapter 9

———◆———

In October, Lynda completed a landscape and Sandy wrote a poem.

The landscape was done in oils. It was a large canvas, measuring two feet tall by three and a half feet wide. It was of a lake, serene and peaceful, throwing back the golden glint of the afternoon sun. The woods on the far side of the water were in shadow, but the immediate foreground was bright with sunlight and wild flowers.

"Where is it?" Kit asked.

"It's in the Catskills," Lynda said.

"A place you've been?"

"I don't think so. I know how it looks though." Lynda regarded the painting with pride. "Don't you think it's pretty?"

Kit nodded. The picture was very good indeed.

"Lynda —" Ruth spoke gently, as one might to a small child. "I want you to think a minute. Try to remember what it was that made you decide to paint this particular scene. Did it come from a calendar, maybe? Or did you once see it on television?"

"I don't know," Lynda said. She frowned, considering

the question. "It's a funny thing, but I don't remember thinking about it at all. I just mixed the paints and took the brush in my hand, and I started painting."

"How did you know how to mix the colors?"

"That's not hard."

"Could you teach me?"

"No," Lynda said. "You just have to know it by yourself. I can do it, but I couldn't explain how to somebody else." She smiled apologetically, that sweet, bland smile that made her look so much younger than her actual years. "I'm sorry, Ruth. I guess a person just happens to be a natural artist, or she doesn't."

She showed the oil to Madame Duret, who admired it greatly and hung it on the wall in the dining room. In the week that followed, Lynda produced two more paintings, small ones. Both were landscapes. One seemed to be of the same lake, but from a different angle, for it showed a footpath leading down to its edge. The other was of fields, green with springtime, lying flat and rich beneath a blue sky.

In the bottom right-hand corner of each picture, Lynda printed the initials T.C.

"T.C.?" Kit said. "Those aren't your initials."

"That's the way I'm going to sign my work," Lynda told her.

"But, why? What do they stand for?" Kit was bewildered.

"Nothing really. I just picked the initials out of the air. People don't have to paint under their regular names, and I'm going to paint under T.C."

It was soon after this that Sandy wrote the poem.

"I did this," she said without preliminaries, tossing herself across the foot of Kit's bed and handing her a sheet of lined paper which had evidently been torn from a spiral notebook. "Read it and tell me what you think."

It was late afternoon and Kit, who was tired of studying, tossed her book aside and picked up the poem. It was titled "Leavetaking."

Quickly she scanned it and then went back to read it again:

I never thought it would be Paradise.
I walked a rugged pathway from the start.
No Ugliness was hidden from my eyes,
Nor was Life's pain a stranger to my heart.
And yet, the earth sprung firm beneath my feet
And summer winds were gentle to my hair.
I breathed upon the dusk, and found it sweet,
I gazed upon the dawn and found it fair.
I know gray moors where shadow mists lie curled
And sunbright streams and night skies rich with stars.
For all its faults, I so have loved this World
And found it beautiful, despite its scars.
Though Angels sing of Glories greater still,
I leave in Sadness, much against my will.

"You wrote that?" Kit turned to her friend in amazement. "Why, Sandy, it's just — just —"

"You don't have to say it," Sandy interrupted. "I know it's good. I also know I didn't make it up."

"You remembered it from somewhere?"

"I must have," Sandy said. "I couldn't have written it myself. On the other hand, I don't recall ever having read it. I never read poetry unless it's for a class assignment."

"I certainly don't recognize it," Kit said. "Perhaps Ruth will know what it's from. She's awfully well read." She started to get to her feet, but Sandy reached out a restraining hand.

"Let's not bring Ruth into this."

Kit was surprised. "Why not?"

"I just don't care for her," Sandy said. "There's something about her that turns me off. I can't put my finger on what it is, but I have this feeling that down inside she's a cold fish and that the only person in life who really matters to her is Ruth Stark."

"She's terribly smart," Kit said.

"I'll give you that. She makes me feel like a moron. Still —" Sandy drew a long breath. "I'm being silly, I guess. Okay, go get her. If this is from something famous, she'll probably know what it is."

Ruth, however, did not recognize the poem.

"It's a type of sonnet," she said, studying the paper. "It has a familiar ring to it, but I've never read it." She glanced across at Sandy. "Where did you get it?"

When Sandy did not answer, Kit spoke for her.

"She wrote it this afternoon."

"Then why —" Ruth stopped as the meaning of the statement became clear to her. Her sharp, dark eyes took on a sparkle of interest. "How did it happen, Sandy? Do you write poetry often?"

"Never," Sandy said shortly. "And I don't know one kind of sonnet from another. That's what's so crazy. I went up to my room after lunch and stretched out on my bed to check over some algebra problems. I must have dozed off, because suddenly I realized that a lot of time had gone by. I had a pencil in my hand, and on the page of my notebook opposite the math problems there was this poem."

" 'Leavetaking,' " Ruth read the title again. Her face was flushed with suppressed excitement. "First Lynda — and now you. It's really incredible."

"What does Lynda have to do with this?" Kit asked her.

"Don't you see a connection? Lynda's never painted

before, and yet she suddenly seems to have this marvelous talent and is turning out pictures that look as though they belong in museums. Sandy's never written poetry, and here she is writing sonnets. And I —"

She paused. Kit regarded her in bewilderment.

"And you?"

"I've been doing some pretty intricate math," Ruth said carefully, "stuff I could never even have conceived of before. At first I thought I was just writing down a lot of numbers. I couldn't see any meaning in them. But now I'm beginning to get glimmers of understanding. It's as though I were being educated by a teacher who is more — much more — capable than Professor Farley."

"What exactly are you driving at?" Sandy's face was dead white beneath her freckles. "Are you trying to say that this is something supernatural?"

Ruth gave her a challenging look. "Do you have a better explanation?"

"Any explanation is better than that," Sandy said shakily.

"There was that woman," Ruth said, "that night in your room when Kit heard you screaming. And there was the time after your parents' death when you knew about the plane crash. If those weren't supernatural occurrences, I'd like to know what you would call them."

"You told her about those things?" Sandy turned to Kit accusingly. "I told you about them in confidence."

"I'm sorry," Kit said. "I didn't think of them as secrets. All these things are part of the mystery of Blackwood. We have to compare our experiences. Perhaps then we'll see some kind of pattern. Ruth thinks that all four of us girls are very sensitive to ESP sort of things, and that that's how we came to be chosen as students here."

"Those entrance exams we took," Sandy said thoughtfully. "They *were* kind of unusual." She paused. "Then, if that should be true — if we were selected for that particular reason — it means that Madame Duret —"

She could not bring herself to complete the sentence.

Ruth finished it for her. "It means that Madame Duret wanted us at Blackwood for exactly that reason."

The room was silent as they digested this statement. Kit thought, this can't be real, this conversation. We're making this up, the three of us; we're inventing a story and giving ourselves roles in it, the way Tracy and I used to do when we were younger.

But she was no longer twelve, and Tracy was not here, and Ruth was not one to play games. Sandy was not playing either; her thin face looked sick.

"We'll have to ask her," Sandy said in a half whisper.

"Ask Madame Duret?" Ruth shook her head. "There'd be nothing to gain by that. Any question we put to her, she's bound to have an answer for. We don't have proof that there's anything wrong. So Lynda's painting and Sandy's turned into a poet — what does that prove? Only that Blackwood is a good school and is bringing out latent talents in its students."

"It's the same with your math," Kit said. "She'll just credit Professor Farley for being such a good instructor. I seem to be the only one here who hasn't developed a new talent." She tried to make her voice light. "I feel sort of left out."

"I wish I were left out," Sandy said. "This whole thing's creepy. If we can't ask Madame Duret outright, then what can we do? If Ruth's theory is right and we're all reacting because we're sensitive personalities, then I want to know what it is we're reacting to. I'm the same person I was when I was back home, but I didn't write poetry then. Why am I doing it here at Blackwood? Is it something about the place itself?"

"What do we know about Blackwood?" Ruth asked.

"Other than the fact that it's an old estate? I don't even know the name of the family that used to own it."

"I know that," Kit volunteered. "It's Brewer. But that doesn't help much."

"I can see no way of getting into town to ask about it," Sandy said. "We haven't been out of this enclosure since we got here. It's a good fifteen miles down to the village, which is farther than I'm about to hike."

"You couldn't get out anyway," Kit said. "The gate's kept closed except when Professor Farley drives down to the town for mail. What about the village help that works here?"

"What help?" Ruth said. "They all quit except for Natalie Culler, and she never opens her mouth."

"She does with me sometimes," Kit said. "We got to be friends on that first day before the rest of you arrived."

"Well, there's nothing to lose," Ruth conceded, "if you want to raise the question to her. The worst she can do is refuse to answer."

"I'll do it," Kit said determinedly, "as soon as I get the chance."

That night it rained. It was a heavy, relentless rain that drummed upon the roof and slashed against the panes and poured in torrents through the rain gullys.

Lying in bed, Kit closed her eyes tightly and tried to pretend that it was a city rain, and that she was in her room at home and the roof above her head was a simple partition that separated her from the next floor of apartments, and that her mother was in the room next door reading, wearing her blue lace bedjacket, with cold cream smeared across her cheeks. In a moment, Kit thought, she will lay her book aside and get out of bed and come into my room to check the window.

But when the bedroom door did open, it was not her mother who slipped through and pushed it closed behind her. "Kit," a voice asked softly, "are you awake?"

"Yes," Kit said. "What is it? Is something wrong? Wait a minute, I'll turn on the light."

"No, don't," Sandy said. "I just want to tell you something. The woman — her name is Ellis."

"The woman in your dream? You've given her a name?"

"Kit, it wasn't a dream." Sandy sounded definite. "It's something else — something more than a dream. This isn't something my mind's made up. Ellis exists. She's a real person. I'm sure of it."

"That's impossible," Kit said. She reached out in the dark and began to fumble for the bedside lamp.

"Don't," Sandy said, sensing her action. "Please, don't. As long as it stays dark I can still see her like a picture on the screen of my mind. She's young — even younger than I thought at first — and she has the most beautiful eyes, dreamy and filled with sorrow as though she's been through a lot of suffering."

"You were afraid of her that first time," Kit said. "You screamed."

"Not now. I'm not afraid any longer. I just wanted to tell you that." Her footsteps brushed on the floor. "Good night, Kit."

The bedroom door opened and closed. Alone once more, Kit shivered and pulled the blankets up over her shoulders. The room was heavy with dampness and the slow, hard beat of the rain.

Chapter 10

———————

The opportunity to talk with Natalie did not come immediately. It was not until several days later, in the evening after dinner, that Kit saw her chance.

The meal had been a subdued one without the usual conversation. Jules had eaten early and driven into town for the evening. Professor Farley had not come to dinner, as he was engaged in doing some writing and did not wish to be disturbed.

"This is how it is with professors," Madame Duret explained lightly. "They must always be publishing something. Perhaps the day will come when some of you girls will be doing the same thing."

Lynda was not at the table either. She had sent word by Ruth that she was not feeling well, and Madame said that a tray should be carried up to her.

"I'll take it," Kit offered, as they were being excused from the table.

"That is kind of you, Kathryn," Madame said. She paused, as though about to add something, and then evidently decided against it.

As she climbed the stairs, Kit realized that it had been

weeks since she had last been inside Lynda's room. The last time she had seen it, she had been impressed by its femininity. The bureau top had been a field of cosmetics, artificial roses had blossomed in a vase on the desk, and the mirror had been edged with a full circle of photographs, all of Lynda herself, smiling coyly up at a variety of admiring boys. The romantic novels that Lynda loved to read had stood in a row on the bedside table, flanked by delicately carved gilt bookends, and a pajama bag, shaped like a pink kitten, had been propped on the pillow of the bed.

Now, when she entered, she was startled to find that, as Ruth had stated, the room resembled nothing so much as an artist's studio. An easel stood by the window where the morning light would fall. The canvas mounted on it was only partially completed; it was a warm, mellow-colored picture of a woodland scene in which a girl's slim figure knelt by a winding stream. Trees bent above her in a great arc of green, and the reflection in the stream gave back the laughing face of a forest nymph.

Other pictures, in various stages of development, leaned against the walls or were piled in a heap in the corner. It was difficult to conceive of the fact that Lynda had created all of them in such a short time.

"Hi," Kit said. "I brought you some dinner. Madame said that you weren't feeling well."

Lynda was stretched, fully clothed, upon the bed. She was wearing no makeup, and her hair lay oily and matted against the pillow, as though she had not bothered to wash it for a long time.

She glanced at the tray and wrinkled her nose.

"Thanks, but I really don't want anything. I'm not at all hungry."

"You need to eat," Kit said. "You're getting thin."

87

The words were true. Lynda's eyes seemed huge in her pretty face, and the delicate tracery of her high cheekbones stood out beneath the normally perfect skin. Now that skin had a yellowish cast.

"I said, I'm not hungry," Lynda said peevishly. "I'm just tired. I've been working hard."

"I should say you have, from the looks of things." Kit nodded toward the picture on the easel. "That's going to be nice."

"Is it?" Lynda said. "I suppose so."

"What are you going to put over there?" Kit gestured toward an unfinished area in the foreground.

"How should I know? It'll come to me when I get the brush in my hand." Lynda turned her face away and threw an arm across her eyes. "Take that food out of here, will you? I can't stand the smell of it."

Kit regarded her with concern. "I hope you're better tomorrow."

"I will be," Lynda said. "I'll have to be. There's so much to be done. He wants so much. There just isn't any stopping."

"*He?*" Kit caught at the word. "What do you mean? Who is it who wants so much?"

"Please," Lynda said, "just let me be, won't you? I'm so tired. We'll talk another time, okay?"

"Okay." Kit stood a moment longer, gazing down at the slender form on the bed. Was this Lynda Hannah, the bright-faced girl with the lilting laugh, whose sole worry less than two months ago had been the fact that Blackwood would not be sponsoring boy-girl parties? She's changed, Kit thought. Not just a surface change, but all the way down inside. She's not the same person.

"Lynda," she said softly, "please, tell me. Something's happened. Can't you tell me about it?"

The girl on the bed did not answer. Her breathing was

slow and deep, and Kit realized suddenly that she was already asleep.

Natalie was scraping plates when Kit brought the tray back down to the kitchen. She glanced at the untouched plate and shook her head.

"Won't eat, huh?"

"She says she's tired," Kit said.

"Funny," Natalie said. "Nobody's eating the way they used to, except for the gentlemen, maybe, and Madame herself. What's with you girls? All coming down with something?"

"I hope not," Kit said, setting the tray on the counter. She paused, knowing that this was the opportunity for which she had been hoping. "Natalie — can I ask you something?"

"You know I'm not supposed to spend time talking to you young ladies." Natalie was silent a moment, then her curiosity got the better of her. "What is it you want to know?"

"About Blackwood. It's been here a long time, hasn't it? You must have heard a lot of things about it."

"It's an old place, sure," Natalie said. "But Blackwood is the new name for it. It used to be called the old Brewer place. Nobody lived here then. It was all grown over so you could hardly see through the fence, just the roof sticking up."

"How do you know?" Kit asked. "Did you look through the fence and see?"

"Well, we all did," Natalie said, with a note of defensiveness in her voice. "All of us kids, I mean. There were so many stories about it. Teenagers used to come up and park in the driveway."

"Did you?"

"Once or twice," Natalie said, flushing slightly. "Nothing happened. We didn't see anything. I figured the ones who said they did were just making up stories to scare the rest of us."

"What did the others see, or pretend to see?" Kit persisted. "Did they ever tell you?"

"Oh, lights in the windows. Shapes moving around. Things like that. Of course, old man Brewer was supposed to have been pretty strange himself back when he lived here. Anybody who'd live alone in a place this size would have had to have been a little bit off."

"He lived here alone?" Kit exclaimed. "Just one person in this huge place?"

"Well, not in the beginning," Natalie said, running the hot water into the sink and dumping in some detergent. "When he first moved here he had a nice family — a pretty wife, they say, and three or four children. The place was kept up fine then with servants and gardeners, and what Madame Duret has made into an apartment for the professor, that was a real carriage house. Then one night there was a fire. Mr. Brewer was away on a business trip at the time, and they never did find out how it started, but it was in the bedroom wing where the family was sleeping. They had to bring the volunteer fire department up from the village, which took a long time because it was a Saturday night and a lot of the volunteer firemen couldn't be located. By the time they got up here and got the fire under control, it was too late."

"You mean Mr. Brewer's whole family died?" Kit asked in horror. "His wife and all the children?"

"They say it was the smoke that did it," Natalie said. "There wasn't that much damage to the house. When old man Brewer got home and found out what had happened, he got rid of all the servants and barred up the gate. From then on he lived here alone.

"He'd go down to the village for church on Sundays and talk about the family like they were still there, still living in the place with him. Or he'd go to the grocery store and say, 'The missus wants me to pick up some things for her,' and he'd buy candy and stuff for the kids and cereal for the baby.''

"That's awful!" Kit gasped. "Just awful! The poor man! How long did this go on?"

"Years and years," Natalie told her. "Talk got started around the town that his family was living here with him, as spirits. Once he called a man to fix the plumbing, and the man said that somewhere in the back of the house he heard a baby crying. After that, he couldn't get people up here to do anything.

"When he died, it was weeks before anybody knew it. Finally they started wondering about his missing church one Sunday after another. So they came up here, and there he was, on one side of the double bed. They say there was a hollow next to him, as though somebody had been lying there.''

"After he died," Kit asked, "what happened then?"

"Oh, they got hold of some distant cousins who came in to bury him. They didn't want the place, and after the funeral they listed it with a real estate agency. It was really weathered down when Madame Duret bought it. She's had a lot of work done — the grounds got in shape and the roof repaired — and, of course, she had the sleeping wing fixed up so you girls could live there."

"The sleeping wing," Kit said slowly. An icy shudder went down her spine. "You mean the wing where we're sleeping is where the fire took place?"

"That's right," Natalie said. "But you'd never know it, she's got it remodeled so nice. The help she hired from the village, though, they didn't like cleaning up there. Said it gave them the creeps. That's why they quit."

"Natalie!" A low, strong voice spoke from behind them.

Kit turned quickly to see Madame Duret standing in the kitchen doorway. The woman's face was pale with anger, and her black eyes were blazing.

"Natalie, you had your instructions not to spend your time talking with our students!"

"I'm sorry, ma'am," Natalie said contritely. "I don't do it often."

There was ice in Madame's voice. "Your instructions were not to do it at all."

"It's not Natalie's fault," Kit said. "I'm the one responsible."

Madame's eyes shifted to rest upon her, and Kit felt the power of them touch her with the force of an electric shock. It was as though two needles had thrust themselves through her body.

"You must have homework to do, Kathryn," Madame said. Her voice was like steel. "I would suggest that you go upstairs to your room and get started on it. Natalie is responsible for her own actions. She does not need you to defend her."

"But, she only —" Kit began, and the words faded from her lips under the penetration of that black stare.

She tried to look at Natalie, but she was unable to move her eyes. Against her will, she found herself moving from her position by the kitchen sink.

As though of their own accord her two legs began to carry her step by step across the kitchen and through the door into the dining room.

And into the outer hall.

And up the stairs.

And down the dark, upstairs hallway to her room.

When she closed her eyes the music began. No longer did it hold back until she slept; it seemed now to lie just behind her eyelids, waiting for them to drop, so that as soon as she went into inner darkness the music was there.

With increasing power, it took over the edges of her mind and crept relentlessly toward its core.

I'm dreaming, Kit told herself firmly, but she was not completely sure that this was true. She was too conscious of the pillow beneath her cheek, of the blanket across her shoulders. She knew that she was cold.

If I open my eyes, she thought, it will be gone.

But will it? an inner voice whispered. Are you certain?

Chapter 11

Dear Tracy —

This is going to seem like a crazy letter. I wish you were here so I could talk to you directly. You're always so sensible, I'm sure you could come up with an answer — and yet, when I think about it, I can't even tell you the *question*. All I know is that something is very wrong. Sometimes I look at myself in the mirror, and it's like looking at a stranger. The face is the same, except thinner — we all seem to be getting thinner — and there is an odd look to it. It may be the circles under the eyes. Can you believe that — me with circles?

But it's not just physical. We're all of us changing in other ways too. Take Lynda, for instance. She has stopped coming to classes and just stays in her room all day, and half the time she doesn't even come down to meals. Madame Duret has a tray sent up to her, but when it comes back there's hardly any food gone from it. When Lynda *does* come down, once in a great while, she looks like a little white ghost, all skin and bones and big staring eyes. And the eyes don't seem to focus on us. They look through us or past us, as though they are seeing something the rest of us can't.

When you talk to Lynda she answers in this odd, vague way, as if her mind is somewhere else, and sometimes the answers don't go with our questions. There are other times when she doesn't seem to know we're here.

It's just plain scary, and yesterday Ruth went to Madame Duret and suggested that Lynda might need a doctor. Madame said she was sure there was nothing wrong. She said Lynda has just awakened to the discovery of her talent as an artist and is working very hard, and that it's no wonder she is tired, but that it is a good kind of tired, the sort that comes when you really accomplish something.

Is it possible that something "good" can make a person look and act the way Lynda does now?

And then, there's Sandy. She, too, is changing. She dreams a lot, and she tells me that it is always the same dream, the one about the woman who comes and stands by her bed. At first it used to frighten her, but somehow it doesn't seem to anymore. She says the woman's name is Ellis, and she speaks of her as though she were a real person.

Tracy, am I going crazy? For I dream too. In my dreams I am at the piano playing — not the way I usually play, but very well — and there's never any sheet music in front of me. In the beginning the music was always soft and beautiful and the dream was a happy one, but it's not like that anymore. Now the music tears through me with so much power that it is a physical pain. When I wake up, I'm tired. My arms and hands ache as though I had really been playing for hours.

I've found out some background information about Blackwood. I don't like it, any of it. Tracy, I don't want to stay here any longer. I don't care if this is all in my imagination, I still don't want to be here. I've written

Mom and asked her if I can't live with you and your family until she and Dan get home. Would that be all right with your folks? I sure hope so.

Write to me. It's been a long time since I've heard from you, and you never answer any of my questions or comment on any of the things I've written about. Is it possible my letters to you are getting lost in the mail? Or might it be that they aren't getting mailed at all? Professor Farley makes the trip into the village each day and carries our letters to the post office. He *must* mail them — mustn't he? I mean, it would be against the law for him not to, wouldn't it? I'm so confused. Tracy, please, please, write.

"I've written another poem," said Sandy.

"Oh?" Kit did not meet her friends eyes, but she felt her stomach begin to tighten in nervous anticipation.

"I'm not doing this alone," Sandy said. "Ellis is helping me. She's a wonderful writer. She's even published a novel."

"Sandy, please," Kit said wearily. "I wish you'd stop talking about this woman as though she were a real person."

"Listen, now," Sandy said. "See if you like this.

Out of the wind that rules the realm of night
And lonely stars held captive in the sky,
I search for Peace, that death may pass me by
Lost in eternity, as light in light
Is lost, beyond the echo of a Sigh.
Where moonlight on the moors in patterns gleams
Against the shadows, only Peace should be,
And there I search, but peace is not for me.
A moment's rest, left undisturbed by dreams,
Is all I ask —

"Stop! Please, stop!" Kit held up a restraining hand. "I don't want to hear the rest. It's morbid. It sounds as though you're *dead*."

"I thought you'd like it," Sandy said in a hurt voice.

"Well, I don't. What's happened to you, Sandy? We used to laugh so much together. Remember the jokes we used to tell and how we planned to short-sheet Ruth's bed? We were going to have a party one night too, and sneak a lot of food up to my room and make it a midnight feast."

"Do you still want to do those things?" Sandy asked in wonder.

"No," Kit admitted. Somehow the plans that had sounded like so much fun in the early days at Blackwood now seemed childish and ridiculous.

Sandy glanced down at the poem in her hands.

"Ellis doesn't think it's very good," she said. "She doesn't want me to submit it to a publisher or anything. She thinks we can do better —"

"You're doing it again!" Kit interrupted in exasperation. "You're talking about this — this dream person — as though she were real!"

"Is she a dream?" Sandy asked slowly. "When she talks to me, it's so sensible and right. I've been thinking — Kit, do you remember what Ruth was saying about our all having various forms of extrasensory perception?"

Kit nodded.

"Well, what if I've used mine to tune in on somebody, a real person who is living somewhere in the world and has a mind that operates on the same wavelength that mine does. Is that so impossible?"

"You mean you think that somewhere there really is a woman named Ellis?" Kit asked incredulously.

"Why not? She doesn't have to be anywhere near here or even in this country. In fact, I have a feeling she *isn't*

97

in this country — the way she speaks and her references to things like moors and yew trees — she may live someplace like England or Scotland."

"It isn't possible," Kit said. "People don't communicate through dreams. They write letters — they make phone calls —"

"Don't yell," Sandy said. "You're making my head hurt. I can't explain this, Kit. Ruth's the one who's the expert on scientific happenings. All I know is that Ellis is real to me, more real than any dream could be. Whether or not you like her poetry doesn't matter. *I* like it, and I'm happy to be the one to whom she communicates it."

Her narrow face was flushed with anger, and Kit felt her own temper flaring in response.

"You sound like a twelve-year-old who has a crush on a movie star! Except that with a movie star at least you can see her on the screen."

"Oh, shut up," Sandy snapped. "I'm sorry for the day I ever told you about Ellis."

"You didn't have to tell me. I heard you screaming, remember? You didn't think this super poet was so great *then!*" Try as she would, Kit could not bite back the sharp words. "It's this place, this awful place! It's doing something to you! You're getting almost as nutty as Lynda!"

But Sandy had already turned on her heel and left the room, shoving the door shut hard behind her.

Exhausted, Kit let herself fall back across her bed. The intensity of the argument left her drained and vaguely frightened. Sandy was her friend, the closest friend she had in this strange, fenced-in world of Blackwood. How could she possibly have spoken to her in such a way, practically accusing her of being crazy? Why were Sandy's rationalizations any less to be respected than her own or Ruth's? If Sandy was crazy, then they all were.

She should call her back and apologize. She knew it, and yet her weariness was so great that the effort was more than she could make. She raised her hands and pressed them tight against her eyelids, and felt the throbbing in her head which was the beginning of the music.

I won't listen, she told herself. This time I'll defeat it. I won't lie here and listen.

But as had happened that night in the kitchen when Madame Duret had ordered her upstairs, her body would not obey her mental command. It lay upon the bed, and like an audience at a concert, Kit felt the music rushing upon her, soft at first, then louder and stronger, picking up pace and volume.

"Sandy!" she longed to cry. "Sandy — come back! Come help me!"

But although she could feel her throat straining with the words, they were lost in the music. Louder, it came — building and building to what she knew would soon be a crashing crescendo.

Too tired to combat it, she stopped resisting and let herself go, to be carried like a leaf in a rushing current of silent sound.

Eventually she slept. She was not conscious of this happening, but when she opened her eyes the afternoon light had faded from the sky beyond the window and the room was dark.

And there was cold. So much cold that she did not know if she could move. Her whole body was leaden with the weight of it. It was the same strange cold that she had felt in Sandy's room on that night so many weeks ago, a chill too intense to be natural, touched with the feel of dampness and a faint odor which she could not place.

For a few moments she lay there, unmoving. Then, with a gigantic effort, she stretched out her hand and found the lamp. The light sprang on, and the familiar room came into being around her — the bureau, the desk, the gilt-edged mirror, the arched red canopy over the bed.

Fighting the lethargy that threatened to drag her back into unconsciousness, Kit got up and went to the closet for a sweater. Taking it from its hanger, she thrust her arms into the sleeves and buttoned it up to the neck. The cold seemed to slide through the heavy material and seep into her very pores.

Shivering violently, she glanced at her watch. Six forty-five. Downstairs in the dining room dinner would be underway. She could picture the great round table under the twinkling chandelier and the group that would be gathered around it — Madame, stately and gracious; friendly, bearded Professor Farley; Jules, handsome and brooding. Ruth would be at the table. And Sandy.

I'd better go down, Kit thought, if only to see Sandy. If I don't, she'll think it's because of our argument. The sooner things could be made right between herself and Sandy the better.

The thought of food made her feel slightly nauseated. Still, anything was better than staying alone in a room that was as cold as a tomb.

Stepping out into the hall, Kit pulled the door closed behind her and locked it. The air was warmer here, but she still found herself shivering. At the far end of the hall the dim bulb threw out its faint circle of light, and the whole corridor seemed made out of shadows.

Slowly, Kit began to walk down the hallway toward the stairs. In the mirror at the hall's end she saw a thin, white-faced girl in a heavy-knit sweater moving toward her.

Is that me? she thought, momentarily startled by the girl's appearance, the dullness of the eyes, the limp, uncombed hair, the heavy, methodical walk. Was this the same Kit Gordy who had bounced down this hallway only a matter of months ago, eyes shining, face alight, to greet her new classmates?

I look awful, Kit thought wretchedly. Just awful.

And then, as she tilted her head, she caught sight of him, the person walking behind her.

In horror she stood there, frozen, one foot lifted for the next step, her eyes staring into the other eyes reflected in the mirror.

It can't be, she told herself. There can't be anyone behind me. The hall was vacant when I came out of my room. Anyone behind me now would have had to have come out of it with me, and that's impossible.

And yet the man was there, his image as clear as her own, standing so close behind her that it was incredible that she did not feel his breath upon the back of her neck.

Dragging in her breath, Kit did the only thing that she could do. She closed her eyes and screamed.

Chapter 12

Once she started, she could not stop. Scream after scream tore from her throat in great, ragged shrieks. For what seemed a million years she screamed, until as though from another world she heard the sound of footsteps pounding on the stairs and a voice calling her name.

Strong hands closed upon her shoulders.

Jules's voice said, "Kit! Kit, what is it? My Lord, what's happened?"

"There —" Kit managed to sob, "there — behind me —"

"There's nothing behind you."

Kit opened her eyes and stared up at him, at the fine-boned, perfectly featured face bent close to her own, at the heavy-lidded dark eyes, filled now with real concern. Gone was the anger that had flared there the day she had intruded upon him in the music room while he was playing the Schubert tape. Gone was the discomfort that had existed between them since.

He cares, she thought, And even through her terror she clutched at the realization. He does care.

"There was someone," she said chokingly. "A man.

He was walking behind me. I saw him reflected in the mirror."

"There can't have been."

"There *was!*"

"There, now — you're okay. It's all right." Jules pulled her against him so that her face was buried against his shirtfront, and his hand ran lightly over her hair. "You saw a shadow. Or perhaps it was your own reflection."

"It was a man!" She tried to cry the words, but they were muffled by the warm bulk of his shoulder.

From somewhere beyond them she heard other voices and she knew that they were coming, all of them, from the floor below. In another moment they would be here surrounding her, patting and comforting her, telling her in rational terms what it was that she had been imagining.

Pressing her hands against Jules's chest, she shoved him away from her so that she could see his face.

"Please," she said frantically, "you must believe me. You have to believe me."

"Kathryn!" The voice was Madame Duret's. "What in the world has occurred?"

"What is it, Kit?"

"Kit, are you all right?"

"Was that *you* we heard?"

She had known it would be this way. Professor Farley, Ruth, Sandy — all of them worried. She felt Sandy's hand touch her arm, a silent reassurance that their friendship was still intact. If no one else did, Sandy would believe her.

"She's frightened," Jules explained. "She thought she saw somebody in the mirror."

"Somebody?"

"A man. I saw a man." Kit struggled to get control of

her voice. "I didn't just think I saw him, I *did* see him. He was just as real as I am."

"What did he look like?" Professor Farley asked her. His keen, old eyes were regarding her intently.

"I — don't know," Kit said haltingly. "The hall's so dark, I couldn't see him well. And my own reflection was partially blocking him. But he was there. There's no doubt about it."

"Then where has he gone?" Madame Duret asked matter-of-factly. She gestured toward the stretch of empty hallway leading back to Kit's door. "If someone had been there, chérie, he would have to be there still. If he had run past you, he would have had to pass us on the stairs."

"He could have gone back," Sandy suggested timidly. She dropped her hand and slipped it into Kit's. "Kit's room and mine are both down at that end of the hall. He might have gone into one of them."

"You keep your rooms locked, don't you?" Ruth asked. She sounded more interested than worried. Her eyes were aglitter with subdued excitement.

"Yes, but still —"

Kit could tell from Ruth's face that she too was remembering the instance of the missing portrait when a locked door had been no deterrent to an invader. She knows something, she thought. Somehow Ruth has gone a step ahead of the rest of us.

"Well, there's one way to be sure of things," said Professor Farley. "Give me your keys, girls, and Jules and I will check your rooms. If there's any possible chance that there is someone in this building who doesn't belong here, we want to know about it."

Sandy and Kit both handed him their keys. In silence they watched the two men go down the hall and enter first one room and then the other.

It did not take long.

"All empty," Professor Farley said. "There's nobody in the closets or under the beds. I'm afraid you were imagining things, young lady. I can see how one might, too, the way the shadows shift about. Walking toward the mirror gives one a strange sensation."

"But I wasn't imagining," Kit exclaimed. And then, a bit doubtfully, "He seemed so real."

"Like my Ellis?" Sandy suggested softly.

"No," Kit said. "Not like that. I was wide awake, not dreaming."

"Are you sure?"

"Of course I'm sure. I was standing right here."

"I think we had best return to the dining room," Madame Duret said firmly. The tone of her voice, pleasant but definite, told them that the issue was now behind them, something that need not be agonized over or discussed any further. "The professor is correct, the light in this hallway is terribly disconcerting. I shall call once again tomorrow about those electricians, and if I cannot get someone from the village, I will call into Middleton.

"Now, do let us return to our dinner before everything is cold. Are you feeling better, Kathryn?"

"Yes, ma'am," Kit said shakily. And though the last thing she felt like doing was eating, she let herself be guided down the stairs and on into the dining room.

The table had been cleared of the soup bowls. They took their seats, and at the tinkle of Madame's silver bell the kitchen door opened and Lola appeared, her gray brows drawn together in a scowl.

"Please to bring the main course now," Madame told her.

Without a word the older women turned and went back through the doorway. Kit stared after her in bewilderment.

"Why is Lola doing the serving?" she asked. "Is Natalie sick?"

"Natalie is no longer in my employment," Madame informed her. Her voice carried no hint of emotion, but Kit, remembering the scene in the kitchen when those two black eyes had struck her like thunderbolts, was filled with a sudden dread suspicion.

"Why?" she asked. "Did you — let her go?"

"Let her go? Why, of course not." Madame took her napkin and spread it in her lap. "Good cooks like Natalie are difficult to acquire these days. No, the girl asked to leave. She is to be married a week from Saturday."

"Married!" Kit exclaimed. It was the last thing she had expected to be told.

"How nice," Ruth commented. "She will probably make somebody a very good wife. Who is she marrying, somebody from the village?"

"I imagine so. Whom else would she find?" Madame said easily. "But with so much of our help gone now, I am afraid we shall all have to do a bit of the work. Nice as it would be, a place like Blackwood does not take care of itself, you know. Starting tomorrow, I must make out a chore list for everyone."

The door swung open again and Lola entered, bearing a platter of overdone chops, and the subject of conversation was terminated.

The phone call came at eight-thirty that evening. The girls were gathered in the parlor watching television when Jules appeared suddenly in the doorway.

"Phone for you, Kit," he said. "Long distance. Your mother."

"It is!" For a moment Kit thought her heart would leap out of her chest. In an instant she was on her feet, hurrying toward him. "Where can I take it?"

"The only phone is in the office," Jules said. "You'd better hurry. Overseas calls cost a mint."

When she entered the office, Kit found Madame Duret seated at her desk. The telephone sat at her right, the receiver off the hook. Madame picked it up and held it out to Kit.

"Are you not the lucky one — a call from Italy! Do give your mother my regards."

Kit snatched for the receiver. She found her hand was trembling as she raised it to her ear.

"Hello — Mom?"

"Oh, honey!" Her mother's tiny voice sounded a million miles away, but the warmth, the inflections, the love, were so familiar that for the second time that evening Kit found her eyes blurred with tears. "It's so wonderful to hear you."

"You too," Kit said. "How are you? How's Dan? Where are you calling from? Are you having fun?"

"So much fun," her mother said, "you can't imagine. We're in Florence now, and tomorrow we leave for Rome. Just think, we'll actually be visiting St. Peter's and the Forum and the Catacombs — all the places you always read about!"

She sounds so young, Kit thought in amazement.

Her mother, with the silver threads in her hair, the soft cobweb of lines at the corners of her eyes, the back that ached after a day of typing, sounded like a young girl, bubbling with enthusiasm and vitality.

"And you, honey? How are you? Do you love it at Blackwood?"

"Mother!" Kit was stunned at the question. "Haven't you been reading my letters?"

"We got one in Cherbourg," her mother said, "but that was almost immediately after we arrived. It's the only letter we've received. That's why I'm calling. Dan said he was sure that you were just too busy to write, but I was worried that you might be ill. You haven't been, have you?"

"No," Kit said. "And I've written every week. I've told you about everything — absolutely everything."

In her chair at the desk, Madame shifted her weight, and Kit moved a few paces away, stretching the telephone cord to its full length.

"It's the mails then," Kit's mother said. "It's so hard to be sure of your timing when you're sending things care of American Express. You must be just missing us every place we go. Well, tell me, how is everything? Are you studying hard? Do you have nice friends?"

"I — I —" Kit could not get an answer out. Instead she said, "Mother, how much longer are you going to stay over there? When are you coming home?"

"The week before Christmas," her mother said. "Don't you remember the plan? We'll coincide with your vacation."

"But, that's months away!" The words burst from her in a strangled cry. "I can't stay here that long, Mom, I just can't! You don't know — you don't understand!"

Madame Duret moved in her chair. Kit felt the intense black eyes boring into her, and she clutched the receiver more tightly against her ear.

"Oh, honey!" There was mild exasperation in her mother's voice. "Are you still upset with us for coming to Europe without you? I thought you'd accepted the situation. You told me —"

"It's not that, really! I swear, that has nothing to do with it. I want to tell you — please, you have to listen —"

There was so much to tell, all the things that she had poured out in her letters and assumed her mother knew, and now realized that she did not know at all. But where could she start? The beginning seemed so long ago, and there was so much — Lynda and her art, Sandy, the dreams, the music, the man in the hall, whom she was sure, really sure, she had not imagined, and yet what other explanation could there be? And her mother was so far away, just a thin, small voice on the other end of a transatlantic cable, with the minutes piling up, each one costing a small fortune.

But most of all there was Madame Duret, seated here beside her, listening to every word that she spoke. Those eyes — those impossible eyes — rested upon her face, and she could not turn from them, could not focus her own gaze anywhere except into their depths. They held her still, impaled, like a bug on two sharp pins.

"Mother —" she said, and she could not go on.

"I think that this conversation must be costing your mother a great deal of money, Kathryn." Madame spoke quietly, but her voice held a note of command. "Do you not think that you should give her your love and say good-bye?"

"Mom!" Kit made one final desperate effort. "I want to stay at Tracy's. Can't I, please? I've written her, and it will be all right, I know it will. I could get the bus in Blackwood Village — Mr. Rosenblum could meet me — and I could stay with them until Christmas, until you and Dan got home —"

"Oh, Kit, really!" The lilting youthfulness was gone from her mother's voice. In its place was a blend of disappointment, concern and weariness. "You'll be seeing Tracy at Christmastime. No matter what you say, it really isn't very far away. Enjoy your other friends now, the new ones you've made at Blackwood. In your one letter you mentioned a girl named Sandy. You seemed to like her. Don't you still?"

"Yes. Yes, sure, I like Sandy."

What shall I do? Kit asked herself frantically. What *can* I do? She looked down into Madame Duret's face, and no further words would come.

"Do write, honey," her mother was saying. "And aim your letters a little further ahead. You have our itinerary. Allow a few extra days for them to reach us, and for goodness sake, don't forget to use airmail. Dan sends his love. He's a fine man, Kit — a good, kind person. I realize it more each day. I'm very lucky."

"Yes," Kit said resignedly. "Yes, I know."

"I love you, honey."

"I love you too." The time was up. There was no way, no possible way. "Tell Dan hello. Have a happy honeymoon."

"We will. You too — be happy, honey. Good-bye for now."

"Good-bye." There was a little click and silence.

Kit lowered the receiver from her ear and placed it carefully back upon the hook. She closed her eyes so that she would not have to see the look of satisfaction on Madame's face, but she could not keep them closed. One could not stand for very long with one's eyes screwed shut.

"That is right, chérie," Madame Duret told her. "You want to leave your mother enough money to purchase some gifts to bring back with her. Are they having a pleasant trip?"

"Yes," Kit said dully. "A wonderful time."

"They seemed so nice, both of them. You would not wish to ruin their trip by having them concerned about you. All girls become a bit homesick on occasion. It is one of those things one must fight against."

"I suppose," Kit said.

Miserably, she turned and started across the room to

the door, and stopped short as her eyes fell upon a painting on the opposite wall over a filing cabinet. A mountain lake reflected light from the sky — green woods, distant hills. The familiarity of the setting struck her like a well-known cry.

"What's that?" she asked.

"That cabinet? It is where I keep my files on former students."

"I didn't mean the cabinet," Kit said. "I meant the picture. Who did it?"

"Do you like the painting? It is a favorite of mine." It was as though there had been no contest between them. "It is a landscape by Thomas Cole. A reproduction, of course."

"I've seen that lake," Kit said.

"Perhaps you have. The picture was painted in the Catskills."

"No, I mean I've seen it painted before. From another angle." Kit continued to stare at the landscape. "There's a footpath over there along the shore, but you can't see it from this direction."

Then the realization struck her.

"It's the same lake that has been in some of Lynda's paintings."

"Why, I do not think so, chérie," Madame Duret said. "Lynda comes from California. I hardly think she would be painting New York scenery."

"But, it is. I know it is," Kit insisted. "Who is this Thomas Cole, anyway? Does he live around here?"

"He did at one time," Madame Duret told her. "Of course, that was many years ago. He died in the middle of the nineteenth century."

Chapter 13

———————

"It's true," Ruth said. "Thomas Cole was a really famous artist. I'm surprised you haven't heard of him. He was the founder of the Hudson River School of landscape painters."

It was late afternoon of the following day, and they had left the house to walk around to the far side of the pond. It was a gray and winterish day, quite different from the bright autumn weather that they had been having, and Kit felt it as an echo of her own spirits. She thrust her hands deep into the pockets of her jeans and stared across at the dead brown stalks that were all that was left of the summer garden.

"And he's dead?" she asked.

"Oh, sure. Ages ago. He died comparatively young too. He was only in his forties. He was one of a batch of American artists we studied in one of the enrichment classes at the last school I went to."

"You learned about him there?" Kit drew a breath of relief. "And Lynda too?"

"No, not Lynda," Ruth said. "She didn't take the enrichment courses. Why is it you're suddenly so hung up on Thomas Cole?"

Kit's head was aching. It seemed to her lately that her head was always throbbing with a dull pressure. Sometimes it was because of the music inside it, ringing and crashing and filling her ears with sounds that no one else could hear.

Other times, like now, the pressure was a thing unto itself, an ache that seemed born of confusion and fatigue.

"I'm so mixed up," she said. "I hardly know where to begin thinking. Nothing makes any sense."

"What's happened?" Ruth asked. "It must be something important if you wanted to come all the way out here to talk about it."

"It was last night," Kit said. "When I was in Madame's office, taking the phone call from my mother. On the wall over a filing cabinet, there was a reproduction of a painting of a lake. Madame said it was by Thomas Cole."

"So?"

"It was the same lake that Lynda paints, and more than that, it looked exactly like one of Lynda's landscapes. The lighting, the colors, the sky — all of it. Lynda might have done it herself."

"That's why you asked if she had studied Thomas Cole?"

"If she had, it would have at least partially explained things. She might have been imitating his work, don't you think? Unconsciously — not even realizing what she was doing? But if she didn't take the course with you, then that's out. There has to be some other answer."

"T.C.," Ruth said softly.

"What?"

"Those are the initials — T.C. It's the way Lynda signs her paintings."

"T.C. — for Thomas Cole?" Kit turned to her incredulously. "Then she must know who he is — she *has* to! She must have seen his work somewhere, perhaps on some television special. And she admires him. She's trying so hard to imitate him that she's using his initials to — well, to sort of bring herself luck."

"No," Ruth said. "I can't buy that. Sorry. I wish it were true, but I'm sure it isn't."

A breeze touched the surface of the pond, making little ripples, and the trees reflected in its surface shimmered and shifted like live creatures in the moving water. Across the pond, the roof of Blackwood rose sharp against the heavy overcast of the sky. The windows stared out at them like empty eyes.

The kitchen door opened suddenly and Lola came out with a bag of trash for the incinerator. Her grayness seemed part of the day itself.

"She'll never quit, at least," Ruth commented. "I bet she's been with Madame since the very beginning."

"Natalie didn't quit," Kit said. "She was fired."

"Madame said she quit."

"I know, but I don't believe it. Natalie needed her job, and if she had a boyfriend, she never bothered to mention him. I'm sure she would have if she had been serious enough to consider getting married."

"But why would Madame have let her go?" Ruth asked. "Lola can't cook. That chicken last night was so greasy I could hardly swallow it. Natalie's meals were the best part of the day."

"Natalie talked," Kit said. "Remember how I was going to ask her about the background of Blackwood? Well, Madame Duret walked in on us while she was telling me, and she was furious. I'm sure that after I left she fired Natalie."

"Then she *did* tell you about it?" Ruth was more interested in this fact than in the fate of Natalie. "What did you find out?"

"Some terrible things. Mr. Brewer's whole family was killed in a fire, and he went off his rocker. He wouldn't admit that they were gone. He lived the whole rest of his life here just as though they were still alive, talking about them and buying toys for the children and everything."

"Did Mr. Brewer die in the house too?"

"Yes," Kit said. "A long time later. Why do you ask that? Ruth —" She stopped at the look on the girl's face. Something was flickering there, a glint of revelation. "Ruth, what is it? Do you know something that I don't?"

"I don't *know* anything," Ruth said. "Anything I came up with right now would just be a guess."

"But you have an idea?"

"It's way-out," Ruth said. "So far out that I don't think you'd accept it. I don't know that I can accept it myself."

"What is it?"

"I don't want to talk about it right now," Ruth said. "I want to think about it a while first. Did you say the woman in Sandy's dream is named Ellis and she comes from England?"

"That's what Sandy has decided. Either there or Scotland, someplace with moors."

"Did she ever mention the woman's last name?"

"No."

"I'm going to check something out in the library," Ruth said. "If it turns out my guess is right, then I'll tell you about it. But you'd better prepare yourself. If I *have* found the answer, you're going to get the shock of your life."

That night, as always, there was the music. Soft, this

time, like a lullaby for a child. Moonlight on a pillow. Tree limbs rustling outside a window in the faint evening breeze. Fireflies on the lawn. Soft laughter from couples sitting on the porch steps.

I am asleep, Kit told herself. I know that I am asleep, lying in the bed with the canopy over it, and the room is dark and still, and this music is not real. It is a dream, only a dream. When I wake, it will be morning with breakfast waiting in the dining room down below and classes to go to, and the music will be gone again as though it has never been.

A voice spoke softly, breaking through the music. A man's voice, gruff, but oddly gentle.

"Gone, for a moment. But not really. Never really gone."

Because she knew it was a dream, Kit was not startled.

"Who are you?" she asked. And then she recognized him, and her heart gave a lurch. "I've seen you before. You were the one standing behind me in the hall, the one I saw in the mirror."

"Of course," the dream man said. He seemed surprised that *she* should be surprised.

"Why were you following me?" Kit asked. "Why are you here now? What is it you want?"

"I am here to give."

"That's no answer."

"It's the only answer," the man said patiently. "You are one of the fortunate ones who are blessed with the ability to receive."

"To receive — what?" Kit asked. And then the answer came to her and she began to understand. "The music? Are you the one who is sending me this music, the way Ellis is sending Sandy poetry? If you are, you must take it back. I don't want it — any of it."

The sounds rose within her, louder now, changing pace and rhythm, beginning to leap and build as they did so often lately into a pressure that swelled her brain.

This is a dream, she reminded herself frantically. Only a dream.

"Of course, it is," the man said and reached for her hand. His fingers closed around her wrist, and it was all that she could do to keep from crying out at the icy touch as he drew her from the bed. She felt the carpet beneath her bare feet and saw him reach for the knob of the door.

"Where are you taking me?"

"You must let it out," the man said.

"Let what out? What do you mean?"

They were in the hall now, and he was leading her down it through the darkness with the assurance of one who knows each step, while the music grew louder and louder, pounding against the inside of her skull.

"You must let it out, or your head will burst with it! You must let it go!"

"How?" Kit sobbed. "How?" She could no longer keep track of where they were going. She knew they were on the stairs — she could feel cold floorboards against the soles of her feet — doors opened and closed. There were other voices, a muted chorus of voices, but the music overwhelmed them.

"Here she is," the dream man said. "I've brought her down."

"It will be my turn now," someone said. "I haven't used her yet."

"No, mine! She must play for me!"

"I want her tonight! She was yours last time — she did that concerto —"

"You forget — I brought her down!"

Kit felt a keyboard beneath her fingers.

"But, I don't know how to play!"

And even as she cried the words she was playing, and it was the old, old dream, with her hands leaping upon the ivory keys and the great thunderous chords rolling forth.

I am dreaming, Kit told herself for one final time. I am — I am — and I must wake up! I *will* wake myself up!

"No," cried the voice of the man in her dream. "You can't — you mustn't —"

"I will!" She turned upon him with every bit of the strength that she possessed, with all the temper and stubbornness which were the mark of Kathryn Gordy — "*I will!*"

The music was gone.

She was seated on a bench in front of a piano, and she was cold — achingly cold. Blinking, she glanced about her and realized that she was in the music room at Blackwood and that she was not alone.

Across from her, at the tape recorder, sat Jules. The tape was moving, and she realized incredulously that he was recording.

"Jules?" She spoke his name sharply.

With a startled movement he reached out and flicked a switch to halt the machine.

"Jules," Kit said shakily, "what am I doing here?"

"You — you walked in your sleep," Jules said haltingly.

"And you were here to record me? You *were* recording me, weren't you? It's my playing that you have on that tape?"

Wordlessly, Jules nodded. His face was pale, and he looked as though he did not know how to combat the question.

"You've done this before, haven't you?" Kit asked.

118

"Other nights — I've come down here and played for you. That's what that tape was I heard you playing the other day. It was a recording of me."

"Yes," Jules said. "Look, Kit, I know this must seem awfully strange to you, but believe me, it's nothing to be upset about. Nothing bad has happened. You've always gotten back to your room safely. The only result is that we have the tapes."

"We? Who is 'we'?"

"Well — all of us. The school."

"Your mother? Professor Farley?"

"Don't look that way, Kit. Nobody's done anything to hurt you. Nothing but good has been happening here. We're giving beautiful music to the world."

"It's not my music," Kit said. "I'm no composer. Where is it coming from? Whose is it?" She watched his face close in, and she could see him struggling to think of an answer. "Don't make something up. I want to know the truth. You owe me that, Jules. Tell me — whose music have I been playing?"

"I don't know," Jules stammered. "This time I — well, I just can't tell."

"And other times?"

"I think — I'm almost sure — that for a while at least, it was Franz Schubert."

"Schubert!" Kit exclaimed. "But he died over a century ago!"

"He died in 1828," Jules said. "He was thirty-one years old. He left so much undone, Kit, so many marvelous pieces of music unwritten. His death was a tragic waste of talent."

"And I've been playing his music? I, who can't even get through 'Dancing Leaves' without mistakes?" Kit's voice was shaking. "And there's the rest — Sandy and the poetry, Lynda —" The parts of the puzzle began to move into place, and the thing that was forming in her mind was too incredible to believe.

"Get them," she said quietly. "All of them — Sandy and Lynda and Ruth, the professor, your mother. I want everybody down here right now. I want to know exactly what has been happening here at Blackwood, the whole story!"

"Now, Kit, look," Jules said desperately. "You're all upset, and I don't blame you. But this isn't the time to talk about anything. It's two o'clock in the morning. Everybody's sound asleep. You don't want to bring them all down here now."

Straightening on the bench, Kit glared at him, as anger swept in to take the place of fear. "If you don't get them, Jules, I will. I'll start yelling and I'll bring the whole house awake. I want to know the answer to the mystery of Blackwood, and I don't intend to wait until morning to get it."

Chapter 14

———————

"It is two o'clock in the morning, scarcely an hour to hold a conference." Madame Duret's voice was crisp and cold. "I must say, Jules, that you are not showing the best of judgment."

"I couldn't help it," Jules said. "Kit woke up while she was at the piano. Of course, she started asking questions."

"But to bring down everyone!"

Madame was wearing a crimson dressing gown. Her long, black hair, loosed from its usual coil, hung down her back in a great cascade, and her face, void of makeup, had an almost skeletal look in the lamplight.

"I made him," Kit said. "Whatever it is that is happening here involves all of us. I don't care what time of night it is."

She spoke with a firmness that surprised her, and she could see a flicker of grudging respect in Madame's eyes.

"And you?" Madame's gesture took in the other three girls who, in robes and slippers, were now gathered in the parlor. Professor Farley, wearing an overcoat over his pajamas, was seated in an armchair by the window. "You wish this — this confrontation?"

Ruth nodded quickly. Her face was flushed with excitement.

Sandy hesitated, her eyes wide and frightened. Then she nodded also.

Lynda glanced blankly at Ruth.

"What is it she's talking about?" she asked. "Why are we all down here?"

Ruth turned back to Madame Duret. "She has to hear it too. She may not understand, but you'll have to tell her. It's only right."

"Very well," Madame said. "I had planned, of course, to disclose everything in good time, just as I did with the girls in my former schools. I had hoped it could wait a bit longer, however. We are still so close to the beginning. There is so much distance still to be covered before your relationships are secure."

"What relationships?" Kit asked. "With whom?"

Madame did not answer immediately. Instead, she turned to gaze past them, out the window into the darkness that lay beyond the pane.

When she did begin to speak at last, it was slowly, as though she were searching for the perfect words.

"Most people in this world are like children. Their lives run on one level only, the physical level of the here and now. From day to day they go, seeing the material things that surround them, believing that there is nothing beyond this.

"But they are not correct. There is a second level of reality, a spiritual level that is as real as the physical. It transcends the first level and exists beyond it. A few special people are blessed with an extraordinary sensitivity to this spirit world and can bridge with their minds the space between these two realities. I" — a note of pride crept into her voice — "I am one of those people."

Kit stared at her. "Do you mean to say that you're a — a — *medium?*"

"I find that word offensive," Madame said stiffly. "It carries with it a flavor of fakery and parlor tricks. I do not lend myself to such demonstrations. I believe my gift is too valuable to be abused in such ways. It must be used only for the good of humanity."

"Which is how?" Kit asked.

Madame continued as though she had not heard the question.

"Today the average lifetime is over seventy years, long enough for a great number of accomplishments. But this development has occurred within the present century. Before that, people tended to die much younger than they do today, and among those early deaths were those of many brilliant and talented people who had much to give the world. It is to these people whom I reach out. It is to them I offer the opportunity to return."

"To return!" It was Sandy who spoke now, her voice expressionless with shock. "But people can't come back once they're dead!"

"Not in physical form," Madame said. "But in spiritual form, they can, if there is a place for them. By this, I mean that there must be a receiver, a young, clear mind, still uncluttered by worldly problems, impressionable and sensitively tuned. Such minds are unusual, but they do exist. They can be found."

"And you found them in us." Ruth made the statement in a matter-of-fact manner. She did not look or sound surprised. "Through those entrance tests, you were able to tell."

Madame nodded. "My tests took years to develop, and they are dependable. Here at Blackwood, I was fortunate in finding a place of perfect atmosphere. There have been spirit occupants here before. Mr. Brewer was in his own way a medium of a sort. He was able to recall and surround himself with the spirits of his deceased family. Their vibrations remain here still, a part of the house. The trip to Blackwood from the plane beyond is a short one, made along a well-traveled path."

The parts of the puzzle were in place now, but Kit could not believe them. I'm going to be sick, she thought, right here on the parlor floor.

But she wasn't. Instead she simply sat there, staring at the tall, red-gowned woman in growing horror. Could they be true — the things that Madame was saying — could they possibly be true?

"I told you," Ruth said, "that you wouldn't be able to accept it."

Kit turned to her in amazement.

"You already knew?"

"I guessed," Ruth said. "Remember, yesterday, when we were walking by the pond, and I told you I wanted to check something out?"

"Yes."

"Well, I did," Ruth said. "Tonight after dinner I went into the library and looked up a few people. One of them was a woman named Emily Brontë who wrote under the name of Ellis Bell."

"Who?" Sandy asked.

"Emily Brontë — you'll know her best as the author of *Wuthering Heights*. She lived in England during the nineteenth century. It was a time when woman writers were not taken seriously, so she and her two sisters decided to write under masculine pen names."

"Ellis — my Ellis — is *Emily Brontë!*" Sandy shook her head. "That's impossible. Emily Brontë has been dead for years."

"She died in 1848," Ruth said. "Of consumption."

"I don't believe it!" Sandy's voice rose hysterically. "Ellis is just as alive as I am. She writes poetry —"

"She dictates poetry," Ruth corrected, "and you write it down for her. You've admitted yourself that those poems don't come out of your own head. She's using you, Sandy, to get onto paper the words she didn't have time to write while she was alive." She turned to Madame. "Isn't that right?"

Madame nodded.

"Control yourself, Sandra. There is nothing for you to become so upset about."

"Nothing to become upset about!" Sandy cried. "With dead people walking through my mind!"

"You haven't been hurt, my child." From his chair in the corner, Professor Farley spoke for the first time. "You have simply been part of a unique experiment. You should feel privileged, not exploited."

"That's what I've been trying to explain to Kit," Jules said.

"Privileged!" Kit exploded. "By having my mind used as a receiving unit?" She turned accusingly to Professor Farley. "And, you — you're in on this also?"

"Of course," the professor said. His kindly old face held no trace of guilt. "I became acquainted with Madame Duret in London while doing research for a paper on psychic phenomena. When I learned about her school in Paris, I was fascinated. I encouraged her to open another, similar institution in England, and later I accompanied her to America to assist with the establishment of Blackwood."

"I think," Kit said, "that it's the most terrible thing I've ever heard of."

"What's so terrible about it?" Jules asked her. "You ought to be proud."

"Proud of what? That I'm being used, like a tool of some kind?" Kit exclaimed incredulously. The voices from the dream came back to her, and she shuddered uncontrollably. " 'She must play for me!' 'I want her tonight!' 'I haven't used her yet!' It's the way you talk about an object, not a person!"

Lynda was looking dazedly from one speaker to another.

"What is all this?" she asked in bewilderment. "Who's an object?"

"You are!" Kit cried. "We all are! Don't you understand at all, Lynda? It's not you who is doing those beautiful pictures we're so impressed by! It's a famous landscape painter who died over a century ago. No wonder they're so good!"

"That's not true," Lynda said. "I painted all day today. Look — I can prove it." She held out a slim, delicate hand smudged with green paint. "That's from doing the grass. There's a lot of grass in my new picture."

"And who wants it there — that grass? Who planned the picture? Who guides the brush?"

"I don't know what you mean."

"The other evening in your room," Kit said in exasperation, "when I brought up your tray, you said, 'There is so much to be done. He wants so much.' Who were you talking about, Lynda? Who is this 'he'?"

"I never said anything like that," Lynda said with a catch in her voice. "I think all you girls are horrid. First Ruth says I'm tracing, and now you say that somebody else is doing the work for me. You're jealous, that's what! Here's the first thing I've ever really been good at in my whole life, and you can't bear to see me get the credit for it."

"Let her be, Kit," Ruth said. "She can't take it in. Can

you blame her? It's an incredible concept. It will take some getting used to for all of us."

"Well, you can get used to it if you want to. Personally, I don't intend to!" Kit turned to Madame Duret. "I'm going home!"

"You cannot do that. Your parents are away."

"I'll stay with friends! The Rosenblums will have me! I'll call Tracy tonight. Her parents will be here by morning. They're that kind of people."

"And they can drop me at the bus stop in the village." Sandy moved to stand beside Kit. "I'm not going to stay in this place a minute longer than I have to. And you'd just better wait until my grandpa hears about this, he'll blow a fuse!"

"Girls, you are being ridiculous." There was a cold edge to Madame's voice. "You cannot back out at this point. The connections are still in the process of being stabilized."

"That's great," Kit said. "I'll break them off before they *do* become stabilized. I'm getting out of here while my brain is still my own. If you think I'm going to sit here and let some wandering spirits take possession of it, you're out of your mind!"

"That is sufficient, Kathryn," Madame said icily. "I ask you to remember, please, that you are a young lady and you will mind your manners accordingly. I do not enjoy listening to yelling, particularly in the middle of the night. It is you who demanded this explanation, and you have now had it, and as far as I am concerned, the discussion is over. You will all please return to your beds. You need your rest in order to be alert for your morning classes."

"I'm not going to be here for classes," Kit told her

angrily. "By tomorrow I'll be with the Rosenblums on the way back to the city!"

And then, she stopped as the realization came to her — there was only one telephone at Blackwood. It was located in Madame Duret's private office.

Chapter 15

The next days moved past in a blur. Nightmare days was the way Kit thought of them. The last of October became the beginning of November, and the final leaves drifted from the branches of the trees around the pond, leaving them stark and bare against the heavy gray of the overcast sky.

Outside the air was damp and chill with the promise of winter, and within the walls of Blackwood a different sort of chill prevailed. Even in the daytime, the house seemed filled with shadows, and in the evenings the girls gathered in the parlor to share the bright reality of the color television set with a sense of relief at finding the banal programs still the same.

"It's as though *this* is the true world," Sandy said thinly, gesturing toward the screen on which a rubber-faced comedienne was imitating a famous opera singer, "and we are the make-believe. Sometimes I wonder if I'm real at all."

"You're real, all right," Kit told her. "We all are. But for how long? We've got to get out of this place as soon as possible."

"How?" Sandy asked hopelessly. "We can't get to the telephone. Madame keeps the office locked at all times. The gate at the end of the drive is padlocked, and there's no way of getting over the fence. I know because I went down to check. Those spikes on top aren't decorations, they're for real."

"I think you're making too much of this," Ruth interjected. She reached over to turn down the volume of the set so that they could talk more easily. "We'll be going home at Christmas. That's not very far off. In the meantime, how many people our age ever get to be intricate parts of such an original experiment?"

"Honestly, Ruth," Sandy said in amazement, "I actually think you're enjoying this. You don't seem to be upset by it at all."

"I was in the beginning," Ruth said, "before I understood what was happening, but now — well, I guess I'm more excited than anything. Imagine having an opportunity to be in on something so significant! It's a true breakthrough in science. And the insight it's giving me is incredible. I have a grasp of mathematical concepts that I never would have believed possible."

"But, it's not you who's grasping them," Kit objected. "It's somebody else, working through your mind!"

"Not entirely," Ruth said. "That's the difference between our situations. You feel that you're being used as a vehicle. You don't have any understanding of the music that's coming through you. You simply 'land' it, mechanically, the way Sandy does her poetry. But in my case, I *am* able, just barely, to begin to get the meaning of the knowledge that is coming through me. Math and science are my thing — they always have been. I feel now as though I have been sitting all my life inside a box, and suddenly someone is lifting the lid and I can look up and see the stars."

"Then there's no actual personality coming into your consciousness?" Kit asked her. "The way there is with Sandy and me?"

"Not that I'm aware of," Ruth told her. "I think perhaps what I'm receiving is a pool of knowledge from a lot of different minds. There may be a hundred different mathematicians and scientists pouring all of their accumulated thoughts and theories into my head, and if I can receive and handle all this and eventually grow to understand it, there will come a time when it will be *my* knowledge too."

"The way Lynda's painting is hers?" Sandy asked bitterly. "She's living in a world that doesn't even touch ours anymore."

"Well, Lynda's different," Ruth admitted. "She's kind of gone under."

"She's possessed," Sandy said.

"We have to escape." Kit made her voice firm. "There has to be a way —"

She broke off the sentence at the sound of voices in the hall.

Professor Farley appeared in the doorway. His crinkled old face was as friendly as ever, and his white hair and little pointed beard gave him the look of an underweight Santa.

"Nine-thirty," he said pleasantly. "It's time for you young ladies to be climbing the stairs to get your beauty sleep."

Glaring at him, Kit got to her feet.

"I don't need beauty sleep. All I need is to get out of here and go home. My stepfather is an attorney, did you know that? You just wait until he finds out I've been held here against my will. He'll have you put in jail."

"Now, Kit," the professor said, "we don't need that kind of talk. Your parents have placed you in our charge for the semester, and it would be very lax of us indeed if we let you go charging off in all directions. You are our responsibility, both legally and morally."

"Morally," Kit growled. "You don't know the meaning of the word. What about all the letters we've written to our friends and families, the ones we've laid out on the hall table for you to mail for us in the village? You stole them, that's what! Do you call that 'moral'? It's not only wrong, it's against the law."

"Nobody has stolen anything," Professor Farley told her calmly. "Your letters are in a neat pile in Madame's office, and you may have them back anytime you so desire. And some of them did go out — the early ones in which there were no disturbing references to 'strange dreams' and 'odd things happening.' I'm sure your parents were delighted to receive them."

"One thing I've been wondering," Ruth said. "What happened to the other schools, the ones in Europe? Madame had two of them there. Why did they close down?"

"For various reasons," the professor told her, "none of which have anything to do with Blackwood."

"What about the girls in those schools?" Sandy asked. "What kinds of talents did they have? Did they compose music and write poetry?"

"Indeed, they did," Professor Farley said. "Many beautiful contributions to the culture of the world came forth from Madame Duret's previous students. I think I may go so far as to say that some of their creations were true masterpieces."

"Then where are they?" Kit asked him. "What was done with them? Why haven't we ever heard about them?" She paused as a thought occurred to her. "The Vermeer — the one Madame said she discovered at an auction! She didn't buy that painting at all! It was painted by one of the girls in her other schools! Madame got a fortune for it! She sold it as an original!"

"It was an original," Professor Farley said. "It was the work of Vermeer, no matter whose hand it was that held the brush."

"But couldn't experts tell the age of the painting?" Ruth asked in bewilderment. "The paint would be different and so would the canvas."

"You are forgetting," Professor Farley said, "that Madame is herself an expert on art. She supplied her students with used canvases of the proper vintage, scraped down to the original gesso. She was also able to supply paints made from lapis lazuli and cochineal. The final look of aging is not difficult to achieve. We baked the paintings in a hundred-degree oven for two hours and then rolled them to bring up the craquelure."

I won't go to sleep, Kit told herself. I may sit here all night, but I will not close my eyes.

It was a futile vow, and she knew it. Sleep waited behind her door like an all-encompassing fog. The moment she stepped into her room a heavy drowsiness would fall upon her, almost as though she had been administered a sleep-inducing drug, and her eyes would be falling closed before she reached the bed.

Tonight she fought it by crossing to the window. Pressing her forehead against the cold glass, she stared out into the night. At first she could see nothing but darkness. Then, as her eyes became adjusted, she saw the black shapes of the trees begin to emerge against the sky and realized that somewhere, too high to be seen from the house, there must be a full moon.

This is the wing, she thought, where the Brewers slept. Perhaps the Brewer babies were born here. This is where they had their nursery and where the parents had their big master bedroom.

Suddenly, there sprang into her mind a vivid picture of a woman, perhaps a little younger than her own mother, standing at this window just as Kit herself was doing now. The woman was plump and dreamy-eyed, and she loved her home — she loved to stand here and gaze out at the summer garden and the stretch of smooth, green lawn leading to the sparkling pond.

The world seemed to shift, the night lifted from Kit's eyes, and she could see before her the same scene that the woman saw — a lush garden abloom with flowers and a sunlit lawn on which three little boys were playing. A baby carriage was parked in the shade of an oak tree, and a white uniformed nurse wearing a sun hat was leaning over it to speak to the tiny occupant.

How lovely, Mrs. Brewer thought. How happy I am! What a beautiful, beautiful life this is!

Kit felt the glow of the woman's happiness sweep through her as though it were her own. Then, as quickly as it had come, the vision was gone. She was herself again, Kit Gordy, and it was November, and outside the night lay thick across the brown lawn.

Turning away, Kit went over and seated herself on the edge of the bed. Madame's words came back to her, "The vibrations still remain a part of the house." Somehow, in his desperate grief over the loss of his family, Mr. Brewer had managed to call them back to him, the gentle, sweet-faced wife, the romping children. He had closed his doors to the outside world and continued to live with his spirit family just as he would have if they had been with him in body.

It was too much to comprehend.

Sleep was pressing upon her now. Kit could feel the weight of it upon her eyelids.

I won't give in, she told herself vehemently. I won't!

Softly, at the edge of her mind, she heard the music, faint and far away, but ready to move closer, to close in upon her and take her over if her consciousness faded even slightly.

Go away, Kit cried silently, whoever you are — go away! You've had your time on earth! This is my time! *Mine!*

The bed was soft, tempting, drawing her backward. Her head touched the pillow and sank helplessly into its feathery depths. Above her the wine-colored canopy seemed to sway, dizzily, hypnotically, and in her ears the music grew louder. It was not just the sound of a piano this time, but strings, the high, sweet voices of violins, the richness of violas, the melodious ripples of a harp. And then there came a flute, shrill and true as the song of a bird.

"No," she wailed. "No!"

But her resistance was gone, and it had closed upon her, and she was a part of it, being carried along on the sweeping tide of sound.

"You must write it down," the dream man told her. How easily he came to her now, as though he belonged there, at home within the confines of her mind. "You must put this on paper. It is too great to lose."

"I can't," Kit replied. "I don't know how to write music."

"I will tell you. Get up from the bed. Here, take my hand — let me lead you over to the desk. Pick up a pencil."

"I don't have any music paper. You must know that."

"You do — you do. See!"

And she did. It was there, a music notebook with the staffs outlined in pale blue, awaiting her use. Someone had brought it and placed it in her room while she was down in the parlor. Madame? Jules? The same person who had come into her locked room on another occasion to remove Lynda's first portrait? Once the question would have seemed important, but now it did not matter. One or the other of them, it was all the same.

"I don't want to," Kit said. "I don't want to write down anything. You can't force me to do something that I don't want to do."

But even as she spoke, her hand was reaching for the pencil. Her fingers closed around it and she lifted it and drew the paper toward her.

"Kit!" Through the pounding of the music there broke a familiar voice, calling her name.

"What — who —" With a decisive wrench, Kit tore through the barrier between the two worlds.

It was Sandy who was standing in the doorway. She was dressed in pajamas, her hair was mussed from the pillow, and her freckles stood out in startling relief against her white skin.

"It's so cold in here," Sandy said, wrapping her arms around herself. "Is your window open? How can you sit there like that when it's like the inside of an ice —"

She did not finish her sentence. The pencil in Kit's hand flew from her grasp and broke with a loud snap in midair. As though fired from a gun, the pointed end shot straight across the room.

Sandy screamed and threw her hands up to cover her face.

In horror, Kit watched the stream of blood burst forth from her friend's forearm.

"Sandy!" she cried. "You're hurt!"

Slowly, the red-haired girl lowered her hands and stood, gazing in bewilderment at the thin shaft of wood protruding from her arm. Dazedly, she reached over with her other hand and drew it out.

"Here, sit down." Kit hurried over to her and, with an arm around her waist, drew her over to the desk chair. "I'll get a washcloth. We've got to stop that bleeding."

She went quickly into the bathroom and grabbed the cloth from the edge of the sink and ran cold water over it. Then she wrung it out and carried it back to the bedroom.

"Press this over the spot. No — I will — I can use both hands."

Sandy stared at her in disbelief. "Why did you do it?"

"Me? You think I did this?" Kit exclaimed, holding the cloth tightly against the injury.

"Well, didn't you? Somebody broke that pencil and threw it at me. If you didn't, who did? There's nobody else —" Her voice broke and understanding came into her eyes. "I'm sorry, Kit. Of course, you didn't. *He* was here, wasn't he? The one with the music?"

"Yes," Kit said. Her hand was shaking as she pressed it upon the washcloth. She felt sick.

"Why?" Sandy whispered. "What does he have against me?"

"It wasn't you," Kit said. "It would have been the same with anybody who had come in just then, who had broken his control. He had me, Sandy. I was going to write down his music for him. When you called out my name your voice came through to me, and I got away."

"Who was it?" Sandy spoke with a choking sob in her voice. "Schubert?"

"I don't think so. It's been a long time since it was Schubert. That is, if I can judge by the music. In the beginning it was lovely, but now it's different, wilder, more discordant. It doesn't *feel* like Schubert."

"It's the same with me," Sandy said. "That's why I came here tonight. I had to tell you. Ellis is gone."

"Gone?" Kit felt a sudden surge of hope. "You're free?"

"No. Oh, no. It's just that Ellis has been replaced. This new one — I don't see him, as I did Ellis, but he's there. I feel him come into my mind, and it's like smoke, thick and gray and dirty."

"Did he tell you who he was?"

"He doesn't tell me anything. He doesn't talk to me, he talks *through* me. He speaks some foreign language. I can't understand him."

"We should have guessed it," Kit said. "That there would be others. Ruth told us it was that way with her right from the beginning, with a whole host of people pouring their thoughts into her. I felt it myself the night I woke in the music room. It wasn't just one voice then but a lot of them, all bidding for me as though I were some sort of community possession."

"But why? I mean, why now, when at the start it was just one?"

"Maybe the road's wider open now, and they can get through."

"Then we can expect it to get worse? More and more of them, crowding into our minds, shoving our own thoughts out, until there's nothing of ourselves left?" Sandy was crying now, soft, hopeless crying which had nothing to do with her injured arm.

Kit lifted the cloth. The blood was stilled. Raising her head, she met the misery in her friend's face with that on her own.

"We've got to fight it," she said. "We can't let down. We can't let them take us over."

"But how can we help it? They're stronger than we are, especially with there being so many of them. They don't have to stop to sleep the way we do, they can keep at us constantly."

"Then we'll have to get out. We'll plan an escape. After all, there are four of us. That's against four of them, if you count Lola. It's even sides."

"You're counting Lynda as one of us. What good would she be? And Ruth — she's more on their side than ours. She likes what's happening." Sandy shook her head. "You're dreaming, Kit. There's no way. We'll never break out of here. Our only hope is Christmas. If we hold out till then, we'll go home for vacation. Our folks expect us. There's no way Madame can hold us here over the holidays."

"That's true," Kit said. "And Madame knows it, and that's what scares me worst of all. Because it doesn't seem to bother her. How can she accept the fact that we'll leave here and tell our parents and never come back again?"

The answer lay there between them in the stillness of the room, too dreadful to acknowledge.

"Don't say it," Sandy said, but Kit spoke the words anyway.

"By Christmas," she said softly, "it won't matter any longer. We won't have to be at Blackwood for them to get through to us. They're digging in deeper every day. By Christmas, they'll be part of us, the spirit people. They'll have such control that no matter where we go, no matter what we do for the rest of our lives, we'll belong to them."

Chapter 16

———————

Dear Tracy —

How strange, to be writing a letter which I know will never reach you. And yet I must; perhaps having you to talk to is what is keeping me sane.

The days go by. I don't even bother to keep track of them any longer; they're all the same. We don't have classes now — they stopped soon after that night when I woke in the music room and forced Madame to tell us the truth about Blackwood. After that, it became impossible. How could we keep going to classes, studying and learning regular everyday schoolwork, knowing that it was just a cover-up for something else? How could we sit at a desk and listen to Madame or Professor Farley lecturing about history and literature and languages, as though they were regular teachers, when we know now what they really are?

And Jules! How could I possibly sit at that piano and play rinky-dink beginners' pieces for Jules, who has heard me playing music that no one has ever heard before, my fingers moving in patterns that some musical genius has arranged for me? Out of everything, what I find hardest to accept is Jules, the fact that he is part of this. Imagine him sitting there in the music room, night after night, making tapes, while I sat on the piano bench in some kind of stupor, being ruled by a ghost! And I thought he liked me. I really did, Tracy — the way he looked at me, and the tone of his voice, and there was something in his eyes that night when I saw the figure in the mirror and started to scream. He came running up the stairs ahead of the others, and he put his arms around me and held me, and he *cared*. I could have sworn it.

How silly I was to think that when all I am to him is part of a weird and awful experiment.

Now that the classes are gone, so too is the pretending. Madame Duret and Professor Farley and Jules no longer sit with us in the dining room. We eat alone — Sandy and Ruth and I — when we eat at all. Most of the time we're not hungry, and when we are it's easier to go out to the kitchen and make a sandwich than to try to choke down the meals that Lola prepares. We spend as much time as we can outside, in the garden and by the pond, but the weather is so bad that the wind and chill soon drive us in again.

Lynda is lost to us completely. We never see her at all. I know she is painting, for every once in a while Professor Farley goes into her room and brings out the canvases and carries them down to Madame's office. What they do with them after that, I don't know. Will they sell them, I wonder, as they did the Vermeer? Is that how Madame managed to finance the purchase of Blackwood — with a brand new manuscript by Hemingway, a poem by Kipling, some music that only Chopin could have composed? Is she even now trying to market the newly discovered pieces by Schubert that Jules has on his tape?

If only I could get into that office to the telephone. I

have dialed your number so many times in my imagination that it is almost a part of me; I write it with my finger in the dust on the bureau top and I see now that I have scribbled it several times over in the margin of this letter. I could dial it in my sleep, I think, if I could reach the phone. But the office door is kept locked.

And Lynda's door also. They keep that locked so that we can't go in and "distract" her. Madame has the key, and she gives it to Lola to use when she brings up the trays. Sandy and I stand outside the room sometimes and try to talk to her, but Lynda doesn't answer. I feel that she might speak to Ruth. If anyone could get through to her, Ruth could — they have been friends for years — but Ruth won't call in to her. She says that the work Lynda is producing is too important to be slowed down by silly conversations.

We stay away from Ruth as much as possible, Sandy and I. Being with Ruth is almost as bad as being in the room with Madame Duret herself. Ruth isn't one of us anymore. She has accepted this thing, and she is riding with it like someone on top of a wave. Her eyes are shining with excitement, and she carries a notebook with her at all times so that she can write down the things that "come" to her. I looked into the notebook once, and it is like a strange code with numbers and signs and odd diagrams.

I won't accept it! Not as long as I'm alive, I won't! I will fight it all the way! I am going to get out of here, Tracy, somehow — some way — I *will* get out of here!"

Kit folded the letter, placed it in the pocket of her jeans, and left the room. She did not bother to lock her door, knowing now how senseless the formality was. She did not look in the mirror at the end of the hall. She did not want to know whom she might see there.

Descending the stairs, she went softly down the hall to Madame's office and tried the knob. It would not turn.

One time, she thought, it will. She cannot keep it locked always. There will come a day when she forgets, and when she does, I will be in there so quickly that no one can stop me. It's just a matter of waiting and watching and trying.

Beyond the office the door to the parlor stood open and there was a fire burning in the grate. Lola was in the room, dusting. Kit paused, but she did not enter. There was no use trying to talk with Lola. She did not know how much Lola understood of the situation at Blackwood, but whatever it might be, she would relate to no one but Madame Duret.

Kit continued down the hall until she reached the music room. From behind the closed door, she could hear the sound of the piano. She listened a moment and then, without knocking, opened the door.

Jules was seated on the piano bench, his back toward her, playing softly to himself. He stopped when the door opened and turned to see who had entered. This time he did not seem irritated by the intrusion.

He said, "Hi."

"Hi." Kit stood staring at him, wondering how she could ever have found him attractive. He looked like his mother, and she hated them both.

"What are you playing?" she asked him bitterly. "Something from Schubert?"

"Kit, please." He made a helpless gesture. "I don't want us to be enemies. I like you a lot. I have right from the beginning. I wish you'd try to understand my position."

"What, exactly, is your position?" Kit asked coldly.

"Well, it's not that of an accomplice in a crime. You're trying to make me feel guilty, and it's not fair. My mother

143

has a gift, a marvelous one. She's given you a chance to help enrich the world. Why do you find that so upsetting?"

"Why do I find it upsetting!" Kit regarded him incredulously. "How would you feel if it were you, being used as a kind of vehicle for dead people! And since the subject's come up, why is it that you're not taking an active part in this experience? Isn't your mind 'young and clear and uncluttered' enough for your mother to want to use it?"

"Evidently not," Jules said stiffly, "or I'm sure she'd have made me a receiver also. Everybody isn't tuned for this sort of thing. You're one of the lucky ones."

"Stop saying that," Kit told him. "There's nothing lucky about it. Jules, I want to ask you something. The two other schools — the ones your mother had in England and in France — what happened to those? What became of the girls who went there? Why did your mother close those schools and come to the United States?"

"I don't know," Jules said. "I've never asked her."

"How can you not know? You were there, weren't you, when the decision was made?"

"No, I wasn't," Jules said. "I was away at the conservatory. I've told you that. The only time I spent at my mother's schools was during vacations, when they were closed. I didn't take much interest in her work. I didn't realize then the extent of what she was doing."

"You didn't know she was a medium?"

"I knew she had talents in that direction," Jules admitted, "but I didn't know she was using her students as subjects. And I had no idea she was doing something as exciting as bringing back the creative geniuses of the world. It wasn't until she closed her school in France and made arrangements to come to the United States that she told me about that. She thought that it would make me want to come with her."

"And is it the way you thought it would be?" Kit asked him. "Are you happy about this, Jules — honestly? Can you look at what's happening to Lynda — to Sandy — to all of us, and think it's right?"

"Kit, you've got to adjust to this," Jules said. "I agree — you girls aren't in good shape. But it's your own fault. You're fighting this so hard that you've got yourselves physically and mentally exhausted. I don't like to see you looking like this, all white and thin and worn out, and I *do* worry about it. But the answer isn't with us, it's with you. If you'd just accept the situation and go along with it, I'm sure you'd be fine."

"You don't see! You don't understand!" Kit cried in frustration. The tears, which she had never used to shed, were welling in her eyes. "Jules, if you do like me — if you're really my friend — then help me! Help us all! Get us out of here!"

Jules shook his head. "I can't. You know that. It would ruin everything."

"Then if you won't do that, will you do something else for me? Will you find out what happened to the other girls, the ones who went to your mother's European schools? There are files on them in her office. She told me so herself."

"What would you learn from that?" Jules asked. "They're probably scattered all over the place by now."

"You could look and see, couldn't you? What harm would that do?"

Jules shook his head. "I can't go plowing through my mother's private files. I'll ask her though, if you want me to, and let you know what she says. Or you can ask her yourself."

"A lot of good that will do," Kit exploded.

The tears were so near the surface now that she knew that if she stayed a moment longer she would not be able to control them. Turning abruptly, she left the music room, slamming the door behind her, and went out again into the hall.

A cold burst of air met her, fresh and damp from the outdoors, and she saw that the great front door was standing open. A familiar figure stood beside it, adjusting the collar of her coat.

Kit gave a startled cry and stretched out her hands.

"Natalie!"

The figure turned, and Natalie Culler gave her a nod of acknowledgment. She completed buttoning the top of the coat and moved as though in preparation to step outside.

"Natalie — wait! Don't go!" Kit hurried over to her. "What are you doing here?"

"Collecting my money," Natalie said shortly. "When your lady fired me, she owed me two weeks' back pay. I was so mad at the time, I just walked out without remembering it, but that money was mine. I earned every penny of it, and I came back today to get it."

"How did you get here?" Kit asked excitedly.

"By car. How else? Think I'm going to walk up from the village?"

"And you were able to get in the gate?"

"I called ahead," Natalie said. "She sent Mr. Jules down to open it. I guess she knew I wasn't about to be put off any." She paused to stare at Kit, and the anger on her face faded slightly, to be replaced by concern. "If you don't mind me saying so, you look awful, miss. You been sick?"

"Yes," Kit said. "We're all sick. The whole place is sick! Natalie, take me with you!"

"With me? You mean to the village?"

"Anywhere! The village would be fine. Just someplace where I can get to a telephone and make a call. Please, Natalie!"

"It's cold out. You don't have a coat on."

"It doesn't matter! I won't be cold!"

"The missus would be furious," Natalie said uncertainly. "She'd likely have me arrested for kidnaping. Why don't you just write your folks and have them come for you, miss? That would be the best way to leave here, if that's what you want to do."

"I can't," Kit told her desperately. "Our letters are all —"

She broke off the sentence as she heard a door open into the hall behind her. There was a moment of silence.

Kit did not have to turn. She could tell from Natalie's expression whom it was that she would see.

"Natalie!" Madame Duret's voice was like ice. "You will please to be on your way. I have given you your wages, and I did not invite you to stay and visit."

"Yes, ma'am." There was a flash of pure hatred across Natalie's face. She turned defiantly to speak to Kit. "Good-bye, miss. You take care of yourself now. I hope you're feeling better soon."

"Wait — please!" Kit struggled to find words, and then, in a final frantic effort, she pulled the letter from her jeans pocket and thrust it quickly into Natalie's work-worn hand.

"Here," she whispered hurriedly, "take this and mail it."

Natalie glanced down at the wadded paper in bewilderment.

"Mail it? To who?"

"Tracy Rosenblum," Kit said. "She lives at —"

"Kathryn!" Madame spoke from directly behind her. "Come inside away from that open door. You will take a chill."

Natalie threw her one startled glance and stepped hurriedly out the door, pulling it closed behind her. She had the letter in her hand, but Kit could feel no thrill of triumph. There was no way possible that Natalie could mail it when it bore no address.

Chapter 17

———————◆———————

That night the winds came. Far and thin at first, like quarrelsome children arguing in the distance, and then closer, shrieking and crying in high, shrill voices in the branches of the trees outside the fence, they made their way to the doors of Blackwood and tried to get in.

All night long, they circled the house, trying the windows, howling around corners, wailing in the eaves, until when morning came Kit was certain she had not slept at all.

Then she realized that her right hand was cramped from writing and that the music book that lay on her desk was half filled.

"It's the same with me," Sandy told her later. "I try to fight it, but there's just so long you can hold out. I don't plan to sleep, and then suddenly it's morning, and I *have* slept."

Apologetically, she offered Kit a sheet of paper.

"Another poem?" Kit glanced at the paper and handed it back. "I can't read that. It's in French."

"I can't read it either. It's in my handwriting, though, so I know I wrote it down."

149

"Shall we get Ruth to translate?"

"I hate to ask her," Sandy said. "She'll enjoy doing it, and I don't want her to enjoy it. That sounds terrible, doesn't it?"

"Yes," Kit agreed. "Still, I know what you mean. She's taking such pleasure in this that I want to smack her." She paused and then said, "We don't have much choice. It's either ask Ruth or Madame or Jules, and Ruth's better than the others. You do want to know what you wrote, don't you?"

"I suppose," Sandy said, pocketing the paper. But she made no effort to go to find Ruth, and neither did Kit, who felt as drained and exhausted as though she had been out-of-doors all night, running with the winds.

They spent most of the day together in Sandy's room, reading, talking a little, and playing a half-hearted game of cards. Late in the afternoon the rain began, lightly at first and then with increased strength, so that by evening the gentle patter on the roof had become a dull roar. At six-thirty they went down to the dining room, not so much from hunger as from the realization that neither of them had eaten since the night before. It was Lola's evening off, and the meal left out on the table consisted of some withered-looking cold cuts and a bowl of soggy potato salad. The candles flickered erratically, and beyond the long windows an occasional flash of lightning streaked the black sky.

The food looked even less appetizing once they had put it on their plates than it had on the serving platter.

"I can't take it," Sandy said. "I'm sorry, I just can't make it go down."

"We've got to eat something," Kit told her. "We need all the strength we can get." But after one or two forced mouthfuls, she too shoved her plate away. A great roll of thunder filled the room, and the chandelier began to sway, moving slowly back and forth like an ornate pendulum, while the hundreds of tiny crystals caught the light from the candles and threw it in a strange, iridescent pattern upon the far wall. Outside the wind screamed and tree branches scratched at the windows like clutching hands.

"Let's go to the parlor," Kit said. "At least there'll be a fire."

Ruth was there ahead of them, leafing through her ever-present notebook and eating a peanut butter sandwich.

"I went out to the kitchen and made it myself," she said, cramming the last wedge into her mouth and swallowing. "I couldn't face that stuff on the table."

"That's a good idea. Maybe we'll do the same thing in a little while." Kit crossed the room to stand before the fire. The heat felt good against her back, and the crackling of the logs was the first cheerful sound she had heard in a long time.

"Why don't you give her the poem," she suggested to Sandy, "and see what she can make of it."

"Another offering from Ellis?" Ruth asked, closing her book.

"No," Sandy said. "It's in French. Ellis's poetry is all in English." She dug the paper out of her pocket and held it out.

Ruth took it and sat for a moment in silence, her eyes flicking from left to right as she scanned the lines.

"Cripes," she said softly, "you don't want me to read you this."

"Why not?"

"You just don't, that's all. It's — not like that other stuff you wrote."

"I don't care," Sandy said. "I want to hear it. I want to know what it is I've been writing."

"Well — okay." Ruth gave a slight grimace. "Just don't say I didn't warn you." She began to read, slowly, in an expressionless voice. As one word followed another, Kit, standing mesmerized in front of the fireplace, could not believe what she was hearing.

Sandy's face grew paler and paler. Finally she made a gesture to cut off the translation.

"No more. Don't read anymore."

"I told you," Ruth said. "I knew you wouldn't want to listen."

"It's sickening," Sandy said in a choking voice. "I've never used words like those in my life. It's just foul, the whole thing. It makes me want to throw up."

"Well, don't blame me for it," Ruth said. "All I did was read it, the way you asked me to. Who's the author, if you don't mind my asking?"

"I hate to think." Sandy turned wretchedly to Kit. "Can you imagine the sort of creepy, demented creature that would spill out garbage like that?" She shuddered. "I feel dirty just for having held the pen. I wish now I'd never —"

She broke off in midsentence as the room went white with a glare of brilliant light. Instantaneously there came a crash of thunder so tremendous that the ceiling seemed to lift with the impact and a picture on the wall by the window lurched from its nail and fell with a clatter to the floor. At the same moment, the electric lights flickered and went out.

In the sudden silence that followed, Kit could hear her heart pounding in rhythm with the drumming of the rain.

"That —" She tried to speak and found that her voice

had to be dragged from her throat. "That was a close one."

Ruth nodded. Her glasses caught the firelight and threw back a reflection of leaping flames. "I bet it hit the chimney."

"And now the lights are out. That's just great," Sandy said shakily. "Can you imagine climbing those stairs and trying to find our rooms in the dark?"

"I don't want to imagine it," Kit said. "I'm going to sleep right here. I'll flip you for the sofa." She meant the words to be light, but they didn't come out that way.

There was the sound of voices in the hall beyond the parlor door. Madame's, sharp and commanding. Professor Farley's. Jules's — raised in a question.

There came another roll of thunder, farther away this time, and the door opened.

"Girls?" the professor said. "Are you all right in here?"

"I guess so," Ruth said. "Do you know what happened?"

"We think it got that big tree outside the dining room window. Jules is going to look, and Madame has gone to the kitchen to hunt for candles. There should be a supply of them there for use on the table."

"At least we have a fireplace," Sandy said. "We can pretend we're at camp and toast marshmallows and tell ghost stories." There was a moment's silence, and then, as the full significance of what she had said came through to her, she began to laugh. It was a high, strange laugh, and once it started it would not be stopped; it poured forth, like carbonated liquid from a bottle that had been shaken and uncorked, gushing out, wild and uncontrolled.

"Stop it," Ruth told her.

But Sandy could not stop. She sat down on the hearth and stared at them out of wide, frightened eyes, and continued to laugh while tears streamed down her cheeks in fire-colored rivulets and the wind shrieked around the corners of the house, straining to be heard over the beat of the rain.

"Sandra? My dear girl." The professor came slowly across the room in his cramped, old-man's walk, grotesquely silhouetted against the glow of the firelight, and bent to gaze into Sandy's face. "Please, my child. You will have to get control of yourself."

"She can't," Ruth said. "She's hysterical."

"She certainly seems to be." The professor raised his head. "One of you girls, go fetch Madame Duret. She'll know how to handle this."

"In the dark?" Ruth objected. "The kitchen's all the way to the back of the house."

"I'll go," Kit said.

"In all this blackness? You'll get lost in the hall."

"No, I won't."

Silently, Kit cursed herself for the eagerness in her voice. How was it possible that they did not hear it and turn to her in suspicious amazement? But, no — they were both bending over Sandy. There was no one to see her, no one to stop her.

She stepped through the door and pushed it closed behind her and started down the hall full of darkness.

She was not afraid. For the first time in weeks, it seemed, there was no fear in her. She was moving purposefully and directly toward the thing that she was going to do. But, quickly, for there was little time. Any moment now Madame might emerge from one of the doors at the far end of the hall, her hands filled with candles.

Kit walked close to the wall, guiding herself with one hand, trying to gauge the distance she had come in comparison with that which she still had to go. She came to the door of the music room; her hand felt the frame, crossed the emptiness of the gaping doorway, found the wall on the far side. She began to count her steps — one, two, three, four — how many feet would it be from the music room door to the door of Madame Duret's office? She attempted to picture it in her mind, but the depth of the darkness around her blotted out all memory of the way the hall looked in the daylight.

Ten, eleven, twelve — had she come too far? Had she somehow missed the doorframe? Or, worse still, might she have lost direction entirely and be working her way toward the entrance to the dining room?

Dear Lord, I hope not, Kit thought. If I end up there, I'll never be able to get myself turned around and started back again.

Thirteen, fourteen — and she was upon it. The paneling of the wall gave way beneath her hand to the smooth, hard wood of the door. With a breath of relief, Kit felt along it, inch by careful inch. On their first trip across, her fingers missed the knob. On the second, they found it.

Offering a silent prayer, Kit closed her hand upon it and gave it a turn. It moved so easily that she almost fell forward as the door swung open into the room beyond.

And she was in the office. She knew it by the feel of the carpeting beneath her feet, by the faint smell of paint from Lynda's canvases, piled there for storage. Although she had been inside this room only once before, Kit could have described every inch of it, and she moved forward without hesitation in the direction of the desk.

Her outstretched hand touched the back of the desk chair. She reached past this and felt the flat, smooth surface of the desk top beneath her palm. She groped onward — over a pile of papers, a portable typewriter — to her goal.

The telephone.

She would not be able to see to dial, but that did not matter. The final digit in the circle would bring her the operator.

In one minute, she thought, just one more minute, I'll hear Tracy's voice. Or her mother's or father's. And I'll say, "This is Kit — Kit Gordy at Blackwood. Help! You've got to help me!"

Her hand was shaking as she lifted the receiver and her other hand felt for the dial. So great was her anticipation that she had already drawn in her breath to speak when she realized that there was no dial tone. Silent and dead, the receiver lay against her ear.

For a long moment she stood there, unmoving, willing it to life. Then, slowly, she lowered it and let it fall from her hand onto the desk.

The clatter was loud. It did not matter. Nothing mattered now.

"It was our one chance," Kit said softly. "Our one last chance."

Never would there be another night like this one, with so much confusion and excitement, with people rushing in different directions and the office door forgotten and unlocked. It was a one-time occurrence. By the time the phone line was repaired, the house would be back to normal and the office secure against invasion.

If I were Sandy, Kit thought miserably, I'd have hysterics. I'd stand here and shriek and laugh and bang my head against the wall. Or I'd cry. I think I could cry from now to eternity and never get done.

But being herself, she did neither. She simply stood there in the darkness, leaning upon the desk, waiting for the inevitable. Madame would return to the parlor with the candles, and as soon as Professor Farley realized that

Kit was not with her, someone would be dispatched to find her. And whoever it was would not have to think long to know where to come.

It was only a matter of minutes. The hall beyond the doorway grew lighter and she heard the footsteps approaching. Then suddenly a flashlight appeared, turned straight into her face.

Jules's voice said, "Kit! What the devil are you doing in here?"

The flashlight beam moved to the desk top and found the telephone, receiver off the hook. She could hear Jules draw in his breath.

"You made a call?"

"Of course." Kit tried to keep her voice steady. "I called the police. They're on their way up from the village now. You'd better tell your mother to get those gates open, Jules."

"Then why haven't you hung up?" Jules came into the room and reached across her to pick up the receiver from the desk. He held it to his ear for a moment, then replaced it on the hook.

"Good try," he said. His voice was oddly gentle. "The lines must be down. Come on, Kit. Let's get back to the others."

"I don't want to go back," Kit said. "I won't sit there in that room with your mother and the professor and make conversation and act as though they're normal people."

"Kit — please — I wish you wouldn't feel this way." He tried to put his arm around her shoulders, but Kit twisted free and stepped quickly around the desk chair so that it stood between them.

"Okay," Jules said stiffly. "If that's the way you want it, I'll take you to your room. You'll have to let me do that because you'll never find your way without a flashlight." He moved so that the beam of light made a pathway across the carpet and bounced against the opposite wall.

It flickered upward across a pile of canvases and stopped — focused upon one that stood propped against the side of the filing cabinet.

It was a moment before either of them could speak.

Then Jules said softly, "Oh, my God!"

Chapter 18

"Who did it? Who painted that — thing? It can't have been Lynda."

"It was," Kit whispered. "Who else?"

She stared at the picture as though hypnotized, nauseated and heartsick, yet unable to tear her eyes away. The scene before her depicted a form of torture more horrible than anything she could ever have imagined. In the foreground, so real that it seemed to be bursting from the canvas, a woman's white face shrieked out at them, contorted into an expression of unbearable agony.

"But I thought —" Jules's voice was hoarse with shock, "I thought she was painting landscapes! Rivers, fields, pretty things —"

"Turn the light away."

Kit closed her eyes and when she opened them again the beam had dropped and the picture was coated with darkness.

"Now, do you see?" she asked quietly. "Do you begin to understand?"

"It's insane! Whoever created that is obscene — horrible!"

"It wasn't Thomas Cole."

"My God, no!" He sounded bewildered. "Who? Do you have any idea? Has she told you?"

"I haven't even seen her for weeks," Kit told him. "Your mother keeps her locked in her room upstairs. She won't speak to us when we call in to her through the door. Didn't you know?"

"I knew she spent most of her time in her room painting, but I thought —" Jules's voice broke. "Can you imagine, being in there alone, painting things like this? Holding a brush and watching them appear before you on canvas?"

"I can imagine it," Kit said, "and so can Sandy. Once the roads to the other world are opened, there's no controlling who travels along them. Can you see now why your mother didn't want to use you for a subject? You're her son. No mother would do this to her own son."

"My mother doesn't realize," Jules said uncertainly. "I'm sure she doesn't."

"She's seen the pictures. They're stored here, right in her office."

"Perhaps this is a new one. Professor Farley might have brought it down today."

"There's a pile of others. Do you want to look at them and see?"

Kit could not see his face, but she knew what must be on it by the sound of his voice.

"No."

"Jules," she said softly, "the other day, I asked you about what happened to the girls who went to your mother's European schools. You couldn't tell me. The files are here, right in that metal cabinet. All we have to do is open it and look."

"I couldn't," Jules said.

"You must! You owe us that!" Kit reached out in the darkness and touched his arm. "Please, Jules, we have to know! Don't you see, whatever it is that happened to them is what is destined to happen to us! Doesn't it matter to you? Don't you *care*?"

"Of course I care." He shifted the light to rest upon the cabinet, and in doing so it flicked across the side of the picture, catching once again the woman's tortured face. Every detail was so real that it seemed that the blood must surely have fallen to stain the carpet beneath it.

Kit swallowed hard against a wave of sickness that rose in her throat, threatening to choke her.

"Okay," Jules said shortly. "Let's look."

They moved together to the cabinet, Jules still holding the flashlight. There were two drawers, one above the other.

Kit dropped to her knees, seized the handle of the top drawer, and pulled it out. It came easily, disclosing a set of ledgers, bound in black leather. Behind these were several piles of canceled checks, held together by rubber bands, and a file of receipts.

Kit regarded them wryly.

"I wonder if there's a record here of what she got for the sale of the Vermeer."

"We'll look at the girls' files," Jules said. "I agreed to that, but not to plowing through the financial records. Shove that closed and pull out the lower drawer."

"All right." Begrudgingly, Kit pushed the drawer back into place and drew forth the one below it. This moved less freely and made a slight creaking sound, as though the grooves along the sides had begun to rust.

"This is it!" Kit exclaimed, feeling her heart begin to beat faster. "It's all names, arranged alphabetically. 'Anderson, Cynthia,' 'Bonnette, Jeanne,' 'Darcy, Mary' — there aren't very many of them."

"She kept the student number small in the other schools," Jules said, "just as she has here. Where do you want to start?"

"With the first in line, I guess." Kit reached for the folder labeled "Anderson." "Shine the light on it, will you? Oh, dear —" She caught her breath in disappointment. "It's in French!"

"Are you surprised? It's my mother's native language. Mine, too, when it comes to that." Jules took the file from her hand. "Here — let me read it."

"Aloud!" Kit said. A moment passed, and she said again, "Aloud, Jules! Translate it for me!"

"Let me skim it first." Slowly Jules moved the flashlight beam down the page, pausing here and there as though to reread certain passages. When he had finished he replaced the file and drew out the next one.

"What did it say?" Kit demanded. "What happened to Cynthia Anderson?"

"Stop pushing me, Kit," Jules said gruffly. "I want to go through the rest of these. You can't tell anything by one particular case."

"Well, hurry. Somebody might come looking for us any minute." Kit bit down on her lip in frustration and lapsed into silence. Outside the storm continued to howl. In the office there was no sound except for the occasional rustle of paper as Jules completed one history and reached for the next.

After what seemed hours, he placed the final folder back into the drawer and pushed it shut.

"Come on," he said. "We're going back to the parlor."

"Is that all you're going to say?" Kit's voice was squeaky with rage. "You go through twenty sets of records, and when you get finished you don't tell me one single thing?"

"I will tell you 'one single thing,' " Jules said. "That thing is that I'm getting you out of here."

"You're — *what?*" Kit stared across at him, trying to make out his face. "Did I hear you right? You're getting us *out?*"

"The sooner, the better," Jules said. "Now — tonight, if that's possible. If not tonight, then first thing in the morning."

"But, what did they say? What was in those files? You have to tell me!"

"I don't have to tell you anything." Jules got to his feet and reached down for her hand. "It doesn't matter what those papers said. What does matter is that you're getting what you want. You're going home, you and the rest of them, if it means I have to drive you there myself."

There was such determination in his voice that Kit did not push the question further. She let him pull her to her feet and, shining the light ahead of them, lead her out of the office and back along the downstairs hall. The glow from the fireplace was a rosy strip under the parlor door.

Jules pulled the door open and, still holding Kit's hand, drew her with him into the room. Glancing quickly about her, Kit saw that the scene had not changed measurably from the one she had left half an hour before. Sandy was still seated on the hearth, but she was quiet now, bent forward with her face buried in her hands, and Professor Farley stood above her, talking to her soothingly. Ruth had shoved a chair over by the fireplace and was trying to read in the flickering light.

Madame Duret stood with her back to the doorway, placing a set of candleholders on the mantel. She turned as she heard the door open and said, "Jules? Where did you find her?"

His voice was low. "She was in the office, just as you suspected, trying to make a phone call. The line must be down, though. The phone was dead."

"Thank goodness for that." Madame turned her icy gaze upon Kit. "Did you really imagine you would accomplish something by that sort of maneuver? I should think by now, Kathryn, that you would have become adjusted to the fact that you are going to remain at Blackwood until you are sent home for the holidays. Nothing you do will change this, and life will become much simpler for you and for the rest of us if you will accept the situation for what it is."

"I don't have to accept it!" Kit cried defiantly. "None of us do! Jules is taking us out of here!"

"That's ridiculous," Madame said firmly. "Jules is doing nothing of the sort. That is something he told you to keep you from making a scene. Jules despises unpleasantness."

"It wasn't!" Kit told her. "He means it! He promised!" She clutched tightly at the strong hand that held hers. "You did promise, Jules — you were telling the truth?"

"Yes," Jules said.

The word fell into the room like a stone into a pond. One single word, but in the silence that followed ripple after ripple rose and went sliding across to splash against the walls. Ruth lowered her book to stare at him unbelievingly. Sandy lifted her face from her hands. Professor Farley turned, his mouth falling open.

Madame Duret stood frozen, a candle in each hand.

"What did you say?" she asked her son.

"I said 'yes.' I am taking them out of here. Tonight, if the storm lets up." Jules spoke quietly. "I read the files, Mother."

"The files?"

"From the cabinet in the office. The ones you kept on the girls from the European schools. I read the records on all of them, the things they did, the things that happened to them."

"Then how is it that you can speak of letting our Blackwood girls go now?" Madame was incredulous. "You saw their accomplishments? That one little Jeanne Bonnette wrote three entire novels. We had them published under a nom de plume and the royalties made possible the purchase of Blackwood. And the black girl from Marseille — what was her name, Gigi? Over fifty oils, straight from the period of the French Impressionists."

"I saw Lynda Hannah's latest oil," Jules said.

"Oh? Well, she is going through a stage. We cannot sell *that*." Madame gave a sigh of regret. "I fear that Lynda's productivity may be reaching its end. But as for the rest of them, they are only beginning! The good months lie still ahead! Who knows what may come forth from them!"

"You think that's important?" Jules asked.

"And *you* do not? That I cannot believe. I heard you yesterday myself, playing over Kathryn's last tape."

"That was yesterday — before I knew." He regarded his mother with amazement. "Do you really think I'd want to go on with it, having read those reports? How can *you* want to?" Jules was fighting to control his voice. "Mother, don't you understand? I know what happened to those girls!"

"What did the reports say?" Kit begged. "Please, Jules — she's not going to give in. You have to tell us."

Jules hesitated, then made his decision.

"Out of the twenty, four of them are dead."

"Dead!" Kit whispered.

"Three committed suicide. One fell, trying to climb

out of a third-story window at the school. That was classified as an accident."

"And — the others?" Kit could hardly bring out the question.

"The others went insane. *Every single one of them is now in a mental institution.*"

From her place on the hearth, Sandy gave a little moan.

Professor Farley shook his head reprovingly. "That was a very unwise statement to make in front of these girls, Jules. It can do nothing but upset them and make them unhappy. It was a cruel thing to tell them."

"Cruel!" Kit cried. "You can call Jules 'cruel'? You, who knew it all along! You and Madame Duret, the two of you — you're not even human! You're like two great big black vultures, feeding on our brains!" She turned frantically to Jules. "Let's leave now! It doesn't matter about the storm. I'd rather get hit by a falling tree or washed off the road or *anything* than spend one more night in this awful place!"

"I'm with you," Sandy cried, pulling herself to her feet. "Ruth?"

"You're darned right, I'm with you," Ruth said. Her face was dark with anger. "This is one little piece of news nobody bothered to tell us. It's one thing to be a receiver — I could go that route fine — but it's something else entirely to know it's going to destroy you."

"Now, girls, calm yourselves," Madame commanded. "Jules, I am furious with you for causing this disruption. Perhaps there was some instability among our past students. We had not perfected our entrance tests at that point and inadvertently selected some emotional types who were too high-strung to be able to adjust to the situation. This has no bearing whatsoever upon what will happen at Blackwood. Each individual is different; you know that."

"Twenty out of twenty is good enough odds for me," Ruth said. She was on her feet now, clutching her notebook against her chest. "If I'm lucky enough to be that one-in-a-million case who pulls through nicely, I don't plan to stick around to find out about it. You were right all along, Kit. I'm ready to go."

"Kit, you go get Lynda," Jules said. "Mother, we'll need the key to her room and the one to the gate. How long will it take you girls to pack?"

"Hardly any time at all," Kit told him. "I'm willing to leave everything I came with except my father's picture, and it'll just take a minute to get that."

"I don't need anything," Sandy said. "I just want to get into that car. We can find out the bus schedule when we get to the village."

"I am afraid you're forgetting something," Madame Duret said quietly. "And that is that the keys are not at your disposal."

"You have them," Jules said.

"Of course I have them, but I do not for a moment intend to give them to you, nor do I plan to tell you where they are. The lock on the front gate will stay locked, and you will remain here, every one of you."

"You can't hold us here!" Kit cried. "Jules won't let you!"

"Jules cannot do very much about it. It distresses me to see him take this unreasonable and sentimental attitude, but young men are inclined to get romantic notions. In this case, I am sure common sense will eventually win out. Jules is an intelligent boy, and the advancement of music is very important to him."

"Not this important," Jules said. "Not when lives and

sanity are at stake. Mother, I can't believe this. Where is your sense of values?"

"Your mother's value system is a good deal more solid than yours, young man," the professor said irritably. "I should hope you would show some respect for her knowledge and experience. If nothing comes from this experiment but one short poem by one of the immortal poets of history, it will be worth more than the lives of four commonplace youngsters."

And there was a time, Kit thought in amazement, when I thought that old man was *sweet!* Anger was building in her to such a point that she was ready to explode with it.

"There's one thing *you've* forgotten," she said to Madame Duret, fighting to keep her voice steady. "That is that we are the ones who receive the material from the world beyond. It's ours — it comes through us — and it doesn't have to go one step farther."

"If that is some kind of threat —" Madame Duret began.

"It isn't a threat, it is a statement of fact." Kit lifted her chin defiantly. "There's no way in the world you're going to get this material if we don't want you to. Do you know what I'm going to do the next time I find myself writing down music? I'm going to tear the paper up into tiny pieces and flush them down the john."

"You would not dare!" Madame's eyes were blazing.

"I would! Just wait and see!"

"And so would I." There was a note of renewed courage in Sandy's voice. "You'll never get another poem of mine, starting with this one!"

Before anyone realized what she was about to do, she pulled a wadded paper from her sweater pocket and threw it into the fire.

The flames leapt high for a moment and there came a

low groan that seemed to rise from all corners of the room at once.

"Was that the one I translated for you?" Ruth asked.

"Yes, and that is just where it belongs — burned to ashes." Sandy made a grimace of disgust. "Horrid thing. I feel cleaner already having gotten rid of it."

"Stop them!" the professor cried. "We can't let them do this! What they're destroying is irreplaceable!"

"They will *not* do it," Madame's voice was a low hiss. "We will simply have to watch them, every minute of every day. We will chain them if necessary and stand over them and remove things from their hands the moment they are completed. We will not be defeated! The stakes are too high! The work is too important!" She turned to Ruth. "Hand me that notebook immediately."

"Go and get it!" Ruth cried.

Ripping the cover from the book, she lunged forward and hurled the pages into the fireplace. Instantly, the edges turned black and began to curl inward.

Madame gave a cry of rage and grabbed for the fire tongs, but Jules moved in to block her.

"It's too late, Mother, can't you see that? The experiment's blown up in your face. This set of girls isn't going to give in. Let them go, let me take them out of here. Holding them isn't going to accomplish anything. It's just not going to work."

The pages from Ruth's notebook burst into a crackling blaze, and from its depths there came a shriek of such agonized fury that it shook the walls. The voice lifted in a scream, and another voice joined it and another, until the room was filled with a chorus of hate-filled wails.

Suddenly, as though lifted by an unseen hand, the burning pages rose from the fireplace and flew straight out into the room in a shower of flaming segments.

Kit instinctively threw up her arms to protect her face

as the deadly missiles whizzed past, and she gave a cry of pain as one brushed her arm. All about her she could hear gasps and cries, and when she lowered her hands she saw to her horror that the draperies over the windows were on fire. The great orange flames gobbled greedily at the rich material and in a moment's time they had spread to the sofa and the overstuffed chair.

"Now, see what you have done! You wretched girls — you have angered them past endurance!" Madame started across the room. "I will call the fire department."

"You can't do that!" Jules flung out an arm to stop her. "The phone's out, remember? Our one chance is to drive to the village for help. Give me the gate key!"

"I know what you intend! You will take the girls with you!"

"Sure, I will," Jules said. "But you don't have a choice. Mother, for God's sake, this old house is an absolute firetrap! It's ancient, the wood is dry — there's nothing to stop it!"

"Oh — damn you! Damn all of you!" Madame glared at them helplessly. Then with a jerk of her hand she reached into her skirt pocket and pulled out a ring of keys. "Here — it is the big, square one. Hurry, Jules! Hurry! If they do not come quickly it will be too late."

"I'll make it as fast as I can," Jules told her. "Now, come on, let's get out of here!"

He threw open the parlor door and led the way through the dark hallway to the front door. A moment later they were outside with the wind wild against their faces and the icy rain full upon them.

"We'll go to my apartment," Professor Farley called, starting across the lawn. "That's detached from the house. Unless the wind changes, we'll be all right there."

Madame's black figure fell into step behind him, and

Jules caught Kit's arm and shoved her toward the driveway.

"You and the other girls wait out there. I'm going to get the car."

"We're leaving!" Sandy was half laughing, half crying. "Can you believe it, Kit, we're actually leaving! By morning we'll be on our way home and we'll look back on Blackwood and the whole thing will seem like a bad dream!"

"I'll call my parents from the village," Ruth said. "They'll wire me plane fare. I can bus to the nearest town that has an airport."

"Home," Kit said. "It sounds like heaven."

And then her heart caught in her chest. She turned and stared back at the house behind them with the flames bright behind the lower windows, and as she watched, she saw a malicious red tongue of fire appear suddenly at the second-floor level, licking up the edge of a bedroom window.

"Sandy! Ruth!" Horror filled her voice. "We're forgetting — *there's Lynda!*"

Chapter 19

"Lynda!" Sandy repeated the name, stunned. "Oh my God! In all the excitement, we forgot about her."

"You wait here," Kit told her, "and tell Jules where we've gone. Ruth and I will go get her."

"Speak for yourself," Ruth said shortly. "I don't plan to commit suicide. Do you see how that fire has spread already? Lynda's room is around on the side, almost directly over the parlor."

"You don't mean we should leave her there!" Kit exclaimed incredulously. "She'll be burned alive!"

"And what do you think will happen to us if we go back into that place to get her?" Ruth shook her head. "I'm sorry. It's tragic, but there's nothing we can do. Perhaps when the fire department gets here —"

"In an hour?" Kit cried. "It will be that by the time we drive the distance to the village and they round up their volunteers and get back here. By that time the place will be ashes!"

"Well, I'm not planning on being ashes with it," Ruth said. "Face it, Kit, the fire's spread all across the front of the house. Look at those windows — they're aglow with it! We'd never even get in the front door."

"We can go through the kitchen," Kit said. "There hasn't been time for it to have got that far. Ruth, think — this is Lynda, your best friend!"

"I'm sorry," Ruth said again. "I honestly am. It's just that there's no chance in the world of our getting up to that second floor and back down again. We wouldn't be saving Lynda, we'd be throwing our own lives away for nothing."

"I'm afraid she's right, Kit," Sandy said shakily. "Our best bet would be to get under Lynda's window and yell up to her. Perhaps we could get her to jump."

"She'd never hear us through the noise of the storm."

"We could throw stones up against the glass."

"Do you really think she'd react to that when she won't even answer us when we call through the door?"

"It's a chance, isn't it?" Ruth said. "It's better than nothing."

"Not *much* better than nothing," Kit retorted. "You can go throw stones if you want to. I'm going to try to get inside through the kitchen."

"You mustn't! You'll get trapped in there!" Sandy grabbed for her arm.

Kit shook her off impatiently.

"I'm not going to let Lynda die up there if there's any possible way to get her out!"

Leaving the other girls behind her, she started on a run around the side of the house. As she rounded the corner the wind struck her full force, whipping the raindrops against her as though they were pellets of steel. Somewhere to her left lay the pond, but she could not see it for the darkness and the driving sheet of rain. Her feet found the familiar gravel path, as dried stalks from the long dead garden raked her ankles and a rosebush threw out a thorny arm to slash her cheek.

"Kit! Wait!" Sandy's voice echoed behind her, thin and far.

I can't wait, Kit called back silently. There's no time to wait!

At the back of the house her way was easier for the planting was less dense and the eaves offered some protection from the rain. She floundered on through the heavy blackness, ran against the incinerator, reversed herself, and found the path that led to the kitchen door. For one panicky instant she was afraid that it might be locked, but it opened easily, and a moment later she was inside, groping her way through the dark kitchen.

She reached the far side, shoved open the door into the dining room, and staggered back, choking, under a great rush of acrid smoke. Letting the door swing closed again, she leaned weakly against the edge of the counter, gasping for breath and wiping the stinging fumes from her eyes.

She would have to mask her face, but how, in the darkness? Frantically she tried to recall the exact layout of the kitchen. There was a drying rack by the sink where Natalie used to hang the dish towels, but did Lola use it now that Natalie was gone?

Working her way back along the counter, Kit kept one arm outstretched, even with the wall. Her hand moved across the smooth tile — found the sink, the faucets, felt the soft touch of cotton cloth.

"Thank heaven," Kit breathed as her fingers closed over the towel and pulled it from the rack. She felt for the faucet and turned it on. The water ran cold, and when the towel was drenched she covered her head with it, letting the front fall forward over her face like a veil, and returned to the dining room door.

Now, when she opened it, she could face the smoke,

at least long enough to reach the stairway. It was not until she was halfway across the room that she realized that she was no longer walking blind. The faint glow of light from the hall beyond should have prepared her for what she would see there, but it didn't. Emerging from the dining room, she felt the heat strike her in one great blast. At the far end of the hall, the wall that had once enclosed the parlor was a solid panel of fire.

The hall was thick with smoke, but through it she could make out the curve of the stair leading to the second floor. She reached the first step and began her ascent, only to stop at the landing, horrified, as a second wall of flame leapt wildly in front of her.

"But it can't be!" she gasped, and then in shaken relief realized that this was only the mirror playing yet another of its devious tricks on her, catching and throwing back the image of the hall below in a blazing reflection.

Continuing her way forward, she reached the second-floor hall. Here it was cooler than on the lower level and the smoke was thinner; the only light was the reflection from the mirror, wavering and pale, but it was enough for her to see her way to Lynda's door.

She reached for the knob, twisted it, and gave a cry of frustration. How could she have forgotten that this door would be locked? There was no way to open it. By the time she could reach the carriage house to get the key from Madame she would not be able to return through the downstairs hall.

Making a fist, she began to pound upon the door.

"Lynda?" she shouted. "Lynda, are you awake in there? Do you hear me, Lynda?"

There was no sound from the room within. Kit pounded more loudly.

"Lynda, answer me! I know you're in there — you have

to be. Lynda, there's a fire! Blackwood is on fire! Do you hear?"

Was it her imagination or was there a faint rustling sound, a movement, a gasp of understanding? Kit began to kick, crashing her foot time and again upon the wood of the lower panel.

"Blackwood is on fire! Blackwood is burning!"

"Who —" The voice on the far side of the door was small and tentative, half dazed as though the speaker were just waking from sleep. "Who — is that?"

"It's Kit! Kit Gordy!" Kit ceased her pounding and brought her face down to the level of the keyhole. "Lynda, listen — you have to get out of there! The door's locked and I don't have the key to open it. The only way is by the window. You'll have to drop from the window."

"From the window?" Lynda echoed blankly. "But I can't do that. It's too high."

"Ruth and Sandy are standing down below," Kit told her. "They'll break your fall. Besides, it's lawn beneath you, not the driveway. You'll have to do it, Lynda, you don't have a choice. There's no other way."

"But, my paintings!" Lynda exclaimed. "I can't leave them!"

"You'll paint new ones." The statement was flatly untrue, but she felt no guilt in uttering it. "Don't waste time talking, get over to the window. Go on, now! I'll stay here until I know you're all right. Go look — are the girls down there?"

There was a moment of silence. When Lynda's voice came again it was faint with increased distance.

"Yes, they're there — Sandy and Ruth — and Jules. Jules is there with them."

"Open the window!" Kit called. "Hurry, get your legs over the sill! If you can lower yourself from the ledge you won't have as far to drop."

"It's raining," Lynda said wonderingly. "I didn't know it was raining. I can see them down there under the window. They're waving and holding their arms up to me. How is it I can see them when it's night?"

"It's the firelight shining from the windows!" The smoke in the hall was getting heavier and the cloth across her face had dried. "Jump!" Kit cried. "Please, Lynda, get on with it! I can't stay here much longer!"

There was no answer. Had the girl done it, or was she standing still by the window, staring down at the firelit figures awaiting her below? Kit rattled the knob.

"Lynda?" she called again.

There was no sound from within. Blackwood lay silent except for a steady crackling noise which, Kit realized suddenly, she had been hearing, half consciously, for some time. She drew a breath and began to cough uncontrollably. The soles of her feet felt hot. Bending, she pressed her hand against the hard wood floor and snatched it away again as quickly as though she had laid it against a hot griddle.

She could wait no longer.

"Good luck!" she called to Lynda, hoping the girl was not there to hear her, and, turning, she started back along the hallway to the stairs.

The hall seemed brighter now and the heat more intense, and in the mirror she could see herself emerging from the darkness like some grotesque apparition, with her rain-dampened clothes molded to her body and the dish towel draped across her head. She reached the top of the staircase, and as she gazed down a low moan escaped her.

"There's no way," Kit whispered. "No way."

Ruth had been right about the impossibility of this mission. In attempting to rescue Lynda, she had sacrificed herself. This stair was the only way down from the second floor, and the fire in the hall below had spread almost to its base.

Then this is how it ends, Kit thought, and somewhere at the edge of her mind she heard someone laughing, a malicious chortle that began softly and rose in a howling frenzy.

"Too good for us, were you!" the dream man cried. "Too good to waste your precious life recording our music! And now, what use will that dear life be to you?"

"It's my own!" Kit shouted back to him, finding strength in defiance. "At least it's my own life, right to the end!" She began to cough again and, half blind with smoke, she pressed her arm across her eyes, feeling the bravado fall away in the horror of reality.

"Mother!" she murmured helplessly. "Daddy, help me! What am I to do now?"

The habit of years, to call upon those two names. A hundred scenes rose from memory to flash upon the screen of her mind — her parents, strong, sure, arms outstretched to her, hands open to catch her own, eyes warm with concern, faces gentle with love. Her mother, regarding her worriedly — "Kit, dear, you will be happy here at Blackwood, won't you? I'd never enjoy a moment of our trip if I thought you weren't." Her father in that strange final visit, standing silent by her bed, gazing down at her —

"Kit, open your eyes."

The voice was low and steady, a never-to-be-forgotten voice, gruff with affection.

"You'll never get out of this place with your head in your arms."

I'm dreaming, Kit thought, and yet she knew that she wasn't. Slowly she raised her head and opened her eyes and stared up into the square, strong-featured face so much like her own.

"Dad!" Kit said softly. "Dad — it's you?"

For an instant longer the vision held, so real that she might almost have reached out and laid her hand against the sun-browned cheek. Then it blurred and was lost as hot tears flooded her eyes.

I'm so glad you're here! I won't be so afraid with you here with me. I should have known you'd come — that you wouldn't let me die alone.

She did not speak the words aloud, but she did not need to. She could feel her father's presence so strongly that he was almost a part of her. When his voice answered it came not from the hall before her but from somewhere within the depths of her own mind —

You are not going to die!

But there's no way out, Kit began — the fire — it's everywhere! No one could make it through that hall —

You must try.

Firm words, spoken in a tone that allowed for no argument. A command that must be obeyed. Kit found herself responding as she had as a child to these words, to his voice —

All right. All right, Dad — I'll try.

She descended the stairs. Later she would try to remember the way it had been, the slow step-by-step progress with the acrid smoke filling her lungs and the walls of Blackwood rising above her to the great arched ceiling, but the memories would not hold true. They would come in fragments. The trip down the stairs. The blazing hallway. The smoldering pit that had once been the parlor. The pressure upon her head —

Bend down. Get as low as you can — the air will be better.

The dining room where the chandelier swung madly above a flaming table, throwing back a million orange lights.

Again — the kitchen.

You must go to the gate. Do not stop for anyone. Go straight to the gate, and when you reach it, the Rosenblums will be waiting.

"The Rosenblums? But, how —"

The letter, she thought. Of course. I had the Rosenblums' phone number scribbled along the margins. Natalie must have read it and realized what the number meant and called them.

She believed him as she had always believed him, and she felt his hand guide hers to the knob of the kitchen door.

She did not remember later, stepping through it. She knew only that suddenly she was outside, running down the driveway, with the silly towel still upon her head and the rain in her face and the wind whipping cold against her shoulders. Ahead of her lay the iron fence and beyond that the black arms of trees waving wild against the sky. She could not see them for the darkness, but she knew that they were there.

Halfway down the drive she stopped and turned to look back at the house. There it stood, as it would stand forever in her nightmares, the great peaked roof outlined in flashes against the lightning-ruptured clouds. It had been from almost exactly this point that she had first glimpsed Blackwood, gray stone upon gray stone like a child's jigsaw puzzle, the windows ablaze in the late afternoon sun as though the interior were alive with flames.

"Can't you feel it?" she had said then to her mother. "There's something about the place — something —"

She knew the answer now.

Kit did not wait to watch the building fall. She turned

and began to run again into the clean, cold strength of the wind.

"Here I am!" she cried. "Here I am!" as headlights came round the curve in the road ahead and drew to a stop against the gate.

The Box Office Hit

Based on the

Novel by

LOIS DUNCAN

Now available on videocassette!

MANDALAY ENTERTAINMENT PRESENTS A NEAL H. MORITZ PRODUCTION "I KNOW WHAT YOU DID LAST SUMMER"
JENNIFER LOVE HEWITT SARAH MICHELLE GELLAR RYAN PHILLIPPE
FREDDIE PRINZE, JR. JOHNNY GALECKI BRIDGETTE WILSON
MUSIC SUPERVISOR ALEX STEYERMARK MUSIC BY JOHN DEBNEY EDITED BY STEVE MIRKOVICH, A.C.E. PRODUCTION DESIGNER GARY WISSNER
DIRECTOR OF PHOTOGRAPHY DENIS CROSSAN, B.S.C. EXECUTIVE PRODUCER WILLIAM S. BEASLEY BASED ON THE NOVEL BY LOIS DUNCAN SCREENPLAY BY KEVIN WILLIAMSON
PRODUCED BY NEAL H. MORITZ, ERIK FEIG AND STOKELY CHAFFIN DIRECTED BY JIM GILLESPIE

Visit our website at www.cthv.com

© 1997 Columbia Pictures Industries, Inc. All Rights Reserved.
© 1998 Layout and Design Columbia TriStar Home Video. All Rights Reserved.

COLUMBIA TRISTAR
HOME VIDEO

COLUMBIA
PICTURES

COLOR R CC

NTSC APPROX. 101 MIN Printed in U.S.A.

BFYR 229

W9-ALT-533

"LOVING TURNS INTO LOVING TOO MUCH WHEN OUR PARTNER IS INAPPROPRIATE, UNCARING, OR UNAVAILABLE AND YET WE CANNOT GIVE HIM UP—IN FACT WE WANT HIM, WE NEED HIM EVEN MORE. WE WILL COME TO UNDERSTAND HOW OUR WANTING TO LOVE, OUR YEARNING FOR LOVE, OUR LOVING ITSELF BECOMES AN ADDICTION."

—Robin Norwood

"Norwood is a persuasive writer with a message so compelling that those readers who see themselves in the book may well be inspired to follow her 10-point recovery plan. . . . Treatment includes finding a support group, recognizing one's problems and—most important—using one's energy to change oneself, not an unwilling man. She also stresses that the less a woman *needs* a partner, the better a partner she will become, and the healthier a partner she will attract. Norwood conveys the authority and sensitivity of a sister sufferer. That she recovered from loving too much—and now enjoys a healthy marriage—is testimony to her program."

—*Philadelphia Inquirer*

"IN MY PERSONAL AND PROFESSIONAL EXPERIENCE, I HAVE NEVER SEEN A WOMAN WHO TOOK THESE STEPS FAIL TO RECOVER. . . . IF THAT SOUNDS LIKE A GUARANTEE, IT IS. WOMEN WHO FOLLOW THESE STEPS WILL GET WELL."

—Robin Norwood

"IF YOU HAVE EVER FOUND YOURSELF OBSESSED WITH A MAN, YOU MAY HAVE SUSPECTED THAT THE ROOT OF THAT OBSESSION WAS NOT LOVE, BUT FEAR . . . FEAR OF BEING UNLOVABLE AND UNWORTHY, FEAR OF BEING IGNORED OR ABANDONED OR DESTROYED."

—Robin Norwood

"WOMEN WHO LOVE TOO MUCH is that rare popular book that exposes the underlying neurotic roots and shows the way out of a life addicted to pain and suffering. We recommend it to all who are burdened and need hope."
—Mildred Newman and Bernard Berkowitz, authors of *How To Be Your Own Best Friend*

"How to distinguish between unwise loving and healthy loving is what Norwood sets out to do. . . . Every woman, no matter how healthy her relationships with men may be, may see a bit of herself in this book."

—*Star Publications*

"IT IS THIS THRILLING POSSIBILITY OF RIGHTING OLD WRONGS, WINNING LOST LOVE, AND GAINING WITHHELD APPROVAL THAT, FOR WOMEN WHO LOVE TOO MUCH, IS THE UNCONSCIOUS CHEMISTRY BEHIND FALLING IN LOVE."

—Robin Norwood

"IF OUR PARENTS RELATED TO US IN HOSTILE, CRITICAL, CRUEL, MANIPULATIVE, OVERBEARING, OVERDEPENDENT, OR OTHERWISE INAPPROPRIATE WAYS, THAT IS WHAT WILL FEEL 'RIGHT' TO US WHEN WE MEET SOMEONE WHO EXPRESSES, PERHAPS VERY SUBTLY, UNDERTONES OF THE SAME ATTITUDES AND BEHAVIORS."

—Robin Norwood

"A LIFE-CHANGING BOOK FOR WOMEN. . . . "

—Erica Jong

"Even if you're not a woman who loves too much, the book is a reminder that we indeed make our lives and that love is supposed to be a happy event."

—*Boston Herald*

"Robin Norwood has written an extraordinary self-help book that reads like a thrilling page-turner. . . . This beautifully written, intelligent book can help women break the pattern of foolish love."

—*Los Angeles Times*

"WE ACHIEVE A SENSE OF SELF FROM WHAT WE DO FOR OURSELVES AND HOW WE DEVELOP OUR OWN CAPACITIES. IF ALL YOUR EFFORTS HAVE GONE INTO DEVELOPING OTHERS, YOU'RE BOUND TO FEEL EMPTY. *TAKE YOUR TURN NOW.*"

—Robin Norwood

Books by Robin Norwood

Letters From Women Who Love Too Much
Women Who Love Too Much

Published by POCKET BOOKS

Most Pocket Books are available at special quantity discounts for bulk purchases for sales promotions, premiums or fund raising. Special books or book excerpts can also be created to fit specific needs.

For details write the office of the Vice President of Special Markets, Pocket Books, 1230 Avenue of the Americas, New York, New York 10020.

ROBIN NORWOOD

WOMEN I WHO LOVE TOO MUCH

When You Keep Wishing and Hoping He'll Change

POCKET BOOKS

New York   London   Toronto   Sydney   Tokyo   Singapore

The author would like to thank the following authors and organizations for their permission to reprint:

"Victim of Love," by Glenn Frey, Don Henley, Don Felder, and J. D. Souther, © 1976 Red Cloud Music, Cass Country Music, Fingers Music, and Ice Age Music. All Rights Reserved. Used by permission.

"My Man," English lyrics by Channing Pollock. Copyright © 1920, 1921 (renewed 1948, 1949) by Frances Salabert. Used by permission of CBS Feist Catalog, Inc. All Rights Reserved.

"The Last Blues Song," by Barry Mann and Cynthia Weil. Copyright © 1972, 1973 Screen Gems—EMI Music Inc. Used by permission. All Rights Reserved.

"Good Hearted Woman," written by Waylon Jennings and Willie Nelson. Copyright © 1971 Hall—Clement Publications (c/o The Welk Music Group, Santa Monica, California 90401) and Willie Nelson Music Co. International Copyright Secured. All Rights Reserved. Used by permission.

The Bleeding Heart, by Marilyn French, Copyright © 1979. Reprinted by permission of Summit Books, a division of Simon & Schuster, Inc.

"She's My Rock," by S. K. Dobbins. Copyright © 1972, 1975 by Famous Music Corporation and Ironsides Music. All Rights Reserved. Used by permission.

"Beauty and the Beast," from *Perrault's Complete Fairy Tales.* Published by Dodd, Mead & Company.

Stanton Peele quote excerpted from a broadcast over University of Minnesota Public Radio Station KUOM, "When Love Is the Drug," broadcast in 1983

POCKET BOOKS, a division of Simon & Schuster Inc.
1230 Avenue of the Americas, New York, NY 10020

Copyright © 1985 by Robin Norwood
Cover photo copyright © 1986 Oudi Photography

Published by arrangement with Jeremy P. Tarcher, Inc./
St. Martin's Press, Inc.
Library of Congress Catalog Card Number: 85-4654

All rights reserved, including the right to reproduce this book or portions thereof in any form whatsoever. For information address St. Martin's Press, Inc., 175 Fifth Avenue, New York, NY 10010

ISBN: 0-671-70862-7

First Pocket Books printing June 1986

37   36   35   34   33   32

POCKET and colophon are registered trademarks of Simon & Schuster Inc.

Printed in the U.S.A.

This book is dedicated to the Anonymous programs in gratitude for the miracle of recovery that they offer.

Contents

CONTENTS

Acknowledgments

THREE PEOPLE ARE OWED MY DEEPEST THANKS FOR THEIR inspiring commitment to the creation of this book. First, there is my husband, Bob Calvert, who cooked dinner every night during the final year of this book's development, and who read everything I wrote—as many as six, seven, or even more times—yet remained energetic, positive, and encouraging, tactfully delivering invaluable feedback, helpful suggestions, and ever-so-gentle criticisms of the work in progress. In spite of the considerable time, effort, and attention that writing this book cost both of us, he was always wonderfully supportive of the project both in words and in deeds.

Second, there is my typist, Stephanie Stevens, who demonstrated a nearly psychic ability to decipher reams of my handwritten material, accompanied by complicated format directions. From these piles of scribbled sheets she consistently produced beautiful manuscript pages in time for every deadline, all the while enthusiastically responding to the material she was typing.

And third, I must thank Laura Golden, the editor at Tarcher, who first saw the manuscript and believed in it. Laura's clear understanding of the concept of loving too much, as well as her insightful, inspiring, and unflagging guidance of a first-time author, vastly improved the relevance, coherence, and overall quality of the book. Working with her has been a great blessing and delight.

Each of these people believed in this book before it was a reality, and I am grateful to them all for their dedication, love, and support.

Preface

WHEN BEING IN LOVE MEANS BEING IN PAIN WE ARE LOVING too much. When most of our conversations with intimate friends are about him, his problems, his thoughts, his feelings—and nearly all our sentences begin with "he . . . ", we are loving too much.

When we excuse his moodiness, bad temper, indifference, or put-downs as problems due to an unhappy childhood and we try to become his therapist, we are loving too much.

When we read a self-help book and underline all the passages we think would help *him*, we are loving too much.

When we don't like many of his basic characteristics, values, and behaviors, but we put up with them thinking that if we are only attractive and loving enough he'll want to change for us, we are loving too much.

When our relationship jeopardizes our emotional well-being and perhaps even our physical health and safety, we are definitely loving too much.

In spite of all its pain and dissatisfaction, loving too much is such a common experience for many women that we almost believe it is the way intimate relationships are supposed to be. Most of us have loved too much at least once and for many of us it has been a recurrent theme in our lives. Some of us have become so obsessed with our partner and our relationship that we are barely able to function.

In this book we will take a hard look at the reasons why so many women, looking for someone to love them, seem inevitably to find unhealthy, unloving partners instead. And we will explore why, once we know a relationship is not meeting our needs, we nevertheless have such difficulty ending it. We will see that loving turns into loving too much when our partner is inappropriate, uncaring, or unavailable and yet we cannot give him up—in fact we want him, we need him even more. We will come to understand how our wanting to love, our yearning for love, our loving itself becomes an addiction.

Addiction is a frightening word. It conjures up images of heroin users jabbing needles into their arms and leading obviously self-destructive lives. We don't like the word and we don't want to apply the concept to the way we relate to men. But many, many of us have been "man junkies" and, like any other addict, we need to admit the severity of our problem before we can begin to recover from it.

If you have ever found yourself obessed with a man, you may have suspected that the root of that obsession was not love but fear. We who love obsessively are full of fear— fear of being alone, fear of being unlovable and unworthy, fear of being ignored or abandoned or destroyed. We give our love in the desperate hope that the man with whom we're obsessed will take care of our fears. Instead, the fears—and our obsessions—deepen until giving love in order to get it back becomes a driving force in our lives. And because our strategy doesn't work we try, we love even harder. We love too much.

I first recognized the phenomenon of "loving too much" as a specific syndrome of thoughts, feelings, and behaviors after several years of counseling alcohol and drug abusers. Having conducted hundreds of interviews with addicts and their families, I made a surprising discovery. Sometimes the patients I interviewed grew up in troubled families, sometimes they did not; but their partners nearly always came from severely troubled families in which they had experienced greater than normal stress and pain. By struggling to cope with their addictive mates, these partners (known in the alcoholism treatment field as "co-alcoholics") were unconsciously recreating and reliving significant aspects of their childhood.

It was mostly from the wives and girlfriends of addictive men that I began to understand the nature of loving too much. Their personal histories revealed their need for both the superiority and the suffering they experienced in their "savior" role and helped me make sense of the depth of their addiction to a man who was in turn addicted to a substance. It was clear that both partners in these couples were equally in need of help, indeed that both were literally dying of their addictions, he from the effects of chemical abuse, she of the effects of extreme stress.

These co-alcoholic women clarified for me the incredible power and influence their childhood experiences had on their adult patterns of relating to men. They have something to tell all of us who have loved too much about why we have developed our predilection for troubled relationships, how we perpetuate our problems, and most importantly how we can change and get well.

I do not intend to imply that women are the only ones who love too much. Some men practice this obsession with relationships with as much fervor as any woman could, and their feelings and behaviors issue from the same kinds of childhood experiences and dynamics. However, most men who have been damaged in childhood do not develop an addiction to relationships. Due to an interplay of cultural and biological factors, they usually try to protect themselves and avoid their pain through pursuits which are more external than internal, more impersonal than personal. Their tendency is to become obsessed with work, sports, or hobbies while, due to the cultural and biological forces working on her, the woman's tendency is to become obsessed with a relationship—perhaps with just such a damaged and distant man.

Hopefully this book will be of help to *anyone* who loves too much, but it is primarily written for women because loving too much is primarily a female phenomenon. Its purpose is very specific: to help women with destructive patterns of relating to men recognize that fact, understand the origin of those patterns, and gain the tools for changing their lives.

But if you are a woman who loves too much, I feel it only fair to caution you that this is not going to be an easy book to read. Indeed, if the definition fits and you nevertheless breeze through this book unstirred and unaffected, or you find yourself bored or angry, or unable to concentrate on the material presented here, or only able to think about how much it would help someone else, I suggest that you try reading the book again at a later time. We all need to deny what is too painful or too threatening for us to accept. Denial is a natural means of self-protection, operating automatically and unbidden. Perhaps at a later reading you will be able to face your own experiences and deeper feelings.

Read slowly, allowing yourself to relate both intellectually and emotionally to these women and their stories. The case histories in this book may seem extreme to you. I assure you that the opposite is true. The personalities, characteristics, and histories that I have encountered among hundreds of women I have known personally and professionally who fit the category of loving too much are by no means exaggerated here. Their actual stories are far more complicated and full of pain. If their problems seem much more serious and distressing than yours, let me say that your initial reaction is typical of most of my clients. Each believes that her problem is "not that bad," even as she relates with compassion to the plight of other women who, in her opinion, have "real" troubles.

It is one of the ironies of life that we women can respond with such sympathy and understanding to the pain in one another's lives while remaining so blinded to (and by) the pain in our own. I know this only too well, having been a woman who loved too much most of my life until the toll to my physical and emotional health was so severe that I was forced to take a hard look at my pattern of relating to men. I have spent the last several years working hard to change that pattern. They have been the most rewarding years of my life.

I hope that for all of you who love too much this book will not only help you to become more aware of the reality of your condition, but will encourage you to begin to change it as well, by redirecting your loving attention away from your obsession with a man and toward your own recovery and your own life.

Here a second warning is appropriate. There is in this book, as in so many "self-help" books, a list of steps to take in order to change. Should you decide that you really do want to follow these steps, it will require—as all therapeutic change does—years of work and nothing short of your total commitment. There are no shortcuts out of the pattern of loving too much in which you are caught. It is a pattern learned early and practiced well, and to give it up will be frightening, threatening, and constantly challenging. This warning is not meant to discourage you. After all, you will most certainly be facing a struggle throughout those years ahead if you don't change your pattern of relating. But in that case, your struggle will not be toward growth but merely toward survival. The choice is yours. If you choose to begin the process of recovery, you will change from a woman who loves someone else so much it hurts into a woman who loves herself enough to stop the pain.

1 • *Loving the Man Who Doesn't Love Back*

> VICTIM OF LOVE,
> I SEE A BROKEN HEART.
> YOU'VE GOT YOUR STORY TO TELL.
>
> VICTIM OF LOVE;
> IT'S SUCH AN EASY PART
> AND YOU KNOW HOW TO PLAY IT
>   SO WELL.
>
> . . . I THINK YOU KNOW
>   WHAT I MEAN.
> YOU'RE WALKING THE WIRE
> OF PAIN AND DESIRE,
> LOOKING FOR LOVE IN BETWEEN.
> —VICTIM OF LOVE

IT WAS JILL'S FIRST SESSION, AND SHE LOOKED DOUBTFUL. Pert and petite, with blond Orphan Annie curls, she sat stiffly on the edge of the chair facing me. Everything about her seemed round: the shape of her face, her slightly plump figure, and most particularly her blue eyes, which took in the framed degrees and certificates on my office wall. She asked a few questions about my graduate school and counseling license, and then mentioned, with obvious pride, that she was in law school.

There was a brief silence. She looked down at her folded hands.

"I guess I'd better start talking about why I'm here," she spoke rapidly, using the momentum of her words to gather courage.

1

"I'm doing this—seeing a therapist, I mean—because I'm really unhappy. It's men, of course. I mean, me and men. I always do something to drive them away. Everything starts out fine. They really pursue me and everything, and then after they get to know me"—she tensed visibly against the coming pain—"it all falls apart."

She looked up at me now, her eyes shining with held-back tears, and continued more slowly.

"I want to know what I'm doing wrong, what I have to change about me—because I'll do it. I'll do whatever it takes. I'm really a hard worker." She began to speed up again.

"It's not that I'm unwilling. I just *don't know* why this keeps happening to me. I'm afraid to get involved anymore. I mean, it's nothing but pain every time. I'm beginning to be really afraid of men."

Shaking her head, the round curls bouncing, she explained with vehemence, "I don't want that to happen, because I'm very lonely. In law school I have lots of responsibility, and then I'm working to support myself too. These demands could keep me busy all the time. In fact, that's pretty much all I did for the past year—work, go to school, study, and sleep. But I missed having a man in my life."

Quickly she continued. "Then I met Randy, when I was visiting friends in San Diego two months ago. He's an attorney, and we met one night when my friends took me out dancing. Well, we just hit it off right away. There was so much to talk about—except that I guess I did most of the talking. But he seemed to *like* that. And it was just so great to be with a man who was interested in things that were important to me, too."

Her brows gathered together. "He seemed really attracted to me. You know, asking if I was married—I'm divorced, have been for two years—if I lived alone. That kind of stuff."

I could imagine how Jill's eagerness must have shown as

she chatted brightly with Randy over the blaring music that first night. And the eagerness with which she welcomed him a week later when he extended a business trip to Los Angeles an extra hundred miles to visit her. At dinner she offered to let him sleep at her apartment so that he could postpone the long drive back until the next day. He accepted her invitation and their affair began that night.

"It was great. He let me cook for him and really enjoyed being looked after. I pressed his shirt for him before he dressed that morning. I love looking after a man. We got along beautifully." She smiled wistfully. But as she continued her story it became clear that Jill had almost immediately become completely obsessed with Randy.

When he returned to his San Diego apartment, the phone was ringing. Jill warmly informed him that she had been worried about his long drive and was relieved to know he was safely home. When she thought he sounded a little bemused at her call, she apologized for bothering him and hung up, but a gnawing discomfort began to grow in her, fueled by the awareness that once again she cared far more than the man in her life did.

"Randy told me once not to pressure him or he would just disappear. I got so scared. It was all up to me. I was supposed to love him and leave him alone at the same time. I couldn't do it, so I just got more and more scared. The more I panicked, the more I chased him."

Soon Jill was calling him almost nightly. Their arrangement was to take turns calling, but often when it was Randy's turn the hour would grow late and she would become too restless to stand it. Sleep was out of the question anyway, so she would dial him. These conversations were as vague as they were lengthy.

"He would say he'd forgotten, and I would say, 'How can you forget?' After all, I never forgot. So then we'd get into talking about why, and it seemed like he was afraid to get close to me and I wanted to help him get through that.

He kept saying he didn't know what he wanted in life, and I would try to help him clarify what the issues were for him." Thus, Jill fell into the role of "shrink" with Randy, trying to help him be more emotionally present for her.

That he did not want her was something she could not accept. She had already decided that he needed her.

Twice, Jill flew to San Diego to spend the weekend with him; on the second visit, he spent their Sunday together ignoring her, watching television and drinking beer. It was one of the worst days she could remember.

"Was he a heavy drinker?" I asked Jill. She looked startled.

"Well, no, not really. I don't know, actually. I never really thought about it. Of course, he was drinking the night I met him, but that's only natural. After all, we were in a bar. Sometimes when we talked on the phone I could hear ice tinkling in a glass and I'd tease him about it—you know, drinking alone and all that. Actually, I was never with him when he wasn't drinking, but I just assumed that he liked to drink. That's normal, isn't it?"

She paused, thinking. "You know, sometimes on the phone he would talk funny, especially for an attorney. Really vague and imprecise; forgetful, not consistent. But I never thought of it as happening because he was drinking. I don't know how I explained it to myself. I guess I just didn't let myself think about it."

She looked at me sadly.

"Maybe he *did* drink too much, but it must have been because I bored him. I guess I just wasn't interesting enough and he didn't really want to be with me." Anxiously, she continued. "My husband never wanted to be around me—that was obvious!" Her eyes brimmed over as she struggled on. "Neither did my father. . . . What is it in me? Why do they all feel that way about me? What am I doing wrong?"

The moment Jill became aware of a problem between her and someone important to her, she was willing not only to try and solve it but also to take responsibility for having created it. If Randy, her husband, and her father all failed to love her, she felt it must be because of something she had done or failed to do.

Jill's attitudes, feelings, behavior, and life experiences were typical of a woman for whom being in love means being in pain. She exhibited many of the characteristics that women who love too much have in common. Regardless of the specific details of their stories and struggles, whether they have endured a long and difficult relationship with one man or have been involved in a series of unhappy partnerships with many men, they share a common profile. Loving too much does not mean loving too many men, or falling in love too often, or having too great a depth of genuine love for another. It means, in truth, obsessing about a man and calling that obsession love, allowing it to control your emotions and much of your behavior, realizing that it negatively influences your health and well-being, and yet finding yourself unable to let go. It means measuring the degree of your love by the depth of your torment.

As you read this book, you may find yourself identifying with Jill, or with another of the women whose stories you encounter, and you may wonder if you, too, are a woman who loves too much. Perhaps, though your problems with men are similar to theirs, you will have difficulty associating yourself with the "labels" that apply to some of these women's backgrounds. We all have strong emotional reactions to words like *alcoholism, incest, violence,* and *addiction,* and sometimes we cannot look at our own lives realistically because we are so afraid of having these labels apply to us or to those we love. Sadly, our inability to use the words when they do apply often precludes our getting appropriate help. On the other hand, those dreaded labels may not apply in your life. Your childhood may have involved problems of a subtler nature. Maybe your father, while providing a financially secure home, nevertheless

5

deeply disliked and distrusted women, and his inability to love you kept you from loving yourself. Or your mother's attitude toward you may have been jealous and competitive in private even though she showed you off and bragged about you in public, so that you ended up needing to do well to gain her approval and yet fearing the hostility your success generated in her.

We cannot cover in this one book the myriad ways families can be unhealthy—that would require several volumes of a rather different nature. It is important to understand, however, that what all unhealthy families have in common is their inability to discuss *root* problems. There may be other problems that *are* discussed, often ad nauseum, but these often cover up the underlying secrets that make the family dysfunctional. It is the degree of secrecy—the inability to talk about the problems—rather than their severity, that defines both how dysfunctional a family becomes and how severely its members are damaged.

A dysfunctional family is one in which members play rigid roles and in which communication is severely restricted to statements that fit these roles. Members are not free to express a full range of experiences, wants, needs, and feelings, but rather must limit themselves to playing that part which accommodates those played by other family members. Roles operate in all families, but as circumstances change, the members must also change and adapt in order for the family to continue to remain healthy. Thus, the kind of mothering appropriate for a one-year-old will be highly inappropriate for a thirteen-year-old, and the mothering role must alter to accommodate reality. In dysfunctional families, major aspects of reality are denied, and roles remain rigid.

When no one can discuss what affects every family member individually as well as the family as a whole—indeed, when such discussion is forbidden implicitly (the subject is changed) or explicitly ("We don't talk about those things!")—we learn not to believe in our own perceptions or feelings. Because our family denies our reality, we begin to deny it too. And this severely impairs the development of our basic tools for living life and for relating to people and situations. It is this basic impairment that operates in women who love too much. We become unable to discern when someone or something is not good for us. The situations and people that others would naturally avoid as dangerous, uncomfortable, or unwholesome do not repel us, because we have no way of evaluating them realistically or self-protectively. We do not trust our feelings, or use them to guide us. Instead, we are actually drawn to the very dangers, intrigues, dramas, and challenges that others with healthier and more balanced backgrounds would naturally eschew. And through this attraction we are further damaged, because much of what we are attracted to is a replication of what we lived with growing up. We get hurt all over again.

No one becomes such a woman, a woman who loves too much, by accident. To grow up as a female in this society and in such a family can generate some predictable patterns. The following characteristics are typical of women who love too much, women like Jill and perhaps like you, too.

1. Typically, you come from a dysfunctional home in which your emotional needs were not met.

2. Having received little real nurturing yourself, you try to fill this unmet need vicariously by becoming a care-giver, especially to men who appear, in some way, needy.

3. Because you were never able to change your parent(s) into the warm, loving caretaker(s) you longed for, you respond deeply to the familiar type of emotionally unavailable man whom you can again try to change, through your love.

7

4.　Terrified of abandonment, you will do anything to keep a relationship from dissolving.

5.　Almost nothing is too much trouble, takes too much time, or is too expensive if it will "help" the man you are involved with.

6.　Accustomed to lack of love in personal relationships, you are willing to wait, hope, and try harder to please.

7.　You are willing to take far more than 50 percent of the responsibility, guilt, and blame in any relationship.

8.　Your self-esteem is critically low, and deep inside you do not believe you deserve to be happy. Rather, you believe you must earn the right to enjoy life.

9.　You have a desperate need to control your men and your relationships, having experienced little security in childhood. You mask your efforts to control people and situations as "being helpful."

10.　In a relationship, you are much more in touch with your dream of how it could be than with the reality of your situation.

11.　You are addicted to men and to emotional pain.

12.　You may be predisposed emotionally and often biochemically to becoming addicted to drugs, alcohol, and/or certain foods, particularly sugary ones.

13.　By being drawn to people with problems that need fixing, or by being enmeshed in situations that are chaotic, uncertain, and emotionally painful, you avoid focusing on your responsibility to yourself.

14.　You may have a tendency toward episodes of depression, which you try to forestall through the excitement provided by an unstable relationship.

15.　You are not attracted to men who are kind, stable,

reliable, and interested in you. You find such "nice" men boring.

Jill displayed nearly all of these characteristics, to a greater or lesser degree. It was as much because she embodied so many of the above attributes as because of anything else she may have told me about him that I suspected Randy might have a drinking problem. Women with this type of emotional makeup are consistently drawn to men who are emotionally unavailable for one reason or another. Being addicted is a primary way of being emotionally unavailable.

Right from the start, Jill was willing to take more responsibility than Randy for initiating the relationship and keeping it going. Like so many women who love too much, she was obviously a very responsible person, a high achiever who was succeeding in many areas of her life, but who nevertheless had little self-esteem. The realization of her academic and career goals could not counterbalance the personal failure she endured in her love relationships. Every phone call Randy forgot to make dealt a serious blow to her fragile self-image, which she then worked heroically to shore up by trying to extract signs of caring from him. Her willingness to take full blame for a failed relationship was typical, as was her inability to assess the situation realistically and take care of herself by pulling out when the lack of reciprocity became apparent.

Women who love too much have little regard for their personal integrity in a love relationship. They pour their energies into changing the other person's behavior or feelings toward them through desperate manipulations, such as Jill's expensive long-distance phone calls and flights to San Diego (remember, her budget was extremely limited). Her long-distance "therapy sessions" with him were much more an attempt to make him into the man she needed him to be than to help him discover who he was. Actually, Randy did not want to help in discovering who he was. If he had been interested in such a journey of self-discovery, he would have done most of the work himself, rather than sitting by passively while Jill tried to force him to analyze himself. She made these efforts because her only other alternative was to recognize and accept him for what he was—a man who was careless of her feelings and of the relationship.

Let's return to Jill's session to better understand what brought her to my office that day.

She was talking about her father now.

"He was such a stubborn man. I swore that someday I'd win an argument with him." She reflected for a moment.

"I never did, though. That's probably why I went into law. I just love the idea of arguing a case and *winning!*" She flashed a wide smile at the thought and then sobered again.

"Do you know what I did once? I made him tell me that he loved me, and I made him give me a hug." Jill was trying to relate it as a light-hearted anecdote from her growing-up years, but it didn't play that way. The shadow of a hurt young girl came through.

"It never would have happened if I hadn't forced him. But he did love me. He just couldn't show me. He never was able to say it again. So I'm really glad I made him. Otherwise I never would have heard him say it to me. I had been waiting years and years. I was eighteen when I said to him, 'You're going to tell me that you love me,' and I wouldn't move until he had said it. Then I asked him for a hug and really I had to hug him first. He just sort of squeezed back and patted my shoulder a bit, but that's okay. I really needed that from him." The tears were back now, this time spilling over her round cheeks.

"Why was that so hard for him to do? It seems like such a *basic* thing, to be able to tell your daughter that you love her."

Again she studied her folded hands.

"I tried so hard. That's even why I argued and fought so hard with him. I thought if I ever won, he'd have to be proud of me. He'd have to admit I was good. I wanted his approval, which I guess means his love, more than anything in the world. . . ."

It became clear in talking further with her that Jill's family blamed her father's rejection of her on the fact that he had wanted a son and had gotten a daughter instead. This facile explanation of his coldness toward his child was far easier for all of them, including Jill, to accept than was the truth about him. But after considerable time in therapy, Jill recognized that her father had had close emotional ties with *no one,* that he had been virtually incapable of expressing warmth or love or approval to anyone in his personal sphere. There had always been "reasons" for his emotional withholding, such as quarrels and differences of opinion or irreversible facts such as Jill's having been a girl. Every member of the family chose to accept those reasons as legitimate rather than to examine the consistently distant quality of their relationships with him.

Jill actually found it harder to accept her father's basic inability to love than to continue in her self-blame. As long as the fault was hers, there was also hope—that someday she could change herself sufficiently to bring about a change in him.

It is true for all of us that when an emotionally painful event occurs, and we tell ourselves it is our fault, we are actually saying that we have control of it: if we change, the pain will stop. This dynamic is behind much of the self-blame in women who love too much. By blaming ourselves, we hold on to the hope that we will be able to figure out what we are doing wrong and correct it, thereby controlling the situation and stopping the pain.

This pattern in Jill became clearly illuminated during a session soon thereafter when she described her marriage. Inexorably drawn to someone with whom she could recreate the emotionally deprived climate of her growing-up years with her father, her marriage was an opportunity for her to try again to win withheld love.

As Jill recounted how she met her husband, I thought of

a maxim I'd heard from a fellow therapist: Hungry people make poor shoppers. Desperately hungry for love and approval, and familiar with rejection though never identifying it as such, Jill was destined to find Paul.

She told me, "We met in a bar. I had been washing my clothes in a laundromat and went next door for a few minutes, to this sleazy little place. Paul was shooting pool and asked me if I wanted to play. I said sure, and that's how it started. He asked me out. I said no, that I didn't go out with men I met in bars. Well, he followed me back to the laundromat and just kept talking to me. I finally gave him my phone number and we went out the next night.

"Now, you're not going to believe this, but we ended up living together two weeks later. He had nowhere to live and I had to move out of my apartment, so we got a place together. And none of it was that great, not the sex or the companionship or anything. But after a year went by, my mother was getting nervous about what I was doing, so we got married." Jill was shaking those curls again.

In spite of this casual beginning, she soon became obsessed. Because Jill had grown up trying to make whatever was wrong right, she naturally carried that pattern of thinking and behaving into her marriage.

"I tried so hard. I mean, I really loved him and I was determined to make him love me back. I was going to be the perfect wife. I cooked and cleaned like crazy, and I was trying to go to school, too. A lot of the time he didn't work. He would lie around or disappear for days at a time. That was hell, the waiting and wondering. But I learned not to ask where he had been because . . ." She hesitated, shifting in the chair. "It's hard for me to admit this. I was so sure I could make it all work if I just tried hard enough, but sometimes I'd get angry after he disappeared and then he'd hit me.

"I've never told anyone about this before. I've always

been so ashamed. I just never saw myself that way, you know? As someone who would let herself be hit."

Jill's marriage ended when her husband found another woman on one of his extended absences from home. In spite of the agony the marriage had become, Jill was devastated when Paul left.

"I knew that whoever the woman was, she was everything I wasn't. I could actually see why Paul left me. I felt like I had nothing to offer him or anyone. I didn't blame him for leaving me. I mean, after all, I couldn't stand me either."

Much of my work with Jill was to help her understand the disease process in which she had been immersed for so long, her addiction to doomed relationships with emotionally unavailable men. The addictive aspect of Jill's behavior in her relationships parallels the addictive use of a drug. Early in each of her relationships there was an initial "high," a feeling of euphoria and excitement while she believed that finally her deepest needs for love, attention, and emotional security might be met. Believing this, Jill became more and more dependent on the man and the relationship in order to feel good. Then, like an addict who must use a drug more as it produces less effect, she was driven to pursue the relationship harder as it gave her less satisfaction and fulfillment. Trying to sustain what had once felt so wonderful, so promising, Jill slavishly dogged her man, needing more contact, more reassurance, more love as she received less and less. The worse the situation became, the harder it was to let go because of the depth of her need. She could not quit.

Jill was twenty-nine years old when she first came to see me. Her father had been dead seven years, but he was still the most important man in her life. In a way he was the only man in her life, because in every relationship with another male to whom she was attracted, she was really relating to her father, still trying so very hard to win love from this man who could not, because of his own problems, give it.

When our childhood experiences are particularly painful, we are often unconsciously compelled to recreate similar situations throughout our lives, in a drive to gain mastery over them.

For instance, if we, like Jill, loved and needed a parent who did not respond to us, we often become involved with a similar person, or a series of them, in adulthood in an attempt to "win" the old struggle to be loved. Jill personified this dynamic as she found herself drawn to one unsuitable man after another.

There is an old joke about a nearsighted man who has lost his keys late at night and is looking for them by the light of a street lamp. Another person comes along and offers to help him look but asks him, "Are you sure this is where you lost them?" He answers, "No, but this is where the light is."

Jill, like the man in the story, was searching for what was missing in her life, not where there was some hope of finding it, but where, because she was a woman who loved too much, it was easiest for her to look.

Throughout this book we will explore what loving too much is, why we do it, where we learned it, and how to change our style of loving into a healthier way of relating. Let's look again at the characteristics of women who love too much, one by one this time.

1. Typically, you come from a dysfunctional home in which your emotional needs were not met.

Perhaps the best way to approach understanding this characteristic is to begin with the second half of it first: ". . . in which your emotional needs were not met." "Emotional needs" does not refer only to your needs for love and affection. Although that aspect is important, even more critical is the fact that your perceptions and feelings were largely ignored or denied rather than accepted and validated. An example: Parents are fighting. Child feels afraid. Child asks mother, "Why are you mad at Daddy?" Mother answers, "I'm not mad," while looking angry and troubled. Child now feels confused, more afraid, and says, "I heard you shouting." Mother replies angrily, "I told you I'm not mad but I'm going to be if you keep this up!" Child now feels fear, confusion, anger, and guilt. Her parent has implied that her perceptions are incorrect, but if that is true, where are these feelings of fear coming from? The child must now choose between knowing that she is right and that her parent has deliberately lied to her, or thinking that she is wrong in what she hears, sees, and feels. She will often settle for confusion, tuning out her perceptions so that she does not have to experience the discomfort of having them invalidated. This impairs a child's ability to trust herself and her perceptions, both in childhood and later in adulthood, especially in close relationships.

Needs for affection may also be denied or insufficiently met. When parents are fighting with each other, or caught up in other kinds of struggles, there may be little time or attention left for the children in the family. This leaves a child hungry for love while not knowing how to trust it or accept it and feeling undeserving of it.

Now for the first part of this characteristic: coming from a dysfunctional home. Dysfunctional homes are those in which one or more of the following occur:

- abuse of alcohol and/or other drugs (prescribed or illicit)
- compulsive behavior such as compulsive eating, working, cleaning, gambling, spending, dieting, exercising, and so on; these practices are addictive behaviors, as well as progressive disease processes; among their many other harmful effects, they effectively disrupt and prevent honest contact and intimacy in a family.
- battering of spouse and/or children

- inappropriate sexual behavior on the part of a parent toward a child, ranging from seductiveness to incest
- constant arguing and tension
- extended periods of time in which parents refuse to speak to each other
- parents who have conflicting attitudes or values or display contradictory behaviors that compete for their children's allegiance
- parents who are competitive with each other or with their children
- a parent who cannot relate to others in the family and thus actively avoids them, while blaming them for this avoidance
- extreme rigidity about money, religion, work, use of time, displays of affection, sex, television, housework, sports, politics, and so on; obsession with any of these can preclude contact and intimacy, because the emphasis is not on relating, but on following the rules.

If one parent displays any of these kinds of behaviors or obsessions, it is damaging to a child. If both parents are caught up in any of these unhealthy practices, the results may be even more detrimental. Often parents practice complementary kinds of pathology. For instance, an alcoholic and a compulsive eater frequently will marry, and then each will struggle to control the other's addiction. Parents also often balance each other in unhealthy ways; when the smothering, overprotective mother is married to the angry and rejecting father each parent is actually enabled by the other's behavior and attitudes to continue relating to the children in a destructive way.

Dysfunctional families come in many styles and varieties, but they all share one effect they have on children growing up in them: these children are to some extent damaged in their ability to feel and relate.

2. **Having received little real nurturing yourself, you try to fill this unmet need vicariously by becoming a care-giver, especially to men who appear in some way needy.**

Think about how children, especially little girls, behave when they are lacking the love and attention they want and need. While a little boy may become angry and act out with destructive behavior and fighting, more often a little girl will turn her attention to a favorite doll. Rocking and soothing it, and at some level identifying with it, that little girl is engaged in a roundabout effort to receive the nurturing she needs. As adults, women who love too much do the same thing, perhaps only slightly more subtly. In general, we become care-givers in most, if not all, areas of our lives. Women from dysfunctional homes (and especially, I have observed, from alcoholic homes) are over-represented in the helping professions, working as nurses, counselors, therapists, and social workers. We are drawn to those who are needy, compassionately identifying with their pain and seeking to relieve it in order to ameliorate our own. That the men who attract us most strongly are those who appear to be needy makes sense if we understand that it is our own wish to be loved and helped that is at the root of the attraction.

A man who appeals to us need not necessarily be penniless or in ill health. Perhaps he is unable to relate well to others, or is cold and unaffectionate, or stubborn or selfish, or sulking or melancholy. Maybe he is a bit wild and irresponsible, or unable to make a commitment or be faithful. Or maybe he tells us he has never been able to love anyone. Depending on our own background, we will respond to different varieties of neediness. But respond we will, with the conviction that this man needs our help, our compassion, and our wisdom in order to improve his life.

3. Because you were never able to change your parent(s) into the warm, loving caretaker(s) you longed for, you respond deeply to the familiar type of emotionally unavailable man whom you can again try to change through your love.

Perhaps your struggle was with one parent, perhaps with both. But whatever was wrong or missing or painful in the past is what you are trying to make turn out right in the present.

Now it begins to be apparent that something very unwholesome and self-defeating is going on. It would be fine if we brought all our sympathy, compassion, and understanding into relationships with healthy men, men with whom there was some hope of getting our own needs met. But we are not attracted to healthy men who could give us what we need. They seem boring to us. We are attracted to men who replicate for us the struggle we endured with our parents, when we tried to be good enough, loving enough, worthy enough, helpful enough, and smart enough to win the love, attention, and approval from those who could not give us what we needed, because of their own problems and preoccupations. Now we operate as though love, attention, and approval don't count unless we are able to extract them from a man who is also unable to readily give them to us, because of his own problems and preoccupations.

4. Terrified of abandonment, you will do anything to keep a relationship from dissolving.

Abandonment is a very strong word. It implies being left, possibly to die, because we may not be able to survive alone. There is literal abandonment, and there is emotional abandonment. Every woman who loves too much has at least experienced profound emotional abandonment, with all the terror and emptiness that implies. As an adult, being left by a man who represents in so many ways those people who first abandoned us brings up all the terror again. Of course, we would do anything to avoid feeling that way again. Which leads into the next characteristic.

5. Almost nothing is too much trouble, takes too much time, or is too expensive if it will "help" the man you are involved with.

The theory behind all this helping is that if it works, the man will become everything you want and need him to be, which means that you will win that struggle to gain what you've wanted so much for so long.

So, while we are often frugal and even self-denying on our own behalf, we will go to any lengths to help him. Some of our efforts on his behalf include

- buying him clothes to improve his self-image
- finding a therapist for him and begging him to go
- financing expensive hobbies to help him use his time better
- going through disruptive geographic relocations because "he's not happy here"
- giving him half or all of our property and possessions so he won't feel inferior to us
- providing him with a place to live so that he can feel secure
- allowing him to abuse us emotionally because "he was never allowed to express his feelings before"
- finding him a job.

This is only a partial list of the ways we try to help. We rarely question the appropriateness of our actions on his behalf. In fact, we spend a great deal of time and energy trying to think up new approaches that might work better than those we've already tried.

6. Accustomed to lack of love in personal relationships, you are willing to wait, hope, and try harder to please.

If another person with a different kind of history found herself in our circumstances, she would be able to say, "This feels awful. I'm not going to continue to do this anymore." But we assume that if it isn't working and we aren't happy then somehow we haven't done enough yet. We see every nuance of behavior as perhaps indicating that our partner is finally changing. We live on hope that tomorrow will be different. Waiting for him to change is actually more comfortable than changing ourselves and our own lives.

7. You are willing to take far more than 50 percent of the responsibility, guilt, and blame in any relationship.

Often those of us from dysfunctional homes had parents who were irresponsible, childish, and weak. We grew up fast and became pseudo-adults long before we were ready for the burdens that role carried. But we were also pleased with the power that was conferred upon us by our families and others. Now as adults we believe it is up to us to make our relationships work, and we often team up with irresponsible, blaming partners who contribute to our sense that it really is all up to us. We are experts at carrying the burden.

8. Your self-esteem is critically low, and deep inside you do not believe you deserve to be happy. Rather, you believe you must earn the right to enjoy life.

If our parents cannot find us worthy of their love and attention, how can we believe that we really are fine, good people? Very few women who love too much have a conviction, at the core of their being, that they deserve to love and be loved simply because they exist. We believe instead that we harbor terrible faults or flaws and that we must do good works in order to make up for this. We live in guilt that we have these shortcomings and in fear of being found out. We work very, very hard at trying to appear to be good, because we don't believe we are.

9. You have a desperate need to control your men and your relationships, having experienced little security in childhood. You mask your efforts to control people and situations as "being helpful."

Living in any of the more chaotic types of dysfunctional families such as an alcoholic, violent, or incestuous one, a child will inevitably feel panic at the family's loss of control. The people on whom she depends are not there for her because they are too sick to protect her. In fact, that family is often a source of threat and harm rather than the source of security and protection she needs. Because this kind of experience is so overwhelming, so devastating, those of us who have suffered in this way seek to turn the tables, so to speak. By being strong and helpful to others we protect ourselves from the panic that comes from being at another's mercy. We need to be with people whom we can help, in order to feel safe and in control.

10. In a relationship, you are much more in touch with your dream of how it could be than with the reality of your situation.

When we love too much we live in a fantasy world, where the man with whom we are so unhappy or so

21

dissatisfied is transformed into what we are sure he can become, indeed *will* become with our help. Because we know very little about being happy in a relationship and have very little experience with having someone we care for meet our emotional needs, that dream world is the closest we dare come to having what we want.

If we already had a man who was everything we wanted, what would he need us for? And all that talent (and compulsion) for helping would have nowhere to operate. A major part of our identity would be out of a job. So we choose a man who is not what we want—and we dream on.

11. You are addicted to men and to emotional pain.

In the words of Stanton Peele, author of *Love and Addiction,* "An addictive experience is one which absorbs a person's consciousness, and as with analgesics, relieves their sense of anxiety and pain. There's perhaps nothing quite as good for absorbing our consciousness as a love relationship of a certain type. An addictive relationship is characterized by a desire for another person's reassuring presence. . . . The second criterion is that it detracts from a person's ability to pay attention to and deal with other aspects of her life."

We use our obsession with the men we love to avoid our pain, emptiness, fear, and anger. We use our relationships as drugs, to avoid experiencing what we would feel if we held still with ourselves. The more painful our interactions with our man, the greater the distraction he provides us. A truly awful relationship simply serves the same function for us as a very strong drug. Without a man on whom to focus, we go into withdrawal, often with many of the same physical and emotional symptoms of that state that accompany actual drug withdrawal: nausea, sweating, chills, shaking, pacing, obsessive thinking, depression, inability to sleep, panic, and anxiety attacks. In an effort to relieve these symptoms, we return to our last partner or desperately seek a new one.

12. You may be predisposed biochemically as well as emotionally to abusing drugs, alcohol, and/or certain foods, usually sugary ones.

The above applies especially to the many women who love too much who are daughters of substance abusers. All women who love too much carry the emotional backlog of experiences that could lead them to abuse mind-altering substances in order to escape their feelings. But children of addictive parents also tend to inherit a genetic predisposition to developing their own addictions.

It may be because refined sugar is nearly identical in molecular structure to ethyl alcohol that so many daughters of alcoholics develop an addiction to it and become compulsive eaters. Refined sugar is not a food but a drug. It has no food value, only empty calories. It can dramatically alter brain chemistry and is a highly addicting substance for many people.

13. By being drawn to people with problems that need fixing, or by being enmeshed in situations that are chaotic, uncertain, and emotionally painful, you keep from focusing on your responsibility to yourself.

While we are very good at intuiting what someone else feels or figuring out what someone else needs or should do, we are not in touch with our own feelings and are unable to make wise decisions about important aspects of our lives that trouble us. We often do not really know who we are, and being embroiled in dramatic problems keeps us from having to hold still and find out.

None of this is to say that we may not emote. We may cry and scream and weep and wail. But we are not able to use our emotions to guide us in making the necessary and important choices in our life.

14. You may have a tendency toward episodes of depression, which you try to forestall through the excitement provided by an unstable relationship.

An example: One of my clients, who had a history of depression and was married to an alcoholic, likened living with him to having a car accident every day. The terrific ups and downs, the surprises, the maneuvers, the unpredictability and instability of the relationship cumulatively presented a constant and daily shock to her system. If you've ever had a car accident in which you weren't seriously injured, you may have experienced a definite "up" feeling the day or so following the event. This is because your body had undergone an extreme shock, and adrenalin was suddenly available in unusually high amounts. This adrenalin accounts for the high. If you are someone who struggles with depression, you will unconsciously seek situations that keep you stirred up, much like the car accident (or the marriage to an alcoholic), so that you stay too high to feel low.

Depression, alcoholism, and eating disorders are closely related and seem to be genetically linked. Most anorexics with whom I have worked, for instance, had *two* alcoholic parents, and many of my women clients with problems of depression had at least one alcoholic parent. If you are someone who came from an alcoholic family, you are likely on two counts to have problems with depression, because of your past and because of your genetic inheritances. Ironically, the excitement of a relationship with someone with that disease may strongly appeal to you.

15. You are not attracted to men who are kind, stable, reliable, and interested in you. You find such "nice" men boring.

We find the unstable man exciting, the unreliable man challenging, the unpredictable man romantic, the immature man charming, the moody man mysterious. The angry man needs our understanding. The unhappy man needs our comforting. The inadequate man needs our encouragement, and the cold man needs our warmth. But we cannot "fix" a man who is fine just as he is, and if he is kind and cares for us then we can't suffer, either. Unfortunately, if we can't love a man too much, we usually can't love him at all.

In the chapters that follow, each of the women you will meet has, like Jill, a story to tell about loving too much. Through their stories perhaps you will be helped to understand the patterns of your own life more clearly. Then you will also be able to employ the tools given toward the end of the book to change those patterns into a new configuration of self-fulfillment, love, and joy. This is my wish for you.

2 • Good Sex in Bad Relationships

> OH MY MAN I LOVE HIM SO—HE'LL NEVER
>   KNOW
> ALL MY LIFE IS JUST DESPAIR— BUT I
>   DON'T CARE
> WHEN HE TAKES ME IN HIS ARMS THE
>   WORLD IS BRIGHT . . .
>
> —MY MAN

THE YOUNG WOMAN WHO SAT IN FRONT OF ME WAS WRAPPED in despair. Her pretty face still displayed yellow and green traces of the terrible bruises she had received a month ago when she had deliberately driven her car off a cliff.

"It was in the newspaper," she told me slowly, painfully, "all about the accident, with pictures of the car dangling there . . . but he never even got in touch with me." Her voice raised a little, and just a hint of healthy anger flickered before she slid back into her desolation.

Trudi, who had very nearly died for love, then brought up what was for her the central question, the one that made the abandonment by her lover inexplicable and nearly unendurable: "How could the sex between us be so good, make us both feel so wonderful, and bring us so close together when we really had nothing else going for us? Why did that work when nothing else did?" As she began to cry, she gave every appearance of a very young, very hurt child. "I thought I was making him love me, by giving myself to him. I gave him everything, everything I had to give." She leaned over, holding her stomach and rocking. "Oh, but it hurts to know that I could do all that for nothing."

Trudi remained doubled up, sobbing for a long time, lost in the empty place where her myth of love had lived.

When she was able to talk again, she continued in the same muted wail. "All I ever cared about was making Jim happy and keeping him with me. I didn't ask for anything except that he spend time with me."

After Trudi had cried again for a while, I remembered what she had told me about her family and asked her softly, "Wasn't that what your mother wanted from your father, too? Basically just that he spend time with her?"

Suddenly she sat upright. "Oh, my God! You're right. I even sound just like my mother. The person I most wanted *not* to be like, the one who ran around making suicide attempts to get her way. Oh, my God!" she repeated and then looked at me, face wet with tears, and said quietly, "That's really awful."

She paused and I spoke. "Lots of times we find ourselves doing the things our same-sex parent did, the very actions we promised ourselves we would never, never do. It's because we learned from their actions, even their feelings, what it is to be a man or a woman."

"But I didn't try to kill myself to get back at Jim," Trudi protested. "I just couldn't stand how awful I felt, how worthless and unwanted." Another pause. "Maybe that's the way my mother felt too. I guess that's the way you end up feeling when you try to keep someone around who has other, more important things to do."

Trudi had tried, all right, and the enticement she had used was sex.

In a later session, when the pain wasn't quite so fresh,

the subject of sex came up again. "I've always been very sexually responsive," she reported with a mixture of pride and guilt, "so much so that in high school I was afraid I was a nymphomaniac.

"All I could think about was the next time my boyfriend and I could be together to make love. I was always trying to arrange everything so that we could have some place to go and be alone together. They say that guys are supposed to be the ones who always want sex. I know I wanted it more than he did. At least, I went to a lot more trouble to make it happen than he did."

Trudi was sixteen when she and her high school steady first "went all the way," as she put it. He was a football player who took the fact that he was in training very seriously. He seemed to believe that too much sex with Trudi was going to diminish his prowess on the playing field. While he made excuses about not staying out too late before a game, she countered by arranging for afternoon babysitting sessions during which she could seduce him on the front-room couch while the infant slept in the nearby nursery. Eventually, though, Trudi's most creative efforts to transmute his passion for sports into a passion for her failed, and this young man, courtesy of a football scholarship, left for a distant college.

After a spell of crying nightly and berating herself for not having been able to persuade him to choose her over his athletic ambitions, Trudi was ready to try again.

It was the summer between high school and college and she was still living at home, a home that was coming apart at the seams. After years of threatening to do so, Trudi's mother had finally initiated divorce proceedings, hiring an attorney known for his willingness to fight dirty. Her parents' marriage had been of the stormiest order, pitting her father's compulsive workaholism against her mother's fervent, sometimes violent, and occasionally self-destructive efforts at coercing him to spend more time with her and their two children, Trudi and her older sister, Beth. He was so rarely home, and for such brief periods, that his wife caustically referred to these sojourns as "pit stops."

"They were the pits, all right," Trudi remembered. "His visits always degenerated into horrible, protracted fights, with Mother screaming and accusing him of not loving any of us, and Father insisting that he worked as hard and as long as he did for our sakes. The times he did spend at home always seemed to end with the two of them screaming at each other. He'd usually leave, slamming the door and yelling, "No wonder I never want to come home!" but sometimes, if Mother had sobbed enough, or had threatened him again with divorce, or maybe taken a lot of pills and gone to the hospital, he would change for a while, come home early and spend time with us. Mother would start making these wonderful meals, to reward him, I guess, for coming home to his family." She frowned. "After about three or four nights, he'd be late again, and there'd be a phone call. 'Oh, I see. Oh, *really?*' Mother would say, all icy. Pretty soon, she'd start screaming obscenities at him, and then bang the phone down. Now here we were, Beth and I, all dressed up because Daddy was supposed to come home for dinner. We probably had set the table especially nicely, the way Mother always told us to when he was supposed to come home, with candles and flowers. And here Mother would be, storming around the kitchen, screaming and banging pots and calling Daddy horrible names. Then she'd calm down, go all icy again, and come out to tell us that we would just eat alone, without him. That was even worse than the screaming. She'd serve us and sit down, never looking at us. We'd get so nervous, Beth and I, with all the quiet. We wouldn't dare speak, and we wouldn't dare not eat. We'd stay there at the table, trying to make it better for Mother, but there was really nothing we could do for her. After those meals I usually got sick in the middle of the night with terrible nausea and vomiting." Trudi shook her head stoically. "Definitely not conducive to healthy digestion."

"Or to learning healthy patterns of relating," I added,

for it was in this climate that Trudi learned what little she knew about dealing with someone she loved.

"What was it like for you when that was going on?" I asked her.

Trudi thought for a while and then nodded as she responded, emphasizing the correctness of her answer. "In the middle of it I was scared, but mostly I felt lonely. No one was looking my way or wondering what I was feeling or doing. My sister was so shy we never talked much. She hid out in her room when she wasn't taking music lessons. She played her flute mostly, I think, to shut out the arguments and to give herself an excuse to stay out of everybody's way. I learned not to make trouble either. I kept quiet, pretended I didn't notice what my parents were doing to each other, and in fact kept everything I was thinking to myself. I tried to do well in school. Sometimes it felt like that was the only time my father ever noticed me. 'Let me see your report card,' he'd say, and we'd talk about it together for a little while. He admired any kind of achievement, so I tried to do well for him."

Trudi rubbed her brow and continued thoughtfully. "There's another feeling too. Sad. I think I felt sad all the time, but I never told anyone. If someone had asked, 'What do you feel inside?' I would have said I was fine, absolutely fine. Even if I could have said I was sad, I could never have explained why. How could I justify feeling that way? I wasn't suffering. Nothing important was missing from my life. I mean, we never missed a meal, never went without anything we needed." Trudi was still unable to fully acknowledge the depth of her emotional isolation in that family. She had suffered from a dearth of nurturing and attention because of a father who was virtually inaccessible and a mother who was consumed by her anger and frustration with him. This had left Trudi and her sister starved emotionally.

Ideally, as she grew up Trudi would have been able to practice sharing who she was with her parents in return for their love and attention, but her parents were unable to be on the receiving end of this gift of herself; they were too caught up in their battle of wills. So, as she grew older she took herself and her gift of love (in the guise of sex) elsewhere. But she offered herself to equally unwilling or unavailable recipients. What else, after all, did she know how to do? Nothing else would have felt "right" or would have fit with the lack of love and attention to which she was already accustomed.

Meanwhile, the conflict between her parents heated up in the new arena of the divorce court. In the midst of the fireworks Trudi's sister ran off with her music teacher. Her parents scarcely paused in their battle long enough to register the fact that their elder daughter had left the state with a man twice her age who was barely able to support himself. Trudi, too, was looking for love, dating men frenetically and going to bed with nearly every one of them. In her heart she believed that the problems at home were her mother's fault, that her mother had driven her father away with nagging and threats. Trudi vowed she would never, ever be the kind of angry, demanding woman she saw her mother to be. She would, instead, win her man with love, understanding, and the total gift of herself. She'd tried once already, with the football player, to be so devotedly loving and giving as to be irresistible, but her approach hadn't worked. She concluded not that her approach was mistaken, or that the object of her approach was a poor choice, but that she hadn't given enough. So she kept trying, kept giving, yet none of the young men she dated stayed around.

The fall semester began and Trudi soon met a married man, Jim, in one of her classes at the local city college. He was a policeman studying law enforcement theory there, to make himself eligible for promotion. He was thirty, had two children and a pregnant wife. Over coffee one afternoon he told Trudi how young he'd been when he married, and how little happiness he felt in his relationship with his wife. He warned her, in a fatherly fashion, not to get caught in the same domestic trap by getting married

early and being tied down to responsibilities. Trudi felt
flattered that he would confide in her about something so
private as his disenchantment with married life. He
seemed kind, and vulnerable somehow, a little lonely and
misunderstood. Jim told her how much talking to her had
meant to him—indeed, how he'd never talked to anyone
quite like her before—and asked if she'd meet him again.
Trudi quickly agreed, for although theirs had been a fairly
one-sided conversation that day, with Jim doing most of
the talking, it was still more communication than Trudi
had ever experienced within her family. Their chat
provided her with a taste of the attention she craved. Two
days later, they talked again, this time walking in the hills
above the campus, and he kissed her at the end of their
stroll. Within a week, they were trysting at the apartment
of an on-duty policeman three afternoons of the five that
Trudi spent at school, and her life began to revolve around
their stolen time together. Trudi refused to look at how
her involvement with Jim was affecting her. She skipped
classes and began, for the first time, to fail scholastically.
She lied to friends about her activities and then avoided
them completely so that she didn't have to keep on lying.
She curtailed nearly every social activity, caring only
about being with Jim when she could, thinking about him
when she couldn't. She wanted to be available to him in
case there was an extra hour here or there that they could
spend together.

In return, Jim gave her a great deal of attention and
flattery when they were together. He managed to say
exactly what she needed to hear—about how wonderful,
how special, how lovable she was, how she made him
happier than he'd ever been before. His words stirred her
to try even harder to thrill and delight him. First she
bought beautiful lingerie to wear just for him, then
perfume and oils, which he cautioned her against using
because his wife might notice their scent and wonder what
was going on. Undaunted, she read books on lovemaking
and tried everything she learned on him. His rapture

spurred her on. There was no greater aphrodisiac for her than being able to arouse this man. She responded powerfully to *his* attraction to *her*. It wasn't her sexuality she was expressing as much as her feelings of being validated by his sexual responsiveness to her. Because she was actually much more in touch with his sexuality than with her own, the more responsive he was, the more gratified she felt. She interpreted the time he stole from his other life to be with her as the validation of her worth for which she hungered. When she wasn't with him she thought about new ways to enchant him. Her friends finally quit asking her to join them, and her life narrowed to a single-pointed obsession: making Jim happier than he'd ever been. She felt a thrill of victory in their every encounter, victory over his disenchantment with life, his inability to experience love and sexual fulfillment. That she could make him happy made her happy. Finally, her love was working its magic in someone's life. It was what she'd always wanted. She wasn't like her mother, driving someone away with her demands. Instead, she was creating a bond built entirely of love and selflessness. She prided herself on how little she asked of Jim.

"I was very lonely when I wasn't with him, which was a lot of the time. I saw him for only two hours three days a week, and he never contacted me in between. He took classes on Monday, Wednesday, and Friday, and we'd meet afterward. The time we had together was mostly spent making love. When we were finally alone we would just rush at each other. It was so intense, so exciting, that sometimes it was hard for either of us to believe that sex could be that thrilling for any other people in the world. And then, of course, afterward we always had to say goodbye. All the other hours in the week when I wasn't with him were empty. I spent most of the time we were apart getting ready to see him again. I'd wash my hair with a special shampoo, do my nails, and just drift along, thinking about him. I wouldn't let myself think too much about his wife and family. I believed that he'd been trapped into a marriage before he was old enough to really know what he wanted, and the fact that he had no intention of leaving, no intention of running away from his obligations, endeared him to me all the more."

"—and made me all the more comfortable with him," Trudi might well have added. She was not capable of a sustained intimate relationship, so the buffer that Jim's marriage and family provided was actually welcome, just as the football player's reluctance to be with her had been. We are only comfortable relating in ways that are already familiar, and Jim provided both the distance and the lack of commitment that Trudi already knew so well from her parents' relationship to her.

The second semester of school was nearly over, summer was coming, and Trudi asked Jim what would happen to them when school was out and they no longer had that convenient excuse for meeting. He began to frown and answered vaguely, "I'm not sure. I'll figure something out." The frown was enough to stop her. All that tied the two of them together was the happiness she was able to give him. If he wasn't happy, it might all come to an end. She mustn't make him frown.

School ended and Jim hadn't figured it out. "I'll call you," he said. She waited. A friend's father offered her a job in his resort hotel for the summer. Several of her friends also had jobs there and urged her to join them. It would be fun, they promised her, working at the lake all summer. She turned down the offer, afraid she'd miss Jim's call. Though she rarely left the house for three weeks, the call never came.

One hot afternoon in mid-July Trudi was downtown, listlessly shopping. She came out of an air-conditioned store, blinking in the bright sunlight, and there was Jim—tanned, smiling, and holding hands with a woman who could only be his wife. With them were two young children, a boy and a girl, and on Jim's chest, in a blue sling, an infant. Trudi's eyes sought Jim's. He stared back briefly, then looked away, walking past her with his family, his wife, his life.

Somehow she made it to her car, even though the pain in her chest nearly prevented her from breathing. She sat there, in the hot parking lot, sobbing and gasping for air until long after the sun went down. Then slowly, dimly, she drove to the college, and up into the hills behind it, the hills where she and Jim had first strolled, first kissed. She drove until the road dropped steeply on one side, and then went straight where she should have turned.

That she survived the crash more or less intact was miraculous. It was also a great disappointment to her. Lying in the hospital bed, she vowed to try again, as soon as they let her out. She got through the transfer to the psych ward, the numbing drugs, the obligatory interview with the psychiatrist. Her parents came to see her in separate shifts, worked out elaborately through the nursing station. Her father's appearances produced stern lectures about how much she had to live for, during which Trudi silently counted the number of times he glanced at his watch. He usually ended with a helpless "Now you know your mother and I each love you, honey. Promise me you won't do this again." Trudi promised dutifully, forcing a small smile, cold with the loneliness of lying to her father about something so important. His visits were followed by her mother's, who paced around the room, demanding insistently, "How could you do this to yourself? How could you do this to us? Why didn't you *tell* me something was wrong? What on earth is the matter, anyway? Are you upset about your father and me?" Then her mother would settle down into one of the chairs provided for visitors and offer a detailed description of how the divorce was proceeding, which was supposed to be reassuring. Trudi was usually sick to her stomach during the night after these visits.

On her last night in the hospital a nurse sat quietly with her and asked her some gently probing questions. The whole story came pouring out. The nurse finally said to her, "I know you're thinking of trying it again. Why shouldn't you? Nothing's different tonight than it was a week ago. But before you do, I want you to see someone." The nurse, a former client of mine, referred her to me.

So Trudi and I began our work together, the work of healing her need to give more love than she received, to give and give from an already empty place inside her. There were a few more men in her life over the next two years, who enabled her to examine how she used sex in her relationships. One was a professor at the university where she was now enrolled. He was a workaholic of her father's caliber, and at first Trudi threw herself into an intense effort to coax him away from his work and into her loving arms. This time, though, she felt keenly the frustration of her struggle to change him, and gave it up after five months. At first the challenge had been stimulating, and each time she "won" his attention for the evening she had felt validated, but Trudi felt herself becoming more and more dependent on him emotionally while he, in return, gave less and less. During one session she reported, "Last night I was with David and I was crying, telling him how important he was to me. He started to give me his usual answer about how I'd just have to understand that he had these important commitments to his work—well, I just stopped listening. I'd heard it all before anyway. It suddenly became very clear to me that I'd played this scene before, with my football-playing boyfriend. I was throwing myself at David the same way I had with him."

She smiled ruefully. "You have no idea, the lengths to which I've gone in order to win men's attention. I've run around throwing off my clothes and blowing in their ears and trying every seductive trick I know. I'm still trying to get attention from someone who isn't very interested in me. I think the biggest thrill I feel with David when we do make love is that I've been able to arouse him enough to distract him from what he'd rather be doing. I hate admitting this, but that has been a big turn-on for me, just being able to get David or Jim or anyone to pay *attention* to me. I guess because basically I have felt so bad about each relationship, the sex has brought a lot of relief. It seems for a few moments to dissolve all the barriers and bring us together. And I've wanted that togetherness so much. But I'm really not willing to keep throwing myself at David. It feels too degrading."

Still, David was not the last of Trudi's impossible men by any means. Her next beau was a young stockbroker who was a dedicated triathalon competitor. She competed as hard as he did, but for his attention, trying to lure him away from his rigorous training schedule with the constant promise of her willing body. Much of the time when they did make love, he was either too tired or too uninterested to achieve or maintain an erection.

One day, in my office, she was describing their most recent failed attempt at lovemaking and suddenly she began to laugh. "When I think about it, it's too much! No one has ever worked harder than I have, to make love to someone who would rather not." More laughter. Then finally, firmly: "I've got to stop doing this. I'm going to quit looking. I seem to always be attracted to the men who have nothing to offer me, and don't even want what I have to offer them."

This was an important turning point for Trudi. She had become more able to love herself through the process of therapy, and now she could evaluate a relationship as unrewarding, instead of concluding that she was unlovable and should try harder. The strong drive to use her sexuality to establish a relationship with a reluctant or impossible partner diminished sharply, and by the time she left therapy after two years, she was casually dating several young men and sleeping with none of them.

"It's so different to be on a date with someone and to actually be paying attention to whether I like him, whether

I'm having a good time, whether I think he's a nice person. I never thought about these things before. I was always trying so hard to make whoever I was with like me, to make sure he had a good time with me and thought I was nice. You know, after a date I never thought about whether I wanted to see the person again. I was too busy wondering if he liked me enough to call me for another date. I had it all backward!"

When Trudi decided to leave therapy, she no longer had it backward. She could spot an impossible relationship easily, and even if a spark of attraction between her and a reluctant suitor flared, it died quickly in her cool assessment of the man, the situation, and the possibilities. She was no longer in the market for pain and rejection. She wanted someone who could really be a partner to her, or no one at all. Nothing in between would do. But the fact remained that Trudi knew nothing about living with the opposites of pain and rejection: comfort and commitment. She had never known the degree of intimacy that comes from being in the kind of relationship she now required. Though she had yearned for closeness with a partner, she had never had to function in a climate of true closeness. That she had been drawn to rejecting men was no accident; Trudi's tolerance for being truly intimate was low. There had been no intimacy in her family as she grew up, only battles and treaties, each treaty more or less marking the beginning of the next battle. There had been pain and tension and occasionally some relief from pain and tension, but never real sharing, real closeness, or real love. In reaction to her mother's manipulations, Trudi's formula for loving had been to give of herself without asking anything in return. When therapy helped her out of the trap of her self-sacrificing martyrdom, she was left knowing clearly what not to do, which was a great improvement. But she was only halfway home.

Trudi's next task was to learn to simply be in the company of men whom she considered nice, even if she also found them a little boring. Boredom is the sensation that women who love too much so often experience when they find themselves with a "nice" man: no bells peal, no rockets explode, no stars fall from heaven. In the absence of excitement they feel antsy, irritable, and awkward, a generally uncomfortable state that is covered over with the label *boredom*. Trudi didn't know how to behave in the presence of a man who was kind, considerate, and really interested in her; like all women who love too much, her skills at relating were honed for a challenge, not for simply enjoying a man's company. If she didn't have to maneuver and manipulate in order to keep a relationship going, she found it difficult to relate to the man, to feel comfortable and at ease. Because she was used to excitement and pain, struggle and victory or defeat, an interchange that lacked these powerful components felt too tame to be important, and unsettling as well. Ironically, there would be more discomfort in the presence of steady, dependable, cheerful, stable fellows than there ever had been with men who were unresponsive, emotionally distant, unavailable, or uninterested.

A woman who loves too much is *used* to negative traits and behaviors, and she will be more comfortable with them than with their opposites unless and until she works very hard to change that fact for herself. Unless Trudi could learn to relate comfortably to a man who considered her best interests as important as his own, she had no hope of ever achieving a rewarding relationship.

Before recovery, a woman who loves too much usually exhibits the following characteristics regarding how she feels and how she relates to men sexually:

- She asks the question "How much does he love (or need) me?" and not "How much do I care for him?"
- Most of her sexual interactions with him are motivated by "How can I get him to love (or need) me more?"

39

- Her drive to give herself sexually to others whom she perceives as needy may result in behavior that she herself labels promiscuous, but her behavior is primarily for another's gratification, rather than for her own.
- Sex is one of the tools she uses for manipulating or changing her partner.
- She often finds the power struggles of mutual manipulation very exciting. She behaves seductively to get her own way and feels great when it works and bad when it doesn't. Failing to get what she wants usually causes her to try even harder.
- She confuses anxiety, fear, and pain with love and sexual excitement. She calls the sensation of having a knot in her stomach "love."
- She takes her excitement from his excitement. She doesn't know how to feel good for herself; in fact, she is threatened by her own feelings.
- Unless the challenge of an unfulfilling relationship is there, she becomes restless. She is not sexually attracted to a man with whom she is not struggling. Instead, she labels him "boring."
- She often teams up with a man who is less experienced sexually, in order that she feel in control.
- She yearns for physical closeness, but because she fears being enveloped by another and/or being overwhelmed by her own needs for nurturing, she is only comfortable with the emotional distance created and maintained by stress in the relationship. She becomes fearful when a man is willing to be there for her emotionally as well as sexually. She either runs away or drives him away.

Trudi's poignant question at the beginning of our work together—"How could the sex between us be so good, make us both feel so wonderful, and bring us so close together when we really had nothing else going for us?"—is one that merits examining, because women who love too much often face the dilemma of good sex in an unhappy or hopeless relationship. Many of us have been taught that "good" sex means "real" love, and that, conversely, sex couldn't be really satisfying and fulfilling if the relationship as a whole were not right for us. Nothing could be further from the truth for women who love too much. Because of the dynamics operating at every level of our interactions with men, including the sexual level, a bad relationship may actually contribute to sex being exciting, passionate, and compelling.

We may be hard pressed to explain to family and friends how someone who is not particularly admirable or even very likable can nevertheless arouse in us a thrill of anticipation and an intensity of longing never matched by what we feel for someone nicer or more presentable. It is difficult to articulate that we are enchanted by the dream of calling forth all the positive attributes—the love, caring, attention, integrity, and nobility—we are sure are lying dormant in our lover, waiting to blossom in the warmth of our love. Women who love too much often tell themselves that the man with whom they are involved has never really been loved before, not by his parents nor by his previous wives or girlfriends. We see him as damaged, and readily take on the task of making up for all that was missing in his life long before we ever met him. In a way, the scenario is a sexually role-reversed version of the tale of Snow White, who slept under a spell, waiting for the liberation that comes with her true love's first kiss. We want to be the one to break the spell, to free this man from what we see as his imprisonment. We take his emotional unavailability, his anger or depression or cruelty or indifference or violence or dishonesty or addiction, for signs that he has not been loved enough. We pit our love against his faults, his failings, even his pathology. We are determined to save him through the power of our love.

Sex is one of the primary ways we try to love him toward health. Every sexual encounter carries all our striving to change him. With every kiss and every touch we work at

41

communicating to him how special and worthy he is, how much he is admired and cherished. We feel sure that once he is convinced of our love he will be metamorphosed into his true self, awakened to the embodiment of everything we want and need him to be.

In a way, sex under such circumstances is good because we need it to be; we put a great deal of energy into making it work, making it wonderful. Whatever response we elicit encourages us to try harder, to be more loving, to be more *convincing*. And there are other factors operating as well. For instance, though it would seem that fulfilling sex would not be very likely in an unhappy relationship, it is important to remember that a sexual climax is a discharge of both physical and emotional tension. While one woman may avoid sexual involvement with her partner when there is conflict and strain between them, another woman in similar circumstances may find sex to be a highly effective way of releasing much of that tension, at least temporarily. For a woman in an unhappy relationship or with a partner to whom she is ill-matched, the sex act may be the one aspect of the relationship that is gratifying, and the one way of relating to him that works.

In fact, the degree of sexual release she experiences may be directly related to the degree of discomfort she feels with her partner. This is easy to understand. Many couples, whether their relationship is healthy or otherwise, experience particularly good sex after a fight. Following a conflict, two elements contribute to especially intense and rapturous lovemaking: one is the aforementioned release of tension; the other involves a tremendous investment, after a fight, in making sex "work," in order to cement the couple's bond that has been threatened by their quarrel. The fact that the couple enjoys a particularly pleasurable and satisfying sexual experience under these circumstances can seem to validate the relationship as a whole. "Look at how close we are, how loving we can be with each other, how good we can make each other feel.

We really *do* belong together," may be the sentiment generated.

The sex act, when it is highly gratifying physically, has the power to create deeply felt bonds between two people. For women who love too much, especially, the intensity of our struggle with a man may contribute to the intensity of our sexual experience with him and thus our bond to him. And the converse is also true. When we are involved with a man who is not so much of a challenge, the sexual dimension may also lack fire and passion. Because we are not in an almost constant state of excitement over him, and because sex isn't used to prove something, we may find an easier, more relaxed relationship to be somewhat tame. Compared to the tempestuous styles of relating that we've known, this tamer kind of experience only seems to verify for us that tension, struggle, heartache, and drama truly do equal "real love."

Which brings us to a discussion of what real love is. Though love seems to be very difficult to define, I submit that this is because we try in this culture to combine two very opposite and even apparently mutually exclusive aspects of love in one definition. Thus, the more we say about love, the more we contradict ourselves, and when we find one aspect of love battling another, we give up in confusion and frustration and decide that love is too personal, too mysterious, and too enigmatic to pin down precisely.

The Greeks were smarter. They used different words, *eros* and *agape,* to distinguish between these two profoundly different ways of experiencing what we call "love." Eros, of course, refers to passionate love, while agape describes the stable and committed relationship, *free of passion,* that exists between two individuals who care deeply for each other.

The contrast of eros and agape allows us to understand our dilemma when we look for both these kinds of love at one time, in one relationship with one person. It also helps us see why eros and agape each have their champions, those who claim that one or the other is the only real way of experiencing love, for indeed each has its very special beauty, truth, and worth. And each type of love also lacks something precious, which only the other has to offer. Let's look at how proponents of each would describe being in love.

Eros: Real love is an all-consuming, desperate yearning for the beloved, who is perceived as different, mysterious, and elusive. The depth of love is measured by the intensity of obsession with the loved one. There is little time or attention for other interests or pursuits, because so much energy is focused on recalling past encounters or imagining future ones. Often, great obstacles must be overcome, and thus there is an element of suffering in true love. Another indication of the depth of love is the willingness to endure pain and hardship for the sake of the relationship. Associated with real love are feelings of excitement, rapture, drama, anxiety, tension, mystery, and yearning.

Agape: Real love is a partnership to which two caring people are deeply committed. These people share many basic values, interests, and goals, and tolerate good-naturedly their individual differences. The depth of love is measured by the mutual trust and respect they feel toward each other. Their relationship allows each to be more fully expressive, creative, and productive in the world. There is much joy in shared experiences both past and present, as well as those that are anticipated. Each views the other as his/her dearest and most cherished friend. Another measure of the depth of love is the willingness to look honestly at oneself in order to promote the growth of the relationship and the deepening of intimacy. Associated with real love are feelings of serenity, security, devotion, understanding, companionship, mutual support, and comfort.

Passionate love, eros, is what the woman who loves too much usually feels for the man who is impossible. Indeed, it is because he is impossible that there is so much passion.

In order for passion to exist, there needs to be a continuing struggle, obstacles to overcome, a yearning for more than is available. Passion literally means *suffering*, and it is often the case that the greater the suffering, the deeper the passion. The thrilling intensity of a passionate love affair cannot be matched by the gentler comforts of a stable, committed relationship, so were she to finally receive from the object of her passion what she has so ardently desired, the suffering would stop and the passion would soon burn itself out. Then, perhaps, she would tell herself she had fallen out of love, because the bittersweet pain would be gone.

The society in which we live and the ever-present media that surround and saturate our consciousness confuse the two kinds of love constantly. We are promised in thousands of ways that a passionate relationship (eros) will bring us contentment and fulfillment (agape). In fact, the implication is that with great enough passion, a lasting bond will be forged. All the failed relationships based initially on tremendous passion can testify that this premise is false. Frustration, suffering, and yearning do *not* contribute to a stable, sustained, nurturing relationship, though they certainly are factors that contribute mightily to a passionate one.

Common interests, common values and goals, and a capacity for deep, sustained intimacy are required if a couple's initial erotic enchantment with each other is to eventually metamorphose into a committed, caring devotion that will endure over time. However, what often happens is this: In a passionate relationship, fraught as it must be with the excitement, suffering, and frustration of new love, there is the feeling that something very important is missing. What is wanted is commitment, a means of stabilizing this chaotic emotional experience and providing a feeling of safety and security. Should the obstacles to their being together be overcome and a genuine commitment forged, these two partners may eventually look at each other and wonder where the passion has gone. They feel safe and warm and kindly toward each other, but a little cheated, too, because they are no longer fired with desire for each other.

The price we pay for passion is fear, and the very pain and fear that feed passionate love may also destroy it. The price we pay for stable commitment is boredom, and the very safety and security that cement such a relationship can also make it rigid and lifeless.

If there is to be continued excitement and challenge in the relationship after commitment, it must be based not on frustration or longing but on an ever-deeper exploration of what D. H. Lawrence calls "the joyful mysteries" between a man and a woman who are committed to each other. As Lawrence implies, this is perhaps best done with one partner, for the trust and the honesty of agape must combine with the courage and vulnerability of passion in order to create true intimacy. I once heard a recovering alcoholic put it so simply and so beautifully. He said, "When I was drinking I went to bed with lots of women, and basically I had the same experience many times. Since I've been sober I've only been to bed with my wife, but each time we're together it's a new experience."

The thrill and excitement that comes not from arousing and being aroused but from knowing and being known is all too rare. Most of us in committed, stable relationships settle for predictability, comfort, and companionship because we fear exploring the mysteries that we embody together as man and woman, the exposure of our deepest selves. Yet in our fear of the unknown within us and between us we ignore and avoid the very gift that our commitment sets within our reach—true intimacy.

For women who love too much, developing true intimacy with a partner can come only after recovery. Later in the book we'll meet Trudi again as she faces this challenge of recovery that awaits us all.

3 • *If I Suffer for You,*
Will You Love Me?

> BABY, BABY, PLEASE DON'T GO.
> I THINK I'M GETTING HIGH ON FEELING
>   LOW.
>
> —THE LAST BLUES SONG

IT WAS NECESSARY FOR ME TO LEAN ACROSS SEVERAL STACKED canvasses in order to read the framed verse that hung in the middle of the cluttered apartment's living room wall. Time-worn and faded, the old-fashioned landscape with its printed poem read:

> *My Dear Mother*
>
> *Mother, dear mother*
> *When I think of you*
> *I want to be all that*
>   *is fine,*
> *That is true.*
> *All that is worthy*
> *Noble or grand*

Has come from you, Mother,
From your guiding hand.

Lisa, an artist of very modest income whose living quarters doubled as her art studio, waved at the poem and laughed lightly.

"It's too much, isn't it? So corny!" But her next words betrayed a deeper sentiment.

"I saved it when a friend of mine was moving and going to throw it out. She'd gotten it from a thrift store as a joke. I think there's some truth to it, though, don't you?" Then she laughed again and said ruefully, "Loving my mother has gotten me into a lot of trouble with men."

At this, Lisa paused and reflected. Tall, with wide-set green eyes and long, straight, dark hair, she was a beauty. She motioned me to sit on a quilt-covered mattress in a relatively uncrowded corner of the floor and offered me tea. As it brewed, she remained silent for a few moments.

Lisa had come to my attention through a mutual friend who had told me some of her history. Because she had grown up with alcoholism in her family, Lisa was a co-alcoholic. The word *co-alcoholic* simply refers to someone who has developed an unhealthy pattern of relating to others as a result of having been closely involved with someone with the disease of alcoholism. Whether the alcoholic has been a parent, spouse, child, or friend, their relationship usually causes certain feelings and behavior to develop in the co-alcoholic: low self-esteem, a need to be needed, a strong urge to change and control others, and a willingness to suffer. In fact, all the characteristics of women who love too much are usually present in the daughters and wives of alcoholics and other addicts.

I already knew that the effects of a childhood spent trying to take care of and protect her alcoholic mother had profoundly influenced how Lisa related to men later in life. I waited patiently, and soon she began to offer some details.

She was the middle of three children, between an older

sister who was the reason for her parents' hasty marriage and a younger brother who was another surprise, born eight years after Lisa, while her mother was still drinking. Lisa was the product of their only planned pregnancy.

"I always thought my mother was perfect, maybe because I needed so badly for her to be. I made her into the mother I wanted and then told myself that I would be just like her. What a fantasy I lived in!" Lisa shook her head and continued. "I was born when she and my father were most in love, so I was her favorite. Even though she said she loved us all the same, I knew that I was very special to her. We always spent as much time together as we could. When I was very young I guess she did take care of me, but after a while we changed roles and I started taking care of her.

"My father was horrible most of the time. He treated her rudely and gambled all our money away. He made a good salary as an engineer, but we never had anything and we were always moving.

"You know, that little poem describes the way I wanted it to be much more than the way it really was. I'm finally beginning to see that. All my life I wanted my mother to be the person that poem describes, but most of the time she wasn't able to even come close to being my ideal mother because she was drunk. Very early, I began pouring all my love and devotion and energy into her, hoping to get back what I needed from her, to get back what I was giving." Lisa paused and her eyes clouded for a moment. "I'm learning all this in therapy, and sometimes it hurts a lot to look at how it really was instead of how I always thought I could make it be.

"My mother and I were so close, but very early—so early I can't remember when it happened—I began to act like I was the mother and she was the child. I worried about her and tried to protect her from my father. I did little things to cheer her up. I tried hard to make her happy because she was all I had. I knew she cared for me because often she would tell me to come sit by her and we'd stay that way for a long time, snuggled up together and not really talking, just holding on to each other. Now, when I look back, I realize I was always afraid for her, always waiting for something awful to happen—something that I should have been able to prevent if only I'd been careful enough. That's a tough way to live when you're growing up, but I never knew anything else. And it took its toll. By the time I was a teenager, I was having serious episodes of depression."

Lisa laughed softly. "What scared me most about the depression was that I couldn't take very good care of my mother when I was in the middle of it. You see, I was very conscientious . . . and so afraid of letting go of her, even for a little while. The only way I could let go of her was by grabbing on to someone else."

She brought the tea on a red-and-black lacquered tray and placed it on the floor before us.

"When I was nineteen, I had the opportunity to go to Mexico with two girlfriends. It was absolutely the first time I had ever left my mother. We were to stay three weeks, and the second week I was there I met this terrifically handsome Mexican man who spoke beautiful English and was very gallant and attentive to me. By the third week of my vacation he was asking me daily to marry him. He said he was in love with me and couldn't bear the thought of being without me now that he'd found me. Well, that was probably the perfect argument to use with me. I mean, he was saying he *needed* me, and everything in me responded to being needed. Besides, I think I knew at some level that I had to get away from my mother. It was so dark and dreary and grim at home. And this man was promising me a wonderful life. His family was wealthy. He had a fine education. He didn't *do* anything that I could see, but I thought that was because they had so much money he didn't have to work. That he had all that money available to him and still thought he needed me to make him happy made me feel terribly important and worthwhile.

"I called my mother and described him in glowing terms to her. She said, 'I trust you to make the right decision.' Well, she shouldn't have. I decided to marry him, which was definitely a mistake.

"You see, I had no idea how I felt about anything. I didn't know if I loved him or if he was what I wanted. I just knew that finally here was someone saying *he* loved *me*. I'd done very little dating, knew almost nothing about men. I'd been too busy taking care of things at home. I was so empty inside, and here was this person offering me what seemed like so much. And he said he *loved* me. I'd been doing all the loving for so long, and now it seemed as if it was my turn to be on the receiving end. And just in time. I knew I was almost totally drained, that I had nothing left to give.

"Well, we were married quickly, without his parents' knowledge. It sounds so crazy now, but at the time it all seemed to show how much he loved me—that he was willing to defy his parents to be with me. I thought then that he was rebelling by marrying me, just enough of a rebellion to make his parents angry, but not enough so they'd throw him out. I see it differently now. After all, he had secrets to keep about his sexual identity and behavior, and having a wife made him look more "normal" than not having one. I guess that was what he meant when he said he needed me. And of course I was a perfect choice, because being an American I would always, in his culture, be wrong, be suspect. Any other woman, especially one from his social class, seeing what I saw would have told someone sooner or later. Then it would have been all over town. But who was I going to tell? Who ever talked to me? And who would believe me?

"I don't think any of this was deliberate or calculated on his part, though, any more than my reasons for marrying him were. We just fit together and we thought, at first, it was love.

"Anyway, after the wedding, guess what? We had to go

home and live with these people who hadn't even been informed we were marrying! Oh, it was dreadful. They hated me and I got the feeling they had been angry with him for quite some time already. I couldn't speak a word of Spanish. His whole family could speak English, but they *wouldn't*. I was totally shut out and isolated, and terribly afraid right from the beginning. He left me alone in the evenings a lot, so I just stayed in our room, and finally learned to go to sleep whether he came home or not. I already knew how to suffer. I'd learned that at home. Somehow, I thought this was the price you paid to be with someone who loved you, that it was normal.

"He often came home drunk, and amorous, and that was really awful. I could smell other women's perfume on him.

"One night I'd already been asleep a long time and some noise woke me. There was my husband, drunk, admiring himself in front of the mirror, in my nightgown. I asked him what he was doing and he said, 'Don't you think I look pretty?' He made a little face and I saw he was wearing lipstick.

"Finally, something snapped. I knew I had to get out of there. Up until then I had been miserable, but I was sure it was my fault, that somehow I could be more loving and make him want to stay with me, make him get his parents to acknowledge me, to like me, even. I was willing to try harder, just like with my mother. But this was different. This was crazy.

"I had no money and no way of getting any, so the next day I told him I would tell his parents what he'd done if he didn't take me to San Diego. I lied and told him I had already called my mother and she was expecting to meet me, and that if he would just take me there I'd never bother him again. I don't know where I got the courage because I actually thought he might kill me or something, but it worked. He was so afraid of his parents knowing, you see. He drove me to the border without a word and gave me bus fare to San Diego and about fifteen dollars. So I ended up in San Diego at a friend's house. I stayed there until I got a job and then I got a place with three roommates and began a pretty wild lifestyle.

"By now I had absolutely no feelings of my own. I was completely numb. But I still had this tremendous compassion, which got me into a lot of trouble. I went home with a great many men during the next three or four years because I felt sorry for them. I'm lucky things didn't ever get really out of hand. Most of the men I got involved with had drug or alcohol problems. I met them at parties or, occasionally, in bars, and again, they seemed to need me to understand them, to help them, which was like a magnet for me."

Lisa's attraction to men of this type made perfect sense in terms of her history with her mother. The closest thing to being loved that Lisa had experienced was being needed, so when a man appeared to need her he was, in effect, offering her love. He did not have to be kind, or giving, or caring. That he was needy was enough to stir the old, familiar feelings in her and kindle her care-giving response.

Her story continued. "My life was a mess, and so was my mother's. It would be difficult to say which of us was sicker. I was twenty-four when my mother got sober. She did it the hard way. All by herself, alone in her living room, she made that phone call to A.A. and asked for help. They sent two people over to talk to her and they took her to a meeting that afternoon. She hasn't had a drink since."

Lisa smiled softly at her mother's courage.

"It must have really gotten unbearable because she was a very proud lady, too proud to call unless she was desperate. Thank God I wasn't there to see it. I probably would have worked so hard to make her feel better that she never would have gotten real help.

"My mother had started drinking really heavily when I

was about nine. I would come home from school and she would be lying on the couch, passed out, with a bottle next to her. My older sister used to get angry with me and tell me that I wouldn't look at reality because I would never admit how bad it was, but I loved my mother too much to even let myself notice that she was doing anything wrong.

"We were so close, she and I. So when things began to fall apart between her and my dad, I wanted to make it up to her. Her happiness was the most important thing in the world to me. I felt I had to make it all up to her for what my father was doing that hurt her, and the only thing I knew how to do was be good. So, I was good in every way I knew how. I would ask her if she needed help with anything. I cooked and cleaned without being asked. I tried not to need anything for myself.

"But nothing worked. I realize now that I was taking on two incredibly powerful forces: my parents' deteriorating marriage and my mother's advancing alcoholism. I didn't have a chance of making it right, but that didn't keep me from trying—and from blaming myself when I failed.

"Her unhappiness hurt me so, you see. And I knew there were still areas where I could improve. My schoolwork, for instance. I wasn't doing too well because, of course, I was under a lot of pressure at home, what with trying to take care of my brother and fixing meals and finally getting a job to help out. In school I only had energy for one brilliant accomplishment a year. I would plan carefully and bring it off to show the teachers I wasn't dumb. But the rest of the time I barely squeaked by. They said I wasn't really trying. Ha! They didn't *know* how hard I was trying—to hold everything together at home. But the report cards weren't good, and my father would yell and my mother would cry. I blamed myself for not being perfect. And I kept trying harder than ever."

In a severely dysfunctional home such as this, where there are apparently insurmountable difficulties, the family will focus on other, simpler problems that hold some promise of being solvable. Lisa's schoolwork and grades thus became everyone's focus, including Lisa's. The family needed to believe that this problem was one which, if rectified, would bring harmony.

The pressure on Lisa was intense. Not only was she trying to solve her parents' problems while saddled with her mother's responsibilities, she was also identified as a *cause* of this unhappiness. Because of the monumental proportions of her task, she never experienced success, in spite of her heroic efforts. Naturally, her sense of self-worth suffered terribly.

"One time I called my best friend and said to her, 'Please let me talk to you. You can read a book if you want. You don't have to listen to me. I just need someone on the other end of the phone.' I didn't believe that I even deserved to have someone listen to my problems! But she did listen, of course. Her father was a recovering alcoholic who went to A.A. She went to Alateen and I think she gave me the benefit of that program just in the way she listened to me. It was so hard for me to admit anything was wrong, unless it was my father's fault. I really hated him."

Lisa and I sipped our tea in silence for a few moments while she struggled silently with bitter memories. When she could continue, she said simply, "My father left us when I was sixteen. My sister was already gone. She was three years older than I, and as soon as she turned eighteen she got a full-time job and left home. That left just my mother, my brother, and me. I think that I was beginning to go under with the pressure I put on myself to keep her safe and happy, and to take care of my brother. So I went to Mexico and got married, came home and got divorced, and then ran around with a lot of men for years.

"It was about five months after my mother got into the A.A. program that I met Gary. The first day I spent time with him he was stoned. We rode around in the car with my girlfriend, who knew him, and he was smoking a joint.

He liked me and I liked him, and we both separately passed on that information through my girlfriend, so pretty soon he called me and came over to visit me. I had him sit for me while I sketched him just for fun, and I remember becoming overwhelmed with feeling for him. It was the most powerful sensation regarding a man I'd ever had.

"He was stoned again, and he was sitting there talking slowly—you know, the way people do on pot—and I had to stop drawing because my hands started shaking so hard I couldn't do anything. I held the sketch pad up at an angle, leaning it against my knees for stability, so he couldn't see my hands shake like that.

"Today I know that what I was responding to was the fact that he talked just like my mother did when she'd been drinking all day. The same long pauses and carefully selected words that came out sort of overemphasized. All the caring and love that I felt for my mother were combined with my physical attraction to him as a good-looking man. But at that time I had no idea why I was responding the way I did, so of course I called it love."

That Lisa's attraction to and involvement with Gary began so soon after her mother stopped drinking was not a coincidence. The tie between the two women had never been broken. Even though considerable geographic distance separated them, her mother had always been Lisa's first responsibility and deepest attachment. When Lisa realized that her mother was changing, recovering from alcoholism without her help, she reacted out of fear at not being needed. Soon Lisa established a new relationship of depth with another addictive individual. After her marriage, her involvements with men had been casual, until her mother's sobriety. She "fell in love" with an addict when her mother turned to members of Alcoholics Anonymous for help and support in getting well. Lisa needed a relationship with an actively addictive person in order to feel "normal."

She went on to describe the six-year relationship that followed. Gary moved in with her almost at once and stated clearly during their first couple of weeks together that if there were ever a choice to be made between buying dope and paying the rent, the dope would always come first with him. Lisa, though, was sure he would change, that he would come to value what they had together and want to preserve it. She was sure she could make him love her the way she loved him.

Gary rarely worked and when he did, true to his word, his income went for the most expensive marijuana or hashish. Lisa joined him in his drug use at first, but when she found it interfered with her ability to earn a living she stopped. She was, after all, responsible for supporting them both, and she took her responsibility seriously. Whenever she thought about telling him to leave—after he'd taken money from her purse again or there was a party going on in their apartment when she came home, exhausted from work, or he hadn't come home all night— he would buy a bag of groceries or have dinner waiting for her or tell her he had gotten some cocaine especially for them to share, and her resolve would melt while she said to herself that he really did love her after all.

His stories of his childhood would make her cry with pity for him, and Lisa was sure, if she loved him enough, that she could make up for all that he had suffered. She felt she must not blame him or hold him responsible for his behavior now, since he'd been so damaged as a child, and she quite forgot her own painful past as she concentrated on remedying his.

Once, during an argument when she refused to give him a check her father had sent her for a birthday present, he plunged a knife into every canvas in the apartment.

Lisa continued with her story. "I was getting so sick by then that I actually thought, *This is my fault; I shouldn't have made him so angry*. I was still taking the blame for everything, trying to fix the unfixable.

"The next day was Saturday. Gary was gone for a while and I was cleaning up the mess, crying and throwing out three years' worth of paintings. I had the television on to distract myself, and this woman who had been beaten by her husband was being interviewed. You couldn't see her face, but she was talking about how her life had been and she described some pretty awful scenes and then said, 'I didn't think it was that bad because I could still stand it.' "

Lisa shook her head slowly. "That's what I was doing, staying in this terrible situation because I could still stand it. When I heard that woman, I said, aloud, 'But you deserve something more than the worst thing you can stand!' And suddenly I heard myself and I started crying really hard because I realized, so did I. I deserved more than the pain and the frustration and the expense and the chaos. With every ruined painting I said to myself, *I won't live this way anymore.*"

When Gary came home, his things were packed and waiting for him outside the front door. Lisa had called her best friend, who brought her husband with her, and the couple helped Lisa to have the courage to tell Gary to leave.

"There wasn't a scene because my friends were there, so he just left. Later he started calling me and threatening me, but I wouldn't respond in any way, so after a while he gave up.

"I want you to understand, though, that I didn't do it by myself—not respond, I mean. I called my mother that afternoon, after all the dust had settled, and told her the whole story. She told me to begin going to Al-Anon meetings for adult children of alcoholics. It was only because I was in so much pain that I listened to her."

Al-Anon, like Alateen, is a fellowship of relatives and friends of alcoholics who come together to help one another and themselves recover from their obsession with the alcoholic in their lives. Adult-children meetings are for the grown sons and daughters of alcoholics who want to recover from the effects of having lived as children with alcoholism. Those effects include most of the characteristics of loving too much.

"That was when I began to understand myself. Gary, for me, was what alcohol had been for my mother: he was a drug that I couldn't do without. Until the day I made him leave, I had always been terrified that he would go away, so I did everything I could to please him. I did all the things that I'd done as a child—work hard, be good, not ask for anything for myself, and take care of what was someone else's responsibility.

"Because self-sacrifice had always been my pattern, I wouldn't have known who I was without someone to help or some suffering to endure."

Lisa's deep attachment to her mother, and the great sacrifice of her own needs and wants that this attachment required, prepared her for later love relationships that involved suffering rather than any kind of personal fulfillment. She had made a profound decision as a child that she would rectify any difficulty in her mother's life through the power of her own love and selflessness. That decision soon became unconscious, but it continued to drive her. Totally unaccustomed to assessing ways of securing her own well-being but expert in promoting the well-being of others, she moved into relationships that held the promise of another opportunity to make everything right for another person through the force of her love. True to her history, failure to win that love through her efforts only made her try harder.

Gary, with his addiction, his emotional dependency, and his cruelty, combined all the worst attributes of Lisa's mother and father. Ironically, that accounted for her attraction to him. If the relationship we had with our parents was essentially a nurturing one, with appropriate expressions of affection, interest, and approval, then as adults we tend to feel comfortable with people who engender similar feelings of security, warmth, and positive self-regard. Further, we will tend to avoid people who make us feel less positive about ourselves through their criticism or manipulation of us. Their behavior will be aversive for us.

However, if our parents related to us in hostile, critical, cruel, manipulative, overbearing, overdependent, or otherwise inappropriate ways, that is what will feel "right" to us when we meet someone who expresses, perhaps very subtly, undertones of the same attitudes and behaviors. We will feel at home with people with whom our earlier unhealthy patterns of relating are recreated, and perhaps awkward and ill at ease with gentler, kinder, or otherwise healthier individuals. Or else, because the challenge of trying to change someone in order to make that person happy or to gain withheld affection or approval is missing, we may simply experience ourselves as feeling bored with healthier people. Boredom often covers mild to intense feelings of awkwardness, which women who love too much tend to feel when out of the familiar role of helping, hoping, and paying more attention to someone else's welfare than to their own. There is in most adult children of alcoholics, and in offspring from other kinds of dysfunctional homes as well, a fascination with people who spell trouble and an addiction to excitement, especially negative excitement. If drama and chaos have always been present in our lives, and if, as is so often the case, we were forced to deny many of our own feelings while growing up, we often require dramatic events to engender any feeling at all. Thus, we need the excitement of uncertainty, pain, disappointment, and struggle just to feel alive.

Lisa ended her story. "The peace and quiet of my life after Gary left drove me wild. It took everything I had not to call him and start it all over again. But I slowly got used to a more normal life.

"I'm not dating anyone now. I know that I'm still too sick to have a healthy relationship with a man. I'd go right out and find another Gary. So I'm making *myself* my project for the first time, rather than trying to change someone else."

* * *

Lisa, in relation to Gary, like her mother in relation to alcohol, suffered from a disease process, a destructive compulsion over which she had no control by herself. Just as her mother had developed an addiction to alcohol and was unable to stop drinking on her own, so Lisa had developed what was also an addictive relationship with Gary. I do not make this analogy, or use the word *addictive* lightly, in comparing the two women's situations. Lisa's mother had become dependent on a drug, alcohol, to avoid experiencing the intense anguish and despair that her life situation held for her. The more she used alcohol to avoid feeling her pain, the more the drug operated on her nervous system to produce the very feelings she was trying to avoid. It ultimately increased rather than diminished the pain. So of course she drank even more. Thus, she spiraled into addiction.

Lisa, too, was attempting to avoid anguish and despair. She suffered from a profound underlying depression, the roots of which traced back to her painful childhood. This underlying depression is a common factor in children from all types of severely dysfunctional homes, and their ways of dealing with it, or more typically, avoiding it, vary depending on their sex, their disposition, and their childhood role in the family. By the time they reach their teen years, many young women, like Lisa, keep their depression at bay through developing the style of loving too much. As they engage in chaotic but stimulating and distracting interactions with unhealthy men, they are too excited to sink into the depression that lingers just under the level of awareness.

In this way, a cruel, indifferent, dishonest, or otherwise difficult partner becomes for these women the equivalent of a drug, creating a means of avoiding their own feelings —just as alcohol and other mood-altering substances create for drug addicted persons a temporary avenue of escape, and one from which they dare not be separated. And as with alcohol and drugs, these unmanageable relationships that provide the needed distraction also contribute their own cargo of pain. In a parallel with the developing disease of alcoholism, dependence on the relationship deepens to the point of addiction. To be without the relationship—that is, to be alone with one's self—can be experienced as worse than being in the greatest pain the relationship produces, because to be alone means to feel the stirrings of the great pain from the past combined with that of the present.

The two addictions are parallel in this way, and equally difficult to overcome. A woman's addiction to her partner, or to a series of unsuitable partners, may owe its genesis to a variety of family problems. Ironically, adult children of alcoholics are more fortunate than those from other dysfunctional backgrounds because, at least in the larger cities, Al-Anon groups often exist to support them as they work through their problems with self-esteem and with relationships.

Recovery from relationship addiction involves getting help from an appropriate support group in order to break the cycle of addiction, and to learn to seek feelings of self-worth and well-being from sources other than a man unable to foster those feelings. The key is in learning how to live a healthy, satisfying, and serene life without being dependent on another person for happiness.

Sadly, for those enmeshed in addictive relationships and those caught in the web of chemical addiction, the conviction that they can handle the problem by themselves often prevents them from seeking help and thus precludes the possibility of recovery.

It is because of this conviction—"I can do it on my own"—that things sometimes must get so much worse before they can begin to get better for so many people struggling with either of these diseases of addiction. Lisa's life had to become hopelessly unmanageable before she could admit that she needed help to overcome her addiction to pain.

And Lisa's condition wasn't helped any by the fact that both suffering for love and being addicted to a relationship are romanticized by our culture. From popular songs to opera, from classical literature to Harlequin romances, from daily soap operas to critically acclaimed movies and plays, we are surrounded by countless examples of unrewarding, immature relationships that are glorified and glamorized. Over and over again we are instructed by these cultural models that the depth of love can be measured by the pain it causes and that those who truly suffer, truly love. When a singer plaintively croons about not being able to stop loving someone even though it hurts so much, there is, perhaps because of the sheer force of repeated exposure to this point of view, something in us that accepts that what the singer expresses is the way it *should* be. We accept that suffering is a natural part of love and that the willingness to suffer for the sake of love is a positive rather than a negative trait.

Very few models exist of people relating as peers in healthy, mature, honest, nonmanipulative, and nonexploitative ways, probably for two reasons: First, in all honesty, such relationships in real life are fairly rare. Second, since the quality of emotional interplay in healthy relationships is often much subtler than the blatant drama of unhealthy relationships, its dramatic potential is usually overlooked in literature, drama, and songs. If unhealthy styles of relating plague us, perhaps it is because that is very nearly all we see and all we know.

Because of the dearth of examples of mature love and healthy communication in the media, I have been entertaining a fantasy for years of taking over the script writing for one day's episode on each of the major soap operas. In my episode, all the characters would communicate with one another in honest, nondefensive, and caring ways. No lies, no secrets, no manipulations, no one who is willing to be someone else's victim, and no one doing the victimizing. Instead, for one day viewers would see people who are committed to having healthy relationships with each other, based on genuine communication.

This style of relating would not only conflict sharply

with the normal format of these programs but would also illustrate, by way of extreme contrast, how saturated we are with depictions of exploitation, manipulation, sarcasm, revenge seeking, deliberate baiting, piqueing of jealousy, lying, threatening, coercing, and so on—none of which contribute to healthy interplay. When you think about what one segment portraying honest communication and mature love would do to the quality of these continuing sagas, consider also what the same alteration in communication style would do in each of our lives.

Everything happens in a context, including the way we love. We need to be aware of the damaging shortcomings of our societal view of love and to resist the shallow and self-defeating immaturity in personal relationships that it glamorizes. We need to consciously develop a more open and mature way of relating than what our cultural media seem to endorse, thus trading turmoil and excitement for a deeper intimacy.

4 • *The Need to Be Needed*

> SHE'S A GOOD-HEARTED WOMAN
> IN LOVE WITH A GOOD-TIMIN' MAN;
> SHE LOVES HIM IN SPITE OF HIS WICKED
> WAYS
> THAT SHE DON'T UNDERSTAND.
> —GOOD-HEARTED WOMAN

"I DON'T KNOW HOW SHE DOES IT ALL. I'D GO CRAZY IF I HAD to cope with what she copes with."

"You know, I've never heard her complain!"

"Why does she put up with it?"

"What does she see in him, anyway? She could do so much better."

People tend to say these kinds of things about a woman who loves too much, as they observe what appear to be her noble efforts to make the best of a seemingly unrewarding situation. But clues that explain the mystery of her devoted attachment can usually be found in her childhood experiences. Most of us grow up and continue in the roles we adopted in our families of origin. For many women who love too much, those roles often meant that we denied our own needs while trying to meet the needs of other family members. Perhaps we were forced by circumstances to grow up too fast, prematurely taking on adult responsibilities because our mother or father was too sick physically or emotionally to carry out the appropriate parental functions. Or perhaps a parent was absent due to death or divorce and we tried to fill in, helping to take care of both our siblings and our remaining parent. Maybe we became the mommy at home while our own mother worked to support the family. Or we might have lived with both parents, but because one was angry or frustrated or unhappy and the other would not respond sympathetically, we found ourselves in the role of confidante, hearing details of their relationship that were too much for us to handle emotionally. We listened because we were afraid of the consequences to the suffering parent if we didn't, and afraid of the loss of love if we failed to fill the role proscribed for us. And so we didn't protect ourselves, and our parents didn't protect us either, because they needed to see us as stronger than we were. Even though we were too immature for the responsibility, we ended up protecting them. When this happened, we learned too young and too well how to take care of everyone but ourselves. Our own needs for love, attention, nurturing, and security went unmet while we pretended to be more powerful and less fearful, more grown up and less needy, than we really felt. And having learned to deny our own yearning to be taken care of, we grew up looking for more opportunities to do what we had become so good at: being preoccupied with someone else's wants and demands rather than acknowledging our own fear and pain and unmet needs. We've been pretending to be grown up for so long, asking for so little and doing so much, that now it seems too late to take our turn. So we help and help, and hope that our fear will go away and our reward will be love.

Melanie's story is a case in point, an example of how growing up too fast with too much responsibility—in this case, filling in for an absent parent—can create a compulsion to nurture.

The day we met, right after a lecture I had given to a group of nursing students, I couldn't help but notice that her face was a study in contrasts. The small, upturned nose with its splash of freckles and the deeply dimpled cheeks of buttermilk skin gave her an appealingly impish air. Those sprightly features seemed out of place on the same countenance that displayed such dark circles beneath her clear gray eyes. From under a cap of dark auburn waves she looked like a pale, tired pixie.

She had waited off to one side as I spoke at some length with each of the half-dozen nursing students who had lingered behind once my lecture had ended. As frequently happened whenever I spoke on the subject of the family disease of alcoholism, several students wanted to discuss matters too personal for the usual question-answer chat period following my presentation.

When the last of her classmates had gone, Melanie allowed me a moment's hiatus and then introduced herself, shaking my hand warmly and firmly for someone as slight and delicate as she was.

She had waited so long and so patiently to speak to me that, in spite of her apparent self-assuredness, I suspected a depth of feeling had been tapped by the morning's lecture. To give her an opportunity to talk at length, I invited her to join me in a walk across campus. As I gathered my belongings and we left the lecture hall, she chatted companionably, but once we were outside in the gray November noon she became quietly reflective.

We walked along a deserted path, the only sound the powdery crackle of fallen sycamore leaves, brittle beneath our feet.

Melanie fell out of step to scuff at a couple of the ragged star-shapes, their pointed tips curling upward like dried starfish, exposing their pale undersides. After a while she said softly, "My mother wasn't an alcoholic, but from what you described this morning about the way that disease affects a family, she might as well have been. She was mentally ill—really very crazy—and it finally killed her. She suffered from deep depressions, went to the hospital a lot, and sometimes stayed away a long time. The drugs they used to "cure" her just seemed to make her worse. Instead of an alert crazy woman, she became a zoned-out crazy woman. But as zonked as those drugs kept her, she finally managed to make one of her suicide attempts stick. Although we tried never to leave her by herself, that day we had all gone off in different directions just for a little while. She hanged herself in the garage. My father found her."

She shook her head quickly, unsettling the dark memories that were gathering there, and continued. "I heard a lot that I could identify with this morning, but you said in your lecture that children of alcoholics or from other dysfunctional homes like ours very often choose partners who are alcoholic or addicted to other drugs, and that's not true of Sean. He doesn't care much about drinking or getting loaded, thank God. But we do have other problems." She looked away from me, lifting her chin.

"I can usually handle anything . . ."—the chin lowered—". . . but it's beginning to get to me." Then she looked squarely at me, smiled, and shrugged. "I'm running out of food and money and time, that's all." She said this as though it were the punch line of a joke, to be responded to with amusement, not to be taken seriously. I had to prod her for the details, which she reported matter-of-factly.

"Sean's gone again. We have three children: Susie, six; Jimmy, four; and Peter, who is two and a half. I'm working part-time as a ward clerk, going for my R.N. in nursing school, and trying to keep it all together at home. Sean usually watches the kids when he's not in art school, or gone." She said this without a trace of bitterness.

"We were married seven years ago. I was seventeen and right out of high school. He was twenty-four, doing some acting and going to school part-time. He had an apartment with three friends. I used to go over on Sundays and make them all these great feasts. I was his Sunday night date. Fridays and Saturdays he was either doing a stage performance or seeing someone else. Anyway, they all loved me at that apartment. My cooking was the greatest thing that happened to them all week. They used to tease Sean, tell him he ought to marry me and let me take care of him. I guess he liked the idea because that's what he did. He asked me to marry him and of course I said yes. I was thrilled. He was so handsome. Look!" She opened her purse and took out a little sheaf of plastic-encased photographs. The first one was of Sean: dark eyes, chiseled cheekbones, and a deeply cleft chin combined in a broodingly handsome face. It was a wallet-size version of what looked like a photograph taken for an actor's or model's portfolio. I asked whether this was the case, and Melanie confirmed that it was, naming a well-known photographer who had done the work.

"He looks like a perfect Heathcliff," I observed, and she nodded proudly. We looked together at the other pictures, which showed three children in various stages of their development: crawling, taking tottering steps, blowing out birthday candles. Hoping to see a less posed photograph of Sean, I commented that he wasn't in any of the children's pictures.

"No, he usually takes the pictures. He's had quite a background in photography as well as acting and art."

"Does he work in any of those fields now?" I asked.

"Well, no. His mother sent him some money so he took off for New York again, to see what opportunities there are for him there." Her voice dropped almost imperceptibly.

Given her obvious loyalty to Sean, I would have expected Melanie to sound hopeful regarding this foray to New York. Since she did not, I asked, "Melanie, what is it?"

With the first trace of complaint, she said, "The problem isn't our marriage. It's his mother. She keeps sending him money. Every time he's about to settle down with us, or is sticking to a job for a change, she'll send him a check and off he goes. She can't say no to him. If she'd just stop giving him money, we'd be all right."

"What if she never stops?" I asked.

"Then Sean will have to change. I'll make him see how he's hurting us." Tears appeared on her dark lashes. "He'll have to refuse when she offers him money."

"Melanie, that doesn't sound too likely from what you're telling me."

Her voice rose and became more determined. "She's not going to ruin this thing. He *will* change."

Melanie found an especially large leaf and for the next several steps she kicked it ahead of her, watching it disintegrate.

I waited a few moments and then asked, "Is there more?"

Still kicking away, Melanie answered, "He's been to New York lots of times and he has someone else he sees when he's there." Softly again, and again matter-of-factly.

"Another woman?" I asked, and Melanie looked away as she nodded. "How long has he been involved?"

"Oh, years, really." At this point Melanie actually shrugged. "It started with my first pregnancy. I almost didn't blame him. I was so sick and miserable and he was so far away."

Amazingly, Melanie assumed the blame for Sean's infidelity to her, as well as the burden of supporting him and their children while he dabbled at various careers. I asked her if she had ever considered divorce.

"Actually, we did separate once. That's silly to say, because we're separated all the time, with his going off the way he does. But once I said I wanted a separation, mostly to teach him a lesson, and so for almost six months we really were apart. He'd still call me, and I would send him money when he needed it, if some opportunity were about to break and he needed something to tide him over until it did. But for the most part we were each on our own. I even met two other men!" Melanie sounded surprised that other men would be interested in her. She puzzled, "Both of them were so nice to the children, and they each wanted to help me around the house, fixing up what needed repairing and even buying me little things that I needed. It was nice having them treat me that way. But the feelings were just never really there on my part. I could never feel anything like the attraction that I still felt for Sean. So eventually I went back to him." She grinned. "Then I had to explain to him why everything was in such good shape at home."

We were halfway across the campus and I wanted to know more about what Melanie's childhood had been like, to understand the experiences that had prepared her for the hardship of her present situation.

"When you remember yourself as a child, what do you see?" I asked and watched her brow furrow as she looked back through the years.

"Oh, that's funny! I see myself in my apron, standing on a stool in front of the stove, stirring a pot. I was the middle child of five, and I was fourteen when my mother died, but I started cooking and cleaning long before that, because she was so sick. She just never came out of the back room after a while. My two older brothers got jobs after school to help out and I sort of took over as mother for everybody. My two sisters were three and five years younger than I, so it was up to me to do almost everything at home. But we managed okay. Daddy worked and shopped. I cooked and cleaned. We did all we could. Money was always scarce, but we made do. Daddy worked awfully hard, frequently holding down two jobs. So he was gone from home much of the time. I think he stayed away partly because he had to, and partly to avoid my mother. We all avoided her as much as we could. She was so difficult.

"My father remarried when I was a senior in high school. Things immediately became easier because his new wife worked too and had a daughter the same age as my youngest sister, who was twelve then. Everything just blended together. Money wasn't such a problem. Dad was much happier. There was enough to go around for really the first time."

I asked, "What were your feelings about your mother's death?"

Melanie set her jaw. "The person who died had not been my mother for many years. She was someone else—someone who slept or screamed and made trouble. I remember her when she was still my mother, but it's vague. I have to go way back to someone who was soft and sweet and used to sing while she worked or played with us. You know, she was Irish and she would sing such melancholy songs. . . . Anyway, I think we were relieved when she finally died. But I felt guilty, too, that maybe if I'd only understood her better or cared more she wouldn't have gotten so sick. I don't think about it if I can help it."

We were nearing my destination, and in the few moments we had left I hoped to help Melanie see at least a glimpse of the origin of her troubles in the present.

"Do you see any similarities between your life as a child and now?" I asked.

She gave an uncomfortable little laugh. "More than ever before, just talking about it now. I see how I'm still waiting—for Sean to come home, just as I waited for my father when he was gone—and I realize how I never blame Sean for what he's doing because I've got his going away all mixed up in my mind with my father going away so that he could take care of us all. I can see how it's not the same thing, and yet I feel the same way about it, as if I should just make the best of it."

She paused, squinting to look harder at the patterns unfolding before her. "Oh, and I'm still the brave little Melanie, holding it all together, stirring the pot on the stove, taking care of the children." Her creamy cheeks flushed pink with the shock of recognition. "So it's true what you said in your lecture about children like I was. We *do* find people with whom we can play the same roles we did when we were growing up!"

As we parted, Melanie hugged me hard and said, "Thanks for listening. I just needed to talk about it a little, I guess. And I do understand better, but I'm not ready to quit—not yet!" Her spirits were obviously lighter as she said, chin up again, "Besides, Sean just needs to grow up. And he will. He's got to, don't you think?"

Without waiting for a reply, she turned and strode through the fallen leaves.

Melanie's insight had, indeed, deepened, but many other similarities between her childhood and her present life still remained outside her awareness.

Why would a bright, attractive, energetic, and capable young woman like Melanie *need* a relationship so fraught with pain and hardship as was hers with Sean? Because for her and other women who have grown up in deeply unhappy homes, where the emotional burdens were too heavy and the responsibilities too great, for these women what feels good and what feels bad have become confused and entangled and finally one and the same.

For instance, in Melanie's home, parental attention was negligible due to the general unmanageability of life as the family tried to cope with the mother's disintegrating personality. Melanie's heroic efforts to manage the household were rewarded with the closest thing to love she was to experience: her father's grateful dependency on her. The feelings of fear and being burdened that would be natural to a child in such circumstances were overshadowed by her sense of competence, which grew out of her father's need for her help and her mother's inadequacy. Heady stuff for a child, to be treated as stronger than one parent and indispensible to the other! This childhood role formed her identity as a savior who could rise above difficulty and chaos, rescuing those around her through her courage, strength, and indomitable will.

This savior complex sounds healthier than it is. While to

have strength in a crisis is laudable, Melanie, like other women of similar backgrounds, *needed* crises in order to function. Without uproar, stress, or a desperate situation to manage, the buried childhood feelings of being emotionally overwhelmed would surface and become too threatening. As a child Melanie was her father's helper, as well as mother to the other children. But she was also a child in need of parenting, and since her mother was too disturbed emotionally and her father too unavailable, her own needs went unmet. The other children had Melanie to fuss over them, worry about them, take care of them. Melanie had no one. Not only was she without a mother, she also had to learn to think and act like an adult. There was no place, no time for expressing her own panic, and soon that very lack of opportunity to take her turn emotionally began to feel right to her. If she pretended hard enough to be a grown-up, she could manage to forget that she was a frightened child. Soon Melanie not only functioned well in chaos, she actually required it to function at all. The burden she shouldered helped her avoid her own panic and pain. It weighed her down and brought her relief at the same time.

Further, the sense of worth she developed resulted from carrying responsibilities that were very nearly beyond her capabilities as a child. She earned approval by working hard, taking care of others, and sacrificing her own wants and needs to theirs. Thus, martyrdom also became part of her personality and combined with her savior complex to make Melanie a virtual magnet for someone who spelled trouble, someone like Sean. It is helpful to very briefly review some important aspects of child development in order to better understand the forces at work in Melanie's life, because, due to the unusual circumstances of her childhood, what would have otherwise been normal feelings and reactions became dangerously exaggerated in Melanie.

For children growing up in a nuclear family, it is natural to entertain strong wishes to be rid of the same-sex parent so as to have the beloved opposite-sex parent all to themselves. Little boys heartily wish that Daddy would disappear so that they could have all of Mommy's love and attention. And little girls dream of replacing their mothers as Daddy's wife. Most parents have received "proposals" from their young children of the opposite sex that express this yearning: A four-year-old boy says to his mother, "When I grow up I'm going to marry you, Mommy." Or a three-year-old girl says to her father, "Daddy, let's you and me have our own house together without Mommy." These very normal yearnings reflect some of the strongest feelings a young child experiences. Yet should something actually happen to the envied rival, resulting in that parent's harm or absence from the family, the effect on the child can be devastating.

When the mother in such a family is emotionally disturbed, severely and chronically ill physically, alcoholic, or drug addicted (or otherwise physically or emotionally absent for whatever reason), then the daughter (usually the oldest daughter, if there are two or more) is almost invariably elected to fill the position left vacant due to the mother's illness or absence. Melanie's story exemplifies the effects of such a "promotion" on a young girl. Due to the presence of debilitating mental illness in her mother, Melanie fell heir to the position of female head of household. During the years when her own identity was forming, she was, in many respects, her father's partner rather than his daughter. As they discussed and managed the problems of the household, they operated as a team. In a sense, Melanie had her father all to herself because she had a relationship with him that was profoundly different from what her siblings had. She was very nearly his peer. She was also, for several years, much stronger and more stable than her sick mother. This meant that Melanie's normal childhood wishes to have her father all to herself were realized, but at the cost of her mother's health and finally her mother's life.

What happens when one's early childhood wishes to be

rid of the same-sex parent and obtain the opposite-sex parent for one's own come true? There are three extremely powerful, character-determining, and unconsciously operating consequences.

The first is guilt.

Melanie felt guilty when she recalled her mother's suicide and her failure to prevent it, the kind of consciously experienced guilt any family member naturally feels in the face of such a tragedy. In Melanie, this conscious guilt was exacerbated by her overdeveloped sense of responsibility for the welfare of all her family members. But in addition to this heavy burden of conscious guilt, she carried another even heavier load.

The realization of her childhood wishes to have her father to herself produced in Melanie an *unconscious* guilt in addition to the conscious guilt she felt for not saving her mentally ill mother from suicide. This in turn generated a drive for atonement, a need to suffer and endure hardship as expiation. This need, combined with Melanie's familiarity with a martyr's role, created in her something close to masochism. There was comfort, if not actual pleasure, in her relationship with Sean, with all its inherent pain, loneliness, and overwhelming responsibility.

The second consequence is unconscious feelings of discomfort at the sexual implications of having the desired parent to oneself. Ordinarily, the presence of the mother (or, in these days of frequent divorce, another companion and sexual partner for the father, such as a stepmother or girlfriend) provides safety for both father and daughter. The daughter is free to develop a sense of herself as attractive and beloved in the eyes of her father, while protected from overt acting out of the sexual impulses inevitably generated between them, by the strength of his bond with an appropriate adult female.

An incestuous relationship did not develop between Melanie and her father, but given their circumstances it certainly could have. The dynamics operating in their family are very frequently present when incestuous relationships develop between fathers and daughters. When a mother, for whatever reason, abdicates her appropriate role as her husband's partner and her child's parent, and causes a daughter to be elevated to that position, she is forcing her daughter not only to take over her responsibilities but also to be at risk of becoming the object of the father's sexual advances. (While this might sound as if all responsibility lies with the mother, in fact it is always the father's *complete* responsibility if incest occurs. This is because, as the adult, it is his duty to protect his child rather than to ever use her for his sexual gratification.)

Further, even if the father never approaches the daughter sexually, the lack of a strong couple bond between the parents and the daughter's assumption of her mother's role in the family serve to heighten feelings of sexual attraction between father and daughter. Because of their close relationship, the daughter may be uncomfortably aware that her father's special interest in her is tinged at some level with sexual overtones. Or the unusual emotional availability of her father may cause the daughter to focus her burgeoning sexual feelings on him more than she would under ordinary circumstances. In an effort to avoid violating, even in thought, the powerful incest taboo, she may numb herself to most or even all of her sexual feelings. The decision to do so is, again, unconscious, a defense against the most threatening impulse of all, sexual attraction for a parent. Because it is unconscious, the decision is not easily examined and reversed.

The result is a young woman who may be uncomfortable with *any* sexual feelings, because of the unconscious taboo violations connected with them. When this happens, nurturing may be the only safe expression of love.

Melanie's primary mode of relating to Sean was to feel responsible for him. This had long since become her way of feeling and expressing love.

When she was seventeen, her father "replaced" Melanie with his new wife, a marriage that she apparently welcomed with relief. That she felt so little bitterness at the loss of her role at home was probably due in large part to the appearance of Sean and his roommates, for whom she performed many of the same functions she had previously performed at home. If that situation had not developed into a marriage between Sean and herself, Melanie might have faced a profound identity crisis at this point. As it was, she immediately became pregnant, thus recreating her caretaking role, while Sean cooperated by beginning, like her father, to be absent much of the time.

She sent him money even when they were separated, competing with his mother to be the woman who took care of him best. (This was a competition she had already won with her own mother, in relationship to her own father.)

When, during her separation from Sean, men appeared in her life who did not require her mothering, who in fact attempted to reverse roles with her by offering her much-needed help, she could not relate emotionally to them. She was only comfortable as the care-giver.

The sexual dynamics of Melanie's relationship with Sean had never provided the powerful bond between them that his need for her caretaking did. In fact, Sean's infidelity simply provided Melanie with another reflection of her childhood experience. Because of her advancing mental illness, Melanie's mother became an increasingly vague, barely visible "other woman" in the back room of the house, emotionally and physically removed from Melanie's life and thoughts. Melanie managed her relationship with her mother by keeping a distance and not thinking about her. Later, when Sean had another love interest, this woman, too, was vague and far away, not perceived as a real threat to what was, like her earlier relationship with her father, a somewhat asexual but practical partnership. Remember, Sean's behavior was not unprecedented. Before they ever married, his established pattern had been to seek other women's company while allowing Melanie to take care of his practical, less romantic needs. Melanie knew this and yet married him.

After marriage, she began a campaign to change him

through the force of her will and her love. Which brings us to the third consequence of Melanie's realization of her childhood wishes and fantasies: her belief in her own omnipotence.

Young children normally believe themselves, their thoughts, and their wishes to be magically powerful, the cause of all significant events in their lives. Ordinarily, however, even though a little girl may passionately wish to be her father's partner for life, reality teaches her that she cannot. Like it or not, she eventually must accept the fact that his partner is her mother. This is a great lesson in her young life—that she cannot always bring about, through the power of her will, that which she wants most. Indeed, this lesson does much to dismantle her belief in her own omnipotence and helps her to come to terms with the limitations of her personal will.

In the case of young Melanie, however, that most powerful wish came true. She did, in many ways, replace her mother. Apparently through the magical powers of her wishes and her will, she won her father for herself. Then, with an undaunted belief in the power of her will to bring about what she desired, she was drawn to other difficult and emotionally charged situations, which she also tried to magically change. The challenges she later uncomplainingly faced, armed with only the weapon of her will—an irresponsible, immature, and unfaithful husband, the burden of raising three children virtually alone, severe money problems, and a demanding academic program coupled with a full-time job—all testified to this.

Sean provided Melanie with a perfect foil for her efforts to change another person through the power of her will, just as he met the other needs fostered by her pseudo-adult role in childhood, in that he gave her ample opportunity to suffer and endure, and to avoid sexuality while exercising her predilection for nurturing.

It should be very clear by now that Melanie was in no way a hapless victim of an unhappy marriage. Quite the opposite. She and Sean met every one of each other's most profound psychological needs. Theirs was a perfect fit. The fact that his mother's timely gifts of money conveniently short-circuited any drive toward growth or maturity in Sean was certainly a problem to this marriage, but not, as Melanie chose to see it, The Problem. What was really wrong was the fact that here were two people whose unhealthy patterns of living and attitudes toward life, though by no means identical, meshed so well that they actually enabled each other to remain unhealthy.

Imagine these two, Sean and Melanie, as dancers in a world in which everyone is a dancer, and grows up learning his or her individual routines. Due to particular events and personalities and, most of all, by learning the dances that were performed with them throughout their childhoods, Sean and Melanie each developed a unique repertoire of psychological steps, movements, and gestures.

Then one day they met and discovered that their dissimilar dances, when performed together, magically synchronized into an exquisite duet, a perfect pas de deux of action and reaction. Each movement made by one was responded to by the other, resulting in choreography that enabled their joined dances to flow, uninterrupted, round and round and round.

Whenever he let go of a responsibility, she quickly picked it up. When she gathered to herself all the familiar burdens of raising their family, he pirouetted away, allowing her plenty of room to do her caretaking. When he searched the stage for other female companionship, she sighed with relief and danced faster to distract herself. While he danced away, exiting off-stage, she performed a perfect waiting step. Round and round and round . . .

For Melanie, it was sometimes an exciting dance, often a lonely one; occasionally, it was embarrassing or exhausting. But the last thing she wanted was to stop the dance she knew so well. The steps, the moves, all felt so right that she was sure the name of the dance was love.

5 • Shall We Dance?

> "HOW DID YOU COME TO MARRY HIM?"
> NOW, HOW COULD YOU TELL SOMEONE
> THAT? HOW HE LOWERED HIS HEAD IN A
> SELF-DEPRECATING WAY AND RAISED HIS
> EYES TO LOOK UP AT YOU COYLY, THE WAY
> A BABY DOES. . . . HOW HE WORMED HIS
> WAY INTO YOUR HEART: SWEET, ADORING,
> PLAYFUL. . . . HE SAID, "YOU'RE SO
> STRONG, HONEY." AND I BELIEVED IT. I
> BELIEVED IT!
> —MARILYN FRENCH, *THE BLEEDING HEART*

HOW DO WOMEN WHO LOVE TOO MUCH *FIND* THE MEN with whom they can continue the unhealthy patterns of relating that they developed in childhood? How, for instance, does the woman whose father was never emotionally present find a man whose attention she continually strives for but cannot win? How does the woman from a violent home manage to team up with a man who batters her? How does the woman raised in an alcoholic home find a man who already has or will soon develop the disease of alcoholism? How does the woman whose mother always depended on her emotionally find a husband who needs her to take care of him?

Out of all the possible partners they encounter, what are the cues that lead these women to the men with whom they can perform the dance they know so well from childhood? And how do they respond (or not respond) when they encounter a man whose behavior is healthier and less needy or immature or abusive than what they are accustomed to, whose dance does not fit so smoothly with theirs?

It is an old cliché in the field of therapy that people often marry someone just like the mother or father with whom they struggled while growing up. This concept is not quite accurate. It is not so much that the mate we choose is just like Mom or Dad, but that *with* this partner we are able to feel the same feelings and face the same challenges that we encountered growing up; we are able to replicate the atmosphere of childhood already so well known to us, and use the same maneuvers in which we are already so practiced. This is what, for most of us, constitutes love. We feel at home, comfortable, exquisitely "right" with the person with whom we can make all our familiar moves and feel all our familiar feelings. *Even if the moves have never worked and the feelings are uncomfortable,* they are what we know best. We feel that special sense of belonging with the man who allows us, as his partner, to dance the steps we already know. It is with him that we decide to try to make a relationship work.

There is no more compelling chemistry than this feeling of mysterious familiarity when a woman and a man come together whose patterns of behavior fit like pieces of a jigsaw puzzle. If, added to this, the man offers the woman an opportunity to grapple with and try to prevail over childhood feelings of pain and helplessness, of being unloved and unwanted, then the attraction becomes for her virtually irresistible. In fact, the more pain from childhood, the more powerful the drive to re-enact and master that pain in adulthood.

Let's look at why this is true. If a young child has experienced a trauma of some kind, it will appear and reappear as a theme in his or her play activities until there is some sense of having finally mastered the experience. A child who undergoes surgery, for example, may re-enact the trip to the hospital using dolls or other toy figures, may make himself the doctor in one such drama and the patient in another, until the fear attached to the event is sufficiently diminished. As women who love too much, we are doing much the same thing: re-enacting and re-experiencing unhappy relationships in an attempt to make them manageable, to master them.

It follows that there really are no coincidences in relationship, no accidents in marriage. When a woman believes that she inexplicably "had to get married" to a certain man, one she would never have deliberately chosen for her husband, for instance, it is imperative that she examine why she chose to be intimate with that particular man, why she ran the risk of pregnancy with him at all. Likewise, when a woman claims that she married on whim, or that she was too young to know what she was doing, or that she wasn't fully herself and could not make a responsible choice, these are also excuses that merit deeper examination.

Actually she did choose, albeit unconsciously, and often with a wealth of knowledge about her future partner even at the outset. To deny this is to deny responsibility for our choices and our lives, and such denial precludes recovery.

But how do we do it? What exactly is the mysterious process, the indefinable chemistry that is sparked between a woman who loves too much and the man to whom she's drawn?

If the question is restated in other ways—What signals flash between a woman who needs to be needed and a man who is looking for someone to take responsibility for him? Or between a woman who is extremely self-sacrificing and a man who is extremely selfish? Or between a woman who defines herself as a victim and a man whose identity is based on power and aggression? Or a woman who needs to control and a man who is inadequate?—the process begins to lose some of its mystery. For there are definite signals, definite cues that are sent out and registered by each of the participants in the dance. Remember, with every woman who loves too much, two factors are operating: (1) the lock-and-key fit of her familiar patterns with his; and (2) the drive to recreate and overcome the painful patterns from the past. Let us take a look at the first hesitant steps of that duet which informs each partner that here is someone with whom it is going to work, to fit, to feel right.

The following stories illustrate clearly the almost subliminal exchange of information that takes place between a woman who loves too much and the man to whom she is attracted, an exchange that instantly sets the stage for the pattern of their relationship, their dance, from then on.

Chloe: twenty-three-year-old college student; daughter of a violent father

I grew up in a really crazy family. I know that now, but when I was young I never thought about it except to hope that no one would ever find out about the way my father hit my mother. He hit all of us, and I guess he sort of convinced us kids that we deserved being beaten. But I knew Mom didn't. I always used to wish he'd hit me instead of her. I knew I could take it, but I wasn't so sure that she could. We all wanted her to leave him, but she wouldn't. She got so little love. I always wanted to give her enough love to make her strong so she could get out, but she never did. She died of cancer five years ago. I haven't been home or spoken to my father since the funeral. I feel that *he* killed her, really, not the cancer. My grandmother on my father's side left each of us kids a trust fund, and that's how I was able to go to college, which is where I met Roy.

We were in an art class together for a whole semester and never spoke to each other. When the second semester began, several of us were together again in another class, and on the first day we all got into this heavy discussion about relationships between men and women. Well, this guy started talking about American women being totally spoiled, wanting to have everything their own way, and how they just used men. He was dripping with venom as he was saying all this, and I thought, *Oh, he's really been hurt. Poor thing.* I asked him, "Do you really think that's true?" and I started trying to prove to him somehow that women weren't all like that—that *I* wasn't like that. Look at how I set myself up! Later on in our relationship, I would not be able to make any demands or take care of myself in any way, or I'd be proving him right in his misogyny. And all my concern that morning in class worked. He was hooked too. He said, "I'll be back. I wasn't going to stick with this class, but I want to talk to you some more!" I remember that right then there was this terrific rush, because already I felt I was making a difference to him.

In less than two months, we were living together. In four months, I was paying the rent and almost every other bill, plus buying the groceries. But I kept trying, for two more years, to prove to him how nice I was, how I wasn't going to hurt him the way he'd already been hurt. *I* got hurt quite a bit in the process, at first just emotionally, then physically too. No one could be as angry as he was at women and not want to push one of them around. Of course, I was sure that was my fault too. It's a miracle I got out. I met a former girlfriend of his and she asked me, right out, "Does he ever hit you?" I said, "Well, not really." I was protecting him, of course, and I didn't want to look like a total fool, either. But I knew she knew because she'd been there too. At first I panicked. It was the same feeling I had as a kid—not wanting anyone to see behind the facade. Everything in me wanted to lie, to act like she had a lot of nerve, asking such a question. But she looked at me with so much understanding that it didn't make sense to go on pretending.

We talked a long time. She told me about a therapy group she was in where all the women were alike in that they were all drawn to unhealthy relationships, and they were working on learning not to do that to themselves.

She gave me her phone number, and after I'd gone through two more months of hell I called her. She got me to go with her to the group and I think it probably saved my life. Those women were just like me. They had learned to put up with incredible amounts of pain, usually starting in childhood.

Anyway, it took me a few more months to leave him, and even with the group's support it was still very hard to do. I had this incredible need to prove to him that he was lovable. I thought that if I could just love him enough he'd change. Thank God I got over that, or I'd be back there again.

Chloe's attraction to Roy

When Chloe, the art student, met Roy, the misogynist, it was as though she was meeting the synthesis of her mother and her father. Roy was angry and hated women. To win his love was to win that of her father, who was also angry and destructive. To change him through her love was to change her mother and save her. She saw Roy as a victim of his sick feelings and wanted to love him into becoming well. She also, like every woman who loves too much, wanted to *win* in her struggle with him and with the important people he symbolized for her, her mother and father. That is what made letting go of this destructive and unfilling relationship so difficult.

Mary Jane: married for thirty years to a workaholic

We met at a Christmas party. I was there with his younger brother who was my age and really liked me. Anyway, there was Peter. He was smoking a pipe and wearing a tweed jacket with patches on the elbows, and he looked so Ivy League. I was terribly impressed. But there was also an air of melancholy about him and really that was as attractive to me as his looks. I was sure he'd been deeply hurt at some time and I wanted to get to know him, to know what had happened, and to "understand." I was sure he was unattainable, but I thought if I could be especially compassionate, perhaps I could keep him talking to me. It was funny, because we did talk rather a lot that first evening, but he never quite squared off with me, face to face. He was always at an angle, slightly preoccupied with something else, and I kept trying to win his complete attention. What happened was that every word he spoke to me became vitally important, almost precious, because I was sure he had better things to do.

It had been just like that with my father. When I was growing up he was never there—literally. We were quite poor. He and my mother both worked in town and left us kids at home alone much of the time. Even on weekends he did odd jobs. The only time I saw Dad was when he was home fixing something—the refrigerator or the radio or something. I remember it always felt like he had his back to me, but I didn't mind because it was just so wonderful to have him around. I used to hang around and ask him lots of questions to try and get him to pay attention to me.

Well, here I was, doing the same thing with Peter, though of course I didn't see it that way then. I remember now how I kept trying to be in his direct line of vision and how he kept sort of puffing away at this pipe, looking off to the side or up at the ceiling, or fiddling with keeping the pipe lit. I thought he was so very mature, with his furrowed brow and faraway look. I was drawn like a magnet.

Mary Jane's attraction to Peter

Mary Jane's feelings about her father were not nearly as ambivalent as those of many women who love too much. She loved her father, admired him, and yearned for his company and attention. Peter, being older and preoccupied, instantly replicated for Mary Jane her elusive father, and winning his attention became all the more important because, like with her father, his was so difficult to capture. Men who willingly listened to her, who were more emotionally present and more affectionate, failed to arouse in Mary Jane the deep yearning to be loved she had felt with her father. Peter's preoccupation offered a familiar challenge to Mary Jane, another chance to win the love of a man who avoided her.

Peggy: raised by a hypercritical grandmother and an emotionally unsupportive mother; now a divorced single parent with two daughters

I never knew my father. He and my mother separated before I was born, and my mother went to work to support us while her mother took care of us at home. Now that doesn't sound too bad, but it was. My grandmother was a terribly cruel woman. She didn't beat my sister and me as much as she hurt us with words, every day. She would tell us how bad we were, how much trouble we caused her, how we were "good for nothing"—that was one of her favorite phrases. The irony was that all of her criticisms just made my sister and me try harder to be good, to be worthwhile. My mother never protected us from her, either. Mother was too afraid Grandma would leave, and that she wouldn't be able to go to work because there would be no one to take care of us. So she just looked the other way when Grandma abused us. I grew up feeling so alone, so unprotected and afraid and worthless, all the while trying to make up for being a burden. I remember I used to try to fix things that broke around the house, wanting to save us money and earn my keep somehow.

I grew up and married at eighteen because I was pregnant. I was miserable from the start. He criticized me all the time. Subtly at first, then more savagely. Actually, I knew I wasn't in love with him and married him anyway. I didn't think I had any other choice. It was a fifteen-year marriage, because it took me that long to believe that being miserable was a good enough reason to get a divorce.

I came out of that marriage desperate for someone to love me but feeling that I was worthless and a failure and sure that I had nothing to offer a good, kind man.

The night I met Baird, it was absolutely the first time I had ever gone out dancing without a date. My girlfriend and I had been shopping. She bought a whole outfit— pants, top, new shoes—and wanted to put them on and go out. So we went to this disco place we'd both heard of. Some businessmen from out of town were buying us drinks and dancing with us and that was okay—friendly, but not very exciting. Then I saw this fellow over next to the wall. He was very tall, very slim, dressed incredibly well, and very good looking. But he also had an air of coldness about him. I remember telling myself, *That is the most elegant, arrogant man I've ever seen.* And then, *I'll bet I could warm him up!*

Incidentally, I can still remember the moment when I met my first husband. We were in high school and he was lounging against the wall when he should have been in class, and I said to myself then, *He looks pretty wild. I'll bet I could settle him down.* See, I was always trying to fix things. Anyway, I went up to Baird and asked him to dance. He was very surprised and I guess a little flattered. We danced awhile and then he said he and his friends were leaving to go to another place. Would I like to go? Though I was tempted, I said no, I was there to dance and that was really all I wanted to do. I kept dancing with the businessmen and after a while he asked me to dance again. So we did. It was incredibly crowded in there. People were just packed in. A little later, my girlfriend and I were leaving and he was sitting with some other people at a table in a corner. He beckoned me over and I went. He said to me, "You have my phone number on your person." I didn't know what he was talking about. He reached over and pulled his card out of the pocket of the pullover I was wearing. It was one of those shirts with a pouch pocket in front and he'd put his card in there when we were coming off the dance floor the second time. I was amazed. I hadn't even known he'd done that. And I was so thrilled to think that this handsome man had taken all that trouble. Anyway, I gave him my card too.

He called me a few days later and we went to lunch. He gave me this terribly disapproving look when I drove up to meet him. My car was kind of old and I immediately felt inadequate—and then relieved that he would have lunch with me anyway. He was very stiff and cold and I took it on myself to put him at ease, as though it was my fault somehow. His parents were coming to town to visit him and he didn't get along with them. He recited a long list of grievances against them, which didn't sound all that serious to me, but I tried to listen compassionately. I left that lunch thinking that here was someone with whom I had nothing in common. I had not had a pleasant time. I had felt uncomfortable and sort of off-balance. When he called two days later and asked me out again, I somehow felt relieved, as though if *he* had had a good enough time to ask me out again, then everything was all right.

We never did have a really good time together. Something was always wrong and I kept trying to make it right. I felt very tense with him and the only good times were when the tension lessened somewhat. That bit of relief from tension passed for happiness. But somehow I was still powerfully attracted to him.

I know it sounds crazy, but I actually married this man without ever liking him. He broke off the relationship several times before we married, saying he just couldn't be himself with me. I cannot tell you how devastating that was. I would beg him to tell me what I needed to do to make him more comfortable. He'd just say, "You know what you need to do." But I didn't. I nearly went crazy, trying to figure it out. Anyway, the marriage lasted only two months. He left for good after telling me how unhappy I made him, and I've never seen him again, except once in a while on the street. He always pretends he doesn't know me.

I don't know how to convey how obsessed I was with him. Each time he left me I felt more drawn to him, not less. And when he came back he would say that he wanted what I had to offer him. There was no rush on earth like that for me. I would hold him in my arms and he would cry and say what a fool he'd been. That kind of scene lasted only one night and then things would start to disintegrate again, with me trying terribly hard to make him happy, so he wouldn't leave again.

By the time he walked out of the marriage, I was hardly functioning. I was unable to work, or to do much at all except sit and rock back and forth and cry. It felt like I was dying. I had to get help in order not to contact him again, because I wanted so badly to make it turn out right, but I knew I couldn't survive another ride on that merry-go-round.

Peggy's attraction to Baird

Peggy knew nothing about being loved, and having grown up without a father, knew virtually nothing about men, either, certainly not kind, loving men. But she knew a great deal, from her childhood with her grandmother, about being rejected and criticized by someone very unhealthy. She also knew how to try as hard as she could to win love from a mother who could not, for her own reasons, give love or even protection. Her first marriage happened because she allowed herself to be intimate with a young man whom she experienced as critical and condemning of her, and for whom she felt little affection. Sex with him was more a struggle to win his acceptance than an expression of her caring for him. A fifteen-year marriage to this man left her even more convinced of her inherent unworthiness.

So strong was her need to replicate the hostile environment of her childhood and continue her struggle to win love from those who could not give it that when she met a man who struck her as being cold, aloof, and indifferent, she was instantly attracted to him. Here was another opportunity to change an unloving person into someone who would finally love her. Once they became involved with each other, his infrequent hints that she was making some headway in teaching him to love her enabled her to keep trying in spite of the devastation to her own life. Her need to change him (and her mother and grandmother, whom he represented) was that strong.

Eleanor: sixty-five; raised by an overly possessive, divorced mother

My mother couldn't get along with any man. She divorced twice in an era when nobody divorced even once. I had one sister, ten years older than I, and my mother said to me more than once, "Your sister was your father's girl so I decided to have one for me." That's exactly what I was to her, a possession and an extension of herself. She didn't believe we were separate people.

I missed my father so much after they divorced. She wouldn't let him near me, and he didn't have the will to fight her. Nobody did. I always felt like a captive, and yet responsible for her happiness at the same time. It was very hard for me to leave her, even though I felt like I was suffocating. I went to business college in a distant town, where I stayed with relatives of ours. My mother was so angry she never spoke to them again.

After school ended, I was working as a secretary in the police department of a large city. One day this good-looking officer in uniform came in and asked me where the drinking fountain was. I pointed it out to him. Next he asked me if there were any cups. I let him borrow my coffee cup. He needed to take a couple of aspirin. I can still see him throwing his head back to swallow those tablets. Then he said, "Whew! I really tied one on last night." Right then I said to myself, "Oh, how sad. He's drinking too much, probably because he's lonely." He was just what I wanted—someone to take care of, someone who needed me. I thought, "I sure would like to try and make him happy." We married two months later and I spent the next four years trying. I used to cook these wonderful meals, hoping to lure him home, but he'd go drinking and wouldn't return until it was very late. Then we'd fight and I'd cry. The next time he stayed out late I'd blame myself for getting upset the last time, and tell myself, *No wonder he doesn't come home.* It got worse and worse until finally I left him. All that was thirty-seven years ago, and just this last year I realized he was an alcoholic. I'd always thought it was all my fault, that I just couldn't make him happy.

Eleanor's attraction to her husband

If you've been taught that men are no good by a mother who hates men, and on the other hand you loved your lost father and find men attractive, you're very likely to grow up fearing that the man you love will leave you. You might therefore try to find a man who needs your help and understanding so that you can have the upper hand in the relationship. This is what Eleanor did when she found herself drawn to the handsome policeman. Although this formula is supposed to protect you from getting hurt and getting left by assuring that your man is dependent upon you, the trouble with it is, you must begin with a man who has a problem. In other words, a man who is already on his way to fitting the "men are no good" category. Eleanor wanted to guarantee that her man would not leave her (as her father had, and as her mother said any man would), and his neediness seemed to provide that guarantee. But the nature of his problem rendered him *more* likely to leave, not less.

Thus, the situation that was supposed to assure Eleanor that she would not be abandoned instead virtually guaranteed that she would. Every night that he did not come home "proved" her mother had been right about men, and finally she, like her mother, obtained a divorce from a "no-good" man.

Arleen: twenty-seven; from a violent family in which she tried to protect her mother and siblings

We were in an acting company together, performing at a dinner theatre. Ellis was seven years younger than I, and not very physically attractive to me. I wasn't particularly interested in him, but one day we did some shopping together and went to dinner afterward. As we talked, all I could hear was that his life was just so messy. There were all these things he wasn't taking care of, and when he talked about them I got this terrific urge to get in there and set it all straight. He mentioned to me that first evening that he was bisexual. Though that didn't fit in with my value system, I turned it into a joke and said I was, too—that when someone got sexual with me I said, "Bye." Actually, I was really afraid of men who came on too strong. My former husband had been abusive to me, and so had another boyfriend. Ellis seemed safe to me. I was as sure that he couldn't hurt me as I was that I could help him. Well, we got heavily involved not long after that. In fact, we lived together for several months before I called it quits, and the whole time I was tense and afraid. Here I thought I was doing him such a favor, and yet I was a wreck. My ego took a beating, too. His attraction to men was always much stronger than his attraction to me. In fact, the night I was hospitalized, deathly ill with viral pneumonia, he didn't visit me because he was involved with a man. Three weeks after I got out of the hospital I ended my relationship with him, but it took an enormous amount of support. My sister, my mother, and my therapist all helped me through it. I became terribly, terribly depressed. I really didn't want to let go. I still felt he needed me and I was sure that with a little more effort on my part, we could make it together.

When I was a kid, I had always felt that way, too, that any minute I'd figure out how to fix it all.

There were five of us kids. I was the oldest, and my mother leaned on me a lot. She had to keep our father happy, which was impossible. He's still the meanest man I know. They finally divorced about ten years ago. I guess they thought they were doing us a favor, waiting until we had left home, but it was miserable growing up in that family. My father hit us all, even my mother, but he was the worst with my sister in terms of violence, and with my brother in terms of verbal abuse. He crippled each of us in one way or another. All I ever felt was that there must be something I could do to make everything better, but I never quite figured out what that would be. I tried talking to my mother, but she was so passive. Then I'd stand up to my dad, but not very much because that was too dangerous. I used to sort of coach my sister and brother on how not to get in Dad's way, not to talk back. We would even come home from school and go through the house just to figure out what might upset him, in order to fix it before he got home in the evening. We were all so scared and unhappy so much of the time.

Arleen's attraction to Ellis

Because she saw herself as stronger, more mature, and more practical than Ellis, Arleen hoped to have the upper hand in her relationship with him and thereby avoid being hurt. This was an important factor in his appeal for her, because she had a history of being physically and emotionally abused starting in childhood. Her fear and rage toward her father made Ellis, in contrast, appear to be the perfect answer to her problems with men, because it seemed unlikely that he would ever respond so strongly toward her as to become violent. Unfortunately, in the few months they were together, she experienced as much hurt and heartache as she had with the heterosexual men she had known.

The challenge of trying to literally and figuratively straighten out the life of a man who was basically gay was commensurate with the level of struggle Arleen knew so well from childhood. The emotional pain inherent in this relationship was familiar too—always waiting for the other shoe to drop, to be hurt or shocked or offended by someone who was supposedly on her side, who supposedly cared for her. Arleen's conviction that she could coerce Ellis into becoming what she needed him to be made it difficult for her to finally let go.

Suzannah: twenty-six; divorced from two alcoholics; daughter of an emotionally dependent mother

I was in San Francisco attending a three-day training seminar to prepare me to pass my state boards for my license as a social worker. At the afternoon break of the second day, I spotted this very handsome man, and when he passed by I flashed him my sunniest smile. Then I went off to sit outside and relax. He came up to me and asked me if I was going up to the cafeteria. I said sure, I could go, and when we got there he said a little hesitantly, "Can I buy you something?" I had the feeling he couldn't really afford it so I said, "Oh, no. That's okay." So I bought myself some juice and we went back and talked for the rest of the break. We told each other where we were from and where we worked and he said, "I'd like to have dinner with you tonight." We made arrangements to meet at Fisherman's Wharf, and when I met him there that evening he looked troubled. He said he was trying to decide whether to be romantic or practical, because he had only enough money with him to either take me on a cruise of the bay or to dinner. Of course I jumped right in and said, "Let's go on the cruise and I'll take you to dinner." So we did, and I felt strong and clever because

I'd made it possible for him to do both things he wanted to do.

It was very beautiful out in the bay. The sun was setting, and we talked the whole time. He told me how afraid he was to be close to someone, that he was in a relationship now that had gone on for years, but he knew it wasn't right for him. He just stayed because he was so fond of the woman's six-year-old son and couldn't bear to think of the boy growing up without a male figure in his life. He also hinted pretty broadly that he was having sexual difficulties with this woman, because he wasn't all that attracted to her.

Well, all my wheels were turning. I was thinking, *This is a wonderful man who just hasn't met the right woman yet. Obviously he's tremendously compassionate and honest.* It didn't matter that he was thirty-seven years old and had probably had plenty of chances to develop a good relationship. That maybe, just maybe, something was wrong with *him.*

Here he'd given me a virtual shopping list of his flaws: impotence, fear of intimacy, and financial problems. And it didn't take much intelligence to figure out that he was pretty passive, too, from the way he operated. But I was too enchanted with the idea that I could be the one to make a difference in his life to be warned off by what he was saying.

We went to dinner and I paid, of course. He protested, saying how much it bothered him, and I just twinkled at him that he could come visit me and take me out to dinner to pay me back. He thought that was a great idea, wanted to know all about where I lived, where he could stay if he came down, what the job opportunities were in my town. He had been a schoolteacher fifteen years before, and after many job changes—each, he admitted, for less money and less prestige—was now working in an out-patient counseling clinic for alcoholics. Well, that was perfect. I'd been involved with alcoholics before and had been torn up in the process, but here was someone safe, someone who couldn't possibly be alcoholic because he counseled them, right? He did mention that our waitress, an older woman with a gravelly voice, reminded him of his mother, who was an alcoholic, and I knew how frequently children of alcoholics develop the disease of alcoholism themselves. But he never drank the whole evening, just kept ordering Perrier. I was practically purring, thinking, *This is the man for me.* Never mind all those job changes and the fact that his career picture in general had been going downhill. That had to be due simply to bad luck. He seemed to have a lot of bad luck and that made him more appealing. I felt sorry for him.

He spent quite a lot of time telling me how attracted he was to me, how comfortable it felt to be with me, how well matched we were. I was feeling exactly the same way. We parted ways that night with him acting the perfect gentleman and *my* kissing *him* goodnight very warmly. I felt so safe; here was a man who wasn't going to push at me to be sexual, who just wanted to be with me because he enjoyed my company. I didn't take this as a sign that perhaps he really did have sexual problems and was therefore trying to avoid the whole thing. I guess I was sure that, given the chance, I could solve any little difficulties he had.

The seminar ended the next day, and afterward we talked about when he could visit me. He suggested he come the week before his exams and stay at my apartment, but he wanted to just study while he was there. I had a few days of vacation coming up and thought it would be great to take it during that time, so we could sight-see together. No, his exams were too important. Pretty soon I was disregarding everything I would want to do, as I tried to make it all perfect for him. I was also more and more afraid he wouldn't come down, even though having someone staying in my apartment studying while I went to work every day didn't sound like a lot of fun. But I had this need to make it right, and already felt guilty if he wasn't happy. And there was this terrific challenge to keep him interested. He had started off so attracted to me that now, if he cooled off, it would feel like I had blown it, so I was standing on my head trying to keep him involved.

Well, we parted ways with things still unsettled, even after I had come up with plan after plan, trying to solve all the problems involved in his coming down. I felt depressed after we said goodbye and I didn't know why, just kind of bad that I hadn't been able to fix it all and make him happy.

He called me the next afternoon, which made me feel wonderful. I felt redeemed.

The following night he called me at 10:30 and began to ask me what he should do about his present girlfriend. I didn't have the answers on that one and told him so. My discomfort was really increasing now. I felt set up somehow, and for once didn't follow an old pattern of mine to jump in and try to fix it. He began to yell at me over the phone and then hung up on me. I was stunned. I began to think, *Maybe this is my fault; I wasn't helpful enough.* And I had this terrific urge to call him back and apologize for making him so angry. But remember, I had been involved with several alcoholics, and because of this I was going regularly to Al-Anon meetings; somehow that program kept me from calling him and accepting all the blame. Well, in a few minutes he called back and apologized for hanging up. Then he asked me all the same questions, which I still couldn't answer. He yelled some more and hung up on me again. This time I realized he had been drinking, but I still had the same urge to call him back and try to make everything all right. If I had taken responsibility for him on the phone that night, we might be together right now, and I shudder to think what that would be like. A few days later I received this very civil note saying he wasn't ready for another relationship at this time—no mention of the yelling or hanging up on me. That was the end.

A year earlier, it would have been just the beginning. He was the kind of man I had always found irresistable: handsome, charming, a little needy, not quite living up to his potential. In Al-Anon, when someone mentions how she was attracted not to what a man was, but to his potential, we all have a great laugh together, because we've all done it—been drawn to someone because we were sure he needed our help and encouragement to maximize his gifts. I knew all about trying to help, to please, to do all the work and take all the responsibility for a relationship. I'd done it as a child with my mother, and then with each of my husbands. My mother and I had never gotten along well. She had lots of men in and out of her life, and when there was someone new she didn't want to be bothered with having to take care of me, so I was trotted off to boarding school. But whenever one of them left her, then she wanted me around to listen while she cried and complained. When we were together it was my job to comfort and soothe her, but I could never do it well enough to take away her pain and she'd get angry at me for not really caring. Then another man would come along and she'd forget all about me again. Of course I grew up making a career of trying to help people. That was the only time I felt important or worthwhile as a child, and I had developed a need to become better and better at it. So it was a great victory for me to finally overcome the urge to pursue a man who had nothing to offer me other than the opportunity to help him.

Suzannah's attraction to the man in San Francisco

A career in social work was nearly as inevitable for Suzannah as her attraction to men who appeared to need her comforting and encouragement. The first hint she had about this new man was that money was a problem for him. When she took his cue and paid for her own juice, they each exchanged vital information: he let her know that he was a little needy, and she responded by paying her own way and protecting his feelings. This theme, that he was lacking and she had enough for both of them, was repeated when they met for their date and she paid for their dinner. Problems with money, problems with sex, problems with intimacy—the very cues that should have been warnings for Suzannah, given her history of involvement with needy, dependent men, were instead the signals that attracted her, because they stirred her nurturing, caretaking behavior. It was very difficult to ignore what was for her a powerful "hook"—a man who was not quite okay as he was but who, it seemed, with her help and attention, could become something special. Suzannah was not able, at first, to ask, "What's in this for me?" but because she was in the process of recovery, she was finally able to assess what was happening in a realistic light. For the first time, she paid attention to what *she* was getting out of the relationship, rather than totally focusing on how she could help this man in need.

It is obvious that each of the women we have talked about found a man who presented her with the kind of challenge she had already known, and who was therefore someone with whom she could feel comfortable and fully herself, but it is important to understand that none of these women *recognized* what was attracting her. If that understanding had been there, there would also have been a more conscious choice about whether to enter such a challenging situation. Many times we believe we are attracted by qualities that appear to be the *opposite* of those our parents possessed. Arleen, for instance, finding herself drawn to a bisexual man much younger than herself, of slight build, and anything but physically aggressive toward her, consciously felt she would be safe with a man unlikely to repeat her father's pattern of violence. But the less conscious struggle to change him into what he was not, to prevail in a situation that from the beginning was obviously not going to meet her needs for love and security—that was the inviting element in developing a relationship with him, and that was what made it so difficult for her to let go of him and the challenge he represented.

Even more convoluted, but just as common, is what happened between Chloe, the art student, and her violent misogynist. Every clue about who he was and how he felt was present in their first conversation, but her need to take on the challenge he represented was so great that instead of seeing him as dangerously angry and aggressive, she perceived him as a helpless victim, needing understanding. I would venture to guess that not every woman meeting this man would see him thus. Most would give him and his attitudes wide berth, but Chloe distorted what she saw, so strong was her drive to engage with this man and all he represented.

Once begun, why is it so difficult to stop these relationships, to let go of the partner who is dragging you through all the painful steps of this destructive dance? A rule of thumb is, The more difficult it is to end a relationship that is bad for you, the more elements of the childhood struggle it contains. When you are loving too much, it is because you are trying to overcome the old fears, anger, frustration, and pain from childhood, and to quit is to surrender a precious opportunity for finding relief and rectifying the ways you have been wronged.

While these are the unconscious psychological underpinnings that make explicable your drive to be with him in spite of the pain, they do little justice to the intensity of your conscious experience.

It would be difficult to overstate the sheer emotional charge that this kind of relationship, once begun, carries for the woman involved. When she tries to cut herself off from relating to the man she loves too much, she feels as though thousands of volts of painful energy are rushing through her nerves and spilling out their severed ends. The old emptiness surges and swirls around her, pulling her down into the place where her childhood terror of being alone still lives, and she is sure she will drown in the pain.

This kind of charge—the sparks, the chemistry, the drive to be with that other person and to make it work—are not present to the same degree in healthier, more satisfying relationships, because they do not embody all the possibilities for settling old accounts and for prevailing over what was once overwhelming. It is this thrilling possibility of righting old wrongs, winning lost love, and gaining withheld approval that, for women who love too much, is the unconscious chemistry behind falling in love.

This is also why, when men come into our lives who are interested in our well-being and in our happiness and fulfillment, and who present the genuine possibility of a healthy relationship, we usually are not interested. And make no mistake: these kinds of men do come into our lives. Each of my clients who has loved too much has been able to recall at least one, often several, men whom she has described wistfully as "really nice . . . so kind . . . actually cared about me. . . ." Then usually comes the ironic smile and the question, "Now why didn't I stick with *him?*" Often she is able, in the next breath, to answer her own query. "Somehow I could never get that excited about him. I guess he was too nice, huh?"

A better answer would be that his actions and our reactions, his moves and our countermoves, didn't mesh into a perfect duet. Although being in his company might be pleasant, soothing, interesting, and affirming, it is difficult for us to regard this kind of relationship as important and worth developing on a more serious level. Instead, such a man has usually been either quickly dropped or ignored, or at best relegated to the "just a friend" category, because he failed to arouse in us the heart pounding and stomach knotting we have come to call love.

Sometimes these men remain in the "friend" category for many years, meeting with us now and then for a drink and drying our tears as we report the latest betrayal, breakup, or humiliation in our current relationship. This sympathetic, understanding kind of man simply cannot offer us the drama, the pain, or the tension that feel so exhilarating and right. This is because, for us, what should feel bad has come to feel good, and what should feel good has come to feel foreign, suspect, and uncomfortable. We have learned, by long and close association, to prefer the pain. A more healthy, loving man cannot play an important part in our life until we learn to let go of the need to relive the old struggle again and again.

A woman with a healthier background has responses and thus relationships that are very different, because struggling and suffering are not so familiar, not so much a part of her history, and therefore not so comfortable. If being with a man causes her to become uncomfortable, hurt, worried, disappointed, angry, jealous, or otherwise emotionally upset, she will experience that as disagreeable and aversive—something to be avoided rather than pursued. On the other hand, she *will* pursue a relationship that offers her caring, comfort, and companionship because it feels good to her. It would be safe to say that the attraction between two people who have the capability of creating a rewarding relationship based on the exchange of healthy responses, while perhaps strong and exciting, is never as *compelling* as the attraction between a woman who loves too much and the man with whom she can "dance."

6 • Men Who Choose Women Who Love Too Much

> SHE'S THE ROCK THAT I LEAN ON,
> SHE'S THE SUNSHINE OF MY DAY,
> AND I DON'T CARE WHAT YOU SAY
>   ABOUT HER
> LORD, SHE TOOK ME IN AND MADE ME
>   EVERYTHING I AM TODAY.
>
> SHE'S MY ROCK

HOW DOES IT WORK FOR THE MAN INVOLVED? WHAT IS HIS experience of the chemistry that occurs in the first few moments of meeting a woman who loves too much? And what happens to his feelings as the relationship continues, especially if he begins to change and becomes either healthier or sicker?

Some of the men whose interviews follow have gained an unusual degree of self-knowledge, as well as a considerable insight into the patterns of their relationships with the women who have been their partners. Several of these men who are recovering from addictions have the benefit of years of therapeutic involvement in Alcoholics Anonymous or Narcotics Anonymous, and are thus able to identify the appeal the co-alcoholic woman held for them as they sank into or were already caught in the web of addiction. Others who have not had problems with addiction have nevertheless had involvement with more traditional kinds of therapy, which helped them understand themselves and their relationships better.

Though the details differ from story to story, always present is the appeal of the strong woman who somehow promises to make up for what each man is lacking in himself or his life.

Tom: forty-eight; sober for twelve years; father died of alcoholism, as did an older brother

I remember the night I met Elaine. It was at a dance at the country club. We were both in our early twenties, and both with dates. My drinking was already a problem. I'd had one arrest for drunken driving at twenty and two years later a serious car accident, which happened because I'd had too much to drink. But of course I didn't think alcohol was doing me any harm at all. I was just a young man on the way up who knew how to have a good time.

Elaine was with an acquaintance of mine, who introduced us. She was very attractive and I was happy when we did that "changing partners for one dance" kind of thing. Naturally, I'd been drinking that night, so I felt a little bold; since I wanted to impress her while we were dancing, I tried some steps that were pretty fancy. I was trying so hard to be suave that I literally ran into another couple and knocked the wind right out of the woman. I was really embarrassed and couldn't say much except to sort of mumble that I was sorry, but Elaine never missed a beat. She took the woman by the arm, apologized to her and her partner, and walked them to their seats. She was so sweet that the husband was probably glad the whole thing happened. Then she came back, very concerned about me, too. Another woman might have been angry and never spoken to me again. Well, I wasn't about to let her get away, after that.

Her father and I always got along great, until he died. Of course, he was an alcoholic too. And my mother loved Elaine. She kept telling her that I needed someone like her to look after me.

For a long time Elaine kept covering up for me the way she had that first night. When she finally got help for herself and stopped making it easy for me to continue drinking, I told her she didn't love me anymore and ran off with my twenty-two-year-old secretary. After that I went downhill fast. It was six months later that I attended my first A.A. meeting, and I've been sober ever since.

Elaine and I got back together after I'd been sober a year. It was real hard, but there was still a great deal of love there. We're not the same people who married twenty years ago, but we both like ourselves and each other better than we did then, and we work on being honest with each other every day.

Tom's attraction to Elaine

What happened between Tom and Elaine is typical of what happens between an alcoholic and a co-alcoholic on first meeting. He gets in trouble and she, rather than being offended, figures out how to help him, how to cover things over and make him and everyone else comfortable. She provides a feeling of safety, which for him has powerful appeal since his life is becoming unmanageable.

When Elaine joined Al-Anon and learned to stop actually helping Tom stay sick by covering up for him, he did what many addicts do when their partners begin to recover. He retaliated as dramatically as he could, and since for every male alcoholic there are plenty of female co-alcoholics looking for someone to save, he quickly found Elaine's replacement, another woman who was willing to continue the kind of rescuing and enabling that Elaine now refused to do for him. He also got so much sicker that his choices narrowed down to two: to begin to recover or to die. Only when his alternatives were that bleak did he become willing to change.

The relationship is currently intact, owing to both these people's involvement in the Anonymous programs, A.A. for Tom, Al-Anon for Elaine. There they are learning, for the first time in their lives, to relate to each other in a healthy, nonmanipulative way.

Charles: sixty-five; retired civil engineer with two children; divorced, remarried, and now widowed

Helen has been dead for two years now, and I'm finally beginning to sort it all out. I never thought I'd see a therapist, not at my age. But after her death I was so angry it scared me. I couldn't stop feeling I wanted to hurt her. I had dreams about hitting her and I'd wake up yelling at her. I thought I was going crazy. Finally I got the nerve to tell my doctor. He's as old and conservative as I am, so when he told me I'd better get some counseling I swallowed my pride and did it. I contacted the Hospice people in town and they put me in touch with a therapist who specializes in helping people get through grief. Well, we worked on my grief and it still kept coming up as anger, so finally I started accepting that I was mad as hell and began with the help of the therapist to look at why.

Helen was my second wife. My first wife, Janet, still lives here in town with her new husband. I guess *new* is a funny word to use. All this happened twenty-five years ago. I met Helen when I was a civil engineer for the county. She was a secretary in the planning department and I used to see her at work sometimes and maybe once or twice a week at lunchtime in a little coffee shop downtown. She was a very pretty woman, always beautifully dressed, and a little shy but friendly, too. I could tell she liked me just by the way she looked at me and smiled. I guess I was a little flattered that she noticed me. I knew she was divorced with two kids, and I felt kind of sorry for her, having to raise them all alone. Anyway, one day I offered to buy her coffee and we had a nice little talk. I made it clear I was married, but I guess I griped a little bit too much about some of the frustrations of married life. I still don't know how she managed to convey the message that day that I was too wonderful a man to ever be unhappy, but I left that coffee shop feeling ten feet tall and wanting to see her again, wanting to feel the way she had made me feel: *appreciated*. Maybe it was because she didn't have a man in her life and she missed that, but I sure felt big and strong and special after our little talk.

Still, I had no intention of getting involved. I'd never done anything like that before. I'd come out of the army after the war and settled down with the wife I'd left waiting for me. Janet and I weren't the happiest couple, but we weren't the unhappiest either. I never thought I'd run around on her.

Helen had been married twice before and had suffered a lot in each marriage. Both men had walked out on her and she'd had a child by each. Now she was raising her children alone, without any support.

The worst thing we could have done was get involved with each other. I felt so sorry for her, but I knew that I had nothing to offer her. In those days you couldn't get a divorce just because you wanted one, and I certainly didn't make enough money to lose everything I had and then start over with another family to support in addition to my own. Besides, I really didn't want a divorce. I wasn't crazy about my wife anymore, but I loved my kids and I liked what we all had together. All that began to change, though, as Helen and I continued to see each other. Neither of us could quit. Helen was lonely and said she'd rather have a little bit of me than nothing, and I knew she meant it. Once I had begun with Helen, there was no way out without hurting someone terribly. Pretty soon I felt like the worst kind of heel. Both these women were counting on me and I was letting both of them down.

Helen was mad about me. She'd do anything to see me. When I tried to break it off I'd see her at work and her sweet, sad face would just break my heart. Well, after a year or so Janet found out about us and told me to stop seeing Helen or leave. I tried to stop but couldn't stick to it. Besides, everything between Janet and me was so different now. There seemed to be less reason than ever to let go of Helen.

It's a long story. Helen and I had a nine-year affair, while my wife tried very hard first to keep me in the marriage, and then to punish me for leaving her. Helen and I lived together on and off several times during those years until Janet finally got tired and agreed to a divorce.

I still hate to think about what it did to all of us. In those days, people did not just live together. I think I really lost all my pride during those years. I was ashamed for myself, for my kids, for Helen and her kids, even for Janet, who had never done anything to deserve all this.

Finally, after Janet quit fighting it and the divorce was final, Helen and I got married. But something was different between us as soon as the divorce was in the works. All those years, Helen had been warm and loving and seductive—very seductive. Of course I loved it. All that loving was what kept me with her in spite of the pain to my kids, my wife, her, and her kids—all of us. She made me feel like the most desirable man in the world. Of course, we had fought before we got married, because the tension was terrible, but our fights always ended with lovemaking and I felt more wanted and needed and cared for than I ever had in my life. Somehow, what Helen and I had together seemed so special, so right, that the price we were paying almost seemed worth it.

But when we finally could be together and begin to hold our heads up, Helen cooled off. She still went to work looking great, but at home she was careless about her appearance. I didn't mind but I did notice. And sex slowed way down. She wasn't interested anymore. I tried not to pressure her, but it was frustrating to me. I was finally feeling less guilty and more ready to really enjoy being with her both at home and out in the world, and she was pulling away.

Within two years we had separate bedrooms. And it went on like that, cool and distant, until she died. I never really thought of leaving. I'd paid such a price to be with her, how could I?

When I look back I realize that Helen suffered probably more than I did through all those years of our affair. She never really knew whether I'd leave Janet or leave her. She used to cry a lot and a couple of times she threatened suicide. She hated being "the other woman." But as awful as those years before our marriage were, they were more loving and caring and exciting and special than anything afterward.

I felt like such a failure after we married, that somehow I couldn't make her happy now that most of our problems were behind us.

I came to understand a lot about myself in therapy but I believe I also became willing to look at some things about Helen I hadn't wanted to face. She functioned better under all the strain and pressure and secretiveness of our affair than she did when things were more normal. That's why the love between us died as soon as the affair was over and the marriage began.

When I could look at all this honestly I began to get over the terrible anger I'd felt toward her since her death. I was angry because being with Helen had cost me so much: my marriage, in many ways my children's love, and the respect of my friends. I guess I felt like I'd been cheated.

Charles's attraction to Helen

Beautiful and alluring when they first met, Helen soon provided Charles with sexual bliss, blind devotion, and love bordering on reverence. His strong attraction to her in spite of a stable, fairly satisfying marriage hardly requires an explanation or justification. Quite simply, Helen made it her life's work from the beginning and throughout all the long years of their affair to deepen Charles's love for her and to make bearable and even worthwhile his long struggle to be free of his marriage.

What does merit explanation is Helen's sudden and patent disinterest in the man for whom she had waited and suffered so long, once he was finally able to freely share a life with her. Why did she love him to distraction while he was married and quickly tire of him when he was not?

Because Helen wanted only what she couldn't really have. To tolerate sustained interaction with a man personally and sexually, she needed the guarantee of distance and unattainability that Charles's marriage supplied. Only under those conditions was she able to give herself to him. She could not comfortably endure a genuine partnership that could, freed of the wracking pressures of his marriage, develop and deepen on a basis other than their mutual struggle against the world. Helen needed the excitement, tension, and emotional pain of loving an unavailable man in order to relate at all. She had virtually no capacity for intimacy, or even much tenderness, once she was no longer embroiled in the struggle to win Charles. Having been won, he was virtually discarded.

Yet through those long years of waiting for him, she gave every appearance of being a woman who loved too much. She genuinely suffered, pined, wept, and wailed for the man she loved but could not truly have. She experienced him as the center of her being, the most important force in her world—until she had him. Then the reality of him as a partner, with the bittersweet romance of their illicit affair removed, failed to rouse her to the thrills of passion she'd enjoyed for nine years with this same man.

Often it is observed that when two people who have been involved for years finally make a commitment to marry each other, something goes out of the relationship; the excitement is lost, and they fall out of love. That this happens is not necessarily because they have stopped trying to please each other. It may be because one or the other or both of them have overstepped their capacity for intimacy by making that very commitment. An open-ended relationship provides the promise of safety from deeper intimacy. With commitment there is often emotional withdrawal in an effort toward self-protection.

This is precisely what happened between Helen and Charles. Charles, for his part, ignored whatever signs there were of Helen's lack of emotional depth because of the flattery he felt from her attention. Far from being a passive victim of her machinations and manipulations, Charles actively refused to acknowledge the part of Helen's character that didn't fit with the view of himself—a view she had fostered and he wanted to believe—that he was enormously lovable and sexually irresistible. He lived in a carefully constructed fantasy world with Helen for many years, unwilling to puncture the illusion his ego had grown to cherish. Much of his anger after Helen's death was at himself, as he belatedly admitted his own denial and the role he had played in creating and perpetuating the fantasy of an all-consuming love, which finally resulted in the most sterile of marriages.

Russell: thirty-two; licensed social worker (having received a pardon from the governor) who designs community programs for youthful offenders

The kids I work with are always impressed with that tattoo of my name on my left forearm. It says a lot about the way I used to live. I got it done when I was seventeen because I was sure that someday I was going to be lying on the ground dead, and nobody would know who I was. I thought I was a helluva bad guy.

I lived with my mother till I was seven. Then she remarried and her new husband and I didn't get along. I ran away a lot and in those days they locked you up for that. First it was juvenile hall, then foster homes and more trips to juvenile hall. Pretty soon it was Boys' Camp and then Y.A., the Youth Authority. As I got older I was in and out of the local jails, and finally prison. By the time I was twenty-five I had been in every kind of correctional facility the state of California had to offer, from forest camp to maximum security.

Needless to say, I spent a lot more time locked up than I did on the outside during those years. But I still managed to meet Monica. One night in San Jose, a buddy I knew from Y.A. and I were cruising around in this "borrowed" car. We pulled into a hamburger drive-in and parked next to these two girls. We got to talking and joking with them, and pretty soon we were sitting in the back seat of their car.

Well, my buddy was a real ladies' man. He had the coolest line, so whenever there were girls around I let him do all the talking. He could always get a couple of girls interested, but he also got first pick because he was so slick and did all the work, and I'd have second choice. I had no complaints that night, because he paired off with this sexy little blond who was driving and I ended up with Monica. She was fifteen, really pretty, all soft and wide-eyed and *interested*. She had this really sweet way, right from the beginning, of *caring* so much.

Now, when you've done time you learn that there are some women who'll think you're a creep and have nothing to do with you. But there are others who get turned on by the whole idea. It fascinates them. They see you as big and bad and they get real seductive, trying to tame you. Or they think you've been hurt and they feel sorry for you and want to help you. Monica was definitely in the category of wanting to help. She was a real nice girl, too. No heavy stuff right away. While my buddy was making it with her girlfriend, Monica and I took a walk in the moonlight and talked. She wanted to know everything about me. I cleaned up my story quite a bit so I wouldn't scare her off, and I told her a lot of the sad things, like how much my stepfather hated me and some of the crummy foster homes I'd been in where they gave me hand-me-downs and spent the money meant for me on their own kids. While I was talking she squeezed my hand real hard and patted it and even got tears in her big brown eyes. Man, by the time we said goodbye that night I was in love. My buddy wanted to tell me every juicy detail of his big score with the blond and I didn't even want to listen. Monica had given me her address and phone number and I was going to call her the next day for sure, but as we were driving out of the city we got stopped by the cops because the car was hot. All I could think about was Monica. I was sure that was the end of it because I'd told her how hard I was trying to clean up my act and go straight.

When I was back in Y.A. I decided to take a chance and write her. I told her I was doing time again, but for something I didn't do—that the cops had arrested me because I had a record and they didn't like me. Monica wrote right back and kept on writing me just about every day for the next two years. All we ever wrote each other about was how much we were in love, how much we missed each other, and what we would do together when I got out.

Her mother wouldn't let her meet me in Stockton when I was released, so I took a bus back to San Jose. I was so excited about seeing her again, but really scared about it too. I guess I was afraid she wouldn't want me after all. So instead of going to see her right away I looked up some old buddies and one thing led to another. We started raising hell, and by the time they finally drove me to Monica's house, four days had gone by. I was pretty wrecked. I'd had to get loaded just to have the courage to come see her, I was so afraid she'd tell me to get lost.

Her mother was at work, thank God, when the guys

dumped me on her sidewalk. Monica came out smiling, so glad to see me even though she hadn't heard from me since I'd hit town. I remember that we went for another of our great walks that day as soon as I wasn't so high. I didn't have any money to take her anywhere and no car either, but she didn't seem to mind then or ever.

For a long time I could do no wrong in Monica's eyes. She made excuses for everything I did and didn't do. I was in and out of jail and then prison for years, and she still married me and stuck by me. Her own dad had deserted the family when she was just a little kid. Her mother was real bitter about that, and she didn't like me too well, either. In fact, that's why Monica and I got married. Once when I'd been busted for bad checks and forgery her mom wouldn't let Monica see me when I was out on bail, so we ran off together and got married. Monica was eighteen then. We lived in a hotel for a little while until my trial. She had a job as a waitress but she quit so she could come to court every day during the trial. Then, of course, I went to prison, and Monica went back home to her mom. They fought so much that she left and moved to the town nearest the prison and worked as a waitress again. It was a college town and I always hoped she'd go back to school; she really liked school and she was so bright. But she said she didn't want to, she just wanted to wait for me. We'd write and she'd come visit as often as they'd let her. She talked to the prison chaplain about me a lot and kept asking him to talk to me and help me, until I finally asked her not to do that anymore. I hated talking to the guy. I just couldn't relate.

Even though she visited she kept on writing, too, and she'd send all these books and articles about improving yourself. She told me constantly that she was praying for me to change. I wanted to stay out of prison, but I'd been doing time for so long it was all I knew how to do.

Well, finally something clicked inside me and I got involved in a program to help me make it out there in the world. I went to school while I was on the inside and learned a trade, plus I finished high school and started on my college education. When I got out, I somehow stayed out of trouble and continued with my education until I had a master's degree in social work. But along the way, I lost my wife. At first when we were really struggling to make it we got along okay, but as things got easier and we began to achieve what we'd always hoped for, Monica got angrier and snappier than I'd ever seen her in all those years through all those troubles. She left me just when we should have been happiest. I don't even know where she is now. Her mother won't tell me and I finally decided that it wasn't my business to look for her if she didn't want to be with me. Sometimes I think it was lot easier for Monica to love an idea of me than to love me in person. We were so in love when we were barely ever together, when all we had were letters and visits and the dream of what we'd have someday. When I started making what we'd wished for a reality, we fell apart. The more middle-class we became, the less she liked it. I guess she couldn't feel sorry for me anymore.

Russell's attraction to Monica

Nothing in Russell's background prepared him to be emotionally or even physically present to another person in a loving, committed relationship. For most of his life he had actively been seeking a feeling of strength and safety by either running away or engaging in dangerous escapades. Through these highly distracting, tension-generating activities, he sought to avoid his own despair. He used involvement in danger to avoid feeling pain and helplessness at having been emotionally abandoned by his mother.

When he met Monica he was enchanted by her softly appealing looks and her tender attitude toward him. Rather than rejecting him for being "bad," she responded to his problems with sincere interest and deep compassion. She immediately communicated that she was willing to be there for him, and it wasn't long before he tested her staying power. When he disappeared, Monica responded by patiently waiting. She seemed to have enough love, stability, and endurance to handle whatever Russell might do. Though it appears that Monica had a great measure of tolerance for Russell and his behavior, actually the exact opposite was true. What neither of these young people consciously realized was that she could be there for him only as long as he was not there for her. As long as he was separated from her, Russell found in Monica the perfect partner, the ideal prisoner's wife. She willingly spent her life waiting and hoping that he would change and that then they could be together. Prison wives like Monica present perhaps the ultimate example of women who love too much. Because they are incapable of any degree of intimacy with a man, they choose instead to live with a fantasy, a dream of how much they will love and be loved someday when their partner changes and becomes available to them. But they can be intimate only in fantasy.

When Russell accomplished the nearly impossible and began to go straight and stay out of jail, Monica drifted away. Having him present in her life demanded a threatening level of intimacy; it made her far more uncomfortable than his absence ever had. Nor could day-to-day reality with Russell ever compete with the idealized vision of mutual love she had entertained. There is a saying among convicts that they all have their Cadillacs parked at the curb waiting for them, meaning they entertain an overly idealized version of what life will be like for them when they are back on the streets. In the imagination of prisoners' wives like Monica, what is probably parked at the curb is not the Cadillac symbolizing money and power, but a coach drawn by six white horses, representing magically romantic love. How these women will love and be loved—that is their dream. Along with their convict husbands, they usually find it easier to live with the dream than to struggle to try to make it come true in the real world.

What is important to understand is that it *appeared* that Russell was unable to love with much depth, while Monica, with all her patience and compassion, seemed to be very good at it. In fact, they were both equally deficient in the ability to love intimately. That is why they became partners when they couldn't be together, and why when they could be together their relationship had to end. It is instructive to note that Russell does not have a new partner in his life at this time. He, too, is still struggling with intimacy.

Tyler: forty-two; business executive; divorced, no children

I used to make a joke when we were still together and tell people that when I first saw Nancy my heart was pounding so hard that I couldn't catch my breath. It was true: she was a nurse who worked for the firm where I'm employed, and I was in her office on a treadmill, having my respiratory system checked—that's what all the heart pounding and heavy breathing was about. I had been sent in by my superior because I gained so much weight and also because I'd been having some pains in my chest. Actually, I was in terrible shape. My wife had left me a year and a half before for another man, and while I know that starts a lot of guys running to the bars at night, I just stayed home and watched TV and ate.

I had always liked to eat. My wife and I had played a lot of tennis and I guess that had taken care of the calories when we were together, but with her gone, playing tennis depressed me. Hell, everything depressed me. That day in Nancy's office I learned I'd gained sixty-five pounds in eighteen months. I'd never even bothered to weigh myself, though I'd gone through several sizes of clothes. I just didn't care.

Nancy was all business at first, telling me how serious

the weight gain was and what I'd have to do to get rid of it, but I was feeling like an old man and I really didn't want to make the effort to change.

I guess I just felt sorry for myself. Even my ex, when she'd see me, would scold me and say, "How can you let yourself go like this?" I half hoped she'd come back to save me, but she didn't.

Nancy asked me if there was any precipitating event tied in with my weight gain. When I told her about the divorce she stopped being quite so professional and patted my hand sympathetically. I remember I felt a little thrill when she did that, and it was special because I hadn't felt much of anything for anybody for a very long time. She advised a diet and gave me lots of pamphlets and charts and told me to come back once every two weeks so she could see how I was doing. I couldn't wait to get back there. The two weeks went by and I hadn't followed the diet or lost any weight, but I sure had gained her sympathy. She and I spent my entire second appointment talking about how the divorce had affected me. She listened and then urged me to do all the things everybody tells you to do: go to classes, join a health club, take a trip with a group, develop new interests. I agreed to everything, did nothing, and waited two more weeks to see her again. It was at this checkup that I asked her out. I knew I was fat and miserable looking, and I really don't know where I got the nerve, but I did, and she accepted. When I picked her up Saturday night she had more pamphlets, along with journal articles on diet, the heart, exercise, and grieving. I hadn't had this much attention in a long time.

We started going out and pretty soon we were getting serious about each other. I thought Nancy was going to make all the pain go away for me. She sure tried, I'll say that. I even moved out of my apartment and into hers. She made a big deal of cooking low-cholesterol meals and watching everything I ate. She even made me lunches to take to work. Although I wasn't eating anything close to what I had been consuming all those nights alone in front of TV, I wasn't losing, either. I just stayed the same, no fatter, no thinner. I tell you, Nancy was working a lot harder than I was to get me to lose that weight. We both sort of acted like it was her project, her responsibility to make me better.

Actually, I think I have a metabolism that requires strenuous exercise in order for me to burn up calories efficiently, and I wasn't getting much exercise at all. Nancy played golf and I would play with her a bit, but it just wasn't my game.

After we'd been together about eight months, I made a business trip back to Evanston, my hometown. Sure enough, after being there two days I ran into a couple of friends from high school. I hadn't wanted to see anyone, looking the way I did, but these guys were old friends and we had a lot to talk about. They were surprised to hear about my divorce. My wife was a hometown girl, too. Anyway, they talked me into playing a set of tennis. They both played, and they knew it was my game from high school. I didn't think I could last through a single game and told them so, but they insisted.

It felt so good to be playing again. Even though the extra pounds really slowed me down, and I lost every game I played. I told them I'd be back next year to whip them both.

When I got home Nancy told me she'd gone to this great seminar on nutrition and she wanted me to try out all this new stuff she'd learned. I told her no, that I was going to do it my own way for a while.

Now, Nancy and I had never fought. Sure, she fussed over me a lot and was constantly on me to take better care of myself, but it wasn't until I started playing tennis again that she and I began to squabble. I played at noon so it didn't take away from the time we spent together, but she and I were never the same.

Nancy is an attractive gal, about eight years younger than I am and once I began to shape up I thought we'd get along better than ever because she'd be proud of me. God knows, I felt better about myself. But it sure didn't work that way. She complained that I just wasn't the same anymore and finally asked me to move out. By that time I weighed only seven pounds more than I had before the divorce. It was really hard for me to leave her. I'd hoped we would eventually get married. But once I was thinner, she was right—it just wasn't the same between us anymore.

Tyler's attraction to Nancy

Tyler was a man with rather pronounced dependency needs, which were exaggerated by the crisis of the divorce. His almost deliberate deterioration, calculated to arouse his wife's pity and solicitude, failed with her but nevertheless attracted a woman who loved too much, who made another's well-being the core of her purpose in life. His helplessness and pain and her eagerness to help were the basis for their mutual attraction.

Tyler was still smarting from his wife's rejection, as well as deeply grieving for the loss of her and the end of their marriage. In this unhappy state common to all those struggling through the throes of separation, he was attracted not so much to Nancy as a person as to her role of nurse and healer, and to the surcease from suffering that she seemed to offer.

Much in the same way he had used great quantities of food to fill his emptiness and smother his loss, he now used Nancy's hovering solicitude to provide a sense of emotional security and bolster his damaged self-worth. But Tyler's need for Nancy's total attention was temporary, a passing phase in his healing process. As time worked its magic, replacing self-obsession and self-pity with healthier self-assertion, Nancy's overprotection, once comforting, now became cloying. Unlike Tyler's temporarily exaggerated dependency, her need to be needed was not a passing phase, but rather a core trait in her personality and almost her sole framework for relating to another person. She was "nurse" both at work and at home. Though Tyler would still be a fairly dependent partner even after recovery from the shock of divorce, the depth of his need to be taken care of could not match the depth of her need to manage and control another's life. His health, for which she had seemed to work tirelessly, was actually the death knell for their relationship.

Bart: thirty-six; former executive; alcoholic since the age of fourteen. Sober two years

I'd been divorced and out doing the singles scene for about a year when I met Rita. She was this long-legged, dark-eyed, hippie-looking girl, and at first we got stoned a lot together. I had lots of money still, and we really had a great time for a while. But you know, Rita was never really a hippie. She was too responsible to let go much. She could smoke a little dope with me, but somehow her proper Bostonian background would never totally disappear. Even her apartment was neat all the time. I had this sense of being safe with her, as if she wouldn't let me fall too far.

The first night we went out we had a great dinner and then came back to her apartment. I got really drunk, and I guess I passed out. Anyway, I woke up on her couch all covered up with this nice, soft quilt, and my head was on a pillow that was scented, and I just felt as if I'd come home—a safe harbor, you know? Rita knew all about taking care of alcoholics. Her father, a banker, had died from his disease. Anyway, I moved in with her a few weeks after that, and came on like the hot shot wheeler-dealer for the next couple of years, for as long as I could get away with it, until I lost everything.

She had quit doing any dope at all after about the first six months we were together. I guess she figured she'd better keep on top of things because I was so out of it. In the middle of all this we got married. Then I really got scared. Now I had another responsibility, and I hadn't done so well with responsibility. Besides, right about the time we got married, I was losing everything financially. I just couldn't hold it together anymore in the shape I was in, drinking all day long. Rita didn't know it was that bad, because I'd tell her I was going to a business meeting in the morning and instead I'd drive out in my Mercedes and park by the beach and drink. Finally, when the bottom really fell out of the business and I owed everybody in town, I didn't know what to do.

I took off on a long trip, intending to kill myself in my car and make it look like an accident. But she came after me, found me in this sleazy hotel, and took me home. All the money was gone but she still got me into an alcoholism treatment hospital. It's funny, but I wasn't grateful. I was angry, confused, very scared—and totally turned off to her sexually for about the first year of sobriety. I still don't know if we'll make it, but it's getting a little better as time goes by.

Bart's attraction to Rita

When on their first date Bart got drunk and passed out, Rita, by making sure that he didn't suffer, seemed to promise him a respite from his headlong rush toward self-destruction. For a while it looked as though she might be able to protect him from the ravages of his own addiction, to subtly and sweetly save him. This seemingly protective attitude actually served to lengthen the time that her partner could practice his addiction and not feel the consequences; by shielding and comforting him, she helped him stay sick longer. An addict who is practicing his disease isn't looking for someone to help him get well, he's looking for someone with whom he can stay sick, safely. Rita was perfect for a while, until Bart got so sick even she couldn't undo what he was doing to himself.

When she tracked him down and entered him into a hospital program for alcoholics, Bart began to give up alcohol and recover. Rita, however, had come between him and his drug. She was no longer performing her usual role of comforting him and making everything all right, and he resented her for that apparent betrayal and also for appearing to be so strong when he felt so weak and helpless.

No matter how badly we're botching the job, each of us needs to feel that we are in charge of our own life. When someone helps us, we often resent that person's implied power and superiority. Moreover, a man often needs to feel stronger than his female partner in order to feel sexually attracted to her. In this case, the help Rita gave Bart by getting him into a hospital only made it clear how very sick he was, and her deeply caring gesture thus undermined, at least for a while, his sexual attraction to her.

Besides this emotional aspect, there may also be an important physiological factor operating here that should be taken into consideration. When a man has been using alcohol and other drugs the way Bart did, and then stops, it sometimes takes a year or more for his body chemistry to right itself and for him to respond sexually in a normal fashion, without the presence of a drug in his system. During this period of physical adjustment the couple may have considerable difficulty understanding and accepting his lack of interest and/or inability to perform sexually.

The opposite can also occur. An unusually strong sex drive may develop in the newly clean and sober addict, perhaps due to hormonal disequilibrium. Or, again, the reason may be more psychological. As one young man, abstinent from alcohol and other drugs for a few weeks put it, "Sex is the only way I can get high now." Sex may thus be substituted for the use of a drug to relieve the anxiety that is typical in early sobriety.

Recovery from addiction and co-addiction is an extremely complex and delicate process for a couple. Bart and Rita might survive that transition, even though they originally came together because their diseases of alcoholism and co-alcoholism called to each other. But to make it as a couple in the absence of active addiction, they must walk separate paths for a while, each focusing on his or her own recovery. They must each look within and embrace the self they tried so hard, through loving each other, dancing with each other, to avoid.

Greg: thirty-eight; clean and sober for fourteen years in Narcotics Anonymous; now married with two children, and working as a counselor to young drug abusers

We met in the park one day. She was reading an underground newspaper and I was just sort of spacing out. It was a Saturday in summer, around noon, really hot and quiet.

I was twenty-two and had dropped out of college my first year, but I kept making noises that I was going to go back. That was so my parents would keep on sending me money. They couldn't let go of their dream that I would finish school and enter a profession, so they bailed me out for a long time.

Alana was pretty fat, about forty or fifty pounds overweight, which meant she wasn't a threat to me. Because she wasn't perfect, if she rejected me it wouldn't count. I started a conversation with her about what she was reading, and it was easy, right from the beginning. She laughed a lot, which made me feel as if I was this charming, entertaining guy. She told me about Mississippi and Alabama, and marching with Martin Luther King, and what it had been like, working with all these people who were trying to make a difference.

I'd never been committed to anything except having a good time. Getting high and getting by was my motto, and

I was much better at getting high than at getting by. Alana was so intense. She said she loved being back in California, but that sometimes she felt she didn't have the right to be so comfortable when other people in this country were suffering.

We sat in the park together for two or three hours that day, just kind of drifting along, telling each other more and more about who we were. After a while we went back to the house I shared to get stoned, but when we got there she was hungry. She started eating and cleaning the kitchen, while I was getting loaded in the living room. There was music on and I remember she came out with this jar of peanut butter, these crackers, and a knife, and sat down real close to me. We just laughed and laughed. I think in that moment we both let ourselves be seen as addicts, more clearly than we ever did after that day. There were no excuses then, just the behaviors. And we were both doing exactly what we wanted to do, plus we'd found someone who wouldn't give us a hard time about it. Without saying a word we knew it was going to work for us to be together.

We had a lot of good times after that, but I don't think there was ever another time when it was all so easy, when both of us were so free of defenses. Addicts are pretty defensive people.

I remember we used to fight a lot about whether I could make love to her without being stoned. She was sure she was repulsive because she was fat. When I got loaded before we made love she thought I had to, in order to stand it. Actually, I had to be stoned in order to make love to anybody. We both had pretty low self-esteem. It was easy for me to hide behind her addiction because her weight *showed* that there was a problem. My lack of motivation and the fact that my life was going nowhere were less obvious than those fifty pounds she was carrying around. So there we'd be, fighting over whether I could really love her even though she was heavy. She'd get me to say that it was who she was inside that counted, not how she looked, and then there would be peace for a while.

She said she ate because she was so unhappy. I said I got loaded because I couldn't make her happy. In this really sick way we were perfect foils for each other. We each had an excuse for what we were doing.

Most of the time we pretended there were no real problems, though. After all, lots of people are fat, and lots of people get loaded. So we'd just ignore the whole thing.

Then I got arrested for possession of dangerous drugs. I spent ten days in jail and my parents got me a hotshot attorney who got me into counseling as an alternative to more jail time. Alana moved out while I was locked up for those ten days. I was so angry. I felt she'd abandoned me. Actually, we were fighting more and more. When I look back now I realize I was becoming pretty hard to live with.

The paranoia that develops in people who do drugs for any length of time had been really beginning to affect me. Also, I was either loaded or wanting to get loaded almost all of the time. Alana had been taking all of it personally, thinking that if she were only different I would want to be more present with her, not stoned every minute. She thought I was avoiding her. Hell, I was avoiding myself!

Anyway, she disappeared for about ten months, on another march, I think. The counselor I saw insisted that I go to Narcotics Anonymous meetings. Since it was either that or jail, I went. I saw some people there I had known from the street and after a while it began to dawn on me that I just might have a problem with drugs. These people were getting on with life and I was still getting stoned every day, all day. So I stopped bullshitting my way through meetings and I asked one guy I thought a lot of if he'd help me. He became my sponsor in N.A., and I'd call him twice a day, morning and night. It meant changing everything I did—friends, parties, everything—but I did it. The counseling helped too, because that counselor knew everything I was going to go through before I did, and he'd warn me. Anyway, it worked, and I was able to stay away from drugs and alcohol.

Alana came back when I'd been clean and sober in N.A. for four months, and right away it was the same old thing. We had this game we played together. The counselor called it "colluding." It was our way of using each other to feel good or bad about ourselves and, of course, to practice our addictions. I knew I'd get loaded if I got into all that behavior with her. Now we're not even friends anymore. It just didn't work if we couldn't be sick together.

Greg's attraction to Alana

Greg and Alana shared a powerful bond right from the beginning. They each had an addiction that was ruling their lives, and from the first day they met they focused on each other's addiction to diminish, in comparison, the importance and power of their own. Then, throughout their relationship, they subtly and not-so-subtly exchanged permission with each other to stay sick, even while protesting each other's condition. This is an extremely common pattern with addictive couples, whether they are addicted to the same substance or to different ones. They use each other's behavior and problems to avoid facing the seriousness of their own deterioration—and the greater the deterioration the more this partner is needed to provide a distraction, to be even sicker, even more obsessed, even less in control.

Along with this dynamic, Alana appeared to Greg as compassionate, willing to suffer for something she believed in. This always has a magnetic allure for an addictive person, because a willingness to suffer is a prerequisite for a relationship with an addict. It guarantees that the addict won't be abandoned when things inevitably start to go bad. After long months of bitter quarreling it was still only when Greg was gone, doing time in jail, that Alana found the strength to leave him, even temporarily. She inevitably returned, ready to begin again where they had left off, as two practicing addicts.

Greg and Alana knew only how to be sick together. With Alana's own addiction to food still out of control she could feel strong and healthy only if Greg were constantly loaded, just as he could feel his drug use was cooly self-controlled compared to her binges with food and extreme overweight. Greg's recovery made her lack of recovery too obvious for them to be comfortable together any longer. She would have needed to sabotage his sobriety in order for them to return to a workable status quo.

Erik: forty-two; divorced and remarried

I'd been divorced a year and a half when I met Sue. An instructor at the community college where I coach football had twisted my arm to come to his housewarming so there I was, on Sunday afternoon, sitting alone in the master bedroom watching a Rams-Forty Niners game while everyone else was out in the living room enjoying the party.

Sue came in to put down her coat and we said hello. She left and then half an hour later came back to see if I was still there. She teased me some about holing up all alone in the back room with the TV, and during the commercial we chatted a bit. Well, she left again and came back with a plate of everything good that was being served out where the party was going on. I looked at her then really for the first time and noticed how pretty she was. When the game was over I joined the party but she had gone. I found out that she was a part-time instructor for the English department, so on Monday I stopped in at her office and asked her to let me pay her back for the lunch she'd brought me.

She said sure, if we could go somewhere with no TV, and we both laughed. But it wasn't really a joke. It would not be an overstatement to say that when I met Sue, sports were my whole life. That's the thing about sports. If you want to, you can pay total attention to them and not have any time left over for anything else. I ran every day. I trained for marathons, I coached my players and travelled with them to games, I followed sports on TV, I worked out.

But I was also lonely, and Sue was very appealing. Right from the beginning she paid a lot of attention to me when I wanted it, and yet didn't interfere with what I wanted or needed to do. She had a son, Tim, who was six, and I liked him okay too. Her ex lived out of state and rarely saw the boy, so it was easy for him and me to be friends. I could tell Tim wanted to be around a man.

Sue and I got married after we'd known each other a year, but pretty soon things started going wrong between us. She complained that I never paid attention to her or Tim, that I was always gone and that when I was home all I cared about was watching sports on TV. I complained that all she did was nag me and that she had known what I was like when she met me. If she didn't like it, what was she doing here? I was mad at Sue a lot of the time but somehow I couldn't be mad at Tim, too, and I knew that the way she and I were fighting was hurting him. Though I never would admit it then, Sue was right. I was avoiding her and Tim. Sports gave me something to do, something to talk about and think about that was safe and comfortable. I'd grown up in a family where sports was the only topic you could discuss with my father, the only way you could get his attention. It was pretty much all I knew about being a man.

Well, Sue and I were just about ready to split up, we were fighting so much. The more she'd pressure me, the more I'd tune her out and escape into my running or the ball games or whatever. Then one Sunday afternoon the Miami Dolphins and the Oakland Raiders were in a play-off and the phone rang. Sue was out with Tim, and I remember how annoyed I felt at the interruption, at having to get up and leave the TV. The call was from my brother, telling me that my father had had a heart attack and that he was dead.

I went to the funeral without Sue. We were fighting so much I wanted to go alone, and I'm glad I did. Going back there changed my whole life. Here I was, at my father's funeral, never having been able to talk to him and on the brink of my second divorce because I didn't know how to relate to my wife, either. I felt like I was losing so much, and I couldn't understand why it was all happening to me. I was a nice guy, I worked hard, I never hurt anybody. I felt sorry for myself and totally alone.

I rode back from the funeral with my youngest brother. He couldn't quit crying. He kept talking about how it was too late now, that he'd never be close to our father. Then, back at the house everybody was talking about Dad, you know how you do after a funeral, and people kept making these little jokes about Dad and sports, how much he loved them, how he was always watching them. My brother-in-law, trying to be funny, said, "You know, this is the first time I've been in this house when the TV wasn't on and he wasn't watching a game." I looked at my brother and he started to cry again, not sadly but bitterly. All of a sudden I saw what my father had done all his life and what I was doing too. Just like him, I wouldn't let anybody be close to me, know me, talk to me. The TV was my armor.

I followed my brother outside and we took a drive together down to the lake. We sat there for a long time. As I listened to him talk about how long he'd been waiting for Dad to notice him, I started really seeing myself for the first time, realizing how much I'd become like my father. I thought about my stepson, Tim, always waiting like a sad little puppy for some of my time and attention, and how I had kept myself too busy for him or his mom.

On the plane ride home I kept thinking about what I wanted people to say about me when I died, and that helped me see what I had to do.

Back home with Sue I talked honestly, maybe for the first time in my whole life. We cried together and called Tim in to be with us, and he cried too.

After that, everything was wonderful for a while. We did things together, bike rides and picnics with Tim. We went out and we had friends in. It was hard for me to back off the whole sports thing, but I had to quit almost cold turkey for a while to get everything in perspective. I really wanted to be close to the people I loved, not to die and leave people feeling the way my father had.

But it turned out to be harder for Sue than for me. After a couple of months had gone by, she told me that she was going to take a part-time job on weekends. I couldn't believe it. That was our time to spend together. Now everything was becoming reversed; she was running away from me! We both agreed to get some help.

In counseling Sue admitted that all our togetherness had been driving her crazy, that she felt like she didn't know how to do it, how to be with me. We both talked about how hard it was to really be with another person. Even though she'd nagged me about my old behavior, she now got uncomfortable when I paid attention to her. She wasn't used to it. If anything, her family had been worse than mine in the attention-affection department. Her father, a ship's captain, was always gone, and her mother liked it that way. Sue had grown up lonely, always wanting to be close to someone, but like me she didn't know how.

We stayed in counseling for a while, and at the therapist's suggestion we joined the Stepfamily Association. As Tim and I got closer, Sue had trouble letting me discipline him. She felt left out and like she was losing control of him. But I knew I had to set my own limits with Tim if he and I were really going to have a relationship.

Being in that association helped me more than anything else. They had group meetings for families like ours. Listening to other men struggling with their feelings was great for me. It helped me keep talking about mine to Sue.

We're still talking and we're still together, learning how to be close and to trust each other. Neither of us is as good at it as we'd like to be, but we keep practicing. It's a brand new game for both of us.

Erik's attraction to Sue

Erik, lonely in his self-imposed isolation, yearned to be loved and cared for without having to risk closeness. When Sue approached him on the day they met, tacitly signaling her acceptance of his chief means of avoidance, his obsession with sports, Erik wondered if he hadn't actually found his ideal woman—one who would care for him and yet leave him alone. Though Sue subtly complained about his inattention by pointedly suggesting that their first date be away from a TV, he still correctly assumed she had a high tolerance for distance. Otherwise, she would have avoided him in the first place.

Actually, Erik's blatant lack of social skills and his inability to relate emotionally were attractive elements to Sue. His clumsiness both endeared him to her and assured her that he wouldn't be able to reach out to other people, including other women, and that was important. Sue, like so many women who love too much, deeply feared abandonment. Better to be with someone who didn't quite meet her needs but whom she wouldn't lose than with someone more loving and more lovable, who might leave her for someone else.

Also, Erik's social isolation provided her with a job to do, to bridge the chasm that stretched between him and other people. She could interpret him and his idiosyncrasies to the rest of the world, attributing to shyness rather than indifference his retreat from social contact. Simply put, he *needed* her.

Sue, on the other hand, was letting herself in for a situation that would replicate all the worse aspects of her childhood years—the loneliness, the hopeful waiting for love and attention, the deep disappointment, and finally the angry despair. As she tried to force Erik to change, her behavior only confirmed his fears about relationships and caused him to retreat further.

But Erik did change dramatically, due to a series of profoundly moving events in his life. He became willing to face his dragon, his fear of closeness, in order to avoid becoming another version of his cold, unapproachable father. That he so strongly identified with lonely little Tim was a major factor in his commitment to change. But this change in him forced a change in each member of the family. Sue, catapulted from being ignored and avoided to being pursued and courted, was forced to face her own discomfort with actually receiving the loving attention she craved. It would have been easy for Sue and Erik to stop at this point, with the tables turned and the pursuer now pursued, the avoider now avoided. They could have simply exchanged roles, kept their proscribed distances, and maintained their comfort level. But Sue and Erik each had the courage to look deeper, and then to try, with the help of therapy and the support of an understanding and empathetic group, to risk really becoming closer as a couple and, with Tim, as a family.

There is no way to overstate how important initial encounters are for us all. As a therapist, the impact a new client has on me during our first meeting provides some of the most important information I will ever receive about that person. Through what is said and what is left unsaid and by everything else that is revealed by physical appearance—posture, grooming, facial expression, mannerisms and gestures, tone of voice, eye contact or lack of it, attitude, and style—I receive an abundance of information about how the client operates in the world, particularly under stress. It all adds up to getting a strong, undeniably subjective impression, providing me with an intuitive sense of what it is going to be like to work with this person in the therapeutic relationship.

While, as a therapist, I very *consciously* try to assess my new client's approach to life, a very similar, though less deliberately conscious, process ensues when any two people meet. Each tries to answer some questions about the other, based on the wealth of information automatically telegraphed during those first few moments together. The questions being silently asked are usually simple: Are you someone with whom I have anything in common? Can I benefit in any way from cultivating a friendship with you? Are you fun to be with?

But often other questions are asked, depending on who these two people are, and what they want. For every woman who loves too much, stronger questions reside beneath the obvious, rational, practical ones, questions we strive all the harder to answer because they come from so deep inside us.

"Do you need me?" the woman who loves too much secretly asks.

"Will you take care of me and solve my problems?" is the silent query behind the spoken words of the man who would choose her to be his partner.

7 • *Beauty and the Beast*

> "THERE ARE MANY MEN," SAID BEAUTY,
> "WHO MAKE WORSE MONSTERS THAN YOU.
> AND I PREFER YOU NOTWITHSTANDING
> YOUR LOOKS . . ."
> —"BEAUTY AND THE BEAST"

IN THE STORIES FROM THE TWO PREVIOUS CHAPTERS, THE women uniformly expressed a need to be of service, to help the men with whom they became involved. Indeed, the opportunity to be of help to these men was the main ingredient in the attraction they felt. The men, correspondingly, indicated that they had been searching for someone who could help them, who could control their behavior, make them feel safe, or "save" them—who would be, in the words of one of my male clients, the "woman in white."

This theme of women redeeming men through the gift of their selfless, perfect, all-accepting love is not a modern idea by any means. Fairy tales, embodying as they do the most important lessons of the culture that creates and

137

perpetuates them, have for centuries been offering versions of this drama. In "Beauty and the Beast," a beautiful young innocent meets a repulsive and frightening monster. To save her family from his wrath, she agrees to live with him. By getting to know him, she eventually overcomes her natural loathing and finally even grows to love him, in spite of his animal persona. When she does, of course, a miracle transpires, and he is freed of his beastly guise and restored to his true, not only human but princely self. As the restored prince, he is a grateful and suitable partner for her. Thus, her love and acceptance of him are repaid a thousandfold as she assumes her proper place by his side, to share a life of blessed good fortune.

"Beauty and the Beast," like every fairy tale that has endured centuries of telling and retelling, embodies a profound spiritual truth in the context of a compelling story. Spiritual truths are very difficult to comprehend and even more difficult to put into practice because they often *go against* contemporary values. Accordingly, there is a tendency to interpret the fairy tale in a way that reinforces the cultural bias. By doing so, it is easy to miss its deeper meaning altogether. Later we will explore the profound spiritual lesson that "Beauty and the Beast" holds for us. But first we must look at the cultural bias this fairy tale *seems* to underscore, that a woman can change a man if she loves him enough.

This belief, so powerful, so all-pervasive, permeates our individual and group psyches to the core. Reflected again and again in our daily speech and behavior is the tacit cultural assumption that we can change someone for the better through the force of our love, and that, if we are female, it is our duty to do so. When someone we care for is not acting or feeling the way we wish, we cast about for ways to try to change that person's behavior or mood, usually with the blessing of others who give us advice and encouragement in our efforts ("Have you tried . . . ?"). The suggestions may be as contradictory as they are numerous, but few friends and relatives can resist making them. Everyone's focus is on how to help. Even the media gets into the act, not only reflecting this belief system but also, with its influence, reinforcing and perpetuating it while continuing to delegate the job to women. For instance, women's magazines as well as certain general-interest publications seem always to be publishing "how to help your man become . . ." articles, while corresponding "how to help your woman become . . ." articles are virtually nonexistent in equivalent magazines for men.

And we women buy the magazines and try to follow their advice, hoping to help the man in our life become what we want and need him to be.

Why does the idea of changing someone unhappy or unhealthy or worse into our perfect partner appeal to us women so deeply? Why is it so alluring, so enduring a concept?

To some, the answer would seem obvious: Embodied in the Judeo-Christian ethic is the concept of helping those who are less fortunate than ourselves. We are taught that it is our duty to respond with compassion and generosity when someone has a problem. Not to judge but rather to help; this seems to be our moral obligation.

Unfortunately, these virtuous motives by no means entirely explain the behavior of millions of women who choose to take as partners men who are cruel, indifferent, abusive, emotionally unavailable, addictive, or otherwise unable to be loving and caring. Women who love too much make these choices out of a driving need to control those closest to them. That need to control others originates in a childhood during which many overwhelming emotions are frequently experienced: fear, anger, unbearable tension, guilt, shame, pity for others and for self. A child growing up in such an environment would be wracked by these emotions to the point of being unable to function unless she developed ways to protect herself. Always, her tools for self-protection include a powerful defense mechanism, *denial,* and an equally powerful sub-conscious motivation, *control.* All of us unconsciously employ defense mechanisms such as denial throughout our lives, sometimes about rather trivial matters and at other times about major issues and events. Otherwise, we would have to face facts about who we are and what we think and feel that do not fit with our idealized image of ourselves and our circumstances. The mechanism of denial is particularly useful in ignoring information with which we do not want to deal. For instance, not noticing (denying) how grown up a child is becoming can be a way of avoiding feelings about that child's leaving home. Or not seeing and feeling (denying) the gain of extra pounds that the mirror and tight clothing both reflect can allow our continued indulgence in favorite foods.

Denial can be defined as a refusal to acknowledge reality on two levels: at the level of what is actually happening, and at the level of feeling. Let's look at how denial helps to prepare a little girl to grow up and become a woman who loves too much. As a child she may, for instance, have a parent who is rarely at home at night because of extramarital affairs. As she tells herself, or is told by other family members, that he is "busy at work," she denies that there is any problem between her parents or that anything abnormal is happening. This prevents her from feeling fear for her family's stability and her own welfare. She also tells herself that he is working hard, which arouses compassion rather than the anger and shame that would be felt if reality were faced. Thus she denies both reality and her feelings about that reality, and she creates a fantasy that is easier to live with. With practice she becomes very skilled at protecting herself from pain in this way, but at the same time she loses the ability to make a free choice about what she is doing. Her denial operates automatically, unbidden.

In a dysfunctional family there is *always* a shared denial of reality. No matter how serious the problems are, the family does not become dysfunctional *unless* there is denial operating. Further, should any family member attempt to break through this denial by, for instance, describing the family situation in accurate terms, the rest of the family will usually strongly resist that perception. Often ridicule will be used to bring that person back into line, or failing that, the renegade family member will be excluded from the circle of acceptance, affection, and activity.

No one using the defense mechanism of denial makes a conscious choice to tune out reality, to wear blinders in order to stop registering accurately what others are saying and doing. Nor does anyone in whom denial is operating *decide* not to feel her own emotions. It all "just happens," as the ego in its struggle to provide protection from overwhelming conflicts, burdens, and fears, cancels out information and input that is too troublesome.

Perhaps a child whose parents frequently quarrel invites a friend to spend the night. During her friend's visit both girls are awakened late at night by the parents' loud arguing. The visitor whispers, "Gee, your parents sure are noisy. Why are they yelling like that?"

The embarrassed daughter, who has lain awake through many such quarrels, answers vaguely, "I don't know," and then lies there in agonized self-consciousness while the shouting continues. The young guest has no idea why her friend begins to avoid her soon thereafter.

The guest is shunned because she was witness to her friend's family secret, and thus serves as a reminder of what her friend would rather deny. Embarrassing events such as the parents' fight during that visit are so painful that the daughter is much more comfortable denying the truth, and so ever more assiduously avoids whatever and whomever may threaten to dismantle her defense against pain. She does not want to feel her shame, her fear, her anger, helplessness, panic, despair, pity, resentment, disgust. But because these strong and conflicting emotions are what she would have to contend with if she let herself feel anything, *she prefers not to feel at all*. This is the source of her need to control the people and events in her life. Through controlling what goes on around her, she tries to create for herself a sense of safety. No shocks, no surprises, *no feelings*.

Anyone in an uncomfortable situation seeks control of it, to whatever degree is possible. This natural reaction becomes exaggerated in members of an unhealthy family because there is so much pain. Remember Lisa's story, when her parents pressured her to get better grades in school: there was some realistic hope that schoolwork could be improved, but little chance that the mother's drinking behavior could be changed; so rather than face the devastating implications of their impotence regarding the mother's alcoholism, they chose to believe that family life would improve if and when Lisa did better in school.

Lisa, too, remember, kept trying to improve (control) the situation by "being good." Her good behavior was not in any way a wholesome expression of her delight with her family and with being alive. Quite the opposite. Each chore she performed unasked represented a desperate attempt to rectify the family's unbearable circumstances, for which she, as a child, felt responsible.

Children inevitably carry the guilt and blame for serious problems that affect their families. This is because through their fantasy of omnipotence they believe both that they are the cause of the families' circumstances and that they have the power to change them, for better or worse. Like Lisa, many unfortunate children are actively blamed by parents or others in the family for problems over which the children have no control. But even without the verbal blame of others, a child will assume a large portion of the responsibility for his or her family's troubles.

It is not easy or comfortable for us to consider that selfless behavior, "being good," and efforts to help may actually be attempts to control, and not be altruistically motivated. I saw this dynamic simply and succinctly represented by the sign on an office door in an agency where I once worked. Shown was a two-tone circle, the top half of which was a bright yellow rising sun and the bottom half of which was painted black. The sign read Help Is the Sunny Side of Control. It served to remind us counselors as well as our clients to constantly examine the motives behind our need to change others.

When efforts to help are practiced by people who come from unhappy backgrounds, or who are in stressful relationships in the present, the need to control must always be suspected. When we do for another what he can do for himself, when we plan another's future or daily activities, when we prompt, advise, remind, warn, or cajole another person who is not a young child, when we cannot bear for him to face the consequences of his actions so we either try to change his actions or avert their consequences—this is controlling. Our hope is that if we can control him, then we can control our own feelings where our life touches his. And of course the harder we try to control him, the less we are able to. But we cannot stop.

A woman who habitually practices denial and control will be drawn into situations demanding those traits. Denial, by keeping her out of touch with the reality of her circumstances and her feelings about those circumstances, will lead her into relationships fraught with difficulty. She will then employ all her skills at helping/controlling in order to make the situation more tolerable, all the while denying how bad it really is. Denial feeds the need to control, and the inevitable failure to control feeds the need to deny.

This dynamic is illustrated in the following stories. These women have gained a good deal of insight into their behaviors through involvement with therapy, and when appropriate because of the nature of their problems, involvement in other support groups as well. They have been able to recognize their helping behavior for what it was, a subconsciously motivated attempt to deny their own pain by controlling those closest to them. The intensity of each woman's desire to be of help to her partner is a clue that it was much more a need than a choice.

Connie: thirty two; divorced, with an eleven-year-old son

Before therapy I could not remember a single issue that my parents fought about. All I could remember was that they constantly fought. Every day, every meal, almost every minute. They criticized each other, disagreed with each other, and insulted each other, while my brother and I looked on. Dad would stay away at work, or wherever, as much as he could, but sooner or later he'd have to come home and then it would begin again. My role in all of this was first of all to pretend nothing was wrong, and second to try and distract either one or both of them by being entertaining. I would toss my head and beam them a big smile and make a joke or do whatever silly thing I could think of to capture their attention. Actually, I was scared to death inside, but being afraid got in the way of putting on a good show. So I clowned and joked, and soon it became a full-time job, being cute. I got so much practice when I was at home that after a while I started acting like that elsewhere, too. I was always polishing my act. Basically, it came down to this: if anything was wrong I ignored it, and at the same time I tried to cover it up. That last sentence encapsulizes what happened in my marriage.

I met Kenneth by the pool at my apartment when I was twenty. He was very tan, very good-looking in a sunburned-surfer sort of way. The fact that he was interested enough to want to live with me shortly after we met made me feel that we had a lot going for us. Also, he was pretty cheerful, like me, so I thought we had all the ingredients for being happy together.

Kenneth was a little vague, a little indecisive about his career, about what he wanted to do with his life, and I gave him lots of encouragement there. I was sure I was helping him blossom, giving him needed support and direction. I made virtually all the decisions concerning us as a couple, too, right from the beginning, but still somehow he did just as he wanted. I felt strong and he felt free to lean on me. It was just what we each needed, I guess.

We had been living together for three or four months when an old girlfriend of his from work called him at home. She was very surprised to hear that I was living with Kenneth. She told me that he'd never mentioned to her that he was involved with anyone else, even though he saw her at least two or three times a week at work. All this came out when she was stumbling around, trying to apologize for calling. Well, that shook me a little, and I asked Kenneth about it. He told me he hadn't thought it was important to tell her. I remember the fear and the pain I felt then, but I felt that way only for a moment. Then I cut off those feelings, and became very intellectual about it. I saw only two choices: I could either fight with him about it or else let it drop and not expect him to see things the way I did. I chose the latter, hands down, and made a joke of the whole thing. I had promised myself that I would never, *ever* fight the way my parents had. In fact, the thought of getting angry literally nauseated me. Because I had been so busy as a child entertaining everyone and didn't dare feel any strong emotions, by now powerful feelings really frightened me, they knocked me off balance. Besides, I liked to keep things smooth, so I accepted what Kenneth said and buried my doubts about how sincerely he was committed to me. We got married a few months later.

Fast-forward twelve years, when one day, at the suggestion of a friend at work, I found myself in the office of a therapist. I thought I was still in total control of my life, but my friend had said she was worried about me and insisted that I see someone for help.

Kenneth and I had been married for those twelve years and I thought we had been very happy, but now we were separated at my suggestion. The therapist probed. What had gone wrong? I talked about lots of different things, and in the midst of my ramblings mentioned that he had been leaving the house in the evening, at first once or twice a week, then three or four times a week, and finally, for the past five years or so, six out of seven nights. Finally I had said to him that it looked as if he really wanted to be elsewhere, so maybe he'd better move out.

The therapist asked me if I knew where he had been all those nights, and I told her I didn't know, that I'd never asked him. I remember how surprised she looked. "All those nights over all those years and you *never* asked?" I told her no, never, that I thought married couples had to give each other space. What I would do, though, was to talk to him about how he should spend more time with our son, Thad. He always agreed with me, and then would go off the same way in the evenings, maybe joining us to do something together on a Sunday now and then. I chose to see him as someone who wasn't very bright, who needed those endless lectures from me to keep him somewhat on the track as a good father. I never could admit to myself that he was doing exactly what he wanted to do and that I was helpless to change him. Actually, it got worse and worse over the years in spite of how perfectly I tried to behave. The therapist asked me during that first session what I thought he'd been doing during the hours he was not at home. I got annoyed. I just didn't want to think about it, because if I didn't then it couldn't hurt me.

I know now that Kenneth was incapable of being with just one woman, though he liked the security of an ongoing relationship. He had given me a thousand clues about this behavior both before marriage and after: at company picnics when he would disappear for hours, or at parties when he'd start talking to some woman and then they'd go off together. Without even thinking about what I was doing in those situations, I'd turn on the charm to distract people from what was happening and to show what a great sport I was . . . and maybe to prove that I was lovable, not someone a boyfriend or husband would want to get away from if he could.

It took me a long time in therapy to be able to remember that other women had been the problem with my parents' marriage, too. Their fights had been about my father going off and not coming home, and my mother, while not saying it outright, would hint that he was unfaithful and then berate him for neglecting all of us. I thought that she drove him away, and decided very consciously that I would never behave the way she did. So I held it all in and worked on always smiling. That's what brought me to therapy. I was still smiling and sunny the day after my nine-year-old son made a suicide attempt. I passed it off as a joke, which really alarmed my friend at work. I had held this magical belief for so long that if I were nice and never got angry, everything would work out fine.

Seeing Kenneth as not too bright helped too. I got to lecture and to try to organize his life, which was for him probably a small price to pay to have someone cook and clean while he did exactly what he wanted, no questions asked.

The depth of my denial that anything was wrong was so great that I couldn't let go of it until I got help. My son was terribly unhappy, and I simply would not let that register. I tried to talk him out of it, made jokes about it, which probably made him feel worse. I also refused to acknowledge that anything was wrong to anyone who knew us. Kenneth was out of the house for six months and I still didn't tell anyone we were separated, which also made it hard for my son. He had to keep the secret, too, and hide his hurt about all of it as well. I didn't want to talk to anyone about it, so I wouldn't let him, either. I didn't see how desperately he needed to let out the secret. The therapist really pushed me to start telling people that my perfect marriage was over. Oh, was it hard for me to admit that. I think Thad's suicide attempt was simply his way of saying, "Hey, everybody! Something *is* wrong!"

Well, we're doing better now. Thad and I are still in therapy together and separately, learning how to talk to each other and feel what we're feeling. There's been a rule in my therapy that I can't make a joke out of anything that comes up during the hour. It's very hard for me to let go of that defense and feel what happens to me when I do, but I'm lots better at it. When I go on dates I sometimes have thoughts about how this man or that needs me to straighten out some little details of his life for him, but I know better than to indulge in that kind of thinking for long. Very occasional snipes at those sick little urges to "help" are the only cracks I'm allowed to make in therapy these days. It feels good, laughing about how sick that behavior has been, rather than laughing to cover up everything that's been wrong.

Connie first used humor to distract herself and her parents from the threatening reality of their unstable relationship. By employing all her charm and wit, she could draw their attention away from each other to her, and thus stop their fighting, at least temporarily. Each time this occurred, she would experience herself as the glue holding these two combatants together, with all the responsibility that role implied. These interactions spawned her need to control others in order to feel safe and secure herself, and she exercised her control by distracting with humor. She learned to be extremely sensitive to signs of anger and hostility in those around her, and to avert any such expression with a well-timed quip or a disarming smile.

She had double cause to deny her own feelings: first, the thought of her parents' potential breakup was too frightening to bear; and second, any emotions of her own would only hamper her delivery of a good performance. Soon she was denying her feelings automatically, just as she was seeking to manipulate and control those around her automatically. Her shallow effervescence undoubtedly alienated some people, but others, like Kenneth, who had no desire to relate on anything but a most superficial level, were attracted to that style.

That Connie could live for years with a man who would leave for hours at a time with increasing frequency, and who finally began disappearing nightly, and *never* question him about his activities or whereabouts during those absences is a measure of her great capacity for denial and the commensurate fear behind it. Connie didn't want to know, didn't want to fight or confront, and most of all didn't want to feel the old childhood terror, that through dissension her entire world would fall apart.

It was very difficult to get Connie to make a commitment to a therapeutic process that demanded she relinquish her chief defense, humor. It was as though someone were asking her to give up breathing air; at some level she was sure she would not survive without it. Her son's desperate plea that they both begin to face the painful reality of their situation barely penetrated Connie's massive defenses. She was out of touch with reality very nearly to the point of being truly crazy, and for a long time in therapy insisted on talking about only Thad's problems, denying she had any of her own. Always "the strong one," she wasn't about to give up that position without a fight. But slowly, as she became more willing to experience the panic that surfaced when she didn't resort to joking, she began to feel safer. Connie learned that she had at her disposal, as an adult, far healthier coping mechanisms than those she had so overused from childhood. She began to question, to confront, to express herself, and make her needs known. She learned to be more honest than she had been in many, many years, with herself and with others. And she finally was able to reclaim her humor, which now included healthy laughter at herself.

Pam: thirty-six; twice divorced, mother of two teenage sons

I grew up in a tense, unhappy home. My father had deserted my mother before I was born, and she became what seemed to me the original "single parent." No one

149

else I knew had divorced parents, and living where we did, in a very middle-class town in the '50s, we were made to feel like the oddity we were.

I worked hard in school and was a very pretty child, so teachers liked me. This helped a lot. At least academically I could succeed. I became a real overachiever, getting straight A's all through grammar school. In junior high the emotional pressure began to build so much that I couldn't really concentrate anymore, so my grades began to slip, although I never dared to do badly. I always had the feeling that my mother was disappointed in me, and afraid that I would embarrass her.

My mother worked hard as a secretary to support us, and I realize now she was exhausted all the time. She also had a great deal of pride, and deep shame, I think, about being divorced. She was very uncomfortable when other children would come to our house. We were poor, struggling to make ends meet, and yet we had this terrific need to keep up appearances. Well, it was easier to do that if people never saw where we lived, so our house was not a welcoming place, to say the least. When friends would ask me to spend the night with them, my mother would tell me, "They don't really want you." She did that partly because she didn't want to have to reciprocate and have them stay at our house, but of course I didn't know that when I was young; I believed what she told me, that I wasn't someone people wanted to be around.

I grew up believing there was something very wrong with me. I wasn't sure what it was, but it had to do with being unacceptable and unlovable. There was no love in our home, just duty. The worst part of it was that we could never talk about the lie we were living, trying when we were out in the world to look better than we were—happier, wealthier, more successful. The pressure to do so was intense, but it was virtually unspoken. And I never felt I could even bring it off. I was so afraid that any moment it would become apparent that I just wasn't as good as everybody else. While I knew how to dress nicely and perform scholastically, I always felt like a fraud. Underneath, I knew I was flawed to the very core. If people liked me it was because I was fooling them. If they knew me well, they would go away.

Growing up without a father made it worse, I suppose, because I never learned how to relate to males in a give-and-take way. They were exotic animals, forbidding and fascinating at the same time. My mother never told me much about my father, but the little she said made me feel he wasn't anything to be proud of, so I didn't ask questions; I was afraid of what I might learn. She didn't like men much at all, and hinted that basically they were dangerous, selfish, and not to be trusted. But I couldn't help it, I found them all fascinating, starting with the little boys in kindergarten my first day of school. I was looking hard for what was missing in my life, but I didn't know what it was. I guess it was that I so badly wanted to be close to somebody, to give and receive affection. I knew that men and women, husbands and wives, were supposed to love each other, but my mother was telling me, in subtle and not so subtle ways, that men didn't make you happy, they made you miserable, and they did that by leaving you, running off with your best friend, or by betraying you in some other way. Those were the kinds of stories I heard from her when I was growing up. I probably decided very early that I would find myself someone who wouldn't, couldn't, go away, maybe someone nobody else would want. Then I guess I forgot that I'd ever made such a decision. I just kept on acting it out.

I could never have put it into words when I was growing up, but the only way I knew how to be with someone, especially someone male, was if he needed me. Then he wouldn't leave me, because I'd be helping him and he'd be grateful.

Not surprisingly, my first boyfriend was crippled. He had been in a car accident and his back had been broken. He wore leg braces and used steel crutches to walk. I used to pray at night that God would make me crippled instead of him. We would go to dances together and I would sit by him all night long. Now, he was a nice enough boy, and certainly a girl could have enjoyed being with him just for his company. But I had another reason. I was with him because it was *safe;* since I was doing him a favor, I wouldn't be rejected and get hurt. It was like having an insurance policy against pain. I was really crazy about this boy, but I know now that I chose him because, like me, he had something wrong with him. His flaw showed, so I could be comfortable feeling all this pain and pity for *him.* He was, by far, my healthiest boyfriend. After him came juvenile delinquents, underachievers—losers, all of them.

When I was seventeen I met my first husband. He was in trouble in school and flunking out. His father and mother were divorced but still fighting with each other. Compared to his background, mine looked *good!* I could relax a little, not feel so ashamed. And of course, I felt so sorry for him. He was quite a rebel, but I thought that was because no one before me had ever really understood him.

Also, I had at least twenty IQ points over him. And I needed that edge. It took all that and more to make me even begin to believe I was his equal, and that he wouldn't leave me for someone better.

My whole relationship with him, and we were married twelve years, was one of refusing to accept who he was and instead trying to make him into what I thought he ought to be. I was sure he would be so much happier and feel so much better about himself if he would just allow me to show him how to parent our children, how to run his business, how to relate to his family. I had continued going to school, majoring, naturally, in psychology. My own life was so out of control, so miserable, and there I was, studying how to take care of everyone else. To be fair to myself, I really was looking hard for answers, but I thought that the key to my happiness was to get *him* to change. He obviously needed my help. He wasn't paying his bills or his taxes. He made the children and me promises he didn't keep. He infuriated his customers who would call *me* to complain about how he hadn't followed through on jobs he had started for them.

I wasn't able to leave him until I could finally see who he really was, instead of who I wanted him to be. I spent the last three months of the marriage just watching—not giving those interminable lectures of mine, but just keeping quiet and watching. That's when I realized I could not live with who he was. All along, I'd been waiting to be able to love the wonderful man that I thought with my help he could become. Only my hope that he'd change for me kept me going all those years.

It still wasn't clear to me, though, that I had a pattern of picking men who were not, in my opinion, fine just as they were, but rather whom I saw as needing my help. I only caught on to that after several more relationships with impossible men: one was addicted to pot; one was gay; one was impotent; and one, with whom I finally had a long relationship, was supposedly very unhappily married. When that involvement ended (disastrously), I couldn't continue to believe it was all bad luck. I knew I must have had a part in what had happened to me.

By this time I was a licensed psychologist, and my whole life revolved around helping people. I know now that my field is full of people like me, who help others all day long at work and still feel the need to "help" in their personal relationships too. My entire method of relating to my sons was to remind them, encourage them, coach them, and worry about them. That was all I knew about loving, to try to help people and to be concerned about them. I hadn't the slightest clue how to accept others as they were, probably because I had never accepted myself.

Life did me a real favor at this point. Everything fell apart for me. When my affair with the married man ended, my boys were both in trouble with the law, and my health was completely shot. I just couldn't keep on taking care of everyone else. It was my son's probation officer who told me I'd better start working on taking care of myself. And I was somehow able to hear him. After all those years in psychology, he was the one who finally got through to me. It took having my whole life fall down around my ears to make me look at myself and the depth of my own self-hatred.

One of the hardest things I had to face was that my mother really hadn't wanted the responsibility of raising me, hadn't wanted me, period. I can understand now, as an adult, how hard it must have been for her. But all those messages she gave me about other people not wanting me around—she was really describing *herself*. And as a child I knew it at some level, but I couldn't face it, I guess, so I ignored it. Pretty soon I ignored a lot. I didn't let myself hear the criticisms she constantly threw at me or how angry she got if I had fun. It was too threatening to let myself experience all the hostility she directed toward me, so I stopped feeling, I stopped responding, and I poured all my energy into being good and helping others. As long as I was working on everybody else, I never had time to pay attention to myself, to feel my own pain.

It was hard on my pride, but I got into a self-help group made up of women who had similar problems with men. The group was the kind I would usually be leading professionally, and there I was, just a humble participant. Though my ego took a beating, this group helped me look at my need to manage and control others, and helped me to stop doing it. I began to heal inside. Instead of working on everybody else, I finally was taking care of myself. And there was so much work to do. Once I began concentrating on trying to let go of fixing everyone in my life, I practically had to stop talking! Everything I had said for so long had been "helpful." It was a terrific shock to me to hear how much managing and controlling I was doing. Altering my behavior has caused even my professional work to change radically. I'm much more able to be with clients in a supportive way while they work out their problems. Before, I felt this huge responsibility to fix them. Now it's more important that I understand them.

Some time passed, and then a nice man came along. He

didn't need me at all. There was really nothing wrong with him. I was very uncomfortable at first, learning how to *be* with him, instead of trying to make him over completely. After all, that had been my whole way of relating to people. But I learned not to do anything except just be myself, and it seems to be working. I feel as if my life has just begun to make some sense. And I keep going to my group to keep from slipping back into my old ways. Sometimes everything in me still wants to run the show, but I know better than to give in to that need anymore.

How does all this relate to denial and control?

Pam began by denying the reality of her mother's anger and hostility toward her. She didn't allow herself to feel what it meant to be an unwelcome object rather than a beloved child in her family. She didn't allow herself to feel, period, because it hurt too much. Later this inability to perceive and experience her emotions actually would enable her to become involved with the men she chose. Her emotional warning system, which would otherwise steer her away from them, was inoperative at the beginning of each relationship, due to highly developed denial. Because she couldn't feel what it was like, emotionally, to be with these men, she could perceive them only as needing her understanding and her help.

Pam's pattern of developing relationships in which her role was to understand, encourage, and improve her partner is a formula often employed by women who love too much, and it usually yields exactly the opposite of the hoped-for result. Rather than a grateful, loyal partner who is bonded to her through his devotion and his dependence, such a woman finds she soon has a man who is increasingly rebellious, resentful, and critical of her. Out of his own need to maintain his autonomy and self-respect, he must cease to see her as the solution to all his problems, and make her instead the source of many if not most of them.

When this happens and the relationship crumbles, the

woman is plunged into a deeper sense of failure and despair. If she cannot even make someone so needy and inadequate love her, how could she ever hope to earn and keep the love of a healthier, more appropriate man? This explains why often such women follow one bad relationship with another that is even worse—because they feel increasingly less worthy with each such failure.

It also makes clear how difficult it will be for such a woman to break this pattern unless she gains an understanding of the basic need that drives her. Pam, like many others in the helping professions, used her career to bolster her fragile sense of worth. She could relate only to neediness in others, including her clients, children, husbands, and other partners. In every area of her life, she sought ways to avoid feeling her deep sense of inadequacy and inferiority. Not until Pam began to experience the powerful healing properties of understanding and acceptance that she got from *peers* in her group did her self-esteem grow so that she could begin to relate in a healthy way to others, including a healthy man.

Celeste: forty-five; divorced, mother of three children who live with their father abroad

I've probably been with more than a hundred men in my life, and I'll bet, looking back, that every one of them was either too many years younger than I or a con artist or dependent on drugs or alcohol or gay or crazy. A hundred impossible men! How did I find them all?

My father was a chaplain in the army. That meant that he pretended to be a kind, loving man everywhere but at home, where he didn't bother to be anything but what he was—mean, demanding, critical, and selfish. He and my mother both believed that we children existed to help him carry off his professional charade. We were supposed to look perfect by getting straight A's, being social charmers, and never getting into trouble. Given the atmosphere at home, this was impossible. You could cut the tension with

a knife anytime my father was in the house. He and my
mother were not close at all. She was furious all the time.
Not loudly fighting with him, just quietly, grimly seething.
Whenever my father did anything she asked him to, he
screwed it up on purpose. Once there was something
wrong with the front door and he fixed it with these nails,
great big nails, which ruined the whole thing. We all
learned to leave him alone.

After retirement he was home every day and every
night, sitting in his chair, glowering. He didn't say much,
but just his being there made life difficult for all of us. I
really hated him. I couldn't see then that he had problems
of his own or that we did, too, in the way we reacted to
him and let him control us by his presence. It was a
continuing contest: who would control whom? And he
always won, passively.

Anyway, I had long since developed into the rebel in the
family. I was angry, just like my mother, and the only way
I could express it was to reject all the values my parents
embodied, to get out and try to be the opposite of
everything and everyone in my family. I think it was the
fact that we looked so normal from the outside that
infuriated me the most. I wanted to scream from rooftops
how awful our family was, but no one else seemed to
notice. My mother and sisters were willing to have me be
the one with the problem, and I obliged by playing my
part to the hilt.

I started an underground newspaper at the base high
school, which stirred up a lot of trouble. Then I went away
to college, and as soon as I had the chance I left the
country. I couldn't get far enough away from home to
satisfy me. I was outwardly very rebellious, but inside
there was nothing but confusion.

My first sexual experience occurred when I was abroad
in Europe, and it was not with another American. It was
with a young African student. He was eager to learn about
the States, and I felt like his mentor—stronger, wiser,
more worldly. The fact that I was white and he was black

caused a lot of waves. I didn't care; it reinforced my view of myself as a rebel.

A few years later, still in college, I met and married a Britisher. He was an intellectual from a wealthy family. I respected that. He was also twenty-seven and still a virgin. Again, I was the teacher, which made me feel strong and independent. And in control.

We were married seven years, living abroad, and I was terribly restless and unhappy but I didn't know why. Then I met a young orphan student and began a really tempestuous affair with him, during which I left my husband and two children. This young man had been involved sexually only with men until he met me. We lived together for two years in my apartment. He had male lovers as well, but I didn't care. We tried all kinds of things sexually, broke all the rules. It was an adventure for me, but after a while I got restless again, and eased him out of my life as a lover, though we're still friends today. After him came a long series of involvements with some real low-life types. They all, at the very least, moved in with me. Most of them also borrowed money from me, sometimes thousands of dollars, and a couple of them drew me into some very illegal schemes.

I had no idea that I had a problem, even with all this going on. Since each of these men was getting something from me, I felt like the strong one, the one in charge of things.

Then I came back to the States and got involved with a man who was probably the worst of the lot. He was so alcoholic that he had suffered brain damage. He was easily roused to violence, he rarely bathed, didn't work, and was facing jail time for offenses related to his drinking. I went with him to the agency where he attended a program for convicted drunk drivers and the instructor there suggested that I see one of their counselors, because it was apparent that I was also having problems. It was apparent to the drunk-driving class instructor, but not to me; I thought it was this man I was with who had all the problems, and that

I was fine. But I did go to a counseling session, and right away this woman got me talking about how I related to men. I'd never looked at my life from that angle before. I decided to continue to see her, and that's when I was helped to begin to see the pattern I'd created.

I had shut off so much feeling as a child that I required all the drama these men provided, just to feel alive. Trouble with the police, involvement with drugs, financial schemes, dangerous people, crazy sex—these had all become the ordinary stuff of life to me. In fact, even with all of that I still couldn't feel anything much.

I stayed with the counseling and began to go to a women's group at the counselor's suggestion. There I slowly began to learn some things about myself, about my attraction to unhealthy or inadequate men whom I could dominate through my efforts to help them. Even though I'd been in analysis in England for years and years, endlessly talking about my hatred for my father and my anger at my mother, I had never related it to my obsession with impossible men. Although I'd always thought analysis benefitted me immensely, it had never helped me change my patterns. In fact, when I examine my behavior, I see I only got worse over those years.

Now, in counseling and group, as I am beginning to get better, my relationships with men are getting a little healthier too. A while back I got involved with a diabetic who wouldn't take his insulin, and I was in there trying to help him, with lectures about the danger of what he was doing and with attempts to improve his self-esteem. It may sound funny, but my involvement with him was a step *up!* At least he wasn't a full-on addict. Still, I was practicing my familiar role as the strong woman in charge of a man's welfare. I'm leaving men alone for a while because I've finally realized that I really don't want to take care of a man, and that's still the only way I know how to relate to them. They've just been my way of avoiding taking care of myself. I'm working on learning to love myself, to take care of me for a change, and to let go of all these distractions, because that's what men have been in my life. It's scary, though, because I was much better at taking care of them than I am at caring for myself.

Again, we see the twin themes of denial and control. Celeste's family was in emotional chaos but that chaos was never openly acknowledged or expressed. Even her rebellion against the family's rules and norms only subtly hinted at the family's deeply troubled core. She was shouting, but none of them would listen. In her frustration and isolation she turned off all her feelings save one, anger: at her father for not being there for her, and at the rest of the family for refusing to acknowledge their problems or her pain. But her anger was free-floating; she did not understand that it stemmed from her helplessness to change the family she loved and needed. She could not get any of her emotional needs for love and security met in this milieu, so she sought relationships that she *could* control, with others who were not as educated or experienced, not as well-off financially or well-set socially as herself. How deep her need for this pattern of relating became is revealed by the extreme inadequacy of her last partner, a late-stage alcoholic who came very close to fitting the stereotype of the skid-row bum. And still Celeste, bright, sophisticated, educated, and worldly, missed all the cues as to how very sick and inappropriate this liaison was. Her denial of her own feelings and perceptions and her need to control the man and the relationship far outweighed her intelligence. A major part of Celeste's recovery involved her letting go of her intellectual analysis of herself and her life and beginning to feel the deep emotional pain that accompanied the tremendous isolation she had always endured. Her numerous and exotic sexual involvements were only possible because she felt so little connection with other human beings and with her own body. Indeed, these involvements actually prevented her from having to risk real closeness with others. The drama and excitement substituted for the threatening intensity of intimacy. Recovery meant holding still with herself, without a man to sidetrack her, and feeling her feelings, including the painful isolation. It also meant having other women who understood her behavior and feelings validate her efforts to change. For Celeste, recovery requires learning to relate to and trust other women, as well as relating to and trusting herself.

Celeste must develop a relationship with herself before she can relate in a healthy way with a man, and she still has some hard work to do in that area. Basically, all her encounters with men were merely reflections of the anger, chaos, and rebellion within her, and her attempts to control those men were also attempts to subdue the inner forces and feelings that drove her. Her work is with herself, and as she gains more inner stability this will be reflected in her interactions with men. Until she learns to love and trust herself, she will not be able to experience either loving or trusting a man, or being loved and trusted by him.

Many women make the mistake of looking for a man with whom to develop a relationship without first developing a relationship with themselves; they run from man to man, looking for what is missing within. The search must begin at home, within the self. No one can ever love us enough to fulfill us if we do not love ourselves, because when in our emptiness we go looking for love, we can only find more emptiness. What we manifest in our lives is a reflection of what is deep inside us: our beliefs about our own worth, our right to happiness, what we deserve in life. When those beliefs change, so does our life.

Janice: thirty-eight; married, mother of three teenage sons

Sometimes, when you've worked so hard to keep up appearances on the outside, it's practically impossible to show anybody what's really going on inside. It's hard to even know yourself. For years and years I'd been hiding

161

what went on at home while putting on a great show out there in public. I began, early as a child in school, taking responsibility, running for office, being in charge. It felt wonderful. Sometimes I think I could have stayed in high school forever. There, I was somebody who could succeed. I was homecoming queen, captain of the drill team, and senior class vice-president. Robbie and I were even voted cutest couple for the yearbook. Everything looked so good.

At home it looked good too. My dad was a salesman and made lots of money. We had a nice big house with a pool and just about everything we wanted in the way of material things. What was missing was all on the inside, where it didn't show.

My dad was on the road nearly all the time. He loved staying in motels, picking women up in bars. Whenever he was home with my mom, they would get into terrible fights. Then she and whoever else was home at the time would have to listen to him compare her with all the other women he knew. They fought physically, too. When that happened, my brother would try to break it up or I'd have to call the police. It was really awful.

After he was gone, back on the road again, my mother would usually have these long talks with my brother and me, asking us if she should leave dad. Neither of us wanted to be responsible for that decision, even though we hated their fighting, so we'd try to avoid answering. But she never did go, because she was too afraid of losing the financial support he provided. She started seeing the doctor a lot and began taking pills instead, in order to stand it. Then she didn't care what dad did. She'd just go off to her room, take an extra pill or two, and stay inside with the door shut. After she was inside her room, I had to take over a lot of her responsibilities, but in some ways I didn't mind. It was better than listening to the fighting.

By the time I met my future husband I was really good at taking over for other people.

Robbie already had a drinking problem when we met in our junior year of high school. He even had a nickname, "Burgie," because he drank so much Burgermeister beer. But that didn't bother me. I was sure I could take care of whatever bad habits Robbie had. I'd always been told that I was mature for my age, and I believed it.

There was something so sweet about Robbie that I was immediately drawn to him. He reminded me of a cocker spaniel, all soft and appealing, with great big brown eyes. We began dating when I let it be known to his best friend that I was interested. I practically arranged the whole thing myself. I felt I had to make it happen because he was so shy. We went together steadily from then on. Occasionally he wouldn't show up for a date, and the next day he'd be very sorry, very apologetic that he'd gotten carried away with drinking and had forgotten. I'd lecture and scold and finally forgive him. He almost seemed grateful that he had me to keep him on the straight and narrow. I was always as much a mother to him as a girlfriend. I used to hem his pants, and remind him about his family members' birthdays, and advise him about what to do in school and with his career. Robbie had nice parents, but there were six kids. His grandfather, who was ill, lived with them too. Everybody was a little distracted with the pressure of it all, and I was more than willing to make up for the attention Robbie wasn't getting at home.

The draft caught up with him after he'd been out of high school a couple of years. It was during the early buildup in Vietnam, and if a young man was married he was exempt from service. I couldn't bear the thought of what would happen to Robbie in Vietnam. I could say I was afraid he would be injured or killed, but if I'm honest I have to admit I was even more afraid that he would grow up over there and not need me anymore when he came back.

I made it very clear that I was willing to marry him to keep him out of the service, and so that's what we did. We got married when we were both twenty. I remember he got so drunk at the wedding reception that I had to drive so we could leave on our honeymoon. It made a great joke.

After our sons were born, Robbie's drinking got worse. He would tell me he needed to get away from all the pressure, and that we had married too young. He went on a lot of fishing trips, and had lots of nights out with the boys. I never really got angry, because I felt so sorry for him. Each time he drank I made excuses for him and tried harder to make it nicer at home.

I suppose we could have gone on forever that way, with things getting a little worse each year, except that his drinking was finally noticed at work. His coworkers and boss confronted him, and gave him the choice of getting sober or losing his job. Well, he got sober.

That's when the trouble started. All those years that Robbie had been drinking and messing up I knew two things: one, he needed me; and two, no one else would put up with him. And that was the only way I could feel safe. Yes, I had to put up with a lot, but that was okay. I'd come from a home where my father did much worse things than Robbie ever did. My dad beat my mother and had lots of affairs with women he met in bars. So having a husband who just drank too much was really not that hard on me. Besides, I could run the house the way I wanted to, and when he really blew it I'd scold and cry and he'd straighten out for a week or two. I didn't really want any more than that.

Of course, I didn't know any of this until he got sober. All of a sudden my poor, helpless Robbie was going to A.A. meetings every night, making friends, having serious talks on the phone with people I didn't even know. Then he got himself a sponsor in A.A., and this man was the one to whom he turned every time he had a problem or a question. I felt like I'd been fired from my job, and I was furious! Again, if I'm going to be honest I have to admit I liked the whole situation better when he was drinking. Before sobriety I used to call his boss with phony excuses when Robbie was too hung over to go to work. I lied to his family and friends about the trouble he got into at work or driving drunk. In general, I ran interference between him and life. Now I couldn't even get in the game. Whenever something difficult had to be handled, he'd get on the phone with his sponsor, who always insisted that Robbie meet problems head on. Then he'd face it, whatever it was, and afterwards he'd call his sponsor again to give him a report. Through it all, I was left on the sidelines.

Although I'd lived for years with an irresponsible, unreliable, and very dishonest man, it was when Robbie had been sober for nine months and was improving in every area that we found we were fighting more than we ever had. What made me angriest was that he would call his A.A. sponsor to find out how to handle *me*. It seemed *I* was the biggest threat to his sobriety!

I was preparing to file for divorce when his sponsor's wife called me and asked if we could meet for coffee. I very reluctantly agreed, and she just laid it out. She talked about how hard it had been for her when her husband got sober, because she could no longer manage him and every aspect of their life together. She talked about how much she had resented his A.A. meetings and especially his sponsor, and that she considered it a miracle that they were still married, not to mention that they were actually happy. She said that Al-Anon had helped her enormously, and urged me to attend a few meetings.

Well, I only half-listened. I still believed that I was fine and also that Robbie owed me a lot for putting up with him all those years. I felt he should be trying to make that up to me, rather than going to meetings all the time. I had no idea how hard it was for him to stay sober, and he wouldn't have dared to tell me because I would have told him how to do it—as though I knew anything about it!

About this time, one of our sons started stealing and having other problems at school. Robbie and I went to a parent conference and somehow it came out that Robbie was a sober alcoholic attending A.A. The counselor strongly suggested that our son go to Alateen and asked if I was in Al-Anon. I felt cornered, but this woman had a lot of experience with families like ours and she was very gentle with me. All our sons started going to Alateen, but I still stayed away from Al-Anon. I went ahead with divorce proceedings and moved myself and the kids to an apartment. When it was time to settle all the details, the boys quietly told me that they wanted to live with their dad. I was devastated. After I left Robbie I had focused all my attention on them, and here they were choosing him over me! I had to let them go. They were old enough to decide for themselves. That left me alone with just me. And I had never been alone with just me before. I was terrified and depressed and hysterical, all at once.

After a few days of being totally out of commission, I called Robbie's sponsor's wife. I wanted to blame her husband and A.A. for all my pain. She listened to me scream at her for a long time. Then she came over and sat with me while I cried and cried and cried. She took me to an Al-Anon meeting the next day and I listened, even though I was terrifically angry and afraid. I began, very slowly, to see how sick I was. I went to meetings every day for three months. After that I went three or four times a week for a long time.

You know, in those meetings I actually learned to laugh at the things I had taken so seriously, like trying to change others, and managing and controlling other people's lives. And I would listen to other people talk about how hard it was for them to take care of themselves instead of focusing all their attention on the alcoholic. That was true for me, too. I had no idea what I needed to make me happy. I'd always believed I'd be happy as soon as everybody else shaped up. I saw people there who were just so beautiful, and some of them were with partners who were still drinking. They'd learned to let go and get on with their own lives. But I also heard from all of them how hard it was to let go of our old ways of taking care of everything and everybody, and acting like a parent to the alcoholic.

Hearing some of these people talk about how they got through the problem of being alone and the feelings of emptiness helped me find my way too. I learned to stop feeling sorry for myself, and to be grateful for what I did have in my life. Pretty soon I wasn't crying for hours anymore and found I had a lot of time on my hands, so I went to work part-time. That helped too. I began to feel good about doing something all by myself. It wasn't long before Robbie and I were talking about getting back together. I was dying to jump right back in, but his sponsor advised him to wait awhile. His sponsor's wife said the same thing to me. I didn't understand it then, but other people in the program all agreed with them, so we held off. I see now why that was necessary. It was important for me to wait until there was somebody home inside me before I went back with Robbie.

At first I was so empty I felt like the wind was blowing through me. But with each decision I made for myself, that empty place filled in a little. I had to find out who I was, what I liked and disliked, what I wanted for myself and my life. I couldn't learn those things unless I had time alone, without anybody else to think about and worry over, because when someone else was around I much preferred running that person's life over living my own.

When we began to think about getting back together I watched myself start phoning Robbie about every little thing, wanting to meet him and talk over every detail. I could feel myself going backward each time I called him, so finally when I needed someone to talk to, I'd go to a meeting or call someone in the program. It was like weaning myself, but I knew that I had to learn to let things flow between us, rather than jumping in all the time and trying to force things to go the way I wanted. This pulling back was incredibly difficult for me. I think it may have been much harder for me to leave Robbie alone than it was for him to leave alcohol alone. But I knew I had to. Otherwise, I would have slipped into all the old roles again. It's funny: I finally realized that not until I *liked*

167

living alone was I ready to go back into the marriage. Almost a year went by, and somewhere in there the kids and Robbie and I all got back together. He had never wanted a divorce, though now I can't understand why not. I was so controlling of all of them. Anyway, I got better, and let go of all of them more, and we're really okay now. The boys are in Alateen, Robbie's in A.A., and I'm in Al-Anon. I think we're each healthier than we've ever been because we're each living our own life.

There is very little to add to Janice's story. Her tremendous need to be needed, to have a weak, inadequate man, and to control that man's life were all ways to deny and avoid the inevitable emptiness at her core, arising from her early years with her family. It has already been noted that children in dysfunctional families feel responsible for their family's problems and also for solving them. There are basically three ways in which these children attempt to "save" their families: by being invisible, by being bad, or by being good.

To be invisible means to never ask for anything, never cause trouble, never make any kind of demand. The child who chooses this role scrupulously avoids adding any burden to her already stressed family. She stays in her room or blends into the wallpaper; she says very little and makes what she does say noncommittal. In school she is neither bad nor good—in fact, she is rarely remembered at all. Her contribution to the family is to not exist. As for her own pain, she is numb, she feels nothing.

To be bad is to be the rebel, the juvenile delinquent, the one who waves a red flag. This child sacrifices herself, agreeing to be the family's scapegoat, the family's problem. She makes herself the focus for the family's pain, anger, fear, and frustration. Her parents' relationship may be disintegrating, but she provides them with a safe topic they can work on together. They can ask, "What are we going to do about Joanie?" instead of, "What are we going to do about our marriage?" This is how she tries to "save" the family. And she has only one feeling, anger. It covers her pain and her fear.

To be good is to be what Janice was, an achiever out in the world, whose accomplishments are aimed at redeeming the family and filling the emptiness inside. Appearing happy, bright, and enthusiastic serves to cover the tension, fear, and anger inside. Looking good becomes much more important than feeling good—than feeling anything.

Janice eventually needed to add taking care of someone to her list of accomplishments, and Robbie, replicating her father's alcoholism and her mother's passive dependency, was a likely choice. He (and after he left, the children) became her career, her project, and her way of avoiding her own feelings.

Without her husband or her sons on whom to focus her attention, a breakdown was inevitable, because they had been the primary means by which she could avoid her pain, emptiness, and fear. Without them, her feelings overwhelmed her. Janice had always seen herself as the strong one, the person who helped, encouraged, and advised those around her, yet her husband and sons actually served a more important role for her than she did for them. Even though they lacked her "strength" and "maturity," they could function without her. She could not function without them. That this family ultimately survived intact is due largely to their good fortune at seeing an experienced counselor and to the honesty and wisdom of Robbie's sponsor and his wife. Each of these people recognized that Janice's disease was as debilitating as Robbie's, and her recovery every bit as important.

Ruth: twenty-eight; married, mother of two daughters

I knew, even before we married, that Sam had problems with sexual performance. We'd attempted to make love together a couple of times, and it never really worked, but both of us blamed it on the fact that we weren't married.

We shared very strong religious convictions—in fact, we met in night classes at a religious college and went together for two years before we ever tried to have sexual relations. By then we were engaged, with the wedding date set, so we shrugged off Sam's impotence as God's way of protecting us from sinning before we were married. I thought that Sam was just a very shy young man, and that I'd be able to help him get over that once we were married. I looked forward to sort of leading him through it all. Except that's not the way it worked out.

On our wedding night Sam was all ready to go, and then he lost his erection and asked me quietly, "Are you still a virgin?" When I didn't answer right away he said, "I didn't think so," and he got up, went in the bathroom, and closed the door. We were each crying, on our opposite sides of that door. It was a long, disastrous night, the first of many more just like it.

I had been engaged, before I met Sam, to a man I didn't even like very much, but he'd swept me off my feet once and we'd had sex together, and after that I felt I had to marry him to redeem myself. He eventually got tired of me and just drifted away. I was still wearing his ring when I met Sam. I guess I expected to be celibate forever after that experience, but Sam was so kind and never pressured me to be sexual with him, so I felt safe and accepted. I could see that Sam was even less sophisticated and more conservative than I was in the area of sex, and that made me feel in control of the situation. That fact, along with our shared religious convictions, assured me we were perfect for each other.

After our marriage, because of my guilt, I took on all the responsibility for curing Sam's impotence. I read every book I could find, while he refused to read any. I kept all those books, hoping he would read them. I found out later that he did read them all, when I wasn't looking. He was frantic for answers too, but I didn't know that because Sam didn't want to talk about it. He'd ask me if I was willing to just be friends and I'd lie and say yes. The worst part for me was not the lack of sex in our lives; I didn't care much about that, anyway. It was my guilt, my feeling that I had ruined everything somehow, right at the beginning.

Something I hadn't tried yet was therapy. I asked him if he'd go. He said absolutely not. I'd become obsessed by then, with the feeling that *I* was depriving *him* of this wonderful sex life he could have had except for the fact that he'd married me. I still felt that maybe there was something a therapist could tell me that would help, something the books had left out. By this time I was desperate to help Sam. And I still loved him. I realize now that a great deal of my love for him at that time was really a combination of guilt and pity, but there was genuine caring for him too. He was a good, sweet, kind man.

Anyway, I went to my first appointment, which was with a counselor who had been recommended by Planned Parenthood as having expertise in human sexuality. I was only there to help Sam, and I told her that. She said that we couldn't help Sam because Sam wasn't there in the office, but we could work with me, and how did I feel about what was and wasn't happening between Sam and me. I wasn't at all prepared to talk about my feelings. I didn't even know I had any. We spent that whole first hour with me trying to shift the topic back to Sam, and she leading me gently back to myself and my feelings. It was the first time I'd ever seen how skilled I was at avoiding myself, and mostly because she was so honest with me I decided to see her again, even though we weren't working on what I was sure was the *real* problem, Sam.

Between our second and third sessions, I had a very vivid and disturbing dream, in which I was chased and threatened by a figure whose face I couldn't see. When I told my therapist about it she helped me work with the dream until I realized that the threatening figure was my father. This was the first step in a long process that finally led to my being able to remember that my father had sexually molested me frequently between the years when I was nine and fifteen. I had completely buried this entire aspect of my life, and when the memories began to return I could let them surface into my awareness only a little bit at a time, because they were so devastating.

My father would often go out in the evening and not come home until late. My mother, I guess to punish him, would lock him out of their bedroom on those nights. He was supposed to sleep on the couch, but after a while, he started coming into my bed. He both cajoled and threatened me never to tell, and I never did because my shame was so great. I was sure that what was happening between us was my fault. Ours was a family where sexual issues were never discussed, but somehow the general attitude that sex was dirty was still communicated. I certainly felt dirty, and I didn't want anyone to know.

I got a job when I was fifteen, working nights, weekends, and summers. I stayed away from home as much as I could, and I bought a lock for my door. The first time I locked my father out, he stood there, pounding on my door. I pretended not to know what was happening, and my mother woke up and asked him what he was doing. He actually said, "Ruth's got her door locked!" and my mother said, "So? Go to sleep!" That was the end of it. No questions from my mother. No more visits from my father.

It had taken every ounce of courage I had to put a lock on my door. I was afraid it wouldn't work and that my father would get in and be angry that I'd tried to lock him out. But even more so, I was almost willing to go on the same way, rather than run the risk of anyone finding out what had been going on.

I left home for college at seventeen and met the man to whom I became engaged at eighteen. I was sharing an apartment with two other girls, and one night they had some friends over whom I didn't know. I went to bed early, mostly to avoid the pot-smoking scene that was developing. Though practically all the students flouted the school's very strict rules about drinking and drugs, I never did get used to being around it or doing it. Anyway, my bedroom door was right next to the bathroom door, and both were at the end of a long hallway. One of the guys at the party who was looking for the bathroom came into my room by mistake. When he saw what he had done, instead of leaving he asked if he could talk to me. I couldn't say no. It's hard to explain that, but I just couldn't. Well, he sat on the side of my bed and talked to me. Then he told me to turn over and he would give me a back rub. Pretty soon he was in my bed making love to me. And that was how I ended up engaged to him. Whether he smoked pot or not, I think he was nearly as conservative as I was and believed as I did that having sex together meant we had to stay together. We saw each other for about four months until, as I say, he just drifted away. I met Sam a little over a year later. Then I assumed, because he and I never talked about sex, that we were avoiding it because of our religious convictions. I didn't recognize we were avoiding it because we were both so sexually damaged. I liked the feeling of helping Sam, of working hard with him to overcome our problem for the sake of my becoming pregnant. I liked feeling helpful, understanding, patient—and in control. Anything less than that total control would have stirred up all those old feelings of my father approaching me and fondling me through all those nights and all those years.

When what had happened between my father and myself began to surface in therapy, my therapist strongly urged me to attend meetings of Daughters United, a self-help group of daughters whose fathers have sexually abused them. I resisted for a long time but finally got involved. It was really a blessing that I did. To learn that there were so many other women who had experiences similar to and often much worse than mine was reassuring and healing. Several of these women had also married men who had sexual problems of their own. These men formed a self-help group, too, and somehow Sam got the courage to join them.

Sam's parents had been obsessed with raising him to be, in their words, a "pure, clean boy." If he had his hands in his lap at the dinner table, he was ordered to keep them on the table "where we can see what you're doing." If he was in the bathroom too long, they would pound on the door and shout, "What are you doing in there?" It was constant. They searched his drawers for magazines and his clothing for stains. He became so afraid of having any sexual feeling or experience that, ultimately, he couldn't even if he tried.

As we began to get better, in some ways life became more difficult for us as a couple. I still had a tremendous need to control Sam's every expression of sexuality (just as his parents had done), because any sexual aggressiveness on his part was so threatening to me. If he reached for me spontaneously I would flinch, or I would turn over or walk away or start talking or do something else to avoid his advances. I couldn't bear having him lean over me when I was in bed because it reminded me so much of the way my father had approached me. But his recovery required that he become fully in charge of his body and his feelings. I had to stop controlling him so that he could, literally, experience his own potency. And yet my fear of being overwhelmed was a big problem too. I learned to say, "I'm getting scared now," and Sam would answer, "What do you need me to do?" Usually that was enough—just to know that he cared about my feelings and would listen to me.

We worked out this deal where we would take turns being in charge of what happened between us sexually. Either of us could say no to anything we didn't like or didn't want to do, but basically one of us would orchestrate the whole encounter. That was one of the best ideas we ever had, because it addressed the need each of us had to be in charge of our own bodies and what we did with them sexually. We really learned to trust each other and to believe that we could give and receive love with our bodies. We also had our groups for support. Everyone's problems and feelings were so similar that it really helped to keep our struggles in perspective. One night our two groups met together and we spent the evening discussing our personal reactions to the words *impotent* and *frigid*. There were tears and laughter and so much understanding and sharing. It took a lot of the shame and the pain away for all of us.

Maybe because Sam and I had already shared so much by that time and there was so much trust, the sexual part of our relationship began to work. We have two beautiful daughters now and we're so happy with them, with ourselves, and with each other. I'm much less of a mother to Sam and much more of a partner. He's less passive and more assertive. He doesn't need me to keep the secret of his impotence from the world, and I don't need him to be asexual. We have lots of choices now, and we freely choose each other!

Ruth's story illustrates another facet of how denial and the need for control manifest themselves. Like so many women who become obsessed with their partner's problems, Ruth knew before her marriage to Sam exactly what his problems were. She was therefore not surprised at their inability to perform sexually together. In fact, that failure was something of a guarantee that she wouldn't ever have to feel out of control of her own sexuality again. She could be the initiator, the one in control, rather than what was for her the only other role in sex, the victim.

Again, this couple was fortunate in that the help they received was tailor-made for their problems. For her the appropriate support group was Daughters United, an offshoot of Parents United, formed to help promote recovery in families where incest has occurred. Luckily, a corresponding group had been formed by the husbands of these incest victims, and in this climate of understanding, acceptance, and shared experience, each of these damaged people could move cautiously toward healthy sexual expression.

For each of the women in this chapter, recovery demanded that she face the pain, past and present, that she had attempted to avoid. As a child, each had developed a style for surviving that included practicing denial and attempting to gain control. Later, in adulthood, those styles ill-served these women. In fact, their defenses had become major contributors to their pain.

For the woman who loves too much, the practice of denial, magnanimously rephrased as "overlooking his faults" or "keeping a positive attitude," conveniently sidesteps the two-to-tango aspect of how his shortcomings allow her to practice her familiar roles. When her drive to control masquerades as "being helpful" and "giving encouragement," what is ignored again is her own need for the superiority and power implied in this kind of interaction.

We need to recognize that the practice of denial and control, called by whatever names, does not ultimately enhance our lives or our relationships. Rather, the mechanism of denial leads us into relationships that allow for the compulsive reenactment of our old struggles, and the need to control keeps us there, striving to change someone else rather than ourselves.

Now to return to the fairy tale highlighted at the beginning of the chapter. As noted before, the tale "Beauty and the Beast" would appear to be a vehicle for perpetuating the belief that a woman has the power to transform a man if she will only love him devotedly. At this level of interpretation, the tale seems to advocate both denial and control as methods for achieving happiness. Beauty, by loving the fearful monster unquestioningly (denial), appears to have the power to change (control) him. This interpretation *seems* accurate, because it fits in with the sexual roles our culture dictates. Nonetheless, I suggest that such a simplistic interpretation widely misses the significance of this time-honored fairy tale. That this story endures is not because it reinforces any era's cultural precepts and stereotypes. It endures because it embodies a profound metaphysical law, a vital lesson in how to live our lives wisely and well. It is as if the story contains a secret map, which, if we are but clever enough to decipher it and courageous enough to follow it, will lead us to a rich cache of treasure—our own "happily ever after."

So what, then, is the point of "Beauty and the Beast?" It is *acceptance*. Acceptance is the antithesis of denial and control. It is a willingness to recognize what reality is and to allow that reality to be, without a need to change it. Therein lies a happiness that issues not from manipulating outside conditions or people, but from developing inner peace, even in the face of challenges and difficulties.

Remember, in the fairy tale, Beauty had no need for the Beast to change. She appraised him realistically, accepted him for what he was, and appreciated him for his good qualities. She did not try to make a prince out of a monster. She did not say, "I'll be happy when he's not an animal anymore." She did not pity him for being what he was or try to change him. And therein lies the lesson. Because of her attitude of acceptance, he was *freed* to become his own best self. That his true self just happened to be a handsome prince (and perfect partner for her) demonstrates symbolically that *she* was rewarded greatly when she practiced acceptance. Her reward was a rich and fulfilling life, signified by living happily ever after with the prince.

True acceptance of an individual as he is, without trying to change him through encouragement or manipulation or coercion, is a very high form of love, and very difficult for most of us to practice. At the bottom of all our efforts to change someone else is a basically selfish motive, a belief that through his changing we will become happy. There is nothing wrong with wanting to be happy, but to place the source of that happiness outside ourselves, in someone else's hands, means we avoid our ability and responsibility to change our own life for the better.

Ironically, it is this very practice of acceptance that allows another to change if he chooses to do so. Let's look at how this works. If a woman's partner has a problem with workaholism, for instance, and she pleads and argues with him about the long hours he spends away from home, what is the usual result? He spends just as much or more time away from her, feeling justified that he has a right to do so in order to escape her endless laments. In other words, by scolding and pleading and trying to change him, she actually enables him to believe that the problem between them is not his workaholism but her nagging—and indeed, her compulsion to change him may become as large a contributing factor to the emotional distance between them as his compulsion to work. In her efforts to force him to be closer to her, she is actually pushing him further away.

Workaholism is a serious disorder, as are all compulsive behaviors. It serves a purpose in her husband's life, probably protecting him from experiencing the closeness and intimacy he fears, and forestalling the upwelling of various uncomfortable emotions, primarily anxiety and despair. (Workaholism is one of the means of avoiding oneself that men from dysfunctional families frequently employ, just as loving too much is one of the primary means of avoidance employed by women from these kinds of families.) The price he pays for this avoidance is a one-dimensional existence that precludes his enjoying much of what life has to offer. But only he can decide if the price is too high, and only he can choose to take whatever measures and risks are required for him to change. His wife's task is not to straighten out his life but to enhance her own.

Most of us have the ability to be far happier and more fulfilled as individuals than we realize. Often, we don't claim that happiness because we believe someone *else's* behavior is preventing us from doing so. We ignore our obligation to develop ourselves while we scheme and maneuver and manipulate to change someone else, and we become angry and discouraged and depressed when our efforts fail. Trying to change someone else is frustrating and depressing, but exercising the power we have to effect change in our own life is exhilarating.

For the wife of a workaholic to be free to live a fulfilling life of her own, no matter what her husband does, she must come to believe that his problem is not her problem, and that it is not within her power, her duty, or her right to change him. She must learn to respect his right to be who he is, even though she wishes he were different.

When she does so, she is free—free of resentment for his unavailability, free of guilt for not being able to change him, free of the burden of trying and trying to change that which she cannot. With less resentment and guilt she may begin to feel greater affection toward him for the qualities in him that she does appreciate.

When she lets go of trying to change him and redirects her energy to developing her own interests, she will experience some measure of happiness and satisfaction, no matter what he does. She may eventually discover that her pursuits are fulfilling enough so that she can enjoy a rich and rewarding life on her own, without much companionship from her husband. Or, as she becomes less and less dependent on him for her happiness, she may decide that her commitment to an absent partner is pointless and may choose to get on with her life free of the constraint of an unrewarding marriage. Neither of these paths is possible as long as she needs him to change in order for her to be happy. Until she *accepts* him as he is, she is frozen in suspended animation, waiting for him to change before she can begin to live her life.

When a woman who loves too much gives up her crusade to change the man in her life, he is then left to ponder the consequences of his own behavior. Since she is no longer frustrated and unhappy, but rather is becoming more and more excited about life, the contrast to his own existence intensifies. He may choose to struggle with disengaging from his obsession and becoming more physically and emotionally available. *Or he may not.* But no matter what he chooses to do, by accepting the man in her life exactly as he is, a woman becomes free, one way or another, to live her own life—happily ever after.

8 • When One Addiction Feeds Another

> THERE IS A GREAT DEAL OF PAIN IN LIFE
> AND PERHAPS THE ONLY PAIN THAT CAN
> BE AVOIDED IS THE PAIN THAT COMES
> FROM TRYING TO AVOID PAIN.
>
> —R. D. LAING

AT OUR WORST WE WOMEN WHO LOVE TOO MUCH ARE relationship addicts, "man junkies" strung out on pain, fear, and yearning. As if this weren't bad enough, men may not be the only thing we're hooked on. In order to block our deepest feelings from childhood, some of us have also developed dependencies on addictive substances. In our youth or later in adulthood we may have begun abusing alcohol or other drugs or, most typically for women who love too much, food. We have overeaten or undereaten or both in order to tune out reality, distract ourselves, and numb the vast emotional emptiness deep inside us.

Not every woman who loves too much also eats too

much or drinks too much or uses too many drugs, but for those of us who do, our recovery from relationship addiction must go hand in hand with our recovery from addiction to whatever substance we abuse. Here's why: The more we depend on alcohol, drugs, or food, the more guilt, shame, fear, and self-hate we feel. Increasingly lonely and isolated, we may become desperate for the reassurance a relationship with a man seems to promise. Because we feel terrible about ourselves, we want a man to make us feel better. Because we can't love ourselves, we need him to convince us that we are lovable. We even tell ourselves that with the right man we won't need so much food or alcohol or so many drugs. We use relationships in the same way that we use our addictive substance: to take our pain away. When a relationship fails us, we turn even more frantically to the substance we've abused, again looking for relief. A vicious cycle is created when physical dependence on a substance is exacerbated by the stress of an unhealthy relationship, and emotional dependence on a relationship is intensified by the chaotic feelings engendered by physical addiction. We use being without a man or being with the wrong man to explain and excuse our physical addiction. Conversely, our continued use of the addictive substance allows us to tolerate our unhealthy relationship by numbing our pain and robbing us of the motivation necessary for change. We blame one for the other. We use one to deal with the other. And we become more and more hooked on both.

As long as we are bent on escaping ourselves and avoiding our pain, we stay sick. The harder we try and the more avenues of escape we pursue, the sicker we get as we compound addictions with obsessions. We eventually discover that our solutions have become our most serious problems. Badly needing relief and finding none, sometimes we can begin to get a little crazy.

"I'm here because my attorney sent me." Brenda was nearly whispering as she made this confession on the occasion of our first appointment. "I . . . I . . . well, took some things and got caught, and he thought it would be a good idea for me to see someone for counseling . . . ," she continued conspiratorially, "that it would look better when I go back to court, if they think I'm getting help with my problems."

I barely had time to nod before she rushed on. "Except, well, I don't think I really have any *problems*. I took a couple of things from this little drugstore and forgot to pay for them. That's pretty awful, having them think I stole from them, but really it was just an oversight. The worst thing about all this is the embarrassment. But I don't have any *real* problems, not like some people do."

Brenda was presenting one of the most difficult challenges in counseling: a client who is not motivated enough to seek help for herself, indeed who denies needing any help, yet is there in the office, referred by someone else who thinks counseling would be beneficial.

While she chatted on breathlessly, I found myself tuning out the words rushing at me. Instead, I studied the woman herself. She was tall, at least five foot ten, and fashion-model thin, weighing at the most 115 pounds. She wore an elegantly simple silk dress of deep coral, accented with heavy ivory-and-gold jewelry. With her honey-blond hair and sea-green eyes she should have been beautiful. The ingredients were all there, but something was off, something was missing. Her brows were chronically knitted, creating a deep vertical crease between them. She held her breath a lot, nostrils constantly flared. And her hair, though carefully cut and coiffed, was dry and brittle. Her skin was papery and sallow in spite of an attractive tan. Her mouth would have been wide and full, but she constantly pursed her lips together, making them appear thin and tight. When she smiled it was as though she was carefully drawing a curtain back across her teeth, and when she spoke she did so with much lip-biting. I began to suspect that she practiced self-induced vomiting along with binge-eating (bulimia) and/or self-starvation (anorexia), because of the quality of her skin and hair as well as her extreme thinness.

Women with eating disorders also very frequently have episodes of compulsive stealing, so that was another clue. I also strongly suspected that she was a co-alcoholic. In my practice, nearly every woman I have seen with an eating disorder has been the daughter of either one alcoholic, two alcoholics (especially those women who practice bulimia) or an alcoholic and a compulsive eater. Compulsive eaters and alcoholics very frequently marry each other, which is not surprising since so many compulsive eaters are daughters of alcoholics and daughters of alcoholics tend to marry alcoholics. The compulsive eater is determined to control her food, her body, and her partner through the force of her will. Brenda and I certainly had some work ahead of us.

"Tell me about yourself," I requested as gently as I could, even though I knew what was coming.

Sure enough, most of what she proceeded to tell me that first day were lies: she was fine, she was happy, she didn't know what happened in the store, she couldn't remember it at all, she'd never taken anything else before. She went on to say that her attorney was very nice, just as I obviously was, and that she didn't want anyone else to know about this incident because no one else would understand, the way the attorney and I did. The flattery was calculated to get me to collude with her that nothing was really wrong, to support her in her myth that the arrest was a mistake, an inconvenient little quirk of fate and nothing more.

Fortunately, there was quite a bit of time between the first appointment and when her case was finally adjudicated, and since she knew I was in contact with her attorney she kept trying to be a "good client." She kept every appointment, and after a while she slowly began to be more truthful almost in spite of herself. Thankfully, when that happened she experienced the relief that came from letting go of living a lie. Soon she was in therapy at least as much for herself as for the effect it might have on a judge hearing the case. By the time she was sentenced (six months suspended and full restitution, plus forty hours of community work that she served at the local Girls' Club) she was working as hard to become truthful as she had previously worked to cover up who she was and what she did.

Brenda's real story, which she at first very hesitantly and cautiously disclosed, began to emerge during our third session. She looked very tired and drawn, and when I commented on this she admitted having had trouble sleeping that week. What had happened to cause that, I queried her.

First she blamed it on the upcoming trial, but that explanation didn't ring entirely true, so I probed. "Is there anything else that's troubling you this week?"

She waited awhile, determinedly chewing her lips, working her way systematically from top lip to bottom and back. Then she fairly blurted out, "I asked my husband to leave, finally, and now I wish I hadn't. I can't sleep, I can't work, I'm a nervous wreck. I hated what he was doing, running around so obviously with that girl from work, but getting along without him is harder than putting up with all of that. Now I don't know which way to turn, and I wonder if it wasn't all my fault anyway. He always said it was, that I was too cold and distant, not enough of a woman for him. And I guess he was right. I *was* angry and withdrawn a lot, but it was because he criticized me so much. I kept telling him, 'If you want me to be warm toward you, then you have to treat me as though you like me and say nice things to me, instead of telling me how awful or dumb or unattractive I am.'" Then she immediately became frightened, those eyebrows climbing even higher up her forehead, and she began discounting everything she had just disclosed. Waving manicured hands, she disclaimed, 'We're not really separated, just taking time off from each other for a while. And Rudy isn't that critical, really, I guess I deserve it. Sometimes I'm tired when I come home from work, and I don't want to cook, especially because he doesn't like what I cook. He likes his mother's cooking so much better that he'll leave the table for his mother's house and then not get home again until two in the morning. I just don't feel like trying so hard to make him happy when it never works anyway. But it's not that bad. Lots of women have it worse."

"What does he do until two? He can't be at his mother's all that time," I questioned.

"I don't even want to know. I guess he's out with his girlfriend. But I don't care. I like it better when he leaves me alone. Lots of time he wants to fight when he finally does get home, and it was more because of that—making me so tired for work the next day—than his carrying on that finally made me ask him to leave."

Here was a woman determined not to feel or reveal her emotions. That they were fairly screaming to make themselves heard only stirred her to create more predicaments in her life in order to drown them out.

After our third session I called her attorney and told him to carefully reiterate to Brenda how important it was that she continue in counseling with me. I was going to take a chance with her and I didn't want to lose her. At the beginning of our fourth session I waded in.

"Tell me about you and food, Brenda," I asked as kindly as I could. Her green eyes widened in alarm, her sallow skin lost even more color, and she pulled back visibly. Then those eyes narrowed and she smiled disarmingly.

"What do you mean, me and food? That's a silly question!"

I told her what it was I saw in her appearance that had alerted me and talked to her about the etiology of eating disorders. Identifying it as a disease shared by many, many women helped Brenda put her own compulsive behavior in better perspective. It didn't take as long as I'd feared to get her talking.

Brenda's story was long and complicated, and it took

quite a while for her to sort out reality from her need to distort, cover up, and pretend. She'd gotten so proficient at dissembling that she'd become caught in her own web of lies. She had worked hard to perfect an image to present to the outside world, an image that would mask her fear, loneliness, and the terrible emptiness inside. It was very hard for her to assess her situation so that she could take steps to meet her own needs. And her neediness was why she stole compulsively, ate compulsively, vomited and ate again, and lied compulsively, desperately trying to cover her every move.

Brenda's mother had also been a compulsive eater, grossly overweight as far back as Brenda could remember. Her father, a thin, wiry, energetic man, long since turned off by both his wife's appearance and her eccentric religiosity, had openly flouted his marriage vows for years. No one in the family doubted that he was unfaithful, and no one ever talked about it. Knowing it was one thing but admitting it was another, a violation of the family's tacit agreement: what we don't acknowledge out loud doesn't exist for us as a family, and therefore can't hurt us. It was a rule Brenda rigorously applied to her own life. If she didn't admit that anything was wrong, then nothing was. Problems didn't exist unless she put them into words. No wonder she tenaciously clung to the very lies and fabrications that were destroying her. And no wonder being in therapy was so hard for her.

Brenda grew up thin, wiry like her dad, and immensely relieved that she could eat a lot yet not get fat like her mother. At the age of fifteen her body began to suddenly show the effects of the enormous amounts of food she ate. By the time she was eighteen she weighed 240 pounds, and was more desperately unhappy than she'd ever been. Daddy now said unkind things to this young woman who had been his favorite child, about how she was turning out to be just like her mother after all. True, he wouldn't have said those things if he hadn't been drinking, but the fact was he was drinking most of the time now, even when he was home, which was seldom. Mom kept on praying and praising the Lord, and Dad kept on drinking and running around, and Brenda kept on eating, trying not to feel the panic rising within her.

When she was away from home for the first time as a college student, and terribly lonely for the comfort of the same mother and father she also deplored, she made an incredible discovery. Alone in her room, in the middle of a binge, she realized that she could vomit up nearly everything she'd eaten, and not be penalized for her enormous consumption of food by gaining weight. She was soon so entranced by the control she now felt over her weight that she began to fast, and to vomit whatever she did eat. She was moving from the bulimic stage to the anorexic stage of her compulsive eating disorder.

Brenda had repeated bouts of obesity interspersed with periods of extreme thinness over the next several years. What she never experienced during that time was a single day free from her obsession with food. She woke with hope each morning that today would be different from yesterday, and she went to bed each night with resolve to be "normal" tomorrow, often to wake in the middle of the night primed for another binge. Brenda had no real understanding of what was happening to her. She did not know that she had an eating disorder, so often present in daughters of alcoholics as well as in children of compulsive eaters. She didn't understand that she and her mother were both suffering from an allergy-addiction to certain foods, principally refined carbohydrates, which almost exactly paralleled her father's allergy-addiction to alcohol. None of them could safely ingest the smallest bit of their addictive substance without setting off an intense craving for more and more and more. And like her father's relationship to alcohol, Brenda's relationship to food, and especially to sugary baked goods, consisted of one long, drawn-out battle to control the substance that instead controlled her.

She continued to practice self-induced vomiting for

years after the time she first "invented" it in college. Her isolation and secretiveness became ever more involved and extreme, and in many ways this behavior was fostered by her family as well as by her disease. Brenda's family did not want to hear anything from her to which they couldn't reply, "Oh, that's nice, dear." There was no room for pain, fear, loneliness, honesty, no room for the truth about herself or her life. Because they constantly skirted the truth, it was implicit that she should too, and not rock the boat. With her parents as silent accomplices, she dived deeper into the lie that was her life, sure that if she could manage to look good on the outside, all would be well—or at least stilled—on the inside.

Even when her appearance was under control for extended periods, the turmoil within could not be ignored. Though she did everything she could to make the outside look good—designer clothes worn with the latest makeup and hair styles—it wasn't enough to still her fear, fill her emptiness. Partly because of all the emotions she refused to recognize and partly because of the devastation to her nervous system that her self-imposed malnutrition was producing, Brenda's mental state was confused, anxious, morbid, and obsessive.

In a search for freedom from this inner turmoil, Brenda, following her mother's pattern, sought solace in a zealous religious group that met on campus. It was within this circle that in her senior year she met her husband-to-be, Rudy, a kind of dark-horse type who fascinated her all the more because of his mystery. Brenda was used to secrets, and he had plenty. There were hints in the stories he told and the names he dropped that he had been on the fringes of mob activities involving bookmaking and numbers in the New Jersey city that was his hometown. He vaguely alluded to large amounts of money he had made and spent, flashy cars and flashy women, the nightclubs, the drinking and drugs. And here he was now, metamorphosed into a serious student living on the campus of a staid midwestern college, active in a religious group for young people, having left his shadowy past behind in search of something better. That he had left in a hurry and under duress was implied by the fact that he had even broken off communication with his family, but Brenda was so impressed with both his dark, mysterious past and his apparently sincere attempts to change that she had no need to ask for detailed explanations of his past exploits. After all, she had her own secrets to keep.

So these two people pretending to be what they were not, he an outlaw in the guise of a choirboy, she a compulsive eater masquerading as a fashion plate, naturally fell in love—with each other's projected illusion. That someone loved what she pretended to be sealed Brenda's fate. Now she had to keep the deception going, and at closer quarters. More pressure, more stress, more need to eat, vomit, hide.

Rudy's abstinence from cigarettes, alcohol, and drugs lasted until he heard from his family that they had moved to California. Apparently deciding that with enough geographical distance between him and his past he could safely return both to his family and his old ways, he packed up himself and his new wife Brenda and headed west. Almost as soon as he crossed the first state line his persona began to alter, to revert to what it had been before Brenda met him. Her camouflage lasted longer, until she and Rudy began living with his parents. With so many people in the house, she was unable to freely continue her self-induced vomiting. While the binges were harder to hide, they nevertheless gained momentum under the stress of her present circumstances, and Brenda's weight began to climb. She quickly gained fifty pounds, and Rudy's beautiful blond wife disappeared into the matronly folds of Brenda's relentlessly fattening body. Feeling cheated and angry, Rudy left her at home while he went out drinking, and looking for someone whose appearance complemented his the way Brenda's once had. In despair, she ate more than ever, promising herself and Rudy that all she needed was for them to have a place of their own and she would be able to become slim again. When they finally got their townhouse, sure enough, Brenda's weight began to drop as precipitously as it had risen, but Rudy was rarely home to notice. She became pregnant, and four months later she miscarried alone while Rudy spent the night elsewhere.

By now Brenda was sure that everything happening was her fault. The man who had once been wholesome and happy and had shared her values and beliefs was like another person now, someone she didn't know and didn't like. They argued over his behavior and her nagging. She tried not to nag, hoping his behavior would change. It didn't. She wasn't fat like her mother, and yet he ran around like her father. Her helplessness in getting her life in order panicked her.

Brenda had stolen as a teenager, not with friends in a shared assault on the adult world's booty, but alone, in secret, rarely ever using or even keeping the items she took. Now in her unhappy marriage to Rudy, she began to steal again, symbolically taking from the world what wasn't being given to her: love, support, understanding, and acceptance. But her thievery only isolated her more, gave her another dark secret to guard, another source of shame and guilt. Meanwhile, the outside packaging was again becoming Brenda's greatest defense against being seen for what she was—a driven, fearful, empty, and lonely person. Once more she was thin, and she held a job primarily to keep herself supplied with the expensive clothes she craved. She modeled some, and hoped it would make Rudy proud of her. While he bragged about his wife, the model, he never bothered actually coming to watch her walk down a single runway.

Because Brenda looked to Rudy for appreciation and validation, his inability to do so drove her self-esteem, already so marginal, even lower. The less he gave her, the more she needed from him. She worked on perfecting her appearance, but felt that she was missing some mysteriously attractive element the dark-haired women with whom Rudy had his affairs all seemed to effortlessly exude. She pushed herself harder to be thinner, because being thinner meant being more perfect. She became a perfectionist about housekeeping as well, and soon was totally occupied with her various obsessive-compulsive behaviors: cleaning, stealing, eating, vomiting. While Rudy was out drinking and running around, Brenda was cleaning the house late into the night, guiltily hopping into bed and feigning sleep if she heard his car pull into the garage below.

Rudy complained about her fastidiousness around the house, and rather aggressively undid the effects of her careful cleaning each evening when he came home, whether early or late. The result was that Brenda couldn't wait for him to leave so that she could clean and straighten what he'd messed up. When he left for the evening's drinking and carousing, she felt relief. Everything was getting crazier.

Her arrest in the drugstore was doubtless a blessing, in that it created a crisis that got her into counseling, where she started looking at what her life had become. She had wanted to get away from Rudy for a long time but hadn't been able to let go of her compulsion to fix the relationship by perfecting herself. Ironically, the more completely she separated from him, the more ardently he pursued her, with flowers, phone calls, showing up at her workplace unexpectedly with tickets to a concert. Her coworkers, who first met him while he was playing this role, thought Brenda was foolish to leave such an adoring, devoted man. It took two hope-filled reconciliations, each followed by painful breakups, for her to learn that Rudy wanted only what he couldn't have. Once they lived together as man and wife, his womanizing quickly resumed. During the second breakup Brenda told him she thought he had a problem with drinking and drugs. He set about getting help to prove he didn't. For two months he was clean and sober. They reconciled again, and on the occasion of their first argument a few days later he drank and stayed out all night. When this happened, Brenda, with the help of therapy, saw the pattern in which they both were caught. Rudy was using the deliberately created turbulence of his relationship with Brenda to both camouflage and justify his addictive pursuit of alcohol, drugs, and women. At the same time, Brenda was using the tremendous tension generated by their relationship as an excuse for surrendering to and indulging in her bulimia and other compulsive behaviors. Each used the other to avoid dealing with themselves and their own addictions. When Brenda finally recognized this, she was able to let go of the hope that she could have a happy marriage.

Brenda's recovery involved three very important and necessary elements. She stayed in therapy, she attended Al-Anon to deal with her lifelong co-alcoholism, and she finally, with the relief that comes from surrender, immersed herself in Overeaters Anonymous, where she received help and support in dealing with her eating disorder. For Brenda, involvement in O.A. was the most important factor in her recovery, and the one she had resisted most vigorously in the beginning. Her compulsive eating, vomiting, and starving comprised her most serious and deep-seated problem, her primary disease process. The obsession with food drained off all the energy that would be required for her to achieve any kind of healthy relationship with herself and others in her life. Until she was able to stop obsessing about her weight, her food intake, calories, diets, and so on, she could feel no real emotions about anything but food, nor could she be honest with herself or others.

As long as her feelings were numbed by her eating disorder, she could not begin to take care of herself, make wise decisions for herself, or really live her own life. Instead, food was her life, and in many ways that was the only life she wanted. Desperate as her battle was to control food, it was a less threatening struggle than the one she faced with herself, her family, her husband. Although she had set limits hourly regarding what she would and wouldn't eat, Brenda had never set limits on what others could do or say to her. In order to recover, she had to begin to define the point where others left off and she, an autonomous person, began. She also had to allow herself to get angry at others, not just at herself, which had been her chronic state.

In O.A. Brenda began to practice honesty for the first time in many, many years. After all, what was the point of lying about her behavior to people who understood and accepted who she was and what she did? In return for her honesty came the healing power of acceptance from her peers. This gave her the courage to carry that honesty to a wider circle outside of the O.A. program, to her family and friends and to possible partners.

Al-Anon helped her understand the roots of her problem in her family of origin and also gave her tools for understanding both her parents' compulsive disorders as well as how their diseases had affected her. There she learned to relate to them in a healthier way.

Rudy went on to marry again, the moment the divorce was final, even while protesting by phone the night before his next wedding that he really wanted only Brenda. That conversation deepened Brenda's understanding of Rudy's inability to honor the commitments he made, of his need to constantly look for a way to avoid whatever relationship he was in. Like her father, he was a wanderer who also liked having a wife and a home.

Brenda soon learned too that it was necessary for her to maintain considerable distance, both geographically and emotionally, between herself and her family. Two visits home, both of which temporarily reactivated her bingeing and purging syndrome, taught her that she could not yet be around her family without resorting to her old ways of handling the tension.

Staying healthy has become her first priority, but she continues to be amazed at how difficult a challenge it is and how few skills she possesses for it. Filling her life with enjoyable work, as well as new friendships and interests, has been a slow, step-by-step process. Having known little about being happy, comfortable, and at peace, she has had to rigorously avoid creating problems that would enable her to feel the old, familiar craziness.

Brenda continues to attend O.A., Al-Anon, and occasionally therapy sessions when she feels the need. She is no longer as thin as she once was, nor as fat either. "I'm normal!" she howls, enjoying a laugh on herself, knowing she never will be. Her eating disorder is a lifelong disease that demands her respect, although it no longer has a stranglehold on her health or her sanity.

Brenda's recovery is still a fragile thing. It takes a long time before the new, healthier ways of living feel right instead of forced. She could again revert to avoiding herself and her feelings through compulsive eating or through obsession with an unhealthy relationship. Because she knows this, Brenda currently interacts with men cautiously, never making a date that would require missing an O.A. or Al-Anon meeting, for instance. Her recovery is extremely precious to her, and she is not about to jeopardize it. In her words, "I've made it a practice not to keep secrets anymore, since that was how I got so sick in the first place. Now when I meet a new man, if it looks like the relationship might go somewhere I always let him know about my disease and the importance of the Anonymous programs in my life. If he can't handle knowing the truth about me or is unable to understand, I see it as *his* problem, not mine. I'm not trying to turn myself inside out to please a man anymore. My priorities are very different today. My recovery has to come first. Otherwise, I have nothing left to offer anyone else."

9 • Dying For Love

> WE ARE ALL, EVERY ONE OF US, FULL OF
> HORROR. IF YOU ARE GETTING MARRIED TO
> MAKE YOURS GO AWAY, YOU WILL ONLY
> SUCCEED IN MARRYING YOUR HORROR TO
> SOMEONE ELSE'S HORROR; YOUR TWO
> HORRORS WILL HAVE THE MARRIAGE, YOU
> WILL BLEED AND CALL THAT LOVE.
>
> —MICHAEL VENTURA,
> "SHADOW DANCING IN
> THE MARRIAGE ZONE"

CHAIN-SMOKING, HER SHOULDERS HELD HIGH AND TIGHT,
Margo swung her crossed leg rapidly back and forth, with
her foot giving an extra jerk at the end of each oscillation.
She sat stiffly forward and stared out the waiting-room
window at one of the most beautiful vistas in the world.
The red-tiled roofs of Santa Barbara climbed the blue and
purple hills above the ocean, but the scene, softly tinted
with pink and gold on that summer afternoon, lent none of
its Spanish-style tranquillity to her face. She looked like a
woman in a hurry, and indeed she was.

As I pointed the way, she walked quickly, heels tapping,
into my office and sat down, again on the edge of her
chair, and looked sharply at me. "How do I know you can
help me? I've never done this before, come to talk with

someone about my life. How do I know it's going to be worth the time and the money?"

I knew she was also trying to ask me, "How do I know whether I can trust you to care about me if I let you know who I really am?" So I tried to answer both questions with my reply.

"Therapy does require a commitment of time and money. But people never even come to the first appointment unless something very frightening or very painful is happening in their lives, something they've already tried hard to handle but haven't been able to manage. No one just casually drops in to see a therapist. I'm sure you thought about it a long time before you decided to come."

The accuracy of that statement seemed to relieve her somewhat, and she allowed herself to sit back with a small sigh.

"I probably should have done this fifteen years ago, or before that even, but how did I know I needed some help? I thought I was doing fine. And in some ways I was—still am, too. I've got a good job and make pretty decent money as an escrow officer." She stopped suddenly, and then, more reflectively, continued. "Sometimes it's as though I have two lives. I go off to work, and I'm bright and efficient, well respected. People ask my advice and give me lots of responsibility and I feel grown up and capable and sure of myself." She looked up at the ceiling and swallowed to gain control of her voice. "Then I come home and my life is like one long, sort of crummy, novel. It's so bad that if it was a book, I wouldn't read it. Too tacky, you know? But here I am, stuck living it. I've been married four times already, and I'm only thirty-five. *Only!* God, I feel so old. I'm beginning to be afraid that I'm never going to get my life together, and that time's running out. I'm not as young as I used to be and not as pretty either. I'm scared no one else will want me, that I've used up all my chances and now I'll have to be alone always." The fear in her voice was matched by the worry lines etched on her brow as she expressed this. She swallowed several times and blinked hard. "It would be difficult for me to say which marriage was the worst. They were all such disasters, but in different ways.

"My first husband and I married when I was twenty. When I met him I knew he was wild. He ran around on me before we got married, and he ran around on me afterward, too. I thought being married would make a difference, but it never did. When our daughter was born I was sure that would slow him down a little, but it had just the opposite effect. He stayed away even more. When he was home he was mean. I could handle him yelling at me, but when he started punishing little Autumn for nothing and everything, I started to interfere. When that didn't work, I got us both out of there. It wasn't easy, because she was so little and I had to find work. He never paid us any kind of support, either, and I was so afraid he'd make trouble for us that I didn't push it with the D.A.'s office or anything. I couldn't move back home, because home was just like my marriage. My mom took a lot of abuse from my dad, physical and verbal, and so did all of us kids. I was always running away when I was growing up. Finally I had run away and gotten married to get out of there, so I sure wasn't going back.

"It took me two years from the time I left to get the courage to divorce my first husband. I couldn't quite let go until I had another man. The attorney who handled my divorce ended up becoming my second husband. He was quite a bit older than I was, and had been recently divorced himself. I don't think I was really in love with him, but I wanted to be, and I thought that here was someone who could take care of Autumn and me. He talked a lot about wanting to start over in his life, begin a new family with someone he could really love. I guess I was flattered that he felt that way about me. I was married to him the day after my divorce was final. Everything was going to be all right now, I was sure. I got Autumn into a good preschool and went back to school myself. My daughter and I spent our afternoons together, then I'd make dinner and go back to school for night classes. Dwayne would stay home in the evenings with Autumn, doing legal work. Then one morning when we were alone Autumn said some things to me that made me realize that something awful, something sexual, was going on between her and Dwayne. I was also suspecting that I was pregnant by now, but I just waited until the next day, as if everything was normal, and after Dwayne went to work I put my daughter and everything of ours I could fit into my car, and left. I wrote him a note telling him what Autumn had told me and warned him not to try to find us or it would come out about what he'd done to her. I was so afraid that he would have some way of finding us and making us come back that I decided, if I was pregnant, not to tell him, not to ever ask anything of him. I just wanted him to leave us alone.

"He did find out where we lived, of course, and sent me a letter, with no reference to Autumn at all. Instead, he blamed me for being cold and indifferent toward him, leaving him alone while I went to school in the evenings. I felt very guilty about that for a long time, thinking that what happened to Autumn was my fault. Here I'd thought I was making everything safe for my daughter, when I'd only put her in a horrible situation." A haunted expression came over Margo's face as she remembered that time.

"Luckily, I found a room in a house with another young mother. She and I had so much in common. We'd both married too young and had come from homes that were unhappy. Our dads were a lot alike and so were our first husbands. She only had one ex-husband, though." Margo shook her head and went on. "Anyway, we babysat for each other a lot, and that enabled us each to continue with school and to go out too. I felt more freedom than I ever had in my life, even though it turned out I was pregnant. Dwayne still didn't know, and I never told him. I remembered all his lawyer stories about the ways he could make trouble for people legally, and I knew he could make trouble for me, too. I wanted nothing to do with him ever again. Before we married that kind of talk from him had made me think he was strong. Now it just made me afraid of him.

"Susie, my roommate, coached me through natural childbirth with my second daughter, Darla. It sounds crazy, but that was one of the best times of my life. We were so poor, going to school, working, taking care of our babies, buying clothes at thrift stores and food with food stamps. But we were free in our own way." She shrugged. "Yet I was so restless. I wanted a man in my life. I kept hoping I could find someone who would make my life turn out the way I wanted it to. I still feel that way. That's why I'm here. I want to learn how to find someone who will be good for me. I haven't done too well at that so far."

Margo's tense face, still pretty though painfully thin, looked at me pleadingly. Could I help her find and keep Mr. Wonderful? That was the question written all over it, her reason for coming to therapy.

She went on with her saga. The next player in her marital round-robin was Giorgio, who drove a white Mercedes Benz convertible and made his living supplying cocaine to some of the wealthiest noses in Montecito. It was a roller coaster ride with Giorgio from the beginning, and soon Margo couldn't distinguish between the chemistry of the drug he so freely provided her with and the chemistry of her relationship with this dark and dangerous man. Suddenly her life was fast and glamorous. It was also hard on her physically and emotionally. Her temper got shorter. She scolded her children over trifles. Her frequent quarrels with Giorgio escalated into physical battles. After complaining to her roommate endlessly about his thoughtlessness, infidelity, and illegal practices, Margo was shocked when Susie finally gave her an ultimatum. Get over Giorgio or get out of the house. Susie wasn't going to listen to it or watch it anymore. It wasn't good for Margo or any of the children. Margo, incensed, flew to Giorgio's arms. He allowed her and her daughters to move into the house where he did most of his dealing, with the understanding that the arrangement would be temporary. Shortly thereafter, he was arrested for drug sales. Before his trial Giorgio and Margo were married, though by that time their interactions were almost always heated to the boiling point.

The reason she gave for her third decision to marry was Giorgio's pressure on her to become his wife so that she couldn't be required to testify against him. The temptation to testify was a distinct possibility, given the inflammatory nature of their interactions and the persistence of the prosecutor. Once they were married, an ungrateful Giorgio refused to have sexual relations with her because, he said, he felt trapped. The marriage was eventually annulled, but not before Margo had met number four, a man four years her junior who had never held a job because he had always been in school. She told herself that this serious student was just what she needed, after her catastrophe with Giorgio, and by now she was terrified of being alone. Margo worked and supported them both, until he left her to join a religious commune. During this fourth marriage, Margo had come into considerable money from a relative's death, which she made available to this husband, hoping by that gesture to demonstrate her loyalty, trust, and love for him (which he constantly questioned). He gave most of her money to the commune, and then made it clear to Margo that he no longer wished to be married to her, and did not want her to join him there, blaming her for the failure of their marriage because of her "worldliness."

Margo had been deeply scarred by these events, and yet she was desperately eager to meet number five, feeling sure it would work out this time if she could just find the right man. She came into therapy haggard and hollow eyed, afraid that she had lost her looks and couldn't attract another man. She was totally out of touch with her lifelong pattern of relating to impossible men, men she didn't trust or even like. Although she admitted to having been unlucky so far in her choice of husbands, she was unaware of how her own needs had trapped her into each marital disaster.

The picture she presented was alarming. Besides being severely underweight (her ulcers made eating a self-imposed torture on the rare occasions when she had an appetite), Margo exhibited a number of other nervous, stress-related symptoms. She was pale (she confirmed that she was anemic) with severely bitten nails and dry, brittle hair. She described problems with excema, diarrhea, and insomnia. Her blood pressure was very high for her age and her energy level was alarmingly low.

"Sometimes it's all I can do to get myself up to go to work. I've taken all my sick leave and used it to stay home and cry. I feel guilty crying when my children are home so it's a relief to be able to let go when they're at school. I really don't know how much longer I can keep going on like this."

She reported that both her children were experiencing problems in school, academically and socially. At home they fought with each other constantly, and her temper with them was quick. She still frequently resorted to using cocaine for the "lift" she had become accustomed to getting from it during the days with Giorgio, a lift that she could ill afford, financially or physically.

None of these factors, however, troubled Margo as much as currently being unattached. Since her teens she had never been without a male in her life. As a child she had battled her father and as an adult she had, in one way or another, battled every man she paired with. Alone four months now, it was only because of her miserable record so far that she found herself as reluctant to go out looking as she was to hold still with herself.

Many women, because of oppressive economic realities, feel they need a man to support them financially, but this was not the case with Margo. She had a well-paying job doing work she enjoyed. None of her four husbands had financially supported her or her children. Her need for another man lay in a different direction. She was addicted to relationships, and bad relationships at that.

In her family of origin there had been abuse of her mother, her siblings, and herself. There had been money problems, insecurity, and suffering. The emotional strain of this kind of childhood had left deep traces on her psyche.

To begin with, Margo suffered from a severe, underlying depression, so often present in women with similar histories. Ironically, because of this depression, as well as the familiar roles she was able to play with each partner, Margo was drawn to men who were impossible: abusive, unpredictable, irresponsible, or unresponsive. In these kinds of relationships would be many arguments, even violent fights, dramatic exits and reconciliations, and periods of tense and fearful waiting in between. There could be serious problems with money or even with the law. Much drama. Much chaos. Much excitement. Much stimulation.

Sounds exhausting, doesn't it? Of course, in the long run it is, but rather like using cocaine or any other powerful stimulant, in the short run these relationships provide a great escape, a great diversion, and certainly a highly effective mask for depression. It is almost impossible to experience depression when we are very excited, either positively or negatively, because of the high levels of adrenalin being released and stimulating us. But too much exposure to strong excitement exhausts the body's ability to respond, and the result is deeper depression than before, this time with a physical as well as an emotional basis.* Many women like Margo, because of their emo-

---

*There are two types of depression, exogenous and endogenous. Exogenous depression occurs in reaction to outside events and is closely related to grieving. Endogenous depression is a result of improperly functioning biochemistry and appears to be genetically linked with compulsive eating and/or alcohol and drug addiction. In tional histories of living with constant and/or severe episodes of stress in childhood (and also because often they may have inherited a biochemical vulnerability to depression from an alcoholic or otherwise biochemically inefficient parent), are basically depressives before they even begin their love relationships as teens and adults. Such women may unconsciously seek the powerful stimulation of a difficult and dramatic relationship in order to stir their glands to release adrenaline—an exercise similar to whipping a tired, overworked horse in order to get a few more miles out of the poor, exhausted beast. This is why, when the strong stimulant of involvement in an unhealthy relationship is removed, either because the relationship ends or because the man begins to recover from his problems and to relate to her in a healthier way, a woman of this type will usually sink into depression. When she is without a man she will either try to revive the last failed relationship or frantically search for another difficult man on whom to focus, because she so badly needs the stimulation he will provide. Should her man begin to seriously address his own problems in a healthier way, she suddenly may find herself yearning for someone more exciting, more stimulating, someone who enables her to avoid facing her own feelings and problems.

Again, the parallels with drug use and withdrawal are obvious. To avoid her own feelings she is literally "fixing" with a man, using him as her drug of escape. For recovery to occur she must gain the support to hold still and allow the painful feelings to come. By this time both her emotions and her body need to heal. It is not an exaggeration to compare this process to a heroin addict's quitting cold turkey. The fear, the pain, and the discomfort are commensurate, and the temptation to resort to another man, another fix, is just as great.

---

fact, these may all be different expressions of the same or similar biochemical disorders.

A woman who uses her relationships as a drug will have fully as much denial about that fact as any chemically addictive individual, and fully as much resistance and fear concerning letting go of her obsessive thinking and high emotionally charged way of interacting with men. But usually, if she is gently but firmly confronted, she will at some level recognize the power of her relationship addiction and know that she is in the grip of a pattern over which she has lost control.

The first step in treating a woman with this problem is to help her realize that, like any addict, she is suffering from a *disease process* that is identifiable, is progressive without treatment, and that responds well to specific treatment. She needs to know that she is addicted to the pain and familiarity of an unrewarding relationship, and that it is a disease afflicting many, many women, having its roots in disordered relationships in childhood.

To wait for someone like Margo to figure out on her own that she is a woman who loves too much, whose disease is becoming progressively severe and may very well ultimately cost her life, is as inappropriate as listening to all the typical symptoms of any other disease and then expecting the patient to guess her condition and her treatment. Even more to the point, it is as unlikely that Margo, with her particular disease and its accompanying denial, could self-diagnose, as it is unlikely that an equally sick alcoholic could accurately self-diagnose. Nor could either of them hope to recover alone, or simply with the help of a doctor or therapist, because recovery requires that they stop doing what seems to give them relief.

Therapy alone does not offer an adequately supportive alternative to the alcoholic's dependency on the drug or the relationally addictive woman's dependency on her man. When anyone who has been practicing an addiction tries to stop, an enormous vacuum is created in that person's life—too great a vacuum for an hour-long session with a therapist once or twice a week to fill. Because of the tremendous anxiety generated when the dependence on the substance or the person is interrupted, access to support, reassurance, and understanding must be constantly available. This is best provided by peers who have been through the same painful withdrawal process themselves.

Another failure of traditional therapy in the treatment of any kind of addiction is the tendency to view the addiction, whether to a substance or to a relationship, as only a *symptom,* rather than recognizing it as the primary disease process that must be addressed *first* in order for therapy to continue and progress. Instead, the patient is usually allowed to continue to practice the addictive behavior while therapy sessions are devoted to uncovering the "reasons" for the behavior. This approach is absolutely backward and usually totally ineffective. By the time someone is in an alcoholic situation, the basic problem is addiction to alcohol, and that is what must be addressed; that is, the drinking must stop before other aspects of life can begin to improve. Searching for underlying reasons for the drinking in the hope that uncovering the "cause" will allow the alcohol abuse to stop *does not work.* The "cause" for the drinking is that this patient has the disease of alcoholism. Only by dealing head-on with the alcoholism first is there a chance of recovering.

For the woman who loves too much, her primary disease is her addiction to the pain and familiarity of an unrewarding relationship. True, this generates from life-long patterns reaching back into childhood, but she *must* first of all deal with her patterns in the present, in order for her recovery to begin. No matter how sick or cruel or helpless her partner is, she, along with her doctor or therapist, must understand that her every attempt to change him, help him, control him, or blame him is a manifestation of *her* disease, and that she must stop these behaviors before other areas of her life can improve. Her only legitimate work is with herself. In the next chapter we will outline the specific steps that a relationally addictive woman must take in order to recover.

The following charts describing the characteristics of practicing and recovering alcoholics and relationally addictive women makes clear the behavioral parallels of these diseases, both in the active phase and in recovery. What a chart cannot truly convey is just how parallel the struggle to recover is in those with either of these diseases. It is as difficult to recover from relationship dependency (or loving too much) as it is to recover from alcoholism. And for those suffering from either disease, that recovery can make the difference between life and death.

Characteristics of Practicing

Alcoholics	Relationally Addictive Women
obsessed with alcohol	obsessed with relationship
denying extent of problem	denying extent of problem
lying to cover how much drinking is going on	lying to cover what is happening in relationship
avoiding people to hide problems with drinking	avoiding people to hide problems with relationship
repeated attempts to control drinking	repeated attempts to control relationship
unexplained mood swings	unexplained mood swings
anger, depression, guilt	anger, depression, guilt
resentment	resentment
irrational acts	irrational acts
violence	violence
accidents due to intoxication	accidents due to preoccupation
self-hate/self-justification	self-hate/self-justification
physical illness due to abuse of alcohol	physical illness due to stress-related diseases

Characteristics of Recovering

Alcoholics	Relationally Addictive Women
admitting helplessness to control disease	admitting helplessness to control disease
ceasing to blame others for problems	ceasing to blame others for problems
focusing on self, taking responsibility for *own* actions	focusing on self, taking responsibility for *own* actions
seeking help for recovery from peers	seeking help for recovery from peers
beginning to deal with *own* feelings rather than avoiding them	beginning to deal with *own* feelings rather than avoiding them
building a circle of well friends, healthy interests	building a circle of well friends, healthy interests

When we are seriously ill, our recovery often requires that the specific disease process from which we are suffering be correctly identified in order that appropriate treatment be given. If we consult professionals, part of their responsibility to us is to be familiar with the signs and symptoms of specific common diseases so that they can diagnose our maladies and treat us accordingly, using the most effective means available.

I want to make a case for applying the disease concept to the pattern of loving too much. This is a tall order, and if you balk at accepting this proposal, I hope you will at least see the strong analogy between a disease such as alcoholism, which is addiction to a substance, and that which occurs in women who love too much, addicted as they are to the men in their lives. I am thoroughly convinced that what afflicts women who love too much is not *like* a disease process; it *is* a disease process, requiring a specific diagnosis and a specific treatment.

First let's examine what is meant, literally, by the word *disease:* any deviation from health with a specific and progressive set of symptoms identifiable across the population of its victims, which may respond to specific forms of treatment.

This definition does not demand the presence of a particular virus or microbe or other physical causative agent, only that the victim of the disease become sicker in a recognizable and predictable fashion unique to that disease, and that recovery may be possible after the application of certain appropriate interventions.

Nonetheless, it is a difficult concept for many in the medical profession to apply when the disease has behavioral rather than physical manifestations in its early and middle stages. This is one of the reasons why most physicians cannot recognize alcoholism unless the victim is in the late stages, when physical deterioration is obvious.

It is perhaps even more difficult to recognize loving too much as a disease, because the addiction is not a substance but to a person. The greatest barrier against recognizing it as a pathological condition requiring treatment, however, is that physicians, counselors, and all the rest of us entertain certain deeply held beliefs about women and love. We all tend to believe that suffering is a mark of true love, that to refuse to suffer is selfish, and that if a man has a problem then a woman should help him change. These attitudes help perpetuate both diseases, alcoholism and loving too much.

Both alcoholism and loving too much are subtle diseases in their early stages. By the time it is obvious that something very destructive is in progress, the temptation is to look at and treat the physical manifestations—the alcoholic's liver or pancreas, the relationally addictive woman's nerves or high blood pressure—without accurately assessing the entire picture. It is vital to view these "symptoms" in the overall context of the disease processes that have created them, and to recognize the existence of these diseases at the earliest possible time in order to halt the continued destruction of emotional and physical health.

The parallel between the progression of the disease of alcoholism and the progression of the disease of loving too much is clearly delineated in the following charts. Each chart demonstrates how addiction, whether to a mind-altering chemical or to an unhappy relationship, ultimately affects every area of the addict's life in a progressively disastrous way. The effects proceed from the emotional to the physical realm, involving not only other individuals (children, neighbors, friends, coworkers) but for the relationally addictive woman often other disease processes as well, such as compulsive eating, stealing, or working. The charts also describe the parallel processes of recovery for chemically addictive and relationally addictive persons. It bears mentioning that the chart for the progression of and recovery from the disease of alcoholism is probably slightly more representative of what happens when the alcoholic is a male, and the chart on relationship addiction is more representative of the disease process and recovery of a woman, rather than a man, who loves too much. The variations due to sex are not major and perhaps can be fairly easily imagined from viewing both charts, but it is not within the scope of this book to explore in detail those differences. The main order of business here is to understand ever more clearly how women who love too much get sick and how they can get well.

Remember, too, that Margo's story was not based on the chart, nor was the chart constructed to reflect her story. She, with several partners, moved through the same progressive stages of the disease that another woman who loves too much would with only one partner. If relationship addiction, or loving too much, is a disease similar to alcoholism, then its stages are equally identifiable and its progression is just as predictable.

The following chapter will examine in detail the recovery side of the chart, but now let us focus briefly on the feelings and behaviors described in the chart that indicate both the presence and the downward progression of the disease of loving too much.

As indicated in each story presented in this book, women who love too much come from families of origin in which they were either very lonely and isolated, or rejected, or overburdened with inappropriately heavy responsibilities and so became overly nurturing and self-sacrificing; or else they were subjected to dangerous chaos so that they developed an overwhelming need to control the people around them and the situations in which they found themselves. It naturally follows that a woman who needs to nurture, control, or both will be able to do so only with a partner who at least allows if not actually invites this kind of behavior. Inevitably, she will involve herself with a man who is irresponsible in at least some important areas of his life because he clearly needs her help, her nurturing, and her control. Then begins her struggle to try to change him through the power and persuasion of her love.

It is at this early point that the later insanity of the relationship is foreshadowed as she begins to deny the reality of the relationship. Remember, denial is an unconscious process, occurring automatically and unbidden. Her dream of how it could be and her efforts to achieve that end distort her perception of how it *is*. Every disappointment, failure, and betrayal in the relationship is either ignored or rationalized away. "It's not that bad." "You don't understand what he's really like." "He didn't mean to." "It's not his fault." These are just a few of the stock phrases that the woman who loves too much uses at this point in her disease process to defend her partner and her relationship.

At the same time that this man is disappointing her and failing her, she is becoming more dependent on him emotionally. This is because she has already become tightly focused on him, his problems, his welfare, and perhaps most important, his feelings for her. As she continues to try to change him he absorbs most of her

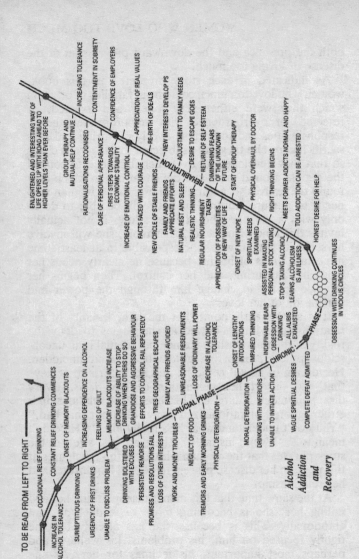

TO BE READ FROM LEFT TO RIGHT

INCREASE IN ALCOHOL TOLERANCE
Occasional relief drinking
Constant relief drinking commences
ONSET OF MEMORY BLACKOUTS
Surreptitious drinking
Urgency of first drinks
Unable to discuss problem
Increasing dependence on alcohol
Feelings of guilt
Memory blackouts increase
Drinking bolstered with excuses
Decrease of ability to stop drinking when others do so
Grandiose and aggressive behaviour
Persistent remorse
Efforts to control fail repeatedly
Promises and resolutions fail
Tries geographical escapes
Loss of other interests
Family and friends avoided
Work and money troubles
Unreasonable resentments
Neglect of food
Loss of ordinary will power
Tremors and early morning drinks
Decrease in alcohol tolerance
Physical deterioration
Onset of lengthy intoxications
Impaired thinking
Moral deterioration
Drinking with inferiors
Unable to initiate action
Indefinable fears
Obsession with drinking
Vague spiritual desires
All alibis exhausted
Complete defeat admitted

CRUCIAL PHASE
CHRONIC PHASE

OBSESSION WITH DRINKING CONTINUES IN VICIOUS CIRCLES

Learns alcoholism is an illness
Stops taking alcohol
Told addiction can be arrested
Honest desire for help
Personal stock taking
Assisted in making
Spiritual needs examined
Meets former addicts normal and happy
Right thinking begins
Physical overhaul by doctor
Onset of new hope
Start of group therapy
Appreciation of possibilities of new way of life
Diminishing fears of the unknown future
Regular nourishment taken
Return of self esteem
Realistic thinking
Desire to escape goes
Natural rest and sleep
Adjustment to family needs
Family and friends appreciate efforts
New interests develop
New circle of stable friends
Re-birth of ideals
Facts faced with courage
Increase of emotional control
Appreciation of real values
First steps towards economic stability
Care of personal appearance
Contentment in sobriety
Confidence of employers
Rationalisations recognised
Increasing tolerance
Group therapy and mutual help continue

REHABILITATION

ENLIGHTENED AND INTERESTING WAY OF LIFE OPENS UP WITH ROAD AHEAD TO HIGHER LEVELS THAN EVER BEFORE

Alcohol Addiction and Recovery

Source: M. M. Glatt, M.D., D.P.M., *The British Journal of Addiction* 54, no. 2

TO BE READ FROM LEFT TO RIGHT

The Progression of "Loving Too Much" and Recovery

Descending phase

- OVERLY RESPONSIBLE, OVERLY NURTURING BEHAVIOR DEVELOPED IN DYSFUNCTIONAL FAMILY OF ORIGIN
- STRONG NEED TO CONTROL OTHERS, CHOOSES IRRESPONSIBLE PARTNER WHO INVITES THIS
- ATTRACTED TO THOSE WHO NEED HER
- TRIES TO "LOVE" HER MAN WELL AS SHE TRIED TO "LOVE" HER SICK PARENTS WELL
- BEGINS TO DENY REALITY OF RELATIONSHIP
- INCREASING EMOTIONAL DEPENDENCY ON MAN
- TRIES TO AVOID UPSETTING MAN
- FEELINGS OF GUILT
- URGENCY TO DISCUSS PROBLEMS WITH MAN
- BEGINS TO DOUBT PERCEPTIONS
- EXCUSES MAN'S BEHAVIOR TO OTHERS
- INCREASING FOCUS ON MAN'S BEHAVIOR
- FEELINGS OF FAILURE
- OBSESSION WITH COVERING UP PROBLEMS
- AGGRESSIVE BEHAVIOR TOWARD MAN, DESIRE FOR REVENGE
- PERSISTENT REMORSE FOR FIGHTS WITH MAN
- EFFORTS TO CONTROL MAN FAIL REPEATEDLY
- ANGER AND RESENTMENT AT UNKEPT PROMISES AND RESOLUTIONS
- TRIES GEOGRAPHICAL ESCAPES WITH MAN
- LOSS OF OTHER INTERESTS
- FAMILY AND FRIENDS AVOIDED
- WORK AND MONEY TROUBLES; ASSUMES MAN'S RESPONSIBILITIES
- UNREASONABLE RESENTMENTS

CRUCIAL PHASE

- COMPULSIVE OVEREATING OR NEGLECT OF FOOD
- MEDICAL PROBLEMS, USE OF TRANQUILIZERS BEGINS
- MAY DEVELOP ALCOHOL OR DRUG DEPENDENCY
- PHYSICAL DETERIORATION
- ONSET OF LENGTHY DEPRESSIONS
- RESENTMENT OF "NORMAL" PEOPLE
- IMPAIRED THINKING, DESPONDENCY
- INDEFINABLE FEARS, PARANOIA
- EXTRAMARITAL AFFAIRS, WORKAHOLISM, OBSESSION WITH OUTSIDE INTERESTS
- UNABLE TO INITIATE ACTION
- INCREASING VIOLENCE TOWARD MAN, CHILDREN
- COMPLETE OBSESSION WITH MAN

CHRONIC PHASE

- SUICIDE THREATS OR ATTEMPTS
- ALL ATTEMPTS TO CONTROL ARE EXHAUSTED
- SERIOUS EMOTIONAL PROBLEMS IN SELF AND CHILDREN
- COMPLETE DEFEAT ADMITTED
- OBSESSION WITH MAN CONTINUES IN VICIOUS CIRCLES

Ascending phase — REHABILITATION

- WILLINGNESS TO SEEK HELP
- HONEST DESIRE FOR HELP NO MATTER WHAT MAN DOES
- LEARNS "LOVING TOO MUCH" IS AN ILLNESS
- TOLD SHE CAN RECOVER WHETHER MAN GETS HELP OR NOT
- RIGHT THINKING BEGINS
- START OF GROUP THERAPY
- FACES POWERLESSNESS
- MEETS RECOVERING WOMEN WHO "LOVE TOO MUCH"
- ONSET OF NEW HOPE
- APPRECIATION OF POSSIBILITIES OF NEW WAY OF LIFE
- OBTAINS HELP FOR HER OWN DRUG, ALCOHOL OR FOOD ADDICTION
- ATTENDS GROUP MEETINGS REGULARLY
- REALISTIC THINKING
- PROGRAM FRIENDS APPRECIATE EFFORTS
- NEW CIRCLE OF STABLE FRIENDS
- IS ASSISTED IN PERSONAL STOCK-TAKING
- INCREASE OF EMOTIONAL CONTROL
- FIRST STEPS TOWARD SELF-RELIANCE
- CARE OF PERSONAL APPEARANCE
- RATIONALIZATIONS RECOGNISED EARLY
- GROUP THERAPY AND MUTUAL HELP CONTINUE
- DESIRE TO ESCAPE GOES, AS ABILITY TO SAY "NO" INCREASES
- DIMINISHING FEARS OF THE UNKNOWN FUTURE
- FOCUS ON SELF RATHER THAN MAN
- RETURN OF SELF-ESTEEM
- STOPS ENABLING MAN TO BE IRRESPONSIBLE
- HEALTHY SELF-INTEREST DEVELOPS
- RE-BIRTH OF IDEALS AND SPIRITUALITY
- APPRECIATION OF OWN PROGRESS
- DIMINISHING NEED TO CONTROL OTHERS
- CONFIDENCE OF CHILDREN REGAINED
- CONTENTMENT NOT BASED ON MAN'S BEHAVIOR
- INCREASING RESPONSIBILITY FOR OWN LIFE
- ENLIGHTENED AND INTERESTING WAY OF LIFE OPENS UP WITH ROAD AHEAD TO HIGHER LEVELS THAN EVER BEFORE

Source: Adapted from M. M. Glatt, M.D., D.P.M.

energy. He soon becomes the source of all good things in her life. If being with him doesn't feel good, she tries to fix him or herself so that it does. She does not look elsewhere for emotional gratification. She is too busy trying to make it work between them. She is sure that if she can make him happy he will treat her better, and then she will be happy too. In her efforts to please she becomes the careful guardian of his well-being. Each time he is upset, she takes his reaction as her failure and feels guilty—for his unhappiness that she hasn't been able to ameliorate, for his inadequacies that she hasn't been able to rectify. But perhaps most of all she feels guilty for being unhappy herself. Her denial tells her that there is nothing really wrong with *him,* so the fault must be all hers.

In her despair, which she judges as founded on trivial problems and petty complaints, she begins to need very badly to talk things over with her partner. Long discussions ensue (if he will talk with her), but the real problems are not usually addressed. If he is drinking too much her denial prevents her from recognizing this, and she pleads with him to tell her why he's so unhappy, assuming his drinking is not important but his unhappiness certainly is. If he is being unfaithful she asks why she isn't enough of a woman for him, accepting the situation as her fault, not his. And so on.

Things are getting worse. But because her partner fears that she may become discouraged and pull away from him and he needs her support—emotional, financial, social, or practical—he tells her she's wrong, that she's imagining things, that he loves her and that their situation is improving but she is too negative to see it. And she believes him, because she needs to so much. She accepts his view that she is exaggerating their problems and becomes further removed from reality.

He has become her barometer, her radar, her emotional gauge. And she watches him constantly. All her feelings are generated by his behavior. At the same time that she gives him the power to rock and sway her emotionally, she runs interference between him and the world. She tries to make him look better than he is and to make them as a couple appear happier than they are. She rationalizes away his every failure, her every disappointment, and while she hides the truth from the world she also hides it from herself. Unable to accept that he is what he is, and that his problems are his, not hers, she experiences a profound sense of having failed in all her energetic attempts to change him. Her frustration erupts in anger and there are battles, sometimes physical ones, initiated by her in her impotent rage at what appears to be his deliberate thwarting of her best efforts on his behalf. Just as she once excused his every failing, she now takes everything personally. She feels that she is the only one who is trying to make the relationship work. Her guilt grows as she wonders where this rage in her is coming from and why she cannot be lovable enough for him to *want* to change for her, for them.

Ever more determined to bring about the changes in him that she seeks, she is now willing to try anything. They exchange promises. She won't nag him if he won't drink or stay out late or run around or whatever. Neither of them is able to stick to the bargain, and she perceives dimly that she is out of control—not only of him but of herself as well. She cannot stop fighting, scolding, wheedling, begging. Her self-respect plummets.

Perhaps they move away, thinking that friends, job, family are to blame for their problems. And perhaps things are better for a while afterward—but only for a while. Too soon, all the old patterns reassert themselves.

By now she is so consumed with this bitter battle that there is no time or energy for anything else. If there are children they are certainly emotionally neglected, if not neglected physically as well. Social activities come to a standstill. There is too much acrimony and too many secrets to keep to make public appearances anything but an ordeal. And the lack of social contact serves to isolate the woman who loves too much even further. She has lost another vital link with reality. Her relationship has become her entire world.

Once upon a time this man's irresponsibility and neediness appealed to her. That was when she was sure she could change him, fix him. Now she finds herself shouldering burdens that are rightfully his to carry, and while she deeply resents him for this turn of events she also revels in the sense of control it gives her over him as she parcels out his money and takes over total control of their children.

You will notice, if you are keeping the chart in mind, that we are well into what is termed the "crucial phase," a time of rapid deterioration, first emotionally and then physically. The woman who has been obsessing about her relationship may now add an eating disorder to her other problems if she hasn't one already. Looking to reward herself for all her efforts and also attempting to muffle the anger and resentment boiling in her, she may begin to use food as a tranquilizing drug. Or she may seriously neglect food due to ulcers or a chronically upset stomach, perhaps combined with a martyred "I don't have time to eat" attitude. Or she may rigidly control her food to make up for the out-of-control feelings she experiences with her life in general. The abuse of alcohol or other "recreational drugs" may begin, and, very frequently, prescribed drugs will become part of her repertoire for coping with the untenable situation in which she finds herself. Physicians, failing to properly diagnose her progressive disorder, may exacerbate her condition by offering tranquilizers to quell the anxiety generated by her living situation and her attitude toward it. Offering these kinds of potentially very addictive drugs to a woman in such circumstances is tantamount to offering her a few stiff shots of gin. Either gin or a tranquilizer will dull the pain temporarily, but its use may create even more problems, while solving none.

Unavoidably, by the time a woman is at this point in the progression of her disease, there will be physical problems as well as emotional ones. Any of the disorders associated with subjection to prolonged and severe stress may manifest themselves. As previously noted, a dependency on food or alcohol or other drugs may develop. There may also be digestive problems and/or ulcers, as well as all kinds of skin problems, allergies, high blood pressure, nervous tics, insomnia, and constipation or diarrhea or both, alternatively. Periods of depression may begin, or if, as is so often the case, depression has already been a problem, the episodes may now lengthen and deepen alarmingly.

At this point, when the body begins to break down due to the effects of stress, we enter the chronic phase. Perhaps the hallmark of the chronic phase is that by now thinking has become so impaired, it is difficult for the woman to be able to assess her situation at all objectively. There is a gradually progressive insanity implicit in loving too much, and by this stage the insanity is in full flower. She is now totally unable to see what her choices are in terms of the life she is living. Much of what she does is *in reaction* to her partner, including love affairs, obsession with work or with other interests, or devotion to "causes" in which she again tries to help/control the lives and conditions of others around her. Sadly, even her turning to people and interests outside the relationship is by now part of her obsession.

She has become bitterly envious of people who don't have her problems, and more and more she finds herself increasingly taking her frustrations out on all those around her, through increasingly violent attacks on her partner and often her children as well. At this point, as the ultimate attempt to control her partner through guilt, she may threaten or actually attempt suicide. Needless to say, by now she and everyone around her is very, very sick, certainly emotionally and often physically as well.

It is instructive to consider too for a moment how a child whose mother suffers from the disease of loving too much would be affected. Many of the women in the stories you have read here grew up under those conditions.

When the woman who has begun by loving too much

finally realizes that she has tried everything to change her man and that her best efforts have failed, perhaps she is able to see that she must get help. Usually the help she seeks involves turning to someone else, perhaps a professional, in one more attempt to change her man. It is *crucial* that the person to whom she turns helps her recognize that *she* is the one who must change, that her recovery must begin with herself.

This is very important, because loving too much is a progressive disease, as has been so clearly demonstrated. A woman like Margo is on her way toward dying. Perhaps death will come from a stress-related disorder such as heart failure or a stroke, or any other physical ailment caused or exacerbated by stress. Or she may die by the violence that has now become so much a part of her life, or perhaps in an accident that wouldn't have occurred if she hadn't been distracted by her obsession. She may die very quickly or spend many years in progressive deterioration. Whatever the apparent cause of death, I want to reiterate that loving too much can kill you.

Now let us return to Margo, dismayed by the turn of events in her life and at least for the moment tentatively looking for help. Margo really has only two choices. She needs to have them delineated clearly for her and then she must choose between them.

She can continue to search for the perfect partner. Given her predilection for hostile, untrustworthy men, she will inevitably be drawn to more of the same types she has already known. Or she can begin the very difficult and demanding task of bringing into conscious awareness her unhealthy patterns of relating, while objectively scrutinizing the ingredients that have added up to "attraction" between herself and various men. She can either continue to look outside herself for the man who will make her happy or she can begin the slow and painstaking (but ultimately far more rewarding) process of learning to love and nurture herself with the help and support of peers.

Sadly, the vast majority of women like Margo will choose to continue practicing their addiction, searching for the magic man who will make them happy, or endlessly trying to control and improve the man they are with.

It seems so much easier and feels so much more familiar to keep on looking for a source of happiness outside oneself than to practice the discipline required to build one's own inner resources, to learn to fill the emptiness from inside rather than outside. But for those of you who are wise enough, weary enough, or desperate enough to want to get well more than you want to either fix the man you are with or find a new one—for those of you who really do want to change *yourself*, the steps of recovery follow.

10 • *The Road to Recovery*

> IF AN INDIVIDUAL IS ABLE TO LOVE
> PRODUCTIVELY, HE LOVES HIMSELF TOO; IF
> HE CAN LOVE ONLY OTHERS, HE CANNOT
> LOVE AT ALL.
>
> —ERICH FROMM, *THE ART*
> *OF LOVING*

HAVING READ IN THESE PAGES OF SO MANY WOMEN WHO ARE so much alike in their unhealthy ways of relating, perhaps you believe by now that this is a disease. What, then, is its appropriate treatment? How can a woman caught in its grip recover? How does she begin to leave behind that endless series of struggles with "him," and learn to use her energies in creating a rich and fulfilling existence for herself? And how does she differ from the many women who do not recover, who are never able to extricate themselves from the mire and the misery of unsatisfactory relationships?

It is certainly not the severity of her problems that determines whether or not a woman will recover. Before recovery, women who love too much are very much alike in character, regardless of the specific details of any present circumstances or past histories. But a woman who has overcome her pattern of loving too much is profoundly different from who and what she was prior to recovery.

Perhaps, until now, it was luck or fate that has determined which of these women would find her way and which wouldn't. However, my observation has been that all women who do recover have eventually taken certain steps in order to do so. Through trial and error, and often without guidelines, they nevertheless, again and again, ultimately followed the program of recovery I will outline for you. Further, in my personal and professional experience, I have never seen a woman who took these steps fail to recover, and I have never seen a woman recover who failed to take these steps. If that sounds like a guarantee, it is. Women who follow these steps will get well.

The steps are simple, but not easy. They are all equally important and are listed in the most chronologically typical order:

1. Go for help.

2. Make your own recovery the first priority in your life.

3. Find a support group of peers who understand.

4. Develop your spiritual side through daily practice.

5. Stop managing and controlling others.

6. Learn to not get "hooked" into the games.

7. Courageously face your own problems and shortcomings.

8. Cultivate whatever needs to be developed in yourself.

9. Become "selfish."

10. Share with others what you have experienced and learned.

One by one, we will explore what each one of these steps means, what it requires, why it is necessary, and what its implications are.

1. Go for help.

What it means

The first step in going for help may involve anything from checking a relevant book out of the library (which can take enormous courage; it feels as if *everyone* is watching!) to making an appointment to see a therapist. It may mean an anonymous call to a hotline to talk about what you've always tried so hard to keep secret, or contacting an agency in your community that specializes in the kind of problem you're facing, whether it is co-alcoholism, a history of incest, a partner who is battering you, or whatever. It may mean finding out where a self-help group meets and getting up the courage to go, or taking a class through adult education, or going to a counseling center that deals with your type of problem. It may even mean calling the police. Basically, going for help means *doing something,* taking the first step, reaching out. It is very important to understand that going for help does *not* mean threatening your partner with the fact that you are thinking of doing so. Such a move is usually an attempt to blackmail him into shaping up so that you don't have to publicly expose him for the terrible person he is. Leave him out of it. Otherwise, going for help (or threatening to do so) is just one more attempt to manage and control him. Try to remember, you are doing this for *you.*

What going for help requires

To go for help you must, at least temporarily, give up the idea that you can handle it alone. You must face the reality that, over time, things have gotten worse in your life, not better, and realize that in spite of your best efforts, you are not able to solve the problem. This means that you must become honest with yourself about how bad it really is. Unfortunately, this honesty comes to some of us only when life has dealt us such a blow or series of blows that we've been knocked to our knees and are gasping for breath. Since that's usually a temporary situation, the moment we're able to function again, we try to pick up where we left off—being strong, managing, controlling, and going it alone. Do not settle for temporary relief. If you start by reading a book, then you need to take the step after that, which is probably to contact some of the sources for help that the book recommends. (For example, see the appendixes at the back of this book for suggested reading as well as a list of places to go to for help.)

If you make an appointment with a professional, find out whether that person understands the dynamics of your particular problem. If, for instance, you've been a victim of incest, someone without special training and expertise in that area is not going to be nearly as helpful to you as someone who *knows* what you've gone through and how it has probably affected you.

See someone who is able to ask questions about your family's history similar to those raised in this book. You may want to know if your potential therapist agrees with the premise that loving too much is a progressive illness and accepts the treatment approach outlined here.

My strong personal bias is that women should see women counselors. We share the basic experience of what it is to be a woman in this society, and this creates a special depth of understanding. We are also able to avoid the almost inevitable man-woman games we might be tempted to play with a male therapist or which, unfortunately, he might be tempted to play with us.

But just seeing a woman is not enough. She must also be aware of the most effective methods of treatment, depending on which factors are present in your history, and be willing to refer you to an appropriate peer support group —indeed, even to make participation in such a group a mandatory element of treatment.

For example, I will not counsel someone who is co-alcoholic unless she becomes involved in Al-Anon. If she is unwilling to do so after several visits, I make an agreement with her that should she become willing to do so I will see her again, but not otherwise. My experience teaches me that without involvement in Al-Anon, co-alcoholics do not recover. Instead, they repeat their patterns of behavior and continue their unhealthy ways of thinking, and therapy alone is not enough to turn this around. With both therapy and Al-Anon, however, recovery happens much more quickly; these two treatment aspects complement each other very well.

Your therapist should have a similar requirement that you join a self-help group that is appropriate for you. Otherwise, she may be enabling you to complain about your situation without requiring that you do all you can to help yourself.

Once you find someone who is good, you must stick with her and follow her recommendations. No one ever changed a lifelong pattern of relating through just one or two visits to a professional.

Going for help may require that you spend money, or it may not. Many agencies have sliding scales for fees according to your ability to pay, and there is no correlation between the most expensive therapist and the most effective treatment. Many very competent and dedicated individuals work for such agencies. What you are looking for is someone who has experience and expertise and is a person with whom you feel comfortable. Trust your feelings and be willing to see several therapists if necessary in order to find one who is right for you.

It is not absolutely necessary that you specifically enter therapy to recover. In fact, seeing the wrong therapist will do more harm than good. But someone who understands the disease process involved in loving too much can be of inestimable help to you.

Going for help does not require that you be willing to terminate your present relationship if you are in one. Nor is that a requirement at any time throughout the process of recovery. As you follow these steps, one through ten, the relationship will take care of itself. When women come to see me, they often want to leave their relationship before they are ready, which means they will either go back or else begin a new, equally unhealthy one. If they follow these ten steps, their perspective on whether to stay or to leave changes. Being with him ceases to be The Problem and leaving him ceases to be The Solution. Instead, the relationship becomes one of the many considerations that must be addressed in the overall picture of how they live their lives.

Why going for help is necessary

It is necessary because you've already tried so hard, and none of your best efforts have worked in the long run. Though they may have brought occasional temporary relief, the overall picture is one of progressive deterioration. The tricky part here is that you are probably not in touch with just how bad it has gotten because you undoubtedly have a great measure of denial operating in your life. That is the nature of the disease. For instance, I've been told countless times by women clients that their children don't know anything is wrong at home, or that these children sleep through the nightly fights. This is a very common example of self-protective denial. If these

225

women faced the fact that their children are truly suffering, they would be overwhelmed by guilt and remorse. On the other hand, their denial makes it very hard for them to see the severity of the problem and get the necessary help.

Take for granted that your situation is worse than you will allow yourself to acknowledge at present, and that your disease is progressing. Understand that you require appropriate treatment, that you cannot do it alone.

What going for help implies

One of the most feared implications is that the relationship, if there is one, may end. This is by no means necessarily true, although, should you follow these steps, I guarantee that the relationship will either improve or end. It, and you, will not stay the same.

Another feared implication is that the secret is out. Once a woman has sincerely sought help, there is rarely regret for having done so, but the fear beforehand can be monumental. Whether the problems a given woman lives with are unpleasant and inconvenient or severely damaging and even life-threatening, she may or may not choose to go for help. It is the magnitude of her fear, and sometimes her pride as well, that determine whether she seeks help, and not the severity of her problems.

For many women, reaching out does not even seem to be an option; to do so feels like taking an unnecessary risk in an already precarious situation. "I didn't want to make him angry" is the classic answer of the beaten wife when questioned as to why she didn't call the police. A deep and profound fear of making things worse and, ironically, a conviction that she can still control the situation somehow prohibit her from reaching out to authorities, or to others who might help her. On a less dramatic scale this is also true. A frustrated wife may not want to rock the boat because her husband's cold indifference to her is "not that bad." She tells herself that he is basically a good man, free of many of the undesirable traits she sees in her friends' husbands, and so she puts up with a nonexistent sex life, his discouraging attitude toward her every enthusiasm, or his preoccupation with sports during every waking moment of the time they share at home together. This is not tolerance on her part. It is a lack of trust that the relationship can survive her unwillingness to continue waiting patiently for his attention, which never comes, and it is, even more to the point, a lack of conviction that she deserves more happiness than she is getting. This is a key concept in recovery. Do you deserve better than your present circumstances? What are you willing to do to make it better for yourself? Begin at the beginning, and go for help.

2. Make your own recovery your first priority.

What it means

Making your own recovery your first priority means deciding that, no matter what is required, you are willing to take those steps necessary to help yourself. Now, if that sounds extreme, think for a moment about to what lengths you would be willing to go to make *him* change, to help *him* recover. Then just turn the force of that energy on yourself. The magic formula here is that although all your hard work and efforts cannot change *him*, you *can*, with that same expenditure of energy, change yourself. So, use your power where it will do some good—on your own life!

What making your own recovery your first priority requires

It requires a total commitment to yourself. This may be the first time in your life that you have regarded yourself as truly important, truly worthy of your own attention and nurturing. This is probably very hard for you to do, but if you go through the motions of keeping appointments, participating in a support group, and so on, you will be helped to learn how to value and promote your own well-being. So for a while just make yourself show up, and the healing process will begin. Soon you will feel so much better that you'll want to continue.

To help the process, be willing to educate yourself about your problem. If you grew up in an alcoholic family, for instance, read the books on that subject recommended in Appendix 3. Go to relevant lectures on the subject and find out what is now known about the effects of that experience in later life. It will be uncomfortable and even painful sometimes to expose yourself to that input, but not nearly as uncomfortable as continuing to live out your patterns without any understanding of how your past controls you. With understanding comes the opportunity for choice, so the greater your understanding, the greater your freedom of choice.

Also required is the willingness to *continue* to spend time and perhaps money, too, to get well. If you balk at spending time and money on your own recovery, if it seems wasteful, consider how much time and money you have spent trying to avoid the pain either from being in your relationship or from having it end. Drinking, using drugs, eating too much, taking trips to get away from it all, having to replace things (either his or yours) that you've broken in fits of anger, missing work, expensive long-distance phone calls to him or to someone you hope will understand, buying him presents to make up, buying yourself presents to help you forget, spending days and nights crying over him, neglecting your health to the point where you become seriously ill—the list of ways you have spent time and money staying sick is probably long enough to make you very uncomfortable if you look at it honestly. Recovery requires that you be willing to invest at least that much in getting well. And as an investment, it is guaranteed to give you considerable returns.

Total commitment to your own recovery also requires that you severely curtail or entirely suspend your own use of alcohol or other drugs while in the therapeutic process. The use of mind-altering substances during this time mitigates against your fully experiencing the emotions you will be uncovering, and it is only through deeply experiencing them that you will also gain the healing that comes with their release. Discomfort with and fear of these feelings may prompt you to want to dull them by one means or another (including using food as a drug), but I urge you not to. Most of the "work" of therapy happens during the hours when you are not in group or in session. My experience with clients is that whatever connections are made during therapy sessions or between them are of lasting value only if the mind is in an unaltered state while processing this material.

Why making your own recovery your first priority is necessary

It is necessary because if you do not, you will never have time to get well. You will be too busy doing all the things that keep you sick.

Just as learning a new language frequently requires repeated exposure to new sounds and patterns of speech that contradict the familiar ways of talking and thinking, and cannot be grasped at all if that exposure is infrequent or sporadic, so recovery goes. An occasional half-hearted gesture of doing something for yourself will not be enough to affect the entrenched ways of thinking, feeling, and relating. Through habit alone, they would reassert themselves without remedial input.

To help put it into perspective, consider the lengths to which you would be willing to go if you had cancer and someone offered you hope of recovery. Be willing to go to those same lengths to recover from this disease, which destroys the quality of life and possibly even life itself.

What making your own recovery your first priority implies

Your appointments with your therapist or your time in group come first. They're more important than

- an invitation to have lunch or dinner with the man in your life
- meeting your man to talk things over
- avoiding his criticism or anger
- making him (or anyone else) happy; getting his (or anyone else's) approval
- taking a trip to get away from it all for a while (so you can return and endure some more of the same)

3. Find a support group of peers who understand.

What it means

Finding a support group of peers who understand may require an effort. If you are or ever have been in a relationship with an alcoholic or drug abuser, go to Al-Anon; if you are the child of an alcoholic or drug abuser, go to Al-Anon meetings for adult children; if you are an incest victim, find meetings of Daughters United (you belong there whether or not your father was the aggressor); if you are or have been the victim of violence, contact shelter services for women in your area regarding ongoing support groups. If you do not fit any of these categories or the specific group that best fits your needs does not exist in your community, find a support group in which women are dealing with their problems of emotional dependency on men, or start your own group. Guidelines for forming your own support group can be found in Appendix 1.

A support group of peers is not an unstructured meeting of women who talk about all the awful things men have done to them, or the unlucky hands that life has dealt them. Group is a place to work on your own recovery. It is important to talk about past traumas, but if you find yourself or others recounting long stories with lots of "he said . . . and then I said . . ." in them, you are probably off the track, and possibly even in the wrong group. Empathy alone will not elicit recovery. A good support group is dedicated to helping all who attend get better, and includes some members who have achieved a measure of recovery themselves and can share with newcomers the principles by which they gained it. This is nowhere better modeled than in Al-Anon. Whether or not alcoholism has touched your life, you may want to attend one meeting or several, to see how the principles of recovery work. They are basically the same for us all, no matter what our past or present circumstances.

What a support group requires

You will be asked to make a commitment to yourself and to the group to attend a minimum of six meetings before you decide that it has nothing to offer you. This is necessary because it takes that long for you to begin to feel like part of the group, to learn the jargon if it exists, and to start to grasp the process of recovery. If you are going to Al-Anon, which often has several meetings each week, try to attend on different days. Different groups will have different characteristics, though the format is basically similar. Find one or two that especially suit you and stick with them, supplementing more meetings when you feel the need.

It will be necessary to attend regularly. Though it is important to the others that you be there, your attendance is for your own benefit. In order to receive what the group has to offer, you must show up.

Ideally, you will feel a certain level of trust, but even if that is not something you are yet able to muster, you *can* be honest. Talk about your lack of trust of people in general, of the group, of the process; ironically, your trust will begin to grow.

Why a support group of peers is necessary

As others share their stories, you will be able to identify with them and their experiences. They will help you to remember what you've blocked from your awareness—both events and feelings. You will become more in touch with yourself.

As you find yourself identifying with others and accepting them in spite of their flaws and their secrets, you will be able to become more accepting of those characteristics and feelings in yourself. This is the beginning of the development of self-acceptance, which is an absolutely vital requirement for recovery.

When you are ready, you will share some of your own experiences, and in doing so you will become more honest and less secretive and afraid. Through the group's acceptance of what has been so unacceptable to you, your self-acceptance will grow.

You will see others using techniques in their lives that work, which you can try for yourself. You will also see people trying things that don't work, and you can learn from their mistakes.

Along with all the empathy and shared experience a group provides, there is an element of humor that is also vital to recovery. The understanding smiles of recognition at yet another attempt at managing someone else, the happy cheering when someone has gotten past an important hurdle, the release of laughter over shared idiosyncrasies—all are truly healing.

You will begin to feel as if you belong. This is critically important for anyone coming from a dysfunctional family, since that experience produces such strong feelings of isolation. To be with others who both understand your experience and share it produces a sense of safety and well-being, which you need.

What finding and joining a support group of peers implies

The secret is out. True, not everyone knows, but a few people do. You walk into Al-Anon and there is the tacit assumption that sometime, somewhere, you've been affected by alcoholism. You show up at Daughters United and it indicates that to some degree you have been a victim of inappropriate sexual advances from someone you trusted . . . and so on.

The fear that others will know keeps many people from getting the help that could salvage their lives and their relationships. Remember, in any valid support group, your attendance there and what is discussed there is information that never leaves the group. Your privacy is respected and protected. If it is not, you need to find a group where it is.

On the other hand, going just once means that others know you have a problem. Hopefully, having read this far, you can see that letting a few others know, especially when they, too, share your problem, is a way out of your painful isolation.

4. Develop your spirituality through daily practice.

What it means

Well, it means different things to different people. For some of you, the whole idea is immediately repellent, and you're probably wondering if you can skip this step. None of that "God" stuff for you. For you, such beliefs seem immature and naive, and you're too sophisticated to take any of it seriously.

Others of you may already be praying determinedly to a God who doesn't seem to be listening. You've told Him what's wrong and what needs fixing and you're still miserable. Or maybe you've prayed so hard for so long with no visible results that you've gotten angry, given up, or feel betrayed and wonder what terrible thing you're being punished for.

Whether or not you have a belief in God, and if you do, whether or not you're on speaking terms with Him, you can still practice this step. Developing your spirituality can mean pretty much following whatever path you choose. Even if you are a 100-percent atheist, perhaps you get pleasure and solace from a quiet walk, or contemplating a sunset or some aspect of nature. Whatever takes you beyond yourself and into a broader perspective on things is what this step is all about. Find out what brings you peace and serenity and commit some time, at least half an hour daily, to that practice. No matter how dismaying your circumstances, this discipline can bring you relief, even comfort.

If you are on the fence about whether there is any such thing as a higher power in the universe, you might want to try acting as if you did believe, even if you don't. Beginning to turn over what you cannot manage to a power greater than yourself can bring enormous relief.

Or, if this feels like you're being coerced into something you don't want to do, how about using your peer support group as a higher power? Certainly there is more strength in the group than any one of you has all by yourself. Allow yourself to use the group as a whole for strength and support, or make a commitment to contact an individual member to help you through it when a rough time comes along. Know that you are no longer all alone.

If you have an active faith, and you regularly worship and frequently pray, developing your spirituality may mean trusting that what is happening in your life has its own reason and its own results, and that *God* is in charge of your partner, not *you*. Take quiet time to meditate and pray, and to ask for guidance in how to live *your own life* while you release those around you to live theirs.

Developing your spirituality, no matter what your religious orientation, basically means *letting go of self-will,* of the determination to make things happen the way you think they should. Instead, you must accept the fact that you may not know what is best in a given situation either for yourself or for another person. There may be outcomes and solutions that you have never considered, or perhaps the ones you've most feared and tried hardest to forestall may be exactly what is necessary in order for things to begin to improve. Self-will means believing that you alone have all the answers. Letting go of self-will means becoming willing to hold still, be open, and wait for guidance for yourself. It means learning to let go of fear (all of the "what ifs") and despair (all of the "if onlys") and replacing them with positive thoughts and statements about your life.

What developing your spirituality requires

It requires *willingness,* not faith. Often with willingness comes faith. If you don't want faith, you probably won't get it, but you still may find more serenity than you've had before.

Developing your spirituality also requires that you use affirmations to overcome old patterns of thinking and feeling, and to replace old belief systems. Whether or not you have any belief in a higher power, affirmations can change your life. Use some of those in the Appendix 4, or better yet, make up your own. Make them totally positive and repeat them silently, or out loud if possible, every chance you get. Just to get you started, here's one: "I no longer suffer. My life is filled with joy, prosperity, and fulfillment."

Why developing your spirituality is necessary

Without spiritual development, it is nearly impossible to let go of managing and controlling and to believe that all will work out as it is meant to.

Spiritual practice calms you, and helps change your perspective from being victimized to being uplifted.

It is a source of strength in crisis. When feelings or circumstances are overwhelming, you need a resource greater than yourself to which you can turn.

Without spiritual development, it is nearly impossible to let go of self-will, and without letting go of self-will you will not be able to take the next step. You will not be able to stop managing and controlling the man in your life because you will still believe it is your job to do so. You will not be able to surrender control of his life to a force higher than yourself.

What developing your spirituality implies

You are freed from the overwhelming responsibility of

fixing everything, controlling the man in your life, and preventing disaster.

You have tools for finding relief that don't require that you manipulate anyone else into doing or being what you want. No one has to change in order for you to feel good. Because you have access to spiritual nourishment, your life and your happiness come to be more under your own control and less vulnerable to the actions of others.

5. Stop managing and controlling him.

What it means

To stop managing and controlling him means not helping and not giving advice. Let's please assume that this other adult whom you are aiding and advising has as much capacity as you have to find himself a job, an apartment, a therapist, an A.A. meeting, or whatever else he needs. He may not have as much *motivation* as you to find these things for himself, or to work out his own problems. But when you take on trying to solve his problems for him, he is freed from his own responsibility for his life. You are then in charge of his welfare, and when your efforts on his behalf fail, *you* will be the one he blames.

Let me give you an example of how this works: I frequently receive calls from wives and girlfriends who want to make an appointment for their partners. I always insist that those men make their own appointments with me. If the person who is supposed to be the client hasn't enough motivation to choose his own therapist and make his own appointment, how will he be motivated to stay in therapy and work on his own recovery? Earlier in my career as a therapist I used to accept these appointments, only to get another call from the wife or girlfriend saying that he had changed his mind about seeing someone, or that he didn't want to see a woman therapist, or that he wanted to see someone with different credentials. These women would then ask if I could recommend someone *else* whom they could call to make another appointment for him. I learned never to take appointments made by someone for anyone else and instead to ask these wives and girlfriends to come in to see me for *themselves*.

Not managing or controlling him also means stepping out of the role of encouraging and praising him. Chances are you have also used these methods to try to get him to do what you'd like, and this means they have become tools for manipulating him. Praising and encouraging are very close to pushing, and when you do that you are trying again to take control of his life. Think about why you are lauding something he's done. Is it to help raise his self-esteem? That's manipulation. Is it so he will continue whatever behavior you're praising? That's manipulation. Is it so that he'll know how proud you are of him? That can be a burden for him to carry. Let him develop his own pride from his own accomplishments. Otherwise, you come dangerously close to playing a mothering role with him. He doesn't need another mother (no matter how bad his mother was!), and much more to the point, you don't need him to be your child.

It means to stop watching. Pay less attention to what he is doing and more attention to your own life. Sometimes, as you begin to let go, your partner will "up the ante," so to speak, to keep you hooked into watching and feeling responsible for the outcome. Things may suddenly go from bad to worse for him. Let them! His troubles are his own to work out, not yours. Let him take the full responsibility for his problems and the full credit for his solutions. Stay out of it. (If you're busy with your own life and you're practicing your own spiritual development, you will more easily be able to take your eyes off him.)

It means detaching. Detaching requires that you get your ego disentangled from his feelings and especially from his actions and their results. It requires that you allow him to deal with the consequences of his behavior, you don't save him from *any* of his pain. You may continue to care *about* him, but you don't take care *of* him You allow him to find his own way, just as you are working to find yours.

What stopping the managing and controlling of him requires

It requires learning to say and do *nothing*. This is one of the most difficult tasks you face in your recovery. When his life is unmanageable, when everything in you wants to take over, to advise and encourage him, to manipulate the situation in whatever way you can, you must learn to hold still, to respect this other person enough to allow the struggle to be his, not yours.

It requires facing your own fears regarding what might happen to him and to your relationship if you let go of managing everything—and then going to work on eliminating your fears rather than manipulating him.

It requires that you use your spiritual practice to uphold you when you become frightened. Your spiritual development is especially important as you learn to let go of feeling that you must run everything. It can actually feel physically as though you are falling off a cliff when you begin to let go of controlling others in your life. The sensation of being out of control of yourself when you release others from your attempts to control can be alarming. Here your spiritual practice can help, because instead of letting go into a void, you can relinquish control of those you love to your higher power.

It requires a hard look at what is, rather than what you hope will be. As you let go of managing and controlling, you must also let go of the idea that "when he changes I'll be happy." He may never change. You must stop trying to make him. And you must learn to be happy anyway.

Why it is necessary to stop managing and controlling him

As long as you are focused on changing someone over whom you are powerless (and we are all powerless over changing anyone but ourselves) you cannot bring your energies to bear on helping yourself. Unfortunately, changing someone else appeals to us much more than working on ourselves, so until we give up the former notion we'll never be able to get to work on the latter.

Most of the insanity and despair you experience comes directly from trying to manage and control what you cannot. Think about all the attempts you've made: the endless speeches, the pleading, threats, bribes, maybe even violence, all the avenues you've tried that haven't worked. And remember how you've felt after each failed attempt. Your self-esteem slipped another notch, and you became more anxious, more helpless, more angry. The only way out of all this is to let go of the attempt to control what you cannot—him and his life.

Finally, it is necessary to stop because he will almost never change in the face of pressure from you. What should be his problem begins to look like your problem, and somehow you end up stuck with it unless you let go. Even if he does attempt to placate you with some promise of changing his ways, he will probably revert back to his old behavior, often with much resentment toward you when he does so. Remember: if you are the reason he gives up a behavior, you'll also be the reason he resumes it.

Example: Two young people are in my office. Referred by his probation officer because of alcohol or drug offenses, he is there because he's in trouble with the law. She's there because she tries to go everywhere with him. She sees it as her job to keep him on the straight and narrow. As is so common in such cases, both of them come from homes where there is alcoholism in at least one parent. As they sit before me, holding hands, they tell me they are going to get married.

"I think getting married will help him," the young woman says, sometimes with shy compassion, sometimes with firm determination.

"Yeah," he nods sheepishly. "She keeps me from getting too wild. She helps me a lot." There is a note of relief in his voice, and his girlfriend glows with pleasure at the faith he has in her, at the responsibility for his life that she has been given.

And I try—gently, in the face of their hope and their love—to explain that if he has a problem with alcohol or other drugs and she is the reason he slows down or stops drinking or using drugs now, she will also be the reason he speeds up or starts drinking and using drugs all over again later. I warn them both that someday he will say to her, in the middle of an argument, "I quit for you and what difference has it made? You're never happy, so why should I keep trying?" Soon they will be torn apart by the very forces that seem now to bring them together.

What the implications are when you stop managing and controlling him

He may become very angry and accuse you of not caring about him anymore. This anger generates from his panic at having to become responsible for his own life. As long as he can fight with you, make you promises, or try to win you back, his struggle is outside, with you, and not inside with himself. (Sound familiar? It's true for you, too, as long as your struggle is with him.)

You may find there is very little to talk about once all the cajoling, arguing, threatening, fighting, and making up stops. It's okay. Say your affirmations quietly to yourself in the silence.

It is very likely that, once you truly let go of managing and controlling him, a great deal of your energy will be freed up that you can then use for exploring, developing, and enhancing yourself. It is important to know, however, that the temptation will be there to again look outside yourself for a raison d'etre. Curb this inclination and stay focused on yourself.

It is only fair to mention that as you let go of the role of smoothing out his life, things may get chaotic, and you may receive some criticism from people who don't understand what you are doing (or not doing). Try not to be defensive, and don't bother going into detailed explanations for them. If you like, recommend they read this book, and then drop the subject. If they persist, avoid them for a while.

Usually, such criticism is far less frequent and far less intense than we both expect and fear. We are our own worst critics, and we project our expectation of criticism out onto those around us, seeing it and hearing it everywhere. Be on your own side in all this, and the world will magically become a more approving place.

One of the implications of letting go of managing and controlling others is that you must relinquish the identity of "being helpful," but ironically, that very act of letting go is frequently the single most helpful thing you can do for the one you love. The identity of "being helpful" is an ego trip. If you really want to be helpful, let go of his problems and help yourself.

6. Learn to not get hooked into the games.

What it means

The concept of games as they apply to dialogue between two people comes from the type of psychotherapy known as transactional analysis. Games are structured ways of interacting that are employed to avoid intimacy. Everybody resorts to games in their interactions sometimes, but in unhealthy relationships, the games abound. They are stereotyped ways of responding that serve to circumvent any genuine exchange of information and feelings, and allow the participants to put the responsibility for their well-being or distress in each other's hands. Typically, the roles played by women who love too much and their partners are varieties of the rescuer, persecutor, and victim positions. Each of the pair plays each of these roles many times in a typical exchange. We will designate the role of rescuer as (R), define it as "trying to help"; the role of persecutor as (P) and define it as "trying to blame"; and the role of victim as (V), defined as "the one who is blameless and helpless." The following script will illustrate how this game works:

Tom, who often comes home late, has just arrived in his bedroom. It is 11:30 P.M. and his wife, Mary, begins.

MARY *(tearfully):* (V) Where were you? I've been so worried. I couldn't sleep, I was so afraid there'd been an accident. You know how I worry. How could you let me lie here like this and not at least call to let me know you were still alive?

TOM *(placating):* (R) Oh, honey, I'm sorry. I thought you'd be asleep and I didn't want to wake you up by calling. Don't be upset. I'm home now and I'll call next time, I promise. As soon as I get ready for bed I'll rub your back and you'll feel better.

MARY *(getting angry):* (P) I don't want you to touch me!

243

You say you'll call next time! That's a joke. You told me the last time this happened that you'd call, and did you? No! You don't care if I lie here thinking of you dead out on the highway. You *never* think of anybody else, so you don't know how it feels to worry about somebody you love.

TOM *(helplessly):* (V) Honey, that's not true. I *was* thinking of you. I didn't want to wake you. I didn't know you'd be upset. I was just trying to be thoughtful. Seems like no matter what I try, I'm wrong. What if I'd called you and you were asleep? Then I'd be a jerk for waking you up. I can't win.

MARY *(relenting):* (R) Now, that's not true. It's just that you're so important to me; I want to know that you're all right, not run over somewhere. I'm not trying to make you feel bad; I just want you to understand that I worry about you because I love you so much. I'm sorry I got so mad.

TOM *(sensing an edge):* (P) Well, if you worry so much, why aren't you glad to see me when I get home? How come you hit me with all this whining about where I was? Don't you trust me? I'm getting tired of having to explain everything to you all the time. If you trusted me you'd go to sleep, and when I got home you'd be glad to see me instead of jumping all over me! Sometimes I think you just like to fight.

MARY *(voice rising):* (P) Glad to see you! After lying here for two hours wondering where you were? If I don't trust you it's because you never do anything to help me build that trust. You don't call, you blame me for being upset, and then accuse me of not being nice to you when you finally drag in the door! Why don't you just turn around and go back wherever you came from, wherever you've been all evening.

TOM *(soothing):* (R) Look, I know you're upset, and I've got a big day tomorrow. How about if I make you a cup of tea? That's what you need. Then I'll take a shower and come to bed. Okay?

MARY *(crying):* (V) You just don't understand how it feels to be waiting and waiting, knowing that you *could* call but don't, because I'm not that important to you. . . .

Shall we stop here? As you can probably see, these two could go on trading places on their triangle of positions as rescuer, persecutor, and victim for many more hours or days, even years. If you find yourself responding to any statement or action of another person from any of these positions, beware! You are participating in a no-win cycle of accusation, rebuttal, blame, and counterblame that is pointless, futile, and degrading. Stop. Let go of trying to make it turn out the way you want it to by being nice, being angry, or being helpless. Change what you can, which means change yourself! Stop needing to win. Stop even needing to fight, or to make him give you a good reason or excuse for his behavior or neglect. Stop needing him to be sufficiently sorry.

What not getting hooked into games requires

Not getting hooked requires that even though you are tempted to respond in any one of the ways you know will keep the game going, you don't. You respond in a way that will end the game. It's a little tricky at first, but with practice you'll easily master it (if you also master your need to play the games in the first place, which is part of the previous step, letting go of managing and controlling).

Let's look again at the situation above and see how Mary could stay off that deadly triangle with Tom. By now, Mary has started developing her spirituality, and she is aware that she has no business trying to manage and control Tom. Because she is working on taking care of herself, earlier this evening, when it began to get late and Tom hadn't come home, instead of allowing herself to get nervous and worked up about it, she called a friend in her support group. They talked about her mounting fear, which helped to calm her. Mary needed someone to hear how she felt, and her friend listened with understanding but without giving advice. After she hung up, she practiced one of her favorite affirmations: "My life is divinely guided, and I grow in peace, security, and serenity every day, every hour." Since no one can hold two separate thoughts at once, Mary found that as she gave her thoughts over to the soothing words of the affirmation, she became calm and even relaxed. By the time Tom got home at 11:30, she was asleep. He woke her when he came into the room, and she immediately felt the annoyance and anger returning, so she repeated her affirmation to herself a couple of times and said, "Hi, Tom. I'm glad you're home." Now, Tom has always been used to a battle under these circumstances, and was a little nonplussed at her casual greeting. "I was going to call you, but . . ." he begins his excuse defensively. Mary waits till he's finished and says, "We can talk about it in the morning if you like. I'm too sleepy now. Good night." If Tom was feeling guilty about the lateness of the hour, a fight with Mary would actually have eased his guilt. He could then tell himself that she was a nagging shrew and the problem would become hers, for nagging, instead of his, for being late. As it is, he's left with his guilt, and she's not suffering because of his actions. That's the way it should be.

It's kind of like a game of ping pong, when you're both doing the rescuer-persecutor-victim thing. You keep hitting the ball back, when it comes your way. In order not to get hooked into playing, you have to learn to let the ball go right past you, off the end of the table. One of the greatest ways of letting it go is to cultivate the use of the word *Oh*. For instance, in response to Tom's excuse, Mary can just respond, "Oh," and go back to sleep. It is an empowering experience not to get caught up in the struggle implicit in the rescuer-persecutor-victim kind of exchange. To not get hooked, to maintain your centeredness, your dignity, feels wonderful. And it means you've taken another step in your own recovery.

Why not getting hooked into the games is necessary

To begin with, understand that the game roles we play are not confined to mere verbal exchanges. They extend to the way we play out our lives, and each of us has a particular role that we may especially favor.

Perhaps yours is the role of rescuer. It is familiar and comforting to many women who love too much to feel that they are taking care of (managing and controlling) another person. Out of their chaotic and/or deprived history they have chosen this path as a way of staying safe and earning some degree of self-acceptance. They do it with friends, family members, and often in their careers as well.

Or perhaps you find yourself playing the persecutor, the woman who is intent on finding the fault, pointing it out, and setting things right. Again and again, this woman must re-create the struggle with the dark forces that defeated her as a child, hoping to have more parity in the battle now that she is an adult. Angry from childhood and seeking to avenge herself in the present for the past, she is a fighter, a scrapper, a debater, a harridan. She needs to punish. She demands apologies, retribution.

And finally, you may, alas, be the victim, the most powerless of the three, seeing no options but to be at the whim of others' behavior. Perhaps there seemed to be no options when you were a child other than being victimized, but now the role is so familiar that there is actually strength to be gained from it. There is a tyranny in weakness; its coin is guilt, and that is the currency of exchange in the victim's relationships.

To play any of these positions, whether in a conversation or in life, keeps the focus off yourself and holds you in your childhood pattern of fear, rage, helplessness. You cannot develop your potential as a fully evolved human being, an adult who is in charge of her life, if you do not give up each of these restrictive roles, these ways of being

247

obsessed with the others around you. As long as you are caught up in these roles, these games, it will appear that another person is keeping you from your goal of happiness. Once you have let go of the games, you are left with total responsibility for your own behavior, your own choices, and your own life. In fact, when the games stop, your choices (both those you've already made and those that are now other options) become more obvious, less avoidable.

What not getting hooked into the games implies

You now must develop new ways of communicating with yourself and others that demonstrate your willingness to take responsibility for your life. Less of "If it weren't for . . ." and lots more of "Right now I'm choosing to . . ."

You will need all the energy that was freed by letting go of managing and controlling when you begin to practice this step, to avoid falling into the games (even announcing "I'm not playing" is playing). It becomes much easier with practice, and after time becomes very self-reinforcing.

You will need to learn to live without all the excitement of the heated battles, those time-consuming, energy-draining dramas in which you've been costarring. This is not easy to do. Many women who love too much have buried their feelings so deeply that they need the excitement of fights, partings, and reconciliations to even feel alive. Beware! Having nothing but your own inner life on which to concentrate may be boring at first. But if you can hold still with the boredom, it will metamorphose into self-discovery. And you will be ready for the next step.

7. Courageously face your own problems and shortcomings.

What it means

Facing your own problems means that, having let go of managing and controlling others and of the games, you now are left with nothing to distract you from your own life, your own problems, and your own pain. This is the time when you need to begin to look at yourself deeply, with the help of your spiritual program, your support group, and your therapist if you have one. It is not always necessary to have a therapist for this process. In the Anonymous programs, for instance, people who have experienced a great deal of recovery may become sponsors to newcomers, and in that role will often help those they sponsor go through this process of self-examination.

It also means that you look hard at your own life in the present, both at what you feel good about and what makes you uncomfortable or unhappy. Write it out in lists. Also look at the past. Examine all the good and bad memories, the accomplishments, the failures, the times you were hurt, and the times you did the hurting. Look at it *all*, again in writing. Focus on areas of particular difficulty. If sex is one of these areas, write out a complete personal sexual history. If men have always been a problem to you, start with your earliest relationships with men, and again, do a complete history. Parents? Use the same technique with them. Start at the beginning and write. Lots of writing, yes, but it is an invaluable tool to help you sort out your past and to begin to recognize the patterns, the repeating themes, in your struggles with yourself and others.

When you begin this process, do as complete a job as you can before you stop. This is a technique you will want to use again later, when problem areas crop up. Perhaps at first you will concentrate on relationships. Later, at another time, you may want to write out your history of jobs, how you felt about each one before you started, during the period of your employment, and afterwards. Just let your memories, thoughts, and feelings flow. Don't examine your writing for patterns as you go; do this afterwards.

What courageously facing your own problems and shortcomings requires

You will have to do a great deal of writing, making the commitment of time and energy necessary to accomplish it. Writing may not be an easy or comfortable means of expression for you. It is, however, the best technique for this exercise. Do not worry about doing it perfectly, or even well. Just do it in a way that makes sense to you.

You will need to be as completely honest and self-revealing as possible in all that you write.

Once you have completed this project as well as you can, share it with one other human being who cares about you and whom you trust. This person should be someone who understands what you are trying to do to recover and can simply listen to what you have written about your sexual history, your relationship history, your history with your parents, your feelings about yourself, and the events in your life, both good and bad. The person you choose as a listener should obviously have compassion and understanding. There is no need for comment at all, and this should be understood from the beginning. No advice, no encouragement. Just listening.

At this point in your recovery, do *not* make your partner the person who hears all this from you. Much, much later you may choose to share with him what you have written, or you may not. But it is not appropriate to share this with him now. You are letting someone hear it so that you can experience what it is like to tell your story, and be accepted. This is not a device for ironing out wrinkles in the relationship. Its purpose is self-discovery, period.

Why courageously facing your own problems and shortcomings is necessary

Most of us who love too much are caught up in blaming others for the unhappiness in our lives, while denying our own faults and our own choices. This is a cancerous approach to life that must be rooted out and eliminated, and the way to do so is to take a good, hard, honest look at ourselves. Only by seeing your problems and your faults (and your good points and successes) as *yours*, rather than related somehow to him, can you take the steps to change what needs to be changed.

What courageously facing your own problems and shortcomings implies

First, you will very likely be able to let go of secret guilt connected with many of the events and feelings of the past. This will clear the way for allowing more joy and healthier attitudes to be manifest in your life.

Then, because someone has heard your worst secrets and you haven't been destroyed by that fact, you will begin to feel safer in the world.

When you let go of blaming others and take responsibility for your own choices, you become free to embrace all kinds of options that were not available to you when you saw yourself as a victim of others. This prepares you to begin to change those things in your life that are either not good for you, not satisfying, or unfulfilling.

251

8. Cultivate whatever needs to be developed in yourself.

What it means

Cultivating whatever needs to be developed in yourself means not waiting for him to change before you get on with life. This also means not waiting for his support—financially, emotionally, or in practical matters—for you to start your career, or change your career, or go back to school, or whatever it is you want to do. Instead of making your plans dependent on his cooperation, make them as though you had no one but yourself on whom to lean. Cover all the contingencies—child care, money, time, transportation—without using him as a resource (or an excuse!). If you are protesting as you read this that without his cooperation your plans are impossible, consider by yourself, or brainstorm with a friend, how you would do it if you didn't even know him. You'll find that it is very possible to make life work for you when you stop depending on him and instead make use of all your other options.

Cultivating yourself means actively pursuing your interests. If you've been too busy for too long with him and you don't have a life of your own at all, then begin by pursuing lots of different avenues to find out what does appeal to you. This is not an easy thing for most women who love too much. Having made that man your project for so long, it feels uncomfortable to switch the focus to yourself and to explore what is good for your own growth. Be willing to try at least one brand-new activity each week. Look at life as a smorgasbord, and help yourself to lots of different experiences so that you can discover what appeals to you.

Cultivating yourself means taking risks: encountering new people, going into a classroom for the first time in years, taking a trip alone, looking for a job . . . whatever you know you need to do, but haven't been able to summon the courage for. This is the time to plunge ahead. There are *no* mistakes in life, only lessons, so get out there and let yourself learn some of what life wants to teach you. Use your support group as a source of encouragement and feedback. (Do not turn to your relationship or to that dysfunctional family of origin for encouragement. They need for you to stay the same, so that they can stay the same. Don't sabotage yourself and your growth by leaning on them.)

What cultivating whatever needs developing in yourself requires

To begin with, do two things each day that you don't want to do, in order to stretch yourself and expand your idea of who you are and what you are capable of doing. Stand up for yourself when you'd rather pretend it doesn't matter, or return an item that is unsatisfactory even if you'd rather just throw it away. Make that phone call you'd like to avoid. Learn how to take better care of yourself and less care of everyone else in your interactions. Say no to please yourself, rather than yes to please someone else. Ask clearly for something you want, and risk being refused.

Then, learn to give to yourself. Give time, give attention, give material objects. Often making a commitment to buy yourself something every day can be a real lesson in self-love. The gifts can be inexpensive, but frankly the less practical and more frivolous, the better. This is an exercise in *self*-indulgence. We need to learn that we ourselves can be the source of good things in our lives, and this is a good way to begin. But if you have no problem spending money on yourself, if indeed you shop and spend compulsively to assuage your anger or your depression, then this lesson in

253

giving to yourself needs to take a different direction. Treat yourself to new experiences rather than gathering up more material objects (and more debts). Take a stroll in the park or a hike in the hills or a trip to the zoo. Stop and watch the sunset. The point is to think about yourself and what you'd like your present for the day to be, then to allow yourself to experience both the giving and the receiving. We are usually very good at giving to others, but very unpracticed at giving to ourselves. So practice!

In taking these steps, you will be required to do something from time to time that is very difficult. You will have to face the terrible emptiness within that surfaces when you are not focused on someone else. Sometimes the emptiness will be so deep, you will almost be able to feel the wind blowing through the place where your heart should be. Allow yourself to feel it, in all its intensity (otherwise you'll look for another unhealthy way to distract yourself). Embrace the emptiness and know that you will not always feel this way, and that just by holding still and feeling it you will begin to fill it with the warmth of self-acceptance. Let your support group help you with this. Their acceptance can also help fill the void, as can your *own* projects and activities. We achieve a sense of self from what we do for ourselves and how we develop our own capacities. If all your efforts have gone into developing others, you're bound to feel empty. Take your turn now.

Why cultivating whatever needs to be developed in you is necessary

Unless you maximize your own talents, you will always be frustrated. And that frustration may then be blamed on him, when it actually issues from your not getting on with your *own* life. Developing your potential takes the blame off him and puts the responsibility for your life squarely where it belongs—with you.

The projects and activities you choose to pursue will keep you too busy to be able to focus on what he is and isn't doing. If you are not currently in a relationship, this will give you a healthy, wholesome alternative to either pining for your last love or waiting for your next one.

What cultivating whatever needs developing in yourself implies

For one thing, you won't need to find a partner who is your opposite in order to bring balance into your life. To explain: Like most women who love too much, you are probably overly serious and responsible. Unless you actively cultivate your playful side, you will be drawn to men who embody what you lack. A carefree, irresponsible man makes a charming acquaintance but is a poor prospect for a satisfying relationship. Nevertheless, until you can give yourself permission to be more free and easy, you'll need him to create the fun and excitement in your life.

For another thing, cultivating yourself enables you to grow up. As you become all you are capable of being, you also take full responsibility for your decisions, your choices, your life, and in this way you embrace adulthood. Until we take responsibility for our own lives and our own happiness, we are not fully mature human beings, but rather remain dependent and frightened children in adult bodies.

Finally, developing yourself makes you better partner material, because you are a fully expressive, creative woman, not someone who is incomplete (and therefore frightened) without a man. Ironically, the less you need a partner, the better partner you become—and the healthier partner you will attract (and be attracted to).

255

9. Become selfish

What it means

Like the word *spirituality* in step 4, *selfish* here requires careful explanation. It probably conjures up an image of exactly what you don't want to be: indifferent, cruel, thoughtless, self-centered. For some people, selfishness may mean all this, but remember, you are a woman with a history of loving too much. For you, becoming selfish is a necessary exercise in letting go of martyrdom. Let's look at what healthy selfishness means for women who love too much:

You put your well-being, your desires, your work, play, plans, and activities first instead of last—before, instead of after, everyone else's needs are met. Even if you are the parent of small children you incorporate into your day some purely self-nurturing activities.

You expect and even require that situations and relationships be comfortable for you. You do not try to adapt yourself to fit uncomfortable ones.

You believe that your wants and needs are very important, and that meeting them is your job. At the same time, you grant others the right to be responsible for meeting their own wants and needs.

What becoming selfish requires

As you begin to put yourself first, you must learn to tolerate other people's anger and disapproval. These are inevitable reactions from those whose welfare you have heretofore put before your own. Do not argue, apologize, or attempt to justify yourself. Remain as even-tempered and cheerful as possible and go on about your activities.

The changes you are making in your life require that those around you change too, and they will naturally resist. But unless you give credence to their indignation, it will be fairly short-lived. It is just an attempt to push you back into your old, selfless behavior, into doing for them what they can and should do for themselves.

You must listen carefully to your inner voice regarding what is good for you, right for you, and then follow it. This is how you develop healthy self-interest, by listening to your own cues. Up to now you've probably been nearly psychic at picking up other people's cues about how they wanted you to behave. Tune those cues out, or they'll continue to drown out your own.

Becoming selfish finally requires that you recognize your worth is great, that your talents are worthy of expression, that your fulfillment is as important as anyone else's, and that your best self is the greatest gift you have to give the world as a whole, and most especially those closest to you.

Why becoming selfish is necessary

Without this strong commitment to yourself, the tendency is to become passive, to develop yourself not for your own greatest expression but for someone else's benefit. Although becoming selfish (which also means becoming honest) will make you a better partner, that cannot be your ultimate goal. Your goal must be the achievement of your own highest self.

Rising above all the difficulties you've encountered isn't enough. There is still your own life to be lived, your own potential to be explored. It is the natural next step as you gain respect for yourself and start honoring your wants and your wishes.

Taking responsibility for yourself and your happiness gives a great freedom to children who have felt guilty and responsible for your unhappiness (which they always do). A child can never hope to balance the scales or repay the debt when a parent has sacrificed her life, her happiness, her fulfillment for the child or the family. Seeing a parent fully embrace life gives the child permission to do the same, just as seeing a parent suffer indicates to the child that suffering is what life is all about.

What becoming selfish implies

Your relationships automatically become healthier. No one "owes" it to you to be other than they are, because you are no longer being other than you are for them.

You free the others in your life to take care of themselves without worrying about you. (It is very likely that your children, for instance, have been feeling responsible for easing your frustration and pain. As you do a better job of taking care of yourself, they are freed to take better care of themselves.)

You now can say yes or no when you want to.

As you make the dramatic shift in roles from caretaker of others to caretaker of yourself, it is very likely that your behavior will be balanced by shifts of roles throughout your relationships. If the role changes are too difficult for the man in your life, he may leave, searching for someone else who is the way you used to be—so you may not end up with the person you began with.

On the other hand, it's ironic that as you become better able to nurture yourself, you may find that you've attracted someone who is able to nurture you. As we become healthier and more balanced, we attract healthier and more balanced partners. As we become less needy, more of our needs are met. As we give up the role of supernurturer, we make space for someone to nurture us.

10. Share with others what you have experienced and learned.

What it means

Sharing your experiences with others means remembering that this is the last step in recovery, not the first. Being too helpful and focusing on others is part of our disease, so wait until you've worked hard on your own recovery before you tackle this step.

In your peer support group, it means sharing with newcomers what it used to be like and how it is now. This does not mean giving advice, only explaining what has worked for you. It also doesn't mean naming names or casting blame on others. By the time you are at this stage of recovery you know that blaming others is not helpful to you.

Sharing with others also means that when you meet someone who is from a similar background, or in a situation similar to what yours was, you are willing to talk about your own recovery without needing to coerce that person into doing what you did to recover. There is no place for managing and controlling here any more than there was in your relationship.

Sharing may mean giving some hours as a volunteer to help other women, perhaps by working on a hotline or meeting one-to-one with someone who has reached out for help.

Finally, it may mean helping to educate the medical and counseling professions about the appropriate treatment approach for yourself and women like you.

What sharing with others what you have experienced and learned requires

You must tap your deep sense of gratitude for having come so far, and for the help others gave you along the way through their sharing.

You need honesty and a willingness to let go of your secrets and your need to "look good."

Finally, you must reveal a capacity to give to others without a motive of personal gratification. Most of the "giving" we did when we were loving too much was actually manipulation. Now we are free enough to be able to give freely. Our own needs are met and we are full of love. The natural thing to do now is to share that love, without expecting anything in return.

Why sharing what you have experienced and learned is necessary

If you believe you have an illness, you also need to realize that like an alcoholic who is sober, you could slip. Without constant vigilance you could resume your old ways of thinking, feeling, and relating. Working with newcomers helps to keep you in touch with how sick you once were, and how very far you've come. It keeps you from denying how bad it really was, because a newcomer's story is going to be much like your own, and you will remember with compassion, for her and yourself, what it was like.

By talking about it, you give hope to others, and validity to all you went through in your struggle to recover. You gain perspective on your courage and on your life.

What sharing what you have experienced and learned implies

You will help others recover. And you will maintain your own recovery.

This sharing, then, is ultimately an act of healthy selfishness, by which you further promote your own well-being through staying in touch with the principles of recovery that will serve you all your life.

11 • Recovery and Intimacy: Closing the Gap

> FOR US MARRIAGE IS A JOURNEY TOWARD
> AN UNKNOWN DESTINATION . . . THE
> DISCOVERY THAT PEOPLE MUST SHARE NOT
> ONLY WHAT THEY DON'T KNOW ABOUT EACH
> OTHER, BUT WHAT THEY DON'T KNOW ABOUT
> THEMSELVES.
>
> —MICHAEL VENTURA,
> "SHADOW DANCING IN
> THE MARRIAGE ZONE"

WHAT I WANT TO KNOW IS, WHERE DID ALL MY SEXUAL feelings go?" Trudi is still in motion, striding toward the couch in my office. She throws the question over her shoulder playfully, but I note a glint of accusation in her eye as she sweeps by me. On her left hand a diamond engagement ring flashes a corresponding glint of its own, and I have a strong hunch about why she made the appointment. It's been eight months since I last saw her, and today she looks better than ever, her warm brown eyes shining and the beautiful cloud of softly waved reddish brown hair longer and fuller than I remember. Her face has the same sweet, almost kittenish appeal, but the two looks between which she once alternated chronically—sad little orphan or brittle sophisticate—have been replaced by a womanly glow of confidence. She has come a long way in the three years since her suicide attempt, when her affair with Jim, the married policeman, ended.

I'm happy to see that her recovery process is still progressing. Trudi doesn't know it yet, but even the problems she is now encountering sexually are part of the inevitable process of her recovery.

"Tell me about it, Trudi," I urge her, and she settles back into the couch.

"Well, I have this wonderful man in my life. You remember Hal? I was dating him when I last saw you."

I remember the name very well. He had been one of the several young men Trudi was dating when she left therapy. "He's nice, but he's a little boring," she had said of him then. "We have great talks and he strikes me as solid and trustworthy. He's good-looking, too, but there are no fireworks so I guess he's not the one." She had agreed with me at that time that she needed to practice being with such a man who was thoughtful and dependable, so she decided to keep on seeing him for a while, "just for drill."

Now Trudi continues proudly, "He's so different from the kind of man I used to get involved with, thank God, and we're engaged to be married in September . . . but we're, well, kind of having some problems. It's not us, actually, it's me. I'm having trouble feeling really turned on, and since that never was a problem for me before, I want to know what's going on. You know how I used to be. I was practically begging for sex with every one of those men who never loved me, but since I'm no longer throwing myself at anyone, I'm like some prudish, inhibited spinster. Here's Hal, handsome, responsible, trustworthy, and really in love with me. And I lie there in bed with him, feeling like a stick of wood."

I nod, knowing Trudi is facing a hurdle most women who love too much must overcome when they recover. Having used their sexuality as a tool to manipulate a difficult or impossible man into loving them, once that challenge is removed they don't know how to be sexual with a loving, giving partner.

Trudi's discomfort is patent. She's pounding her fist softly on her knee, emphasizing almost every word. *"Why* can't I get excited about him?" And then she stops pounding, and looks at me fearfully. "Is it because I don't really love him? Is that what's wrong between us?"

"Do you think you love him?" I ask.

"I think I do, but I'm confused because everything feels different from what I've known before. I enjoy being with him so much. We can talk about anything. He knows my whole story, so there aren't any secrets between us. I don't pretend with him about anything. I'm completely myself, which means that I'm more relaxed with him than I've ever been with any man before. I'm not always putting on a great big show, which is nice, but sometimes those performances were easier than just relaxing and trusting that being myself will be enough to keep somebody interested.

"We enjoy a lot of the same things—sailing and bicycling and hiking. We share almost identical values, and when we do have a quarrel, he's a clean fighter. In fact, having an argument with Hal is almost a pleasure. But at first even the open, frank talks we had about our disagreements were scary for me. I wasn't used to someone being so honest and up front about how he felt and expecting me to be the same way. Hal helped me not to be afraid to say what I thought or ask for what I needed from him, because he's never punished me for being honest. We always end up settling whatever it's about and feeling closer afterward. He's the best friend I've ever had, and I'm proud to be seen with him. So, yes, I think I love him, but if I'm in love with him, why can't I have a good time in bed with him? There's nothing wrong with the way he makes love, either. He's very considerate, really wants to please me. That's very new for me. He's not as aggressive as Jim was, but I don't think that's the problem. I know he thinks I'm wonderful, and gets really excited about me, but nothing much happens on my end. I'm cold and kind of embarrassed a lot of the time. After the way I used to be, it doesn't make any sense, does it?"

I'm glad to be able to reassure her. "Actually, Trudi, it makes perfect sense. What you're going through now is something that many women who have similar histories to yours, and who have been able to recover, find themselves facing when they begin to relate to a man who is an appropriate partner. The excitement, the challenge, the old knot in the stomach just aren't there, and since that is what "love" has always felt like before, they are afraid that something very important is missing. What's missing is the craziness, the pain, the fear, the waiting, and the hoping.

"Now, for the first time, you've got a nice, steady, reliable man who adores you, and you don't have to go to work on him to change him. He already has the qualities you've wanted in a man, and he's made a commitment to you. The trouble is, you've never experienced having what you wanted before. You've only known what it was like not to have it, and to work like crazy to try and get it. You're used to the yearning and the suspense, which creates a lot of heart-pounding excitement. Will he, won't he? Does he, doesn't he? You know what I'm talking about."

Trudi smiles. "Do I ever. But how does all this relate to my sexual feelings?"

"It relates because not having what you want is much more stimulating than having it. A kind, loving, devoted man will never get your adrenaline running the way Jim did, for instance."

"Oh, it's true! I keep questioning the whole relationship because I'm not always obsessed with Hal. I've wondered whether I'm just taking him for granted." Trudi is no longer angry. She's excited now, a detective unraveling an important mystery.

I affirm, "Well, you probably do take him for granted somewhat. You know that he'll be there for you. He's not going to desert you. You can count on him. So there's no need to be obsessed. Obsession isn't love, Trudi. It's just obsession."

She nods, remembering. "I know! I know!"

"And sometimes," I continue, "sex works very well when we're obsessed. All those strong feelings of excitement and anxious anticipation, even dread, contribute to a powerful package that gets called love. Actually, it's anything but. Still, it's what all the songs tell us love is. The 'I can't live without you, baby' stuff. Hardly anyone writes songs about how easy and comfortable a healthy love relationship is. They're all writing about fear and pain and loss and heartache. So we call that love, and we don't know what to do when something comes along that isn't crazy. We begin to relax and then we're afraid it isn't love, because we're not obsessed."

Trudi agrees. "Exactly. That's exactly what happened. I didn't start out calling it love because it was too comfortable—and I wasn't used to anything being comfortable, as you know." She grins, and continues. "He just grew on me over the months that we saw each other. I felt as if I could relax and be totally myself and he still wouldn't go away. That alone was incredible. I'd never had someone not go away. We waited a long time before we got sexually involved, actually got to know each other first as people. I liked him more and more, and being with him was such a good, happy time for me. When we finally did go to bed together it was very tender, and I felt *so* vulnerable. I cried a lot. I still do sometimes, but he doesn't seem to mind." Trudi lowers her gaze. "I guess there are still a lot of painful memories that come up for me around sex, of being rejected and feeling so hurt." After a pause, she adds, "As far as sex now, I'm more troubled than he is. He'd like it to be more exciting for both our sakes, but he's really not complaining. I am, though, because I know how it could be."

"Okay," I respond, "tell me how it *is* between you and Hal now."

"He's in love with me. I can see it by the way he treats me. Whenever I meet a friend of his for the first time I can tell Hal's already said wonderful things about me just by the way I'm greeted. And when we're alone, he is so affectionate, so eager to make me happy. But I get stiff, cold, rigid almost. I cannot seem to really warm up to him. I don't know what stops me . . ."

"What do you feel when you and Hal start to make love, Trudi?"

She sits quietly for a while, thinking. Then she looks up at me. "Afraid, maybe?" Then, answering herself, "Yes, that's it. I'm scared, really scared!"

"Of . . ." I prod.

More thoughtful silence. Finally she continues, "I'm not sure. Being *known,* somehow. Oh, that sounds so Biblical. You know how they always talk about that in the Bible. 'Then he knew her.' That kind of thing. But somehow I feel like, if I let him, Hal would really know me, not just sexually, but in other ways too. I can't seem to surrender to him. It's just too scary for me."

I ask the obvious question. "What will happen if you do?"

"Oh, God, I don't know." Trudi starts to squirm in her chair. "I feel so vulnerable, so naked when I think about it. I feel silly talking about sex this way, after all my exploits. But this is different, somehow. It's not as easy to be sexual with someone who really wants to be close to me in every way. I close up like a clam, or else go through the motions while part of me is holding back. I'm acting like this shy virgin or something."

"Trudi," I reassure her, "when it comes to the kind of intimacy you and Hal already have, and what you can have together in the future, you're very much like a virgin. It's all new, and you're very inexperienced at this way of being with a man, with anyone in fact. You *are* scared."

"Well, that's exactly how I feel—self-protective, as though I'm going to lose something very important," she agrees.

"Yes, and what you're afraid of losing is all your armor, your protection against being really hurt. Even though you threw yourself at men before this, you never really risked getting close to any one of them. You never had to deal with being close because none of *them* could be close either. Now you're with Hal, who'd like nothing better than to be close in every way with you, and you are panicking. It's fine when you're talking and enjoying each other's company, but with sex, when every possible barrier between the two of you is removed, it's different. With your other partners, not even sex removed the barriers. In fact, it helped to keep them in place because you used sex to avoid communicating about who you really were and how you really felt. So no matter how much sex you had, you never really got any closer to knowing each other. Because you used sex once to control relationships, my guess is that it is very hard for you to let go of that control, by being sexual rather than using sex as a tool.

"I like your phrase, Trudi—'to be known'—because that is what your sexual sharing means now. You and Hal have shared so much about yourselves already that sex has become a deepening of the way you know each other, not an avoidance."

Trudi's eyes gleam with tears. "Why does it have to be this way? Why can't I just relax? I know this man isn't going to hurt me deliberately. At least I don't think he is . . ." When she hears her self-doubt, she quickly changes her tack. "Okay, you're telling me I only know how to be sexy with someone who doesn't really want me, not all of me anyway, and that I can't be sexy with someone like Hal, who is good and kind and thinks I'm wonderful, because I'm afraid of the closeness. So what do I do?"

"The only way out is *through*. First of all, let go of the idea of 'being sexy' and allow yourself to just be sexual. Being sexy is an act. Being sexual is relating intimately on a physical level. You'll need to tell Hal exactly what's happening to you as it happens—all your feelings, no matter how irrational. Tell him when you're afraid, when you need to back away, and when you're ready to let the closeness happen again. If you need to, take more control of the lovemaking and go only as fast and as far as is comfortable for you. Hal will understand if you ask for his help with your fears. And try not to judge anything that's happening to you. Love and trust are not areas you've had much experience with till now. Be willing to go very slowly, and build your willingness to surrender. You know, Trudi, in all that sex before, there was very little surrender, but there was a whole lot of managing and controlling someone else, manipulating him through sex, and practicing lots of self-will. You were performing, hoping for rave reviews. Look at what you did before and what you're trying to do now as the difference between playing the part of a great lover and allowing yourself to be loved. Playing the part can be very exhilarating, especially when you've got your audience's attention. Allowing yourself to be loved is much more difficult because it has to come from a very private place, the place where you already love yourself. If there's lots of love already there, it's easier to accept that you deserve another's love. If there's very little self-love, it's much harder to let love in that comes from outside yourself. You've come a long way in loving yourself. Now you're at the next step: trusting enough to let yourself be loved by this man."

Trudi reflects. "All that wild abandon I used to practice was actually very calculated. I can see that. There really wasn't much letting go at all, even though it was an exciting performance. So now I have to stop trying and start just being. Funny, how that's even harder. Being loved . . ." Trudi muses. "I know I still have a long way to go with that one. Sometimes I look at Hal and wonder how he can be so enchanted with me. I'm not sure there's anything that's wonderful about me when I'm not putting on a great big, spectacular show." Trudi's eyes widen. "That's what has made it so difficult for me, right? Not having to put on that show. Not having to do much of anything special. Not having to *try*. I've been afraid to be loving to Hal because I was sure I didn't know how. I thought that unless I went into my seductive routine whatever I did with him wouldn't be enough and he'd be bored. I couldn't use the seductive act because we were such good friends before we became lovers that it was totally inappropriate for me to suddenly start breathing heavily and throwing myself at him. Plus it wasn't necessary. He already was very interested without my doing any of that.

"It's just like the rest of what we have together. The whole thing is so much easier than I ever thought love could be. Just being myself *is* enough!" Trudi stops, and then she looks at me sheepishly. "Do you see this kind of thing happening all the time?" she asks.

"Not nearly as often as I'd like," I reply. "What you are struggling with now is only an issue for a woman who's really recovered from loving too much . . . and most women do not recover. They spend their time, their energy, their lives, using their sexuality as a tool, in trying to change someone who's not able to love them into someone who is. It never works, but it's safe, because as long as they're all wrapped up in the struggle, they never have to deal with real intimacy, with letting another human being know them in the deepest sense. Most people are so frightened of that. So while their loneliness drives them toward relationships, their fear causes them to choose people with whom it won't ever really work."

Trudi asks, "Has Hal done that with me? Chosen someone with whom he can't be close?"

"Maybe," I answer.

"So I'm now on the other end of this thing, being the one who resists being close. That's a switch."

"It happens a lot. We all have the ability to play both roles, you know. The pursuer, which is what you used to be, or the distancer, which is what your partners used to be. Now, to some degree, you're the distancer, the one who is fleeing from intimacy, and Hal is doing the pursuing. If you stopped running, it would be interesting to see what would happen. You see, what will tend to stay the same through all this is the gap between you and another person. You may trade roles, but the gap will remain constant."

"So no matter who is chasing and who is running away, neither person has to deal with being close," Trudi says. Then, softly, cautiously, "It's not the sex, is it? It's the closeness that is so frightening. But I really think I want to hold still, and let Hal catch up to me. It scares me and it feels threatening as hell, but I want to close the gap."

Trudi is talking about being willing to enter a state of being with another person that very few people ever achieve. The need to avoid it is behind all the struggles in which women who love too much and men who love too little engage. The positions of pursuer and distancer are reversible, but for two people to eliminate them completely demands a rare courage. I give the only guidance I can offer for their journey.

"Well, I suggest that you talk about all this with Hal. And don't stop talking when you two are in bed together. Let him know what you are going through. That's a very important form of intimacy, you know. Stay very, very honest and the rest will take care of itself."

Trudi looks immensely relieved. "It helps so much to understand what's been going on. I know you're right, that this is all new for me and I don't know how to do it yet. Thinking that I should be just as wild as I used to be hasn't helped either. In fact, that's caused more problems. But I already trust Hal with my heart and with my feelings. Now I just need to trust him with my body." She smiles, shaking her head. "None of this is easy, is it? But it's all exactly what has to happen. I'll let you know how it goes . . . and thanks."

"My pleasure, Trudi," I answer, meaning it with all my heart, and we hug good-bye.

* * *

To see how far Trudi has come in her recovery, we can compare her beliefs about herself and her style of relating in an intimate relationship with the characteristics of a woman who has recovered from loving too much. Keep in mind that recovery is a lifelong process and a goal toward which we strive, rather than one we achieve once and for all.

These are the characteristics of a woman who has recovered from loving too much.

1. She accepts herself fully, even while wanting to change parts of herself. There is a basic self-love and self-regard, which she carefully nurtures and purposely expands.

2. She accepts others as they are without trying to change them to meet her needs.

3. She is in touch with her feelings and attitudes about every aspect of her life, including her sexuality.

4. She cherishes every aspect of herself: her personality, her appearance, her beliefs and values, her body, her interests and accomplishments. She validates herself, rather than searching for a relationship to give her a sense of self-worth.

5. Her self-esteem is great enough that she can enjoy being with others, especially men, who are fine just as they are. She does not need to be needed in order to feel worthy.

6. She allows herself to be open and trusting with *appropriate* people. She is not afraid to be known at a deeply personal level, but she also does not expose herself to the exploitation of those who are not interested in her well-being.

7. She questions, "Is this relationship good for me? Does it enable me to grow into all I am capable of being?"

8.   When a relationship is destructive, she is able to let go of it without experiencing disabling depression. She has a circle of supportive friends and healthy interests to see her through crises.

9.   She values her own serenity above all else. All the struggles, drama, and chaos of the past have lost their appeal. She is protective of herself, her health, and well-being.

10.   She knows that a relationship, in order to work, must be between partners who share similar values, interests, and goals, and who each have a capacity for intimacy. She also knows that she is worthy of the best that life has to offer.

There are several phases in recovering from loving too much. The first phase begins when we realize what we are doing and wish we could stop. Next comes our willingness to get help for ourselves, followed by our actual initial attempt to secure help. After that, we enter the phase of recovery that requires our commitment to our own healing and our willingness to continue with our recovery program. During this period we begin to change how we act, think, and feel. What once felt normal and familiar begins to feel uncomfortable and unhealthy. We enter the next phase of recovery when we start making choices that no longer follow our old patterns but enhance our lives and promote our well-being instead. Throughout the stages of recovery, self-love grows slowly and steadily. First we stop hating ourselves, then we become more tolerant of ourselves. Next, there is a burgeoning appreciation of our good qualities, and then self-acceptance develops. Finally, genuine self-love evolves.

Unless we have self-acceptance and self-love, we cannot tolerate being "known," as Trudi so aptly put it, because without these feelings we cannot believe we are worth loving just as we are. Instead, we try to earn love through giving it to another, through being nurturing and patient, through suffering and sacrifice, through providing exciting sex or wonderful cooking or whatever.

Once the self-acceptance and self-love begin to develop and take hold, we are then ready to consciously practice simply being ourselves without trying to please, without performing in certain ways calculated to gain another's approval and love. But stopping the performances and letting go of the act, while a relief, can also be frightening. Awkwardness and a feeling of great vulnerability come over us when we are just being rather than doing. As we struggle to believe that we are worthy, *just as we are,* of the love of someone important to us, the temptation will always be there to put on at least a bit of an act for him, and yet if the recovery process has progressed there will also be an unwillingness to go back into the old behaviors and old manipulations. This is the crossroads Trudi faces now: no longer able to employ her old style of relating sexually but frightened to go forward into a more genuine, less controlled (all that wild abandon having been a most controlled performance) mode of sexual experience. To stop performing feels at first like being frozen. When we are no longer willing to make the moves calculated to produce an effect, there is a period of time during which we suffer from not knowing what to do until our *genuine* loving impulses have a chance to be heard and felt and to assert themselves.

Letting go of the old strategems does not mean we never approach, never love, never nurture, never help, never soothe nor stimulate nor seduce our partner. But with recovery, we relate to another person as an expression of our own essence, rather than because we are trying to elicit a response or create an effect or produce a change in him. What we have to offer instead is who we genuinely are when we are not hiding or calculating, when we are undisguised and unvarnished.

First we must overcome our fear of being rejected if we

allow someone to truly see us, truly know us. Then we must learn not to panic when all our emotional boundary lines are no longer in place, surrounding and protecting us. In the sexual realm, this new quality of relating requires not only that we be naked and vulnerable physically, but that we be emotionally and spiritually naked and vulnerable as well.

No wonder this degree of connecting between two individuals is so very rare. Our terror is that without those boundaries we will dissolve.

What makes the risk worthwhile? Only when we truly reveal ourselves can we ever be truly loved. When we relate as we genuinely are, from our essence, then if we are loved it is our essence that is loved. Nothing is more validating on a personal level and more freeing in a relationship. It must be noted, however, that this kind of behavior on our part is only possible in a climate that is free of fear, so we must not only conquer our own fears of being genuine but also avoid people whose attitudes and behaviors toward us produce fear. No matter how willing to be genuine you become with recovery, there will still be people whose anger, hostility, and aggression will inhibit you from being honest. To be vulnerable with them is to be masochistic. Therefore, lowering our boundaries and eventually eliminating them should happen only with those people—friends, relatives, or lovers—with whom we have a relationship bathed in trust, love, respect, and reverence for our shared, tender humanity.

What frequently happens with recovery is that as our patterns of relating change, so do our circles of friends as well as our intimate relationships. We change in how we relate to our parents and to our children. With our parents we become less needy and less angry, and often less ingratiating as well. We become much more honest, often more tolerant, and sometimes more genuinely loving. With our children we become less controlling, less worried, and less guilty. We relax and enjoy them more because we are able to relax and enjoy ourselves more. We feel more freedom to pursue our own needs and interests, and this frees them to do the same.

Friends with whom we could once commiserate endlessly may now strike us as obsessed and unhealthy, and while we may offer to share what has been helpful for us, we will not allow ourselves to carry the burden of their troubles. Mutual misery as a criterion for friendship is replaced by more rewarding mutual interests.

In short, recovery will change your life in more ways than I can predict for you on these pages, and sometimes that will be uncomfortable. Don't let the discomfort stop you. The fear of change, of relinquishing what we've always known and done and been, is what holds us back from our metamorphosis into a healthier, higher, more truly loving self.

It is not the pain that holds us back. We're already enduring alarming levels of pain with no prospect of relief unless we change. What holds us back is the fear, fear of the unknown. The best way I know to confront and combat fear is to join forces with fellow travelers who are on the same journey. Find a support group of those others who have been where you are and who are headed for or have already arrived at the destination you want to reach. Join them on the path toward a new way of living.

APPENDIX 1

How to Start Your Own Support Group

FIRST, LEARN WHAT RESOURCES ARE ALREADY AVAILABLE IN the area you live in. Often communities have a directory listing all service agencies and sources of help. If you don't know whether such a publication exists or how to find it, call your library or your community crisis hotline. (Also, see the Sources of Help section, Appendix 2, for a listing of national organizations. You can call or write to them and they will advise you regarding local service agencies.) Even if there is no such publication, your community hotline should be able to give you the names of various counseling agencies and self-help groups that may be appropriate for you. In addition, most telephone directories now include a "human services" listing, so you can check that as well.

Do not, however, assume that one phone call to one agency or professional will result in all the information you need to have. It is difficult for any professional in a large community to stay in touch with all the resources that the area has to offer, and unfortunately many professionals are woefully uninformed about what is currently available.

Do your own homework. Make all the calls you need to, anonymously if you wish. See if the group you need already exists. There's no point reinventing the wheel or going into competition with a group that is already functioning and could use your involvement. If you are a candidate for Daughters United or Overeaters Anonymous or Al-Anon or Shelter Services groups for battered women or Rape Crisis groups for rape survivors, be willing to take some time and go to some trouble, maybe travel some distance to attend the meetings they offer. It will be worth it to you.

If, after diligent searching, you are quite certain that the group you need doesn't exist, start one yourself.

Probably the best way to begin is to run an ad in the Personals section of your newspaper. It might go something like this:

> WOMEN: HAS FALLING IN LOVE MEANT BEING IN EMOTIONAL PAIN SOONER OR LATER? A FREE SELF-HELP GROUP IS NOW FORMING FOR WOMEN WHOSE RELATIONSHIPS WITH MEN HAVE, UP TO NOW, USUALLY BEEN DESTRUCTIVE. IF YOU WANT TO OVERCOME THIS PROBLEM, CALL [YOUR FIRST NAME AND PHONE NUMBER] FOR INFORMATION AND LOCATION OF MEETING.

You should be able to fill a group by running such an ad just a few times. Your group ideally would have about seven to twelve members, but start with fewer if necessary.

Remember, at that first meeting the women who show up are there because this is a serious problem for them and they are looking for help. Don't spend too much of the meeting time talking about how to organize future meetings, even though that too is important. The best way to start is to share your stories, because doing so will forge an immediate bond and a sense of belonging. Women who love too much are much more alike than different, and that will be felt by all of you. So make sharing your stories your first priority.

Try this agenda for your first meeting, which should last no more than an hour.

1. Start on time. This lets everyone involved know that they must be prompt for future meetings.

2. Introduce yourself as the person who ran the ad and

explain that you would like the group to develop into a continuing source of support for yourself and everyone present.

3. Emphasize that everything that is said during the meeting is to remain in the meeting, that no one who is seen there or anything that is said there should be discussed elsewhere, *ever*. Suggest that those present simply use their first names to introduce themselves.

4. Explain that it would probably help everyone there to hear one another's reasons for coming to the group and that perhaps each person could talk for up to five minutes about what made her decide to come. Emphasize that no one has to talk for that much time but that it is available to each person should she want it. Volunteer to begin by giving your first name and telling your own story briefly.

5. When everyone who wants to has shared her story, go back to any who did not want to talk when it was their turn, and gently ask if they would like to now. Do not pressure anyone to speak. Make it very clear that each woman is welcome whether or not she is ready to talk about her situation yet.

6. Now talk about some of the guidelines that you would like to see the group follow. I recommend the following, which should be copied down and given to each participant:

- No advice giving. All are welcome to share their experiences and what has worked to help them feel better, but no one should advise another as to what she should do. Advice giving should be gently pointed out if anyone indulges in it.
- Leadership should rotate within the group weekly, each meeting led by a different member. It is the leader's responsibility to start the meeting on time, to pick a topic to be discussed, to save a few minutes at

the end for any business matters, and to choose another leader for the following week before she closes the meeting.

- Meetings should last a specific length of time. I recommend one hour. No one is going to solve all her problems in one meeting and it is important not to try. Meetings should start promptly and end on time. (It is better that they be too short than too long. Members can decide to lengthen the meeting if they wish, later on.)

- The meeting place should be a neutral setting rather than someone's home, if at all possible. Homes are full of distractions: children, telephone calls, and lack of privacy for the group members, especially the hostess. Moreover, the role of hostess should be avoided. You are not entertaining each other socially; you are working together as peers to recover from your common problems. Many banks, savings and loans offices, other businesses, and churches make rooms available free of charge to groups for meetings in the evening hours.

- No eating, smoking, or drinking any beverages while your meeting is in progress: these all serve to distract from the business at hand. Such things may be made available before and after the meeting if your group decides that this is important. *Never* provide alcohol. It distorts people's feelings and reactions and impedes the work to be done.

- Avoid talking about "him." This is *very* important. Group members must learn to focus on themselves and their own thoughts, feelings, and behaviors, rather than on the man who is their obsession. Some talking about him is inevitable at first, but each person as she shares should strive to keep this to the strictest minimum.

- No one should be criticized about what she does or does not do, either when she is present or when she is absent from the group. Although members are free to ask for feedback from each other, this should never be given unsolicited. Like advice, criticism has no place in a support group.

- Stick to the topic at hand. Virtually any topic a leader wants to introduce is fine except anything having to do with religion, politics, or outside issues such as current events, celebrities, any causes, treatment programs, or therapeutic modalities. There is no room for debate or devisiveness in a support group. And remember, you are not meeting to gripe about men. You are interested in your own growth and healing, in sharing how you are developing new tools for coping with old problems. Below are some topic suggestions:

Why I need this group
Guilt and resentment
My worst fears
What I like best about myself and what I like least
How I take care of myself and meet my own needs
Loneliness
How I cope with depression
My sexual attitudes: what they are and where they come from
Anger: how I handle my own and others'
How I relate to men
What I think people think of me
Examining my motives
My responsibilities to myself; my responsibilities to others
My spirituality (this is *not* a discussion of religious beliefs but of how each group member experiences her own spiritual dimension or doesn't)
Letting go of blame, including self-blame
Patterns in my life

It is recommended that group members read *Women Who Love Too Much,* but this is *not* a requirement, only a suggestion.

The group may decide to add an extra fifteen minutes on to the meeting time once a month to deal with business matters or changes in format, how well the guidelines are working, or any other problems.

Now, back to the suggested format for the first meeting:

7. Discuss the list of guidelines together as a group.

8. Ask if someone would be willing to lead the group the following week.

9. Ascertain where the group will meet the following week and decide on the issue of refreshments before or after the meeting.

10. Discuss whether more women should be invited to join your group, whether to run the ad one more week, or whether the women present might invite other women.

11. Close the meeting by standing silently in a circle, holding hands with eyes closed for a few moments.

A final word regarding these guidelines: The principles of confidentiality, rotation of leadership, no criticism, no advice-giving, no discussions of controversial subjects or outside issues, no debating, and so on are all very important to group harmony and cohesion. Do not violate these principles in the interest of pleasing a group member. What is best for the group as a whole must always be considered first.

With this in mind, you have the basic tools for starting a group for women who love too much. Do not underestimate how very healing this simple hour's meeting of personal sharing will come to be in all your lives. Together you are offering each other the opportunity to recover. Good luck!

APPENDIX 2

Sources of Help

WHEN YOU ARE LOOKING FOR HELP, IT IS OFTEN DIFFICULT TO know the names for the agencies and programs you need. For instance, if your husband is battering you, and you are ready to talk to someone who understands but don't know that the agency for dealing with your situation is listed under Shelter Services for Women, you may feel frustrated and helpless. Therefore, this list is prepared to aid you in knowing where to look when you are ready to go for help.

A good way to begin is to call your local hotline if your area has one. You can find that number by calling Information or by looking in your phone book in the section listing community services. Sometimes this information is listed in the blue pages that divide the directory's personal and business numbers; sometimes it is in the information section at the beginning of the white pages. You may also call your local library and ask if there is a publication that lists community resources. This is an excellent source of information about what counseling services and self-help groups exist in your area. Also, most agencies offering help to the community know about other sources of help, so sometimes one call to one agency, even if it isn't the right one, will start you in the direction of finding the help you need.

If all else fails, you may want to write these national offices for information about what is available in your community:

A.A. World Service (Alcoholics Anonymous)
P.O. Box 459, Grand Central Station
New York, NY 10163
(212) 686-1100

Alcoholics Anonymous is listed in nearly every telephone directory in the United States and in many countries abroad as well, so getting in touch with this organization should be very easy. It is the most effective and successful program of help for those with a serious desire to stop drinking. It is also an excellent source of accurate information about the disease of alcoholism. Call your A.A. central office for a directory of local meetings or to obtain their free literature or to talk to someone in the program.

Al-Anon Family Group Headquarters
World Service Office
P.O. Box 182, Madison Square Station
New York, NY 10159-0182

Based on the principles of A.A., Al-Anon is for the families and friends of alcoholics. Al-Anon is usually listed in the phone book or in the Personals section of the newspaper as Al-Anon Family Groups. If there is no listing, call A.A. Central Office and ask for Al-Anon's number, or ask to talk to a member of A.A. who can put you in touch with someone in Al-Anon. The meetings and literature are an invaluable source of help, and they are free.

National Coalition Against Domestic Violence
1500 Massachusetts Avenue, NW, Suite 35
Washington, DC 20005

Local shelter services offer a refuge for battered women and their children as well as ongoing support groups and a domestic violence hotline. Usually staffed in part by volunteers who have themselves been victims of domestic violence, these shelters are an excellent source of help for the woman who is being physically abused. Look in your phone book under Shelter Services, use your local community information directory, or call the district attorney's office or the Legal Aid office for the number. If there are no shelter services in your community, you might consider trying Al-Anon. Eighty percent of those who batter their wives and/or children abuse alcohol, and their violent episodes are related to their drinking. Al-Anon has a great deal to offer victims of domestic violence whose partners are alcoholic.

National Coalition Against Sexual Assault
Austin Rape Crisis Center
P.O. Box 7156
Austin, TX 78712
(512) 472-8858

Not all rape crisis centers are affiliated with this coalition. Your local health department or a nearby college or university women's center may be able to aid you in finding the nearest source of help. Or try your District Attorney's office or police department. Of course, you may call anonymously.

Contacting a rape crisis center or hotline is appropriate whether the rape occurred ten minutes ago or twenty years ago. Women who have been raped tend to feel that they do not deserve to be loved and may, from this experience alone, become women who love too much.

Free information and support services are usually provided by volunteers who have themselves been victims of rape. Sometimes a nominal fee or a sliding-scale fee is charged for ongoing support group involvement.

Overeaters Anonymous
World Service Office
2190 190th Street
Torrance, CA 90504
(213) 320-7941

Based on the principles of A.A., O.A. provides a support group for men and women whose eating is out of control. *Not* another diet, O.A. teaches how to eat without starving or bingeing, one day at a time. It is usually listed in the phone book or the Personals section of your newspaper or with your hotline. You may call or write the above listing for a schedule of meetings in your area. Free.

Narcotics Anonymous
World Service Office
16155 Wyandotte Street
Van Nuys, CA 91406
(818) 780-3951

Also based on the principles of A.A., Narcotics Anonymous offers help to those who abuse drugs other than alcohol. Although alcoholics and addicts used to be separate populations, this has not been the case in the last generation. Most young people who are addictive are polydrug abusers. N.A. meetings thus tend to have a somewhat younger population than A.A. meetings. N.A. is a great source of help to the addict and provides valuable information to the co-addict on the nature of drug addiction and the steps necessary for recovery. Free.

Parents United
P.O. Box 952
San Jose, CA 95108

Daughters United
(Same address as above)

Sons United
(Same address as above)

Parents United is a support group for couples in which one
partner has been the aggressor in an incestuous involvement. Mothers of incest victims need to attend whether or
not the aggressor does. Daughters United and Sons
United are support groups for those who have been
victims of sexual advances by parents or other trusted
adults or family members. Child Protective Services or the
department of social services in your area may have the
number if none is listed in your directory. Your local
agency that deals with child abuse should have information regarding these groups. By writing to the above
address you can obtain a listing of the areas in which
Parents United, Daughters United, and Sons United meetings are held. Information is free. Send a stamped,
self-addressed envelope. There may be a nominal charge
or sliding-scale fee for services.

Stepfamily Association of America
28 Allegheny Avenue, Suite 1307
Baltimore, MD 21204
(301) 823-7570

The national Stepfamily Association provides information
about local chapters and issues a newsletter, while local

chapters offer classes, workshops, and support groups for blended families. Membership in the association provides an excellent way for these families to find each other and form support networks for dealing with the problems and feelings unique to their situation. Fee for membership. Some classes, workshops, and services free.

APPENDIX 3

Suggested Reading

SINCE I FREQUENTLY FIND MYSELF RECOMMENDING THAT MY clients read one or several of the books listed below, I am also recommending these books to you. In no way is this short list intended to be inclusive of all the books that might be of help to you. It does, however, include some of my favorites.

Love and Addiction, by Stanton Peele
New York: Taplinger, 1975

This book amply illustrates and documents the addictive nature of many "love" relationships. Required reading for every woman who loves too much.

Love and Limerance, by Dorothy Tennov
New York: Stein & Day, 1978

Tennov coins a new word, *limerance,* to denote the state of being obsessed with another person. After reading this book you will never be able to be quite as "crazy" about any man again. Another absolute must on your reading list.

How to Survive the Loss of a Love, by Melba Colgrove and others
Scarsdale, NY: Lion Press, 1976 (distributed by Simon & Schuster)

Since women who love too much are often left broken-hearted by their men, this handy little booklet can help you pick up the pieces and go on—at least until you learn not to fall for men who can't love you back.

The Art of Selfishness, by David Seabury
New York: Pocket Books, 1981

Written in a charmingly British style and with strong spiritual overtones but no preaching, this is a good textbook on how to become selfish in a healthy way—a lesson every woman who loves too much needs to learn.

Mega-Nutrients for Your Nerves, by H. L. Newbold
P. H. Wyden, 1975

A highly readable source of information about the physiological and biochemical factors that contribute to endogenous depression. Two cautions regarding this book: It contains some misleading information about alcoholism, and it also advises self-testing for vitamin and mineral deficiencies, which is a very confusing process. Consult an orthomolecular specialist for help with this. Newbold provides information on how to contact these specialists.

I'll Quit Tomorrow, by Vernon Johnson
New York: Harper & Row, 1973

An excellent work on the progression of the disease of alcoholism. The intervention process, by which many alcoholics have been helped to seek treatment for their disease, was created by Vernon Johnson, and this book explains the technique. Very readable and informative.

It Will Never Happen to Me! by Claudia Black
M.A.C., 1981

So many women who love too much are adult children of alcoholic parents. Ms. Black, in this already classic work, describes the effects of living in an alcoholic family, both in childhood and later in adulthood. A *must* for all who grew up with alcoholism in a parent or caretaker.

Betrayal of Innocence: Incest and Its Devastation, by Susan Forward and Craig Buck
Los Angeles: J. P. Tarcher, 1978

A good introductory book on the subject of incest for those who have been victims of sexual abuse by a parent or family member or other trusted adult.

The Dynamic Laws of Prosperity, by Catherine Ponder
Englewood Cliffs, NJ: Prentice-Hall, 1962

This is one of my favorite books on metaphysics. Though it has a definite '50s flavor, the basic spiritual lessons are timeless. Contains many, many positive and healing affirmations. Through their use you can begin to believe that you *deserve* a wonderful life!

The Game of Life and How to Play It, by Florence Scovell Shinn
Rickard, 1941

This short masterpiece on metaphysics gives you guidelines for living life successfully. If you don't have a spiritual practice and you wish you did, this book may be a good place to start. On the other hand, a full appreciation of Mrs. Shinn's work requires a good deal of spiritual development.

APPENDIX 4

Affirmations

I WILL START WITH AN AFFIRMATION THAT ADDRESSES WHAT IS both most important and also most difficult to do, for some women who love too much. Twice daily, for three minutes each time, maintain eye contact with yourself in a mirror as you *say out loud,* "[your name], I love you and accept you exactly the way you are."

This is also an excellent affirmation to repeat out loud to yourself while you are in your car alone driving, or silently whenever you are feeling self-critical. One cannot hold two thoughts at the same time, so replace your negative statements about yourself, such as "How could I be so dumb?" or "I'll never get this right," with positive affirmations. Repeated diligently, positive affirmations actually have the power to cancel out destructive thoughts and feelings, even when the negativity has been going on for years.

Other affirmations that are short and easy to remember, and which can be used in the time you spend driving, exercising, waiting, or simply holding still, follow:

I am free of pain, anger, and fear.
I enjoy perfect peace and well-being.

In every aspect of my life I am guided to my highest happiness and fulfillment.

All problems and struggles now fade away: I am serene.

292

The perfect solution for every problem now manifests.
I am free and filled with light.

If you have a belief in God or a higher power, make that belief an important part of your affirmations:

God loves me.
God blesses me.
God is working in my life.

The serenity prayer is one of the best affirmations possible when said thus:

God grants me the serenity
To accept the things I cannot change,
The courage to change the things I can,
and the wisdom to know the difference.

(Remember, you *cannot* change others; you *can* change yourself.)

If you do not have a belief in God you may be more comfortable with an affirmation like the following:

All things are possible through love.
Love is working in me to heal me and strengthen me,
To calm me and guide me to peace.

It is important that you also make up your own affirmations. Those which feel and sound exactly right to you will work best for you, so practice some of the ones listed here until you are ready to design your own 100-percent positive, unconditional, fully validating affirmations, tailor-made by you, for you. Do not create affirmations such as "Everything works out perfectly between Tom and me and we get married." The "and we get married" may not be the perfect solution for whatever goes on between you and Tom. Leave it at "Everything works out perfectly," maybe adding "for my highest good." Stay away from demanding specific results. Simply affirm yourself, your life, your worth, and your wonderful future. When you make affirmations, you are programming your unconscious to become willing to let go of the old patterns and move into new, healthy, joyous, and prosperous ways of living. In fact, that's not bad as an affirmation:

> I release all the pain of the past and welcome the health, joy, and success that are mine to claim.

See how it's done? Okay, here's some room for your own creations.

Index

INDEX

INDEX